I0646457

Broken Cradle

Corrupted Coil Series: Book 4

Theo Mann

The Invisible Publishing Company

Corrupted Coil Series

Contents

Chapter 1

Yann Dilnao grabbed Eliska and yanked her out of the way just in time as a massive wave surged out of the ocean, changed into a giant grinning mouth, and smashed down on the gravel beach right next to where Eliska had just been standing.

The two travelers lost their footing on the uneven ground and pitched sideways. Yann still clasped Eliska in his arms when she landed on top of him.

Icy cold saltwater soaked his clothes from the gravel underneath him as the wave surged up the beach and then pulled back.

More colossal waves reared out of the ocean, transformed into monstrous faces, cracked their jaws wide open to swallow the pair, and smashed down on the beach. The same upheaval raged up and down the beach for miles in both directions.

Yann and Eliska scrambled to their feet. "We have to get out of this Island!" he bellowed. "Can you take us somewhere else?!"

She yelled something back at him, but he didn't hear her.

They staggered farther up the gravel to the dunes. They met low foothills rising to the countryside beyond the beach coastline.

Yann didn't know what he and Eliska would find up there, but it had to be better than this.

She stumbled again and he caught her to help her balance. They tripped over driftwood and climbed toward the dunes, but at the same instant, another wave of instability swept over the hills up there.

Random ejections of wild magic spouted from holes in the ground. They fired rockets and starbursts everywhere that hit the nearby hills and the place went haywire right in front of Yann and Eliska.

The friends staggered to retreat as the hills started to fold over and under each other. They submerged and ruptured each other and the whole landscape rolled and undulated in every direction.

Yann grabbed Eliska a second time and realized with a sinking knot of horror in the pit of his stomach that she didn't have her staff with her. She must have dropped it when they landed in this Island.

He couldn't even call it an Island anymore. The instability hit the beach this time and it pitched and tossed the same way the hills did.

Eliska dove for him, and without warning, her magic whisked both of them all the way down the beach to a headland jutting out into the raging ocean.

Yann and Eliska landed on top of it. The instability didn't hit the headland for some reason. At least—it didn't hit it the same way.

Another rolling wave tumbled across the hills, cracked down onto the headland where it met the rest of the continent, and smashed the bedrock to smithereens.

The part of the cliff with Yann and Eliska standing on it split away and floated out to sea.

Massive waves attacked the headland in fury. Huge mouths towered over the spot.

Eliska dove onto her knees, planted her hands flat on the ground, and ejected a sheet of magic around the headland. Her whole body trembled from the effort, but she held the headland together against thunderous booming waves.

They tossed the headland up, pitched Yann onto his back, and then he flipped onto his stomach.

He had to hold onto the grass as the whole headland tipped up almost vertically before it plunged down the other side of a wave.

Freezing spray rained on top of him and soaked his clothes. He shut his eyes and channeled all his effort into just staying on this thing. He couldn't let himself fall off.

He heard Eliska screaming in the background, but he couldn't see her. Magic crackled through the grass right under his face as she left off one discharge after another.

He only prayed to High Heaven that she was still holding the headland together—at least until they got somewhere safe.

He didn't understand why she didn't shatter this Island and send them somewhere else, but he didn't get a chance to ask.

He pried his eyes open just in time to see an absolutely gargantuan wave rise out of the sea. It spread its mouth to a huge size. Yann couldn't see anything else. Would he and Eliska even survive this?

She took one hand off the grass and raised her arm above her head, but the wave was already plunging down on top of her. She fired a burst of magic into the wave's mouth and the wave detonated with an ear-splitting boom before it smashed down on top of the headland.

Yann came to his senses lying on a hard wooden floor somewhere. He still smelled seawater in his nose and mouth. He coughed and sat up.

His brain took a minute of blinking at the surroundings before he could bring himself to accept that he was on a boat.

He was on a boat in the middle of the ocean. The breeze chilled him through his wet clothes. Sea water drenched his hair.

The minute he sat up, he spotted Eliska huddled a few feet away from him. She cowered in a corner hugging her knees to her chest while her features went through a rapid series of excruciating grimaces of pure misery.

She whined and sobbed, choked on her own tears, and then started shaking violently. Water saturated her clothes and hair. Her teeth chattered, but something told Yann it wasn't the breeze that made her so cold.

He stared at her for a minute trying to understand how someone could fall apart so completely in just the few days since she and Anríq had been gone.

That collapse on the beach shouldn't have bothered her this much. She'd gone through much worse with the Watchmen and held the whole group together. She'd practically been in charge of the group since they left Middleborough.

He ran through a bunch of different possibilities while he tried to decide what to do about her. He didn't dare to ask her what the problem was—not now.

He scooted over next to her. He couldn't think of one intelligent thing to say that might make this easier for her.

He was starting to hope he never found out what the problem was—but he would have to. He would have to find out in case there was anything he could do to help her.

He wouldn't be able to. Anríq must have already tried. He cared about Eliska too much to let her suffer like this.

Yann made up his mind and put his arms around her the way he did in the lava fields. What else was he supposed to do?

She crumbled in his arms, burst into tears, and collapsed across his chest. Her wet clothes and hair squelched into his jacket. The wind made him shiver, too, but he just stayed there and held her.

Sitting like this gave him all the time he needed to look around this boat he was on.

The deck couldn't have been more than twenty feet long and he was the only other person on board. A triangular sail billowed from the one mast.

The wind filled the sail and drove the boat on a straight course toward a vast, empty horizon. Yann didn't see any land, beach, rolling hills, or headland in sight.

Sunshine sparkled on the ocean and glowed through the white sail. Not a single cloud floated in the sky. Did that upheaval on the beach send Yann and Eliska to another Island?

He couldn't exactly call this an Island when he was on a boat in the middle of the ocean. But this was a stable Layer, so technically it must be an Island of sorts.

He stayed where he was until Eliska passed out into an exhausted sleep. Yann's own fatigue caught up with him and the sunshine made him sleepy enough to fall asleep, too.

Chapter 2

Yann woke up lying on his side on the deck. He pried his eyes open, sat up, and looked around before he remembered why he was on a boat in the middle of the ocean.

Just then, he heard a banging noise somewhere.

A wooden ladder descended from the deck hatch to the cabin below deck. The noise came from down there.

He started to shiver again. He was just making up his mind when Eliska climbed the ladder carrying a bunch of random nautical equipment in her arms.

"Oh, good, you're awake," she told him. "Take your clothes off. We need to dry them out."

"Um...where the hell are we....?" he stammered. "And what are you doing with all that stuff?"

"We're on a boat in the middle of the ocean...."

"I'm well aware that we're on a boat in the middle of the ocean," he snapped back. "How did we get here? We were on that beach...."

"The Island must have shattered. Now we're in a different Island."

"Did you bring us here?" Yann asked.

"No, I woke up here the same way you did. Now take your clothes off before you catch a chill. Here. You can put these on while I dry your clothes."

He frowned at her. "Your clothes aren't wet."

"That's because I dried them before you woke up. Did you think I was going to strip off naked in front of you?"

"So you want me to strip off naked in front of *you?*" he countered.

She smirked at him in a way he really didn't like. "I've seen it all before. Trust me."

"You haven't seen me before."

She laughed at him. "Fine. Freeze to death for all I care....or I can dry you out like that."

He froze. "What do you mean? What are you going to do?"

She gasped in exasperation. "Honestly, Yann. I really had no idea you were such a prude."

She stalked over to him and squatted down in front of him.

He cringed when she extended her arms toward him, but she didn't give him a chance to escape.

She clamped her hands on his shoulders and a flash of searing heat raced through his clothes. It burned him, but it evaporated all the water in seconds.

He screamed, but the heat died an instant later and left his clothes perfectly dry.

She stood up and walked away from him. "You're welcome," she muttered.

"Um...thank you. What did you do?"

"I used my magic to dry you. Isn't that obvious?"

"But...." He frowned at nothing. "If you could do that all along, why did you.....?"

He went through a series of memories of her drying people's clothes on sticks by the fire.

He decided not to ask. She'd been doing so many things differently just in the last day or two.

He glanced out at the ocean. "Do you know where we are?"

"We're in the Coil," she mumbled without turning around.

"Aren't we supposed to be finding the Shard of Hotha?"

"We are finding it," she replied over her shoulder.

He frowned at her the back of her head. "How can we be finding it if we're here?"

She pointed up at the sail and then behind him. "I think this boat must be alive or something. It steers itself and it's heading straight for an Island where the White Spire is now. I can't be sure, but this boat might be an Island that takes people where they want to go."

"It's...." He faltered when he realized what she just said. He looked over his shoulder.

The ship's wheel held itself steady and made minor adjustments to itself to keep the boat on course.

The prow kept skimming over the smooth ocean with no help or interference from Yann or Eliska.

She finished screwing around with the pile of junk in front of her and came back over to sit down in front of him.

"What are you doing?" he asked.

"It's daytime now, but the sun will go down and then it will get dark and cold. I was thinking of lighting a fire...here...."

"You want to light a fire—on a boat?! Are you insane?"

She bit back another grin. "Do you remember how the Watchmen used that sheet of metal in the barn to protect the floor? I was planning to do that."

"Maybe we should just stay warm by going below," he suggested. "The boat must have berths down there."

She cocked her head and frowned. "You're right. It does."

"Don't tell me you've never spent any time on a boat before," he exclaimed.

"Well, when have *you* ever spent time on a boat? You spent your whole life in Middleborough."

"At least I got an education. I read about boats in books."

She grimaced. "It isn't my fault I didn't get an education and read about boats in books. So you know more about it than I do. You can be the captain for all I care. I'll be your dutiful passenger."

He had to laugh. "Then my first decision as captain is that you won't light a fire on this boat. Boats and fire do not mix. That's rule number one."

"I thought rule number one was to always keep the boat between you and the water."

"You're supposed to be dutiful—not snarky, remember? We'll spend the night down below. We'll be warmer there."

"But we won't be able to see if something comes."

"We'll have to trust the boat for that."

She stared at him for a second. He waited for her to say something else, but instead, she jerked her head away and stared out over the water. Her features spasmed from that hidden pain she carried inside her.

"Are you okay?" he asked.

"Just....." She fought to control her mouth. "I wish I knew what happened to Anríq."

"If he's still alive, he'll go for the Shard, too. We might even meet him there when we get to the Island where the White Spire is."

"He doesn't know how to get there. My Coil projection is the only thing guiding us."

"Don't lose hope yet."

She glanced at him only once, but her eyes betrayed a depth of misery that stabbed him in the guts. Anríq was gone....and so was Marine.

Yann had come to feel something for her that he never dreamed he would ever feel for anyone.

He joked around with her about her marrying a handsome prince, but Yann never let her see how jealous that made him.

She would never marry a prince as long as the four friends continued to carry on this campaign against the Voyant.

Yann didn't want this journey to end because he didn't want to lose Marine. He didn't want to stand by and watch her marry someone else.

She would never marry Yann. If he ever entertained the possibility that he might leave the Black Watch and find a wife, he never dared to dream it might be her. He would never be good enough for her.

Now he lost her anyway. He found his eyes being drawn back to the horizon. Was she still out there? Were Marine and Anríq alive and alone together trying to find their way to the White Spire?

They wouldn't be able to break into it.

Eliska's magic might be strong enough to get Yann into the White Spire, but the friends stood the best chance by working together. Now they lost that advantage.

Eliska would have taken herself and Yann straight back to Anríq and Marine if she could have. Yann didn't doubt that even for a second. She would have done anything to find Anríq if it was at all possible.

Yann should have felt jealous about that, but he couldn't even care. Losing Anríq and Marine stung worse than anything—almost anything. It stung only slightly less than losing Marine.

Eliska shook herself and went below again. She came back with a bunch of sealed packages.

She dumped them on the deck in front of Yann. "This is some kind of food. I guess this boat provides everything the passengers need."

She tore open one of the packages and sniffed it.

"What does it smell like?" he asked.

"It smells like some kind of cured meat." She held up the package. "What does the label say?"

He read the faded letters. "It says, 'Brined Lionfish'—whatever that is."

She handed it to him and tore open another one. He ate in silence and so did she.

He really hoped this trip wasn't going to turn into an awkward silence with neither of them daring to speak to the other.

Yann felt himself developing some kind of relationship with Eliska before they got separated. Then everything started to develop between him and Marine.

Should Yann tell Eliska about that? Would she get murderously jealous toward her own friend?

He decided not to say anything. He didn't know if he and Eliska would ever see Marine again. Then he would only have Eliska—the way he did before he found out who Marine really was.

He fell into another brooding silence about the way she acted in Savaré. He slept with his arms around her. He kissed her and she touched his bare body. He would cherish those memories forever.

Would he ever be able to think about Eliska that way? She was no princess, but he didn't come to feel this way about Marine because she was a princess.

Chapter 3

Eliska finished her food, got up, and went back to messing around with all her stuff. He couldn't imagine what she was trying to do with it.

He watched her for a while. "What are you doing?" he asked.

"I'm trying to untangle this rope."

He waited a little longer. "You don't have the first idea what you're doing, do you?"

"I told you I don't know anything about boats."

"Bring it here," he growled. "I'll do it for you."

She dragged over her pile of stuff. A length of rope had gotten tangled around a few different kitchen appliances, a buoy, and a large empty cask with the word, *Water,* printed on the side.

Yann found the end of the rope and started the laborious process of feeding it through all the tangled knots.

Eliska sat back out of the way and watched him. "Don't tell me you learned all this from books."

"You can learn a lot from books. You should try it."

"I don't need to try it. I don't need to read if I'm living out in the Coil."

"Is that what you plan to do? Do you plan to be a Coil rat all your life?"

"I don't see why everyone treats that as an insult. I had a good life before all of this started."

"I don't know enough about your life before this started, but that doesn't mean you have to keep living that way. You could change. You could become a nurse—or a teacher—or a nun."

He meant it as a joke to make her laugh, but he got the opposite response. Her face screwed up in misery, but only for a split second.

She almost burst into tears before she floundered back under control and turned away to stare across the water.

"I'm sorry," he blurted out. "I didn't mean to.....I didn't know...."

He faltered to a stop and stopped himself from saying anything else. She refused to look at him. She shot to her feet, scrambled down the ladder, and vanished below.

He sighed. Now what was he supposed to do?

He finished untangling the rope, wound it into a byte, and hung it from a belaying pin in the starboard gunwale.

He checked the wheel and then studied a compass that had been built into the wheel pedestal. The ship held a steady course even when the wind changed.

The mast and spars creaked and the ropes twanged into the wind. It made a haunted sound.

The sun started to slip toward the horizon. Eliska was right. The air cooled rapidly.

He took the rest of the stuff down below to put it away. Eliska sat on one of the aft berths She didn't look up when he came down the ladder.

He hung the frying pan on the bulkhead and stashed the buoy in a footlocker under a different beath.

Then he slid the hatch shut to keep out the cold air.

The water hissed along the hull. Every thump and creak of the rigging translated through the ship's timbers. Yann held onto one of the deck frames while he listened to it.

This boat had a unique sound that reminded him of a person's voice. He didn't understand the words, but the sound comforted him.

Eliska kept her head down. Did the sound bother her—or was it something else—something neither of them would talk about?

He threw caution to the wind, went forward, and sat down on the berth across from her. She didn't look up. Her hair hung on either side of her face.

He took a long time to decide what to say to her. He wouldn't go through this trip tiptoeing around her and pretending there was no elephant in the room, especially not if he was going to be stuck with her alone from now on.

He'd come too far with her to pull his punches. Whatever was wrong with her affected him, but that wasn't the reason he wanted to know.

"Do you think you'll be able to sleep tonight?" he finally asked.

She went through the same sequence of jolting, grimacing, coming within inches of bursting into tears, glancing around in terror, clamping her eyes shut, and shuddering as though her skin crawled.

He couldn't stand to watch her. He shot to his feet and swiveled over to her berth.

He barely kept his voice down to a strained whisper. "What the hell happened to you? Why are you so jumpy and messed up? You're really starting to scare me."

Her wild eyes darted everywhere but to him. "I......I keep.....I don't know how to....I just....."

"Hey!" he breathed. "It's me! Look at me! You know me! I'm right here!"

He tried to turn her by the shoulders. When that failed, he wound up cupping both her cheeks in his hands to force her to turn around and look at him.

"What's going on?" he murmured. "Tell me what's wrong. I can't stand seeing you like this."

"Yann...." she choked.

"Something happened with you and Anríq, didn't it? Something happened while you two were alone together. I need to know what it was. If something hurt you...."

She tore herself out of his hands and forced herself to her feet, but she didn't walk away. She took a few steps down the cabin and stopped there with her back to him.

She bowed her head and her hair draped the sides of her face again. She stared down at her hands while she knit her knuckles together again and again. She wrenched them so hard she must have been hurting herself.

"He seems fine," Yann went on. "Whatever happened must have only happened you."

"Nothing happened to him," she choked. "He's always the same."

"So what happened to you? Whatever it was must have been really bad. Maybe I can help you."

"No one can help me," she croaked. "I'm beyond help."

That broken murmur tore his heart out. "Then just tell me what happened. I care about you. Let me do something. Anríq says talking can be healing."

She burst into another fit of jerking shudders at those words. She squirmed inside her clothes, paced farther away, and came back.

She stopped in front of him, ran her fingers through her hair, clamped her eyes shut, and then scraped her palm across her eyes before she shook her head like she needed to get something out of her mind.

"Do you remember.....?" She looked away into a corner so she wouldn't have to make eye contact with him. "Do you remember when I healed Barsali and I took his poison on myself?"

"Yeah, but you got better after that. You even acted like you were happy sometimes. This is so much worse than that ever was."

She mumbled down at her hands. "I guess my magic recovered after that, but it can't heal me from this. Nothing can."

Yann watched her in mounting desperation. He couldn't let her go through this. He had to do something—but what?

"And......Anríq couldn't do anything about it?" he finally asked.

"He wanted to, but I wouldn't let him. I didn't want it to poison him, too."

That word sent a prickle up Yann's scalp. Poison.

It brought up so many nightmare scenarios.....but it somehow made sense. Something was poisoning her from the inside.

He forced himself to sit up straight. "Tell me what happened."

She sat down on the berth next to him and stared down at the floor.

She propped her arms against the bulkhead on either side of her hips, locked her elbows, and kept her back and shoulders tensed to the breaking point. Her whole body wound up with tension.

She rocked back and forth a few times and then her cheeks screwed up in agony. "There was a city.....under attack......from the Dark....." She lost her struggle to control herself and started crying again. Her voice spiked to a husky shriek. "I.....I healed...the city...."

Yann gasped. "You healed a whole city—by yourself?!"

Racking sobs tore her apart, but she wouldn't look at him. She stared at something horrifying that he couldn't see. "There were chil dren.....dying....nightmares.....terrible memories.....I took their Darkness on myself to save their lives.....and now I can't get rid of their memories. I keep seeing them....and more people who are even still alive....and people whose Darkness I didn't take. It poisoned me....and I went into the Dark. A Dark Layer attacked the town.....and I took all that Darkness on myself.....and now I'll be like this forever. He said I was a Servant and I tried to serve....and now I'm nothing but poison to everyone...."

She broke down sobbing hard. Every muscle and fiber in her body shook from the misery and anguish coming out of her.

Her story didn't even scratch the surface of what she'd seen—the horrors she'd witnessed.

Now Yann understood why Anríq didn't tell him. Maybe not even Anríq understood the full depth of how far she'd gone. He would have been able to guess based on how she acted.

Watching her made Yann want to cry, but he couldn't do that to her.

Overwhelming love and protective fury consumed him when he saw her like this. He would have done anything—sacrificed anything—even his own life—just to give her some relief.

He couldn't, though. Every instinct he'd ever had to become a Servant—it all came down to this. It came down to sitting here loving her, caring for her, and not being able to do a damn thing to help her.

Now he was alone with her—maybe forever. He would be the one to watch her go through this torment.

He might spend years watching her suffer, but at least he would know why. He would know she got like this by saving a whole city.

She might even have saved more than that and just not told him. He wouldn't be surprised. She might hide the worst from him to protect him.

The painful convulsions going through her body made him hurt just as much. She was one of the strongest people he'd ever met. Whatever she went through must have been truly horrific.

He swallowed hard before he dared to speak. "Anríq.....he took care of you, didn't he? Let me do the same thing. Will you let me do that? Let me serve by taking care of you."

She was crying too hard to answer. He didn't have to wait anymore.

He put his arm around her shoulders again, but she didn't collapse the way she did earlier.

She stayed sitting bolt upright. Spasms and brutal contortions twisted her muscles in all the wrong directions while she poured out all her inner pain in hot, endless tears. She might cry like this forever.

He couldn't wait for that, either.

He closed his hands around her wet cheeks again and pulled her to turn around and face him.

"Listen to me," he murmured. "We're Servants—all four of us. We pledged to follow this path and that's what we're going to do. Your magic is stronger now. It's stronger than anything I've ever seen or even heard of. You stand the best chance of getting to the White Spire and taking the Shard—so that's what we're going to do. This Darkness—it might turn out to be a good thing. You would save the whole Coil, not just one city. Okay? We're going to keep going. We're going to do what we promised to do. We're going to stop the Voyant and stabilize the Coil. All right? Are you with me on that?'

She nodded, but she didn't stop wincing and shaking in agony. The sight of her wrung Yann's heart more than he could stand.

"Lie down here and try to get some rest," he told her. "I'll be with you in case you wake up with nightmares. Okay? I'm not going anywhere."

He pulled her down on the berth. He didn't want to let go of her. He couldn't.

She needed him more now than she ever did before, but he needed her just as much. He needed to help her even if he could only do that by being here for her. Someone had to, now that Anríq wasn't here to do it.

He drew her down onto his chest and stretched out next to her with his arms around her. She cowered against his shoulder.

He didn't think twice about comforting her like this. He didn't even think to stop himself from kissing her on the head or running his fingertips down her hair again and again.

He never thought once that he might be betraying whatever he started with Marine.

He settled back on the mattress and prepared himself to spend all night like this. The ship kept rocking, creaking, and groaning all around him.

Its voice told him he was doing the right thing. The boat would take care of them until tomorrow. He could put aside all other concerns and just deal with her.

He shut his eyes and let himself drift with the current right on the other side of the hull.

Eliska's voice floated out of the darkness and brought him back to the present, but he didn't open his eyes.

"Yann....." she croaked.

"Yeah?" he whispered.

"I know....." Her body jolted from some inner shock. "I know ......you shared something special....with Marine......"

He turned his head aside and bit back a sudden torturous stab of cruel longing for Marine.

Did he actually start to love her in Savaré? Was that why the joke about her marrying a handsome prince made him so jealous?

"I'm sorry...." Eliska whispered. "I'm sorry....."

He couldn't stand that. He forced himself to turn back and kiss her hair again. "I know you shared something special with Anríq, too. I'm glad you had him with you. I'm glad he was there for you so you didn't have to go through it alone."

She didn't say the rest of it. Neither of them mentioned that she and Yann might never see Marine and Anríq again.

Now Yann and Eliska only had each other. They would have to continue on this path and try to take the Shard of Hotha on their own with no other help from anyone.

Chapter 4

Yann bent over the compass and checked the boat's heading. It stayed a few hundred yards offshores and followed the coastline in the same direction.

Yann scanned the horizon, but he didn't see any other boats around—or any people on the coast.

Eliska sat on a footlocker nearby and studied her Coil projection.

"Can you tell how close we are to the next Island?" he asked.

"I was looking at something else. I'll check."

"What were you looking at?" he asked.

"This thing is amazing. It's so detailed. I can see so much more in it than I ever could before."

"That's a good thing, right? You'll be able to find Anríq and Marine when this is all over with."

"We can only hope."

She changed the image and brought up another image of a beautiful city landscape shining with sunshine. Flowering trees lined all the avenues and the White Spire glistening on the skyline.

"That's the same thing we saw last time," Yann pointed out. "That isn't the Island we found with the White Spire in it. Maybe it's an illusion."

She rotated the picture in all directions. She studied it much more closely than he would have. "I was thinking….maybe this is what it's supposed to look like."

"What do you mean?"

"Maybe when two people take the Shards and the Coil stabilizes, maybe the White Spire stays in one place—in this landscape. Do you remember the picture we saw in that book? It was in the same city. I'm certain of it. The buildings were in the same places."

"Maybe the instability is affecting the White Spire, too. In fact, I'm sure it is because it keeps moving around. This is the Island the White Spire is in when the Coil is working the way it should be—when both Shards are taken by two people who are in congress with each other—or whatever you want to call it."

"It's an interesting theory, but then how do we find it? If it keeps moving around and your projection is showing you the Island it's supposed to be, how do we find the Island it's actually in at any given time? We could be sailing for an illusion right now instead of the real thing."

"Hmm." She studied the picture for a little while. "Maybe I can change it by adding more power to it."

She raised her other hand, let it hover over the image, and sent a flow of magic into it from her left hand.

The image expanded even more.

The picture of the landscape with the White Spier on the horizon changed into a dark, smoky, wasteland with another carpet of bleached bones covering every inch of the flat, featureless desert.

The bones didn't lie in piles, though. They kept leaping out of position, fitting together with each other into different shapes, and tottering around the landscape before they fell apart and scattered where they had been lying a second before.

"That's probably what it really looks like," Eliska murmured. "I wouldn't be surprised based on what we've seen lately."

"Can't you just add your power to it through your right hand?" he asked. "Do you really have to use your left hand?"

She shot him a smirk. "It looks more dramatic this way."

He turned back to studying the coastline. "I wonder why this Island is so stable. I wonder if there is any reason why any Island stays stable longer than another."

"The situation will probably keep disintegrating as time goes on." She stood up and closed her projection. "Everything will fall apart and become more chaotic until someone takes the second Shard."

He cocked his head to study her again. She held herself together a little better this morning. She really needed to spend a few months in bed—and she needed to put on some weight. She barely ate any of the brined Lionfish.

She wouldn't spend months in bed. Sleeping must have been the very last thing in the world she wanted to do.

She saw him watching her. "What?"

"You probably don't want to hear this....."

"You're right. I don't."

"Just hear me out, okay? When I was with Marine, she and I tried to get into the White Spire."

"You said that. You said you saw the Voyant manipulating the Coil."

"I did. He used a projection like yours—except that it wasn't a projection. It was some kind of large model. He could manipulate it, collapse some Layers, and expand others to create new Islands."

"Uh-huh? What about that is something we don't already know?"

"I didn't recognize it before because Marine and I weren't with you—but I recognize it now. It looked like your projection—the larger projection you use now. See what I mean?"

"No, I don't. What does this have to do with anything?"

"Maybe there's a connection between you and the Voyant....."

She jolted and spun away from him. "There is NOT a connection between me and the Voyant! Don't even suggest that!"

"Why not? What would be so bad about it if there was? You don't know who your parents are....."

"So you're saying the Voyant is my....what? My father?"

"Why not? Why else would he be trying to find you?"

"The Voyant is not trying to find me?!" she roared. "We already know that. The Voyant didn't come after me and Anríq even once when we were alone together."

Yann frowned. "He didn't?"

"No!" she snapped. "Next question?"

Yann furrowed his brow in thought. "That's strange. He didn't come after me and Marine while we were alone together, either."

"The Voyant is not my father!" she snarled. "Don't even suggest that!"

"It doesn't mean you have to go along with whatever he's doing. You have all this extra power now. Why don't you try again to find out who your parents are? You said before that you searched and couldn't find them. Maybe that's because you didn't have the power to find them."

She snorted. "It isn't....and I am NOT going to search for my parents. We're searching for the Shard of Hotha, remember? What happened to that?"

"Just hear me out, okay? Imagine you had this power when you were little—like right after you got separated from your parents.

Imagine you used these lines to track them down—or at least to the place where you got separated from them. You could have at least found out who they were."

She glared at him and then turned away to stare across the water. "That was decades ago. I couldn't do it now."

"How do you know? How do you know these lines are perishable? They might last forever."

She refused to answer him at all or even look at him. She simmered in resentment while she glared out at the coastline passing the boat.

He didn't regret bringing it up. She could have all kinds of power she didn't even know about—power just waiting for her to tap into it. She might be able to end this war a lot more quickly than she realized.

He let the subject drop and pretended to study the compass. The boat had an uncanny way of maneuvering itself and adjusting its course to accommodate the slightest breath of wind or change in the landscape.

The boat tacked farther out to seat when it came to a promontory. Yann and Eliska had to duck under the boom when it swung to the other side. Then the ship tacked back to the same distance from shore as soon as it passed the headland.

Eliska opened her Coil projection again. She didn't use her left hand this time to make it big enough to see the real Island where the White Spire was.

"Could you use that to find the Sacred Shrine?" Yann asked.

"I already tried that," she mumbled over her shoulder. "It doesn't show up and I can't read anything inside the White Spire at all."

"The Voyant must have protections around it," Yann remarked. "You could read the layout of that maze Island perfectly well."

She surprised him by spinning around and facing him. Was this the first time she'd ever made full eye contact with him since they wound up on this boat?

"This is what I don't understand," she exclaimed. "If the Voyant wants to find someone to take the second Shard—why hide it? Why would he set up protections around the spire to stop someone from finding the Shard? You would think he would do the opposite and make it as easy to find as possible."

"You're right," Yann replied. "Maybe something else is hiding it."

She narrowed her eyes at the coastline again, but she didn't really see it. "I'm starting to agree with Marine. I don't think the Shard is in the White Spire at all."

"Then was that book lying?" Yann asked.

"No, not lying. The Shard is in some magical dimension that may or may not coincide with the White Spire—but it isn't exactly *in* the White Spire if you know what I mean."

"No, I don't know what you mean. How can it be in the White Spire and not in the White Spire at the same time?"

"Because the Sacred Shrine is a magical dimension—like a Layer. Some of the more stable Islands have names—like the Ancestral Empire or the Hallowed Vales or the Sojourner's Sanctum. The Sacred Shrine sounds like one of those, doesn't it?"

"If it's a Layer, then it should show up in the Coil, shouldn't it?"

"Not if it can only be accessed by magical means—and not if the person who takes the Shard has to go on a quest to find it."

"So what's the quest? The records don't say the person has to go on a quest. The records just said......"

Yann broke off. Now he was the one to stare off into space.

"What?" she asked again. "Did you remember something?"

"The records where Marine found out about the Shard of Hotha were more detailed genealogies of the Kings in the White Spire. They only said, 'He took the Shard of Hotha from the Sacred Shrine and entered the Hall of Light to become King.' They didn't say anything about how the person finds the Sacred Shrine, but the information might be recorded somewhere else."

She went back to brooding and so did he. He studied the landscape. The coastline looked so quiet and serene—too quiet and serene. Its very quietness and serenity didn't look right.

She surprised him again by breaking the silence. "I guess I could," she mumbled.

"Could what?" he asked.

"I could try to find out if.....you know......"

They both jumped out of their skins when a blazing halo of brilliant golden light erupted over the ocean to the right in front of the boat. The Voyant Mendicat appeared out of nowhere.

Chapter 5

The ocean exploded in chaos the instant the Voyant appeared. Massive waves erupted out of the sea and the boat veered hard to the left—which took it straight toward the beach.

Yann pounced on the wheel. Eliska shot to the prow. She tried to raise her staff, but she didn't have it anymore.

She glanced around for anything she could use to fight the Voyant and grabbed a random belaying pin sticking out of the ship's starboard rail.

She pointed it at the Voyant, but at that moment, the giant wave shapes seethed out of the ocean the way they did when she and Yann got trapped on that headland.

Massive faces with wide, devouring mouths plunged down on top of the boat. Yann fought the wheel to steer the ship away from the shore.

The hills beyond the coastline went nuts at the same time. They started folding, rolling, and churning the same way they did last time.

Eliska pointed the belaying pin at the Voyant, but right then, another gigantic wave plastered the ship from behind.

Spray pelted all over the deck and the impact knocked Eliska off balance. She slammed into the mast and struggled to stand up straight so she could get a clear shot at the Voyant.

He never moved. He hovered over the waves glaring out at everything with the same brutal scowl on his face.

The storm built to a hurricane out on the ocean and another wave slapped the boat sideways.

Yann yelled something. Eliska glanced in his direction and saw the boat sailing full speed into a huge rock cliff against another promontory.

The waves reared taller than ever and struck harder if that was even possible.

A colossal wave rose out of the ocean right behind the boat and lifted it high in the air. It would smash down right onto that cliff. The blow would destroy the boat in seconds.

Eliska didn't hesitate long enough to explain what she was going to do. She saw the whole scene disintegrating before her eyes.

She spun away, sprinted down the deck, and collided with Yann where he stood behind the wheel. He yelled out again.

"Hold on!" she bellowed, slammed him down flat on his back on the deck, nailed her belaying pin into the deck boards, and detonated the Island full force.

The boat exploded and Yann and Eliska plunged through into another Layer.

She held onto him with all her strength and he held onto her just as hard. He crushed her in his arms, and the next second, they dropped through into another scene of full-scale chaos.

A ton of water fell through the breach when the boat Island imploded.

Yann and Eliska crashed down hard on a stone floor and all that water dumped on top of them before Eliska realized where they were.

She dragged herself out of a lake of water and immediately had to duck under her arms to protect herself from flying debris.

She spotted a few empty bookshelves across a room built into a stone tower. Books, torn papers, and random trash pelted through the air and hammered both her and Yann.

She fired a bolt of magic from her belaying pin to cover both of them, but the next instant, the room exploded with them inside it.

Yann charged her and threw his arms around her. "We gotta get out of here!" he bellowed. "Take us to another Island!"

"This is the Layer with the White Spire in it!" she yelled back.

"How can it be?!" he roared.

"We have to find our way out of this without destroying the Layer! Come on!"

She seized his hand, but she couldn't hold onto him, protect him with her shield, and deflect all the stuff zooming at her at the same time.

She let go of him, used her left hand to keep up the shield, and aimed her belaying pin through the shield to shoot at books, chairs, desks, and broken stone blocks tumbling in confusion.

They hurtled at the two friends, crashed into her shield, bounced off, and sprang right back up to come at her again.

She fired at a granite boulder and smashed it to dust, but the dust kept whizzing around the room and circling back to bombard the shield all over again.

This happened so often that she couldn't deny the truth anymore. Everything in this room was trying to attack her.

"Stay with me!" she yelled over her shoulder. "I can't hold onto you and protect us at the same time! Make sure we don't get separated!"

He inched up behind her and took hold of the back of her cloak. At least she could feel him there. He was still with her even when she turned her back on him.

She fought her way across the room, but all the stuff flying around doubled down its assault when she got near the door.

The rain of thumps and smashes on her shield escalated to a steady pounding din. Everything in this room hammered the shield trying to get through. Why?

Yann tugged her cloak to turn her around. He moved behind her and turned her back to the door.

She backstepped to push him toward it while she defended his retreat. "I got the door open!' he yelled in her ear. "Come on! We can get out now!"

He dove through, yanked her backward to pull her with him, and they both stumbled onto a stone landing before he slammed the door shut.

The wind died immediately, but the stuff inside the room didn't stop pounding on the door from the other side. All the books and stuff tried to get out to come after the pair.

Eliska backed away aiming her belaying pin at the door, but nothing came through. Everything on the landing sounded way too quiet.

Yann looked behind them toward the stairs. "The rest of the building looks okay. Come on. Let's see if we can find a way out."

Eliska took at least a minute before she dared to put her belaying pin down. She didn't want to turn her back on that door.

Heavy thuds banged the thick boards and rattled the lock in the wall, but the books and granite blocks didn't break the door down. Yan pulled her away.

They climbed down the stairs to the next landing, but he didn't see any more instability or even any sign of people.

"This is spooky," she murmured. "I wonder what's wrong with this place."

"This isn't the Layer where you saw the White Spire before," Yann pointed out. "That place was destroyed by fire. This obviously hasn't been."

She nudged him. "There's another room over there with a window. Let's see if we can locate the spire from here."

She led the way into a stone room with no furniture in it.

"It doesn't look like anyone has lived here for a long time," Yann remarked. "I haven't seen any furniture in any of the rooms."

"The room with all those flying books had plenty of furniture," she told him. "Just none of it was nailed down."

He laughed and approached the window. She went over to him.

They both stood and stared through it at the surrounding landscape churning in chaos. Dark vapors and clouds of colored gas swirled past the window along with Layers, landscapes, Islands, and Dark forces caught in the confusion.

Eliska bent through the window. She couldn't see any ground this building might be standing on—or any roof or sky above, either.

When she looked up, she saw part of the stone tower flying apart as instability hit it.

"It looks like this tower is going to disintegrate pretty soon, too," she pointed out. "We should find a way to get out of here before that happens."

Yann pointed out the window. "There's the White Spire. We won't be able to get to it through all of that."

The clouds of vapor parted just long enough for Eliska to see the spire, too, and at that moment, another forest Island tumbled past.

It looked like a nice, green place with plenty of lush vegetation. She caught a split-second glimpse of Anríq and Marine before the Island somersaulted off to nowhere. She didn't even get a chance to see what they were doing. Then they were gone.

She couldn't have spoken if her life depended on it. Yann didn't say a word, either.

They both stood and stared, but neither of them could see Anríq or Marine in the chaos anymore.

Chapter 6

Yann walked away, left the tower room, and went back to the stairs.

Eliska followed him in a numb daze. Knowing Anríq and Marine were still alive out there somehow made it worse that Yann and Eliska couldn't rejoin them.

She created her Coil projection behind his back to find Anríq's and Marine's location, but the lines blurred again in all the collapsing Layers. She couldn't locate Anríq and Marine from here.

Yann climbed down the stairs, entered a dozen identical rooms, and eventually worked his way all the way down to the very lowest halls.

This tower resembled the cloud tower where Marine first found the information about the Kings.

Vast decorative halls for dining and gathering branched off from tall, vaulted colonnades.

This tower didn't have any fires crackling in the fireplaces or dishes set for people to eat from. The whole place echoed with cold silence.

"This tower has the same layout as a Guardian Temple," Eliska remarked when they got to the fourth gathering hall.

"I noticed that, too. If that's true, we should be able to get out through the stable tunnel."

"We can try it. If we can't, I say we shatter this Layer and try to get to the White Spire another way."

He nodded. "I was just about to suggest that myself."

The pair found the kitchens, but before they went for the tunnel leading out to the stable yard, Eliska made a detour into a broom closet.

"Don't tell me you're getting interested in domestic cleaning," Yann teased.

"Hardy-har-har," she sneered. She picked up a broom. "I need a staff. I am NOT leaving this Island with *that.*" She threw the belaying pin on the floor.

Yann snorted with laughter. "You could wave your wand at the Voyant like a real wizard."

She glared at him. "You better shut your mouth."

She turned her attention back to the broom so she wouldn't see him smirking at her. She tore off the broom head and used the handle as a staff. "We can go now."

"Are you sure you don't want to search this place for a pointed hat and a long blue robe with stars on it?" he asked.

"I have a better idea. We can search this place for a bridle and saddle for you to wear, but we'll put them on backward so everyone can see what a horse's ass you are."

He only laughed at her and they left the kitchen for the tunnel.

They stopped inside it and looked out at the chaos. It surrounded the tower on all sides and left no solid land anywhere.

"I guess that settles it," Yann remarked. "Can you decide ahead of time which Layer to go to?"

"I don't suppose it matters," she replied. "This is the Layer with the White Spire in it—which is where we're trying to go. We'll just have to find a stable Island somewhere and try to get to the White Spire the next time it moves."

He nodded again. "That sounds like as good a plan as any."

She glanced up at him....and their eyes met. She would have to use a binding spell to hold him near her while they fell through the Layers.

He held out his hand instead. She found herself smiling at him when she took it.

She would have liked to tell him right then how glad she was to be with him, but words failed her.

She would have been unbelievably relieved to be stranded in the Coil with any of her three friends—Anríq, Yann, or Marine. Any of them would be better than getting stranded out here alone.

They would have been so much better than that. She was really starting to understand how desperate and bare her life had been before she went to Middleborough.

She had been living so close to the wind, barely keeping herself alive, and treating everyone she met as an enemy. She never relied on anyone for help.

She would never be able to go back to that. She really didn't care anymore if she got stranded with an imp like Yann.

She squeezed his hand and he squeezed back. She read the same gratitude and affection in his eyes when he gazed down at her.

She raised her staff and stabbed it into the floor at her feet. The tower around her evaporated in a cloud of mayhem and all the stone walls hurtled inward to crush the pair.

She dove for him at the same instant he dove for her. They grabbed onto each other and wheeled off into the Layer.

Eliska had to continuously magick her and Yann from one place to another to keep out of the way of more landscapes imploding on all sides.

Whole Islands thundered nearer. They came perilously close to crushing the two friends before she magicked herself and Yann out of the way to the last second.

They smashed through a blast of spikes ripping out of thin air before Yann and Eliska crashed down hard in a dense patch of trees at the bottom of a steep ravine.

Yann landed on top of her and they both grunted in pain when the fall knocked the air out of their lungs.

"Get off me, you big oaf!" she roared.

"Quit whining!" he countered. "You're the one who brought us here—not me."

She wound up laughing and squirmed out from under him before she floundered to her feet.

Neither of them could stand up very well on the ravine's steep sides. Leaf litter and fallen branches made the surface even more uneven.

"Well, here we are." Yann searched the area. "I guess we're in a stable Island—for now."

"Hold on," she told him. "I can get us somewhere better than this."

He grinned at her. "I wasn't going to say...."

She wound up laughing again, grabbed his hand, and magicked both of them to the top of the ravine.

They landed on a hilltop overlooking an immense wilderness stretching into the distance around them. Giant snowcapped mountains faded to a cloud of blue horizon.

Eliska opened her Coil projection. "There are some towns and cities down in the valleys. We can head for those."

"Where are we in relation to the White Spire?"

She revolved the image. "The Layer we just left is still collapsing. I don't see the Spire appearing anywhere else just yet. It looks like we just have to wait for it to show up."

They headed off in the direction where she'd seen the towns. She didn't tell him how far away they were.

The wind bit much colder up here. Both Yann's and Eliska's clothes were still wet from falling through the boat Island, so she used her magic to dry them.

"You could use your magic to create a town like Tenby with all the fixings," he suggested.

"I might be able to create a town like Tenby if I understood how any of that stuff worked."

"You're right. I don't think even the people of Tenby knew how it worked."

"Marine might," Eliska pointed out. "She seems to understand a lot about that stuff."

"I should have asked her when I had the chance—or she could have shown me how to look it up on the computers.'

She cocked her head to study him, but she didn't ask about what happened between him and Marine while they were alone.

The change in him had more to do with that than with him taking command of the Black Watch in Tenby—or anywhere else.

Eliska didn't blame Yann for being interested in Marine. Any sane man would be. It only surprised Eliska that Yann didn't try to start something with Marine sooner.

He didn't deny it when Eliska said he shared something special with Marine. It might have been something really special—like life-changing special—kind of like what happened between her and Anríq.

If Yann and Eliska never met back up with Anríq and Marine....if Yann and Eliska got stuck together for good......

Each of them would be the other's second choice.

She would never regret getting together with Yann. He was one of the best men she'd ever met. Any woman would be lucky to get with him.

He wasn't Anríq, though. No one ever could be.

She wasn't Marine, either. Even Eliska understood that. She would never be able to live up to Marine's standard.

She wouldn't mind being a man's second choice if the first choice was Marine. Eliska would never want to take Marine's place in Yann's heart—assuming it came to that.

He felt the same way about Anríq. She already knew that. Yann worshiped Anríq—and for good reason.

Neither of them broke the silence on their way through the mountain wilderness. He must be thinking the same thing. He must be evaluating what would happen between them if they never met up with Anríq and Marine.

Eliska knew Yann cared about her. He loved her as much as he could love anyone who wasn't Marine.

Eliska would never be his dream come true, but maybe she didn't need to be.

They could care for each other, protect each other, help each other, and be there for each other.

They could each know the secret truth burning a hole in the other's heart and it would be all right.

Chapter 7

D usk came early to the mountains. The wind bit even colder once the sun slipped behind the peaks.

Yann searched the tops. Hardly any vegetation grew up here. "We should find a place to make camp for the night."

Eliska looked into a pool of magic in her hand. "There's a cave over there. We should use that."

The two of them worked together in silence to get ready for the night. Yann gathered armloads of firewood and a few extra piles of tinder for him and Eliska to sleep on.

She set fire to the branches to make a fire and then went out hunting a biturong while he looked for water.

He found a trickle coming off the snowmelt. He had to use his hands to cup it into his mouth. Then he got her to use her magic to fashion a bowl out of a tree branch so he could bring more water back to the cave.

She settled into a squat and started down at the flames. He found himself studying her in the firelight.

She didn't spasm in as much distress as she did on the boat. She acted calmer, but the shadow still hung over her. It never went away.

"What's on your mind?" he asked.

She didn't look up. "I was just thinking about all the people who should be here with us who aren't. They were all such wonderful men."

Yann cast his gaze down into the flames, too. He just had to ask. Now he couldn't get his fellow Watchmen out of his head.

"I'm glad I'm not the only one who remembers them," he murmured. "I'm glad I'm with someone who knew them enough to appreciate them."

She shut her eyes and shook her head to clear her thoughts. "Let's not talk about that. Let's talk about something else. Unfortunately, I don't have Marine's gift for music.....but I do have this."

She took a glistening green stone out of her bag and held it up over the flames. The light refracted through it and cast a bunch of different colored glimmers around the cave.

Yann leaned back and marveled at them revolving on the ceiling. "That's amazing! Where did you get it?"

She smiled down at the stone in her hand. "I found it in a stream bed.....when Anríq and I were out with the children."

"That's so beautiful!" he exclaimed.

She beamed at him, but plenty of sadness crept into her expression.

She pretended to poke the coals under the biturong.

"What else happened between you and Anríq while you were out together?" he asked for no particular reason. "Were you in the city the whole time?"

"No, we wound up in his home Island. We wound up with his home tribe." She looked away. "Maybe I shouldn't tell you this."

"You can tell me—because he already did."

She looked up. "What did he tell you?"

"Just about his family shunning him....and what they did to him when he decided to become a Servant."

She looked down into the flames. She didn't say what else happened and Yann didn't ask.

He decided to change the subject again. "Do you want to try to use your Coil projection to see if you can find out anything about your family?"

She actually brightened up when he suggested it. Maybe she so dreaded talking about Anríq that she would jump at the chance to talk about something else.

She started to smile and raised her hand when, without warning, a blast of white-hot magic forked into the cave from out in the dark.

The shot smashed the biturong off the spit and barely grazed Yann's shoulder before the jet of magic exploded the opposite wall.

It ricocheted back, but not before more bursts of scorching energy erupted from outside. They dumped into the cave shattering rock and deflecting in all directions.

Eliska screamed, dove aside, and barely snatched her staff before another blast burst right next to her.

Yann wound up diving in the other direction. "ELISKA!!" he roared.

She roared, too, but not at him. She pivoted onto her back, plastered herself flat to the floor, and rotated her staff to the cave opening.

She unloaded into the darkness outside, but Yann couldn't see anything out there. He didn't even see where the shots came from.

She bellowed in feral rage and swiped a torrential jet of magic back and forth across the cave mouth. Yann didn't see her hit anything.

As soon as she started shooting, the mystery assailants out there stopped. Yann scrambled onto his knees and hustled over to her. "Are you all right?!" he bellowed.

She kept ejecting her magic through the cave opening, sweeping her staff back and forth, and thundering in insane fury for what seemed like a long time.

She didn't stop until he shook her by the shoulder. "Hey! They're gone! You can stop now!"

She broke off shooting, but she didn't lower her staff. She stayed there contracting her midsection and panting hard.

Her crazed eyes stared out into the darkness beyond the cavemouth. There was nothing there.

"I think they're gone," Yann gasped.

She bolted upright and opened her hand to look into her magical window.

The pool showed a dozen hooded figures racing down the mountain. The image in her window rushed up behind them and rotated in front of them so she and Yann could see the attackers head-on.

Blurry sheets of magic covered the places under their hoods where their faces should have been.

"Bastards!" she snarled. "They're concealing their identities."

"Why did they attack us? Are they with the Voyant?"

"They're human." She traced the assailants' movements for a while. "They're heading for the same towns we were heading for."

"Should we divert somewhere else?

"If they came after us once, they'll come after us again." She shut her hand and scrambled to her feet.

She and Yann surveyed the wreckage of the cave. That first blast hurled the biturong into the dirt. A few embers smoldered where the fire had been.

Boulders and rubble lay all over the floor where the magical bombardment chipped those stones out of place.

"We shouldn't stay here," Yann told her. "We should move."

"I was just going to say the same thing," she murmured. "We're too obvious here."

He turned away first. They didn't even try to clean up the mess.

They left the cave and continued on their way down the mountain. He caught her checking her hand window a few times to find out where the hooded figures went.

"Can you find out who they are?" he asked.

"Not really," she replied. "They're using more than one kind of magical concealment."

"This isn't like the Voyant," he pointed out. "He takes a much more direct approach."

"He hired the Barbarians," she argued. "Maybe these are just another band of assassins or guns for hire."

"We should find another place to spend the night."

She drifted to a halt. They'd been following a ridge all day with the ravine on their right.

Now the ridge dropped away. The downward slope met up with the undergrowth spilling out of the ravine. It followed a streambed out of the wilderness to flat country in the valleys below.

"Come over here," Yann murmured. "We'll just settle down here and wait for morning."

He sat down under a tree and pulled her down next to him.

"I don't think we should light another fire," she whispered.

"No, you're right. I agree with you."

She glanced around in the darkness.

He saw her demons creeping up on her and he made the decision again to put his arms around her. He pulled her against him and tightened her cloak around her.

He would have given her his jacket, too, but she placed her hand flat on the ground between them and sent a flow of magic into the soft soil around the tree roots.

The ground heated up and radiated warmth into both of them.

"Thank you," he breathed. "That would have been so useful in the snow Island."

She burst into a grin. "I didn't know I could do it then—or maybe I couldn't do it then." She looked away. "So many things are different now."

He didn't ask again if she wanted to try to find out about her family. He didn't want her to create the Coil projection in case it attracted unwanted attention.

They cuddled up together and the warmth made both of them fall asleep.

Chapter 8

Yann and Eliska both woke up at sunrise, got to their feet, and set off down the mountain.

Yann didn't ask if they were heading for the same town the mystery attackers fled to. In fact, neither Yann nor Eliska broke the silence all morning.

They made it to the flat land by early afternoon and joined up with a road leading to one of the towns.

A few people passed on their way into town, but as the travelers got closer, Yann sensed again that something was wrong with this place.

It didn't breathe with the same kind of rot and menace as the Hall of Magical Learning. Yann couldn't find anything wrong with this town except that there weren't nearly enough people in it.

Eliska tensed as she and Yann drew level with the first houses. This town didn't look any bigger than Middleborough—which only made it more obvious that it wasn't functioning the way it should have.

One man stood in front of his house chopping firewood with an axe. These people didn't have the fantastical machines the friends saw in other Layers.

A few doors down, Yann and Eliska passed a bony woman with a scarf tied around her thinning hair. She carried a laundry basket on her hip and led a little boy with her other hand.

The boy glared up at Yann and Eliska. The hostility blasting out of the kid's face almost made Yann stop in his tracks.

Eliska's eyes darted around the town taking it all in. She saw it, too.

The two friends eventually made it as far as the blacksmith's forge, but the blacksmith wasn't there. Maybe that was the problem. The constant ring of the blacksmith's hammer didn't send its usual lively music through the town.

Four men stood talking in front of the forge. Hardly anyone else moved around in this town. They all either hid in their houses....or they weren't here at all.

These men all wore beaten, dirty work clothes, muddy boots, and left their hair and beards uncut and uncombed.

Eliska went over to the men. "Good afternoon," she began.

"Good afternoon," one of the men replied politely enough.

"I was wondering if you could help me. We're looking for a group of men—about ten or twelve of them. They were wearing black hoods and used magic to conceal their faces. They ran into this town last night just after sundown. Did any of you see them?"

The same man raised his bushy eyebrows. "We would have seen something like that."

"But then again," another man added, "none of us would have been out and about then. We wouldn't have seen if we'd been in our houses."

"I was just wondering in case one of you might not have been in your houses at the time."

"I wasn't." The first man raised his eyebrows again. "Why do you want to know?"

"These strangers attacked me and my friend last night....in the mountains up there. We tracked them to this town....."

"If they used magic to conceal their faces, maybe they used magic to make it look like they came here when they didn't," a third man suggested.

Eliska nodded. "I thought of that. I just thought I'd ask. Thank you for your help."

She started to turn away, but the fourth man darted forward and grabbed her elbow. "You're a magic-user, aren't you? You must be if you tracked those men here."

Yes, I am," she replied. "What of it?"

"Maybe you could help us. This town is under a curse."

Eliska made a face and grimaced at the surroundings. "I can see that it is. What's the problem, anyway? Where is everyone?"

"We don't know," the third man replied. "They just keep disappearing one after another. We don't know why."

"It's been going on for years," the first man added. "Everything's fine and then, one day, you wake up and your wife is gone."

Eliska gasped. "That's awful! I'm so sorry."

"Can you help us?" the fourth man asked. "Could you find out what's causing it?"

"I'll try." Eliska spread her palm in front of her.

She created her Coil projection, revolved it until she found this Island, and examined it from all sides.

"Can you locate the source of the curse?" Yann asked.

"There is no curse," she replied. "The Island is destabilizing at its edges. The population disappearing is just a symptom of instability taking over the Island."

"So....there's nothing we can do?" the first man's voice shook. "We can't.... you know....get our loved ones back?"

She turned around to face them. "I don't think so. Your families will be lost in the Layers if they're still alive at all. I'm sorry I can't tell you anything more promising than that. If I was you, I'd evacuate this Island before anyone else gets taken."

"Evacuate!" the third man gasped. "You mean...just leave?"

"The instability will keep growing until the Island disintegrates completely. Then all the rest of you will be lost, too."

"But that means....." The first man shot a flinty glance around the town. "That would cause panic."

"I could help you," Eliska offered. "My friend and I will leave this Island soon, too. I could take you with us to another stable Island."

The four men held a hasty conference amongst themselves. Yann watched the interchange without getting involved.

She didn't tell these men that whatever stable Island she took them to would also destabilize at some point—probably sooner rather than later.

The four men came to some decision and returned to where Yann and Eliska waited for them.

"We'll....just....gather our people....." the first man stammered.

"Take your time," Eliska told him. "There's no rush. We'll wait here until you're ready."

The four men scattered in different directions. The noise in the town changed as they went from house to house passing the word to evacuate.

Eliska consulted her Coil projection as soon as they left. She expanded it and studied a few different nearby Layers.

"What are you looking for?" Yann asked.

"I'm looking for the men who attacked us. They must have gone to a stable Layer. I'm going to track the bastards down and find out why they attacked us. I can't think of any other reason unless it had something to do with this whole war against the Voyant. He's our only enemy."

Yann watched her adjust the image a few different times. She created lines from the cave where she and Yann originally planned to spend the night.

The lines scattered and separated before each one dropped into the next Layer below this one.

The lines faded out at different points, but she added more magic to the image and made them clearer.

They eventually rejoined in another city Island five Layers away. She used her hand window to bring up a picture of the hooded figures with their faces blurred by magic.

"Can't you penetrate their protection?" Yann asked.

"I might be able to, but I want to find them first. I'll unmask them when I catch them. Then we'll be able to question them about why they're after us. It doesn't make sense that the Voyant is trying to kill us if he wants one of us to take the second Shard."

"Why try to kill us all the other times, then?" Yann asked.

"I'm not so sure that he did. He might have hired the Barbarians to come after us, but they were supposed to hand their target over to their client—not kill the person."

Yann looked away. "They sure acted like they wanted to kill us."

"That might have been because the Barbarians don't know how to fight any other way. They don't normally try to keep a person alive once they start fighting. They aren't in the habit of even thinking about whether a person stays alive."

Yan made a face. "I might be able to accept that if the Voyant didn't keep coming after us."

"We know the single Shard coincides with upheaval and instability. Maybe he can't control any of that. Maybe he just shows up and whatever Island or Layer he shows up in starts to collapse no matter what he does. Maybe he doesn't have any control over that."

Yann spun around and frowned at her. "Why are you defending him? You're the one who said he was after us."

"He is after us—assuming we're right about the whole Shard thing."

"Does this have anything to do with what I said about you being related to him?"

Now she was the one to turn away. "Maybe it does—but you have to admit that it fits what we've seen from him. We've been wondering all this time why he didn't just kill us outright—and he doesn't. He has never really tried to kill us—not really. He could have done it dozens of times."

"These strangers certainly tried," Yann pointed out.

"That's exactly my point. If they don't come from him, who are they and why did they really try to kill us?"

Just then, the townspeople came over to the pair and started to assemble in front of the forge. A few women and children came first. They shuffled their feet and looked around at everything other than Yann and Eliska.

She shut her Coil projection. Yann and Eliska just stood around and waited for the rest of the townsfolk to show up.

Some brought baskets or bundles of goods. Others came with nothing but the shirts on their backs.

A hundred people gathered from every direction. The four men came last. They went through every house from one end of town to the other, stuck their heads inside, and occasionally went in to search and make sure everyone got out.

The four men finally reassembled at the forge. They had to go through the crowd answering a million questions and reassuring everyone.

The first man finally came over to Eliska. "We're ready to go now. Thank you for doing this."

"Don't mention it." She raised her voice to call over the crowd so everyone could hear her. "I'm going to create a binding spell to hold all of us together so we don't get separated in the Layers. You'll all get squashed together. It might be a little bit uncomfortable, but it won't last long and it will make sure no one gets lost. I'll transport us through the Layers to another city. It's a stable Island. You'll be safe there for now. What you do after that will be up to you. Does everyone understand?"

The townsfolk nodded and a few murmured to each other.

"Do whatever you have to do," the man told her. "We're really grateful to you for doing this."

She didn't acknowledge him. She shouldered her way into the crowd, took her place at the very center, and pushed everyone outward and away from her to clear a space.

Yann tried to follow her and got smashed into the crush of bodies.

"Don't worry about standing too far away," Eliska told everyone. "I'll be able to hold onto you. Don't worry. You're going to be fine."

Her assurance didn't ease the townsfolks' agitation. Their murmuring turned to outright protests and some of the children started crying.

She ignored them, raised her staff above her head, circled it over the townsfolk, and spread a wide net around the whole group.

Yann fell into a shocked silence watching her. The depth of her new power had been startling enough before now.

She went through this process so methodically—almost lazily. She must have done this before. She treated it as a non-event.

She circled her staff around and around. The fountain of magic shooting from the end spread above the townspeople's heads and started to curl down toward the ground. It surrounded the crowd in a ball of crackling, flashing, blazing light.

The crowd became progressively more hysterical as the ball closed them inside it. A few people screamed, but Eliska didn't stop.

She swept her staff around faster and faster. The magic pouring from it came stronger and crackled louder. It built to a crescendo until she slammed the other end of her staff down hard in the middle of the circle.

A powerful force tugged Yann and the townspeople inward. They all crushed in on Eliska standing at the center, but she didn't let up even for a second.

The ground rumbled beneath Yann's feet. Brilliant forks of lightning shot through the soil and cracked it away from the rest of the town.

The fountain of magic kept jetting from the top end of Eliska's staff. She hunkered under it with her eyes clamped shut and her face screwed up in intense concentration.

The wind whipped her hair and clothes in all directions and then a tempest of chaos struck the ball full force.

The town Island disintegrated around the ball and everyone in town wheeled off into the mayhem.

Screams and terrified yells echoed through the ball. It tumbled away into nothing.

Darklings lunged for the ball, tried to crush it in their teeth, and roared in fury when they couldn't penetrate it.

The townspeople cringed and shrieked every time some monster came too close. Eliska didn't even try to deflect the Darklings. She poured all her magic into the ball.

It smashed through one chaos Layer, plunged into a vast ocean, sank to the bottom, touched down, and another blast fractured the ocean floor.

Millions of tons of water pounded through the breach and carried the ball with it, but none of that water touched the townspeople.

The ball tumbled, somersaulted, and wheeled through dozens of Layers. Fire pelted the ball's outer edge.

Countless strikes from unseen assailants smacked the ball back and forth, but the gravity holding everyone's feet on the ground stayed the same through it all.

The ball eventually bounced off a stone wall, slowed to a stop, and then hurtled at the wall with unbelievable force.

The ball punched straight through it, shattered another Layer, and landed on a hillside outside a giant city somewhere deep in the Coil.

Chapter 9

Eliska lost control of her magic when her ball of protection hit the hillside and started to roll down it. One of the nearby townswomen bumped into Eliska and knocked her staff out of place.

The ball started to fail and then someone else crashed into her from behind.

The ball fell apart and everyone sprawled down the hill grunting and groaning in pain. She rolled onto her stomach and smelled grass under her nose.

She scrambled to sit up. Yann lay on his back next to her. She touched his shoulder and felt that he was unhurt. None of the other townspeople were injured, either.

She landed outside a city only a few miles away. This new magic building inside her told her without checking that the men she wanted to find were inside that city. They fled here to hide so she wouldn't be able to find them, but they were still here.

The townsfolk blundered to their feet and stumbled over to her. "Thank you so much!" one of the men told her. "We are so grateful!"

She stood up and brushed the grass off her pants. "I'm just glad you're all safe. You should be fine here for now. Good luck. My friend and I will go on our way now."

She extended her hand to Yann to pull him up and the two of them set off for the city.

The townspeople took longer to straighten themselves out, gather into a group, and decide what to do.

They were still standing there in the same place by the time Yann and Eliska made it halfway to the city.

"That was amazing," Yann breathed on the way.

"What?" she asked.

"What you just did. You surrounded all those people with your magic."

She shrugged that away. "That was nothing. I could have taken the whole town if I needed to—including the houses, the land, live-stock—everything."

He looked away with a shake of his head. "Should I be worried about this?"

"About what?"

"About how powerful you're getting. Everyone always said you had amazing magic before, but you're so much stronger now. It's really starting to worry me."

"You don't have anything to worry about. I'm the one who has to control it."

"Can you?" he asked.

She grimaced at him. "Do you see me losing control of it?"

"I guess not," he muttered.

"I control it all the time," she mumbled. "If I can control it now, I can control it all the time. Controlling it isn't the problem."

He frowned at her. "I don't understand. What you do you mean?"

She stopped and turned to him. "Do you really want to know? Do you really want me to tell you?"

"Of course. I always want to know what's going on with you."

She compressed her lips and glanced away before she made up her mind to tell him. She still wasn't sure if she should.

Her new power scared her, too, but not the way he said. "This power....." she began.

He waited for her to finish. "Yeah? What about it?"

She opened her mouth and stopped herself from telling him point blank that it came from the Dark. Maybe he would have already figured that out, but she didn't want to really scare him by saying it out loud.

"It's a lot stronger than you think," she finally blurted out. "It's a lot stronger than what you've seen—like a lot stronger. I could....well, I won't tell you what I could do. That's all you need to know. It's a lot stronger than anything I've used. I don't let myself use it because I don't know how. I only use a small part of it—the part I know I can control. See? I'm already controlling it—probably more than I need to. You have nothing to worry about unless I start flying off the handle and doing crazy stuff out of control. Now do you understand?"

He nodded, turned away, and started walking. "I guess it doesn't really make me feel better to know it's as strong as that."

"That's why I didn't tell you before."

He didn't answer the rest of the way to the city. She actually really hoped he did figure out that this magic came from her Dark poison. Where else would it come from? It was the only thing that changed while she and Anríq were alone together.

Yann and Eliska entered the city. It definitely didn't suffer from any population loss.

Men, women, and children packed every square inch of the place. They could barely walk down the streets without bumping into each other. Thick, jostling crowds packed every street.

This was one of the machine cities with vehicles running along the ground and flying in the air.

Heavy traffic made it difficult for so many people to get through on foot. The ground vehicles had to drive extra slowly to avoid running over anyone.

Airborne vehicles clouded the skies between tall buildings.

Eliska squinted up at them.

"Is something wrong?" Yann asked.

"Something's wrong with this Island," she muttered.

"Is it the same thing we felt with the Hall of Magical Learning?"

"I don't know. I guess it might be."

"What do you want to do?" he asked.

"I guess we just keep going and see what happens. We're already here and we're safe. I don't see any reason to leave yet."

"Maybe we should," he pointed out. "If this place is Dark and Dark forces come after us......"

"If these mystery men are really after us, they'll follow us to whatever other Island we go to. I say we go on the offensive and hunt them instead."

He burst into a grin. "Okay. How do you want to do it?"

She expanded her Coil projection, she zeroed in on this particular Layer, located the golden lines attached to the men she wanted to find, and found where they were in the town.

"They're in that hotel. Three of them are in the bar. Another two are outside on the terrace."

"How many of them do you want to capture?" Yann asked.

"We only need one to tell us what they're doing and who they're working for. You use the front door and go into the bar. I'll sneak around the back of the hotel over here, jump the wall, and approach the terrace from the garden. That way, if they run for it, we'll box them in from both sides."

"And then what?" Yann asked. "Are you going to open fire on them with all those other people around?"

"I'm not going to open fire to kill these men. I just told you that. I'm going to try to capture one of them." She caught him looking at her sideways. "I won't harm anyone else in the hotel. On my honor."

"Okay. If you're sure....."

They split up. Eliska circled the hotel. She had to climb through a few different yards and scale a brick wall behind the hotel.

She climbed up it just enough to peek over the side. A giant garden separated her from the terrace.

Dozens of people in fancy clothes milled around, sipped their drinks, talked, and laughed out there.

A stone fountain tinkled farther down the terrace. Its water flowed down an artificial series of channels to a silver pool at the bottom.

She didn't see the men she was looking for from here.

She checked her hand window one more time. One of the men looked like a powerfully built middle-aged man six inches taller than anyone in front of her.

Two others were much younger. They all wore plain black suits without the colorful brocade jackets and silk hats of the men she saw on the terrace.

She used the trees and shrubbery to conceal herself so no one saw her jump over the wall. She inched closer to the terrace and searched every face.

Half the people out here were women wearing dresses in the Tenby style.

Everyone at this party looked like they stepped out of Tenby except that this Island seemed even richer and more extravagant.

She snuck a little closer and hid behind a tree before she located the men she wanted. They had moved from the bar to another inner gathering hall. Yann approached them from the opposite side of the hotel.

The men she'd seen on the terrace had already gone inside, too. They met up with their friends. All five men were in one place. This was perfect. They played right into Eliska's hands.

The scene in the gathering hall looked even more luxurious. Some of the women in there wore elaborate sleeveless gowns with wide ruffled skirts spilling all the way to the floor.

Some of the men wore gold-braided uniforms covered in medals and decorations. One even wore a huge hat with gold ruffles around the corners.

Eliska advanced the rest of the way to the terrace. A few of the guests gave her strange looks, but she ignored them and shouldered her way inside.

The men she was looking for were in there.

She entered the hotel itself and stopped on the threshold to the gathering hall. The five men she'd seen earlier stood with some of the fanciest men and women in the hall. They talked easily and even laughed. What were these mystery attackers doing here?

Those five men looked even more out of place than Eliska herself.

Right then, Yann stepped into another doorway at the opposite end of the big hall. So many people stood between him and Eliska that she wouldn't have seen him otherwise.

Everyone definitely noticed him even though he wasn't dressed nearly as extravagantly as all the other guests.

Everyone saw his uniform and the glaive in his hand. People stopped talking and turned around to stare at him in stunned shock.

Dead silence fell over the hall. Everyone pulled back to get away from him when he stepped into the room.

A bubble of space surrounded him as he advanced slowly into the room. His eyes traced every face and measured every decoration and frilly ruffle.

He got closer to the men in question.

They must have been using magic to spy on Yann and Eliska because they definitely recognized him, too.

The five men waited where they were. They didn't react at all until he got right near them.

The crowd parted in exactly the same way to let him through....and all five lunged forward to attack him.

These men didn't use staffs nor did they fight barehanded the way the Guardian Templars did.

The strangers opened their hands to create some kind of glowing magical crystals that hovered over their palms.

The strangers' magical blasts ejected from the points of the crystal and bombarded Yann—or they would have if he didn't dodge out of the way in time.

He dove sideways to avoid the shots and somersaulted into the crowd. The strangers' shots hit some of the surrounding bystanders.

People screamed and ran, scurried for the exits, and left Yann sitting there exposed.

He spun around and raised his glaive, but he wouldn't be able to fight these wizards with just a glaive.

People charged for the other exit where Eliska stood waiting.

She shoved her way through them, entered the hall behind the strangers' backs, and raised her staff.

The instant she sent her magic into it, the five strangers spun around to confront her. They completely ignored Yann and all five of the strangers concentrated on her alone.

Each man used a different colored crystal, but none of that concerned Eliska.

She felt in that moment just how powerful she was. She didn't usually let herself become aware of the real depth of Darkness she'd become.

She didn't know who these men were, but they didn't hold a candle to her Darkness. Not even all of them combined could touch this.

She raised her staff over her head. All five of them fired their magic at her at the same time. Five different colored forks of power jetted at her.

She pointed her staff at them, sucked all five beams into her staff, and blasted them back at their owners.

The forks smashed all five crystals and left the five men defenseless.

They tried to recover by scattering. It took each of them a split second to recreate their crystals.

One of them strangers ran in Yann's direction, but these strangers must have completely discounted him. He raised his glaive to fight back, but the stranger didn't even look at Yann.

Eliska couldn't risk one of them shooting at him or anyone else in this hall getting hurt.

She swept her staff over her head one more time and fired it at the five strangers. She surrounded them with another binding spell, sucked them all together so their bodies squashed into a tight bunch, and slammed them down on the floor.

She added another spell to the binding charm to stop any of them from using their magic.

Chapter 10

Y ann hustled over to Eliska. The five strangers sat crumpled on the gathering hall floor.

"Are you okay?" Yann panted.

"I'm fine." She curled her lip at the wizards in front of her. "They aren't as special as they think they are. That was way too easy."

He followed her gaze. A sheet of magic surrounded the five men and bound them to each other. They couldn't move or use their magic to break out.

"What do you want to do with them now?" Yann asked.

"We have to get them out of the hotel, but we can't go through the terrace. Everyone will see us. Hold onto me."

She shot out her hand and took his. The feeling of her holding his hand brought back so many memories, but now wasn't the time.

She aimed her staff at the strangers, and the next instant, Yann, Eliska, and the five men magicked out of the hotel into what looked like a park somewhere.

Yann looked all around him. "Where are we?"

"We're just in another part of the same city. No one will bother us here." She turned to the strangers. "Who are you? Why are you hunting for us? You tried to kill us last night. Why?"

"No one tried to kill you, young one," the older man countered. "We only wanted to capture you."

"Don't you dare call me that," she snapped back. "You concealed your identities to hide what you were doing—which means you were doing something you shouldn't have. Now tell me who you are and don't lie about it or I'll flatten you. Why did you want to capture us?"

"Not him. Just you." The old man inclined his head to one side and examined Eliska extra closely. "You don't remember me, do you? You were too young then."

She frowned at him. "What are you talking about?"

"We met you.....a long time ago...when you were only small. You must have been five years old at the time. You were already wandering alone in the Coil. You met up with our party and traveled with us for two days. I taught you a few things about how to use your magic to navigate the Coil and find food." His eyebrows came together. "You don't remember?"

Eliska scowled at him and then turned away. "Now I do."

"My name is Miloji Evic. We belong to the order of the Keepers of the Dawn," the old man went on. "We've been looking for you."

"Why now?" Yann interjected. "If you met her back then, you could have helped her. What kind of people are you that you would let a five-year-old wander alone in the Coil?"

"We had nothing to do with it," the old man replied. "She left us of her own free will. She magicked herself away from us to another part of the Coil where we couldn't follow."

Yann glanced over at her. She wouldn't look at her prisoners.

She said she moved around a lot when she lived alone in the Coil. She never stayed with anyone for very long.

Maybe she didn't want to get attached to these wizards. Maybe she didn't trust them or maybe she just treated everyone like that.

Miloji turned his attention back to her. "We sensed a great Dark force developing....about a week ago. Our task was to eliminate the source to protect the rest of the Coil. Then we discovered that the force came from you, young one. You have taken this Darkness on yourself....."

She rounded on him snarling. "What do you want from me? Did you come here to rub it in my face? Do you think I wanted to get like this? You just admitted you wanted to destroy the Dark force....."

"We wanted to destroy it before we found out it was you," Miloji corrected. "After we found out it came from you, we decided to capture you. Come back to our monastery with us. We can heal you of this Darkness. You'll be free. You can go your own way. Then we can destroy the Darkness the way we set out to."

She jerked away and paced a few steps aside. She stopped there with her back to the men.

"You have incredible magic, young one," Miloji went on. "You always did, but it's so much stronger now. We can teach you to use it. We offered to take you into our order way back then. Do you remember? Then you slipped away that same night. If you've ever regretted that decision, you can change it now. You don't have to go alone. We can teach you how to use this magic. You don't have to live in fear—of the power or yourself."

Eliska didn't move for a second. Yann studied her on the side. It sure sounded like the answers to her prayers—to all their prayers.

When she did move, she glanced over at Yann. Their eyes met.

Her face went through a series of rapid emotional contortions. Her expression changed so fast that Yann couldn't read exactly what she might be thinking or feeling.

She didn't ask him what he thought. This sounded like their best bet, but that was her decision.

She finally hardened her features and faced her prisoners. "All right. I'll go with you. You better not be messing with me...."

Miloji smiled up at her. "I wouldn't do that. We want to destroy this Darkness as much as you do, but we don't want to destroy you. You're too valuable the way you are. I told you that the last time. Don't you remember?"

She didn't answer. She passed her hand across the air in front of her and broke the binding spell holding the men together.

They got to their feet, dusted themselves off, and Miloji went from man to man checking that none of them was hurt.

Eliska stood back by Yann's side and watched them.

"Do you trust these guys?" Yann murmured out the side of his mouth.

"Not one inch, but if they have that much power, I might as well try it. Maybe they can help us in other ways. It's worth it to me to find out as long as we're separated from Anríq and Marine—and we can't find the White Spire, either What else do we have to do?"

He smiled down at her. "It will be worth it to help you even without all that other stuff."

Her face pinched, but they had to cut their conversation short when the wizards stood up.

They called themselves the Keepers of the Dawn. That meant nothing to Yann. It didn't tell him whether these men were good, bad, or indifferent.

He didn't see anything that would specifically make him mistrust these men. He didn't see anything that would make him specifically mistrust them, either.

They gathered around Eliska. Miloji smiled at her and patted her on the shoulder once. "We should get started right away. We'll take you to our monastery in the mountains. We can begin there."

"Where is it?" she asked.

"It's in another Layer. We can transport you there."

Eliska's eyes widened. "You can transport across Layers?! I've never been able to do that."

"You have a lot to learn about this new power." Miloji turned to Yann. "It's been a pleasure meeting you, young man. I'm sure you can find your way back to the city from here." Miloji waved to Eliska. "Let's go, young one."

"Hold it," she interrupted. "Yann is coming with us."

"I'm afraid that's impossible. We don't allow imps inside the monastery."

Eliska reared back in alarm. Every muscle stiffened to the breaking point.

She tightened her grip on her staff. "I'm not going anywhere without Yann. You take both of us or we leave together. If I see you anywhere near us again, I'll kill you next time. Thanks for nothing." She took hold of Yann's elbow to turn him away. "Come on, Yann. Let's get out of here."

"Stop, young one," Miloji shot out his hand to block her way. "You can't keep living with this Darkness. It will destroy your whole life."

"I was living with it just fine before I met you. At least I have one friend in the world—and that didn't change just because you showed up. See you around."

She turned away for the second time.

This time, Miloji actually dove in front of her to stop her. "All right, young one. You win. You can bring your imp friend."

"His name is Yann," she snapped. "Treat him with some respect. He's the one who has been getting me through this—not you—and he's saved my life more than once."

Miloji only nodded. He let his arms flop at his sides. "Have it your way. You can bring him with you, but he won't be involved in your training nor will he be allowed to enter any of the sacred areas of the monastery."

"Fine," she snapped. "I'll come as long as I can see him every day. I would rather live with this Darkness than let anything separate us."

"Very well. I agree to your conditions."

"So how do you want to take us to the other Layer?"

The Keepers of the Dawn surrounded Yann and Eliska. She shrank a little nearer to him when the strangers came too close.

He considered if he should put his arm around her shoulders. He didn't want anything to separate him from Eliska again, either.

He never imagined he could mean this much to her. She had been ready to walk away from her one chance at healing—for him.

This kind of help and training must have been a dream come true for her, but it wasn't as important to her as he was.

He loved her for that. He just hoped these strangers came through on their promise. They better—as if Yann would have been able to do anything to them if they didn't.

Chapter 11

The Keepers of the Dawn formed a circle around Yann and Eliska in the center. The men raised their hands, but they didn't join them.

Each man placed his right hand over the left hand of the man next to him. They sent a flow of magic into each other's hands and new crystals formed over each pair of hands.

The crystals glowed with multi-faceted prismatic colors. These crystals were much bigger than the ones the Keepers of the Dawn used in the hotel.

The wizards added more and more magic to the crystals to make them shine with brilliant light. The color got lost in that blinding white glow.

Without no warning, a sudden flash burst inward from all the crystals.

The flash magicked the whole party to a completely different landscape. This was not a lush park in the middle of an advanced city.

The group materialized on a high rock ledge in the middle of a vast wilderness of bare stone mountains. Yann didn't see a single stick or leaf of vegetation anywhere.

Jagged cliffs towered to a white-blue sky scuttered with clouds. That was it. Yann didn't see any life here except for himself, Eliska, and the five men from the Keepers of the Dawn.

Miloji pointed across a steep chasm dropping over vertical cliffs. Miles of the same rocky, lifeless wilderness separated the group from huge stone mountains over there.

Some kind of fortress had been carved straight out of the rock. It clung to the cliff face miles above the canyon floor. Yann didn't see any road or even a path leading up to it.

"That's our monastery," Miloji announced. "We'll go inside."

The Keepers of of the Dawn answered Yann's questions by forming a circle again, creating their crystals, and magicking the group to the monastery's front steps.

Miloji led the way into the monastery's main central entrance foyer. Monks in full-length black cassocks glided around everywhere.

They all walked with their hands tucked into their sleeves. It gave them a very dignified, almost holy air.

Miloji turned to face Yann and Eliska and pointed out the two younger wizards from the hotel. "This is Andrija Vasic and Milic Uljani. They'll will show you where to go." Miloji nodded to Eliska. "I'll see you very soon, young one."

He walked off. The other two strangers went with him and left Andrija and Milic alone with Yann and Eliska.

"Follow me," Andrija told Yann.

"But what about....?" Yann glanced at her.

Eliska looked up at him with a desperate pleading expression.

"Initiates to the order stay in the dormitory upstairs," Milic explained. "You couldn't go there. Miloji said you could see each other every day. He didn't say you could live together."

Yann frowned. "I guess not." He turned to Eliska. "I guess....I'll see you soon."

She nodded fast, but she had to pinch her lips together too tightly to say anything.

He would have liked to tell her to be careful, but he didn't see anything here to threaten them.

Andrija and Milic both backed off in different directions. Yann and Eliska had no choice but to separate.

He walked backward to keep her in sight until the last possible second. She did the same thing.

He really didn't want to leave her alone, especially when he saw how scared she was. She'd been alone all her life before she came to Middleborough.

This would be the first time she'd gone anywhere alone since she joined the Watch. She had become as dependent on the group as they had become dependent on her.

Yann didn't trust these Keepers of the Dawn and his feeling had nothing to do with whether they were good people or not.

He'd spent so much time and invested so much energy and attention in protecting Eliska and taking care of her. He didn't want to hand her over to some strangers who didn't even know her.

He backed up so far that he bumped into the wall. He had to turn around.

Andrija waited for him in another corridor leading behind the foyer.

Yann entered it and lost sight of Eliska, but he couldn't forget that terrified expression on her face.

He didn't know what the Keepers of the Dawn would do to help her, but he really wanted to be there with her when it happened. She deserved that much.

He tried to shake that off. The monks would heal her in a few minutes. The sooner the better. He wouldn't begrudge them if they didn't want an imp in the room when they did it.

Andrija brought him back to reality. "Your sweetheart is very pretty."

Yann snapped out of his trance in a heartbeat. "She isn't my sweetheart. She's just my friend."

Andrija snorted. "You don't have to gloss it over. We can all see the way you act around each other."

Yann didn't argue to change the guy's mind.

Yann studied Andrija more closely. He was a tall, strapping blond-haired, blue-eyed guy of eighteen, but he had the build of a man much older than that.

Milic was smaller with dark hair and eyes, olive skin, and a compact, more dangerous kind of energy.

"How did you wind up joining the Keepers of the Dawn?" Yann asked.

"I was born here," Andrija replied. "My father was one of the senior Rectors."

Yann raised his eyebrows. "How did he manage to have you, then?"

"Anyone of the rank of Rector or above can take a wife. I'd say half the Rectors have wives and children living in the Tenth Wing."

Yann gaped at him. "They do? That's incredible."

"Why is it incredible? Miloji has five children and his brother has six.'

Yann shook his head and looked away. "I'm used to the Black Watch. They don't have children or get married. They live as celibates."

Andrija stopped in his tracks, dipped his eyes to Yann's uniform, and then pierced him with a harsh glare.

"Then how is it possible that you travel with this woman—and don't tell me you're only friends. I'm not so stupid that I can't see. You're much more than that."

Yann broke eye contact and kept walking. "We might be more than that, but we aren't sweethearts. Besides, I haven't taken the oath yet. I'm still underage."

Andrija sized him up. "You can't be too far off from it."

"I'm not—but since I'm alone, I don't have any other senior Watchmen to take the oath to—so I've just been trying to get through each day with my life intact. I guess that's the best I can do right now."

Andrija walked in silence for a long time. Yann didn't see where they were going.

"She's extremely powerful," Andrija finally remarked. "I've never seen anyone as powerful as she is."

"So I keep hearing," Yann muttered.

"How does a magic-user as powerful as that wind up with an imp like you?"

Yann shrugged. "It wasn't intentional—believe me."

"Why did she leave Miloji's group behind and she doesn't leave you behind?"

"You would have to ask her that. Anyway, we're on a mission to stop the Voyant Mendicat. We've been working together...."

Yann didn't tell this stranger about the friends' suspicions that Yann was either related to the last King in the White Spire or that he might become the next King.

Andrija made a face and turned off at the next corner. "No one can defeat the Voyant Mendicant. That's a fool's errand."

"Not even Eliska?" Yann asked. "Could she defeat him?"

Andrija only grimaced again, opened a door at the end of the corridor, and waved Yann through it.

"Go down these stairs. You'll find another hall with the kitchen on one side and a dormitory on the other. You can stay there. Vesna will show you which bunk to take."

Yann didn't know or care where he stayed. He only knew he wouldn't be staying with Eliska.

Andrija didn't go with him when Yann trotted down the stairs.

He found Vesna working in the kitchen. She was a heavy-set middle-aged woman wearing a grubby white apron and a handkerchief tied around her hair.

She wiped her hands on her apron when Yann told her what he wanted. "Are you the new stableboy?" she asked.

"No, a friend of mine is upstairs with the monks. I'm here with her."

Vesna frowned. "Everyone who comes here has to have a job. If you aren't an initiate to the order, you better take over as the stableboy until we find out what job you're supposed to do."

She led him across the hall to the dormitory. It consisted of one long room with double bunks a few feet apart.

She waved to different sections of the dormitory. "The kitchen staff stays over there. The housekeeping staff stays there. The maintenance crew stays there. The stable staff stays over there. You can take this bunk here."

"So...." Yann hesitated. "So this is the servants' quarters? Is that it?"

"Of course! What did you think?" She beamed at him and turned away. "Now I know why they sent you. You aren't very bright, are you? You better get out there and get to work. The stables won't clean themselves."

She went back to the kitchen. She didn't explain where the stables were or how he should clean them out. He would just have to figure it out.

At least if he had a job, the monks wouldn't think about throwing him out and keeping Eliska here on her own.

He didn't bother Vesna again. He explored around this understory and found the stables on the next level down.

A giant courtyard occupied the monastery's lowest level. Towers, battlements, and giant wings extended from all sides of the huge fortress.

Stable boxes surrounded a gargantuan courtyard built into the monastery from the back. Whoever built this fortress carved out the whole mountain so sunshine would stream between the rocks and light up the stable courtyard.

Monks in cassocks led magnificent horses out of stalls surrounding the courtyard. The stables had been constructed out of the mountain's bare rock.

The monks exercised the horses and even rode them out there.

The animals glistened with health. Yann had never seen such impressive horses anywhere, not even among the Corsairs who were famous for their horses.

He didn't understand why a bunch of magic-users would need horses like this, but he didn't ask.

He went to the nearest empty stall. It definitely needed cleaning. He sighed and rested his glaive against the wall. He could put up with this for Eliska's sake.

He had to hunt around before he found a shovel and wheelbarrow.

He also found what might have been a barn if it hadn't been part of the same stone fortress. Hay packed the barn to the rafters.

Heaven only knew where the monks got this hay. They must have gotten it from another Island. They couldn't have gotten it from this landscape.

He got to work shoveling out the stalls, but he had to look around before he found where to dump his wheelbarrow loads of dirty hay and muck.

He rolled the wheelbarrow down a long ramp behind the courtyard. The manure pile occupied a lonely spot behind the fortress where the steep walls met up with uncarved mountain cliffs.

The very first time he went down there, he discovered two young boys hiding from the monks. These boys couldn't have been more than eleven and they both wore cassocks.

They jumped a foot in the air when Yann showed up, but the boys wilted in relief when they saw who it was. "We thought you were Grugur coming to find us!" one of the boys panted.

"What are you doing down here, anyway?" Yann asked. "Shouldn't you be inside?"

The taller boy put his hands behind his back way too fast. "Nothing!" he blurted out. "We aren't doing anything."

Both boys had brown hair. The taller one had curly hair and a long, thin, bony face. The shorter boy had straight, shoulder-length hair and was kind of chubby.

Yann eyed both boys while he dumped his wheelbarrow. "If you don't tell me what you're doing, I'll assume you were up to no good and I'll have to tell Grugur that I found you down here. If you tell me what you were doing and you *weren't* up to anything bad, I might leave you alone and not tell anyone what I know."

The boys exchanged glances. "Promise you won't tell anyone," the chubby boy insisted.

"I can't do that. You might have been doing something dangerous."

The tall boy hung his head. "You show him, Zvedan."

"No way! You show him. This was all your idea, Lemir. If anyone gets in trouble, it will be you."

"You'll both get in trouble if you were doing something dangerous," Yann interrupted. "Now tell me what it was."

Lemir, the tall boy, stepped forward, but he didn't raise his head to make eye contact with Yann. Lemir held out his hand and created one of those magical windows like the one Eliska used.

The window looked in on a different courtyard of the same fortress. This place must be a lot bigger than Yann realized.

The monks might have used magic to add wings, courtyards, and side turrets that wouldn't have been possible in real the world.

The window looked in on a beautiful sparkling pool full of a bunch of teenage girls swimming, splashing, playing, and laughing with each other.

Yann didn't see any boys or adults with them. The girls were alone, but they were all dressed in swimming outfits.

Their suits covered them from shoulder straps down to thigh-length shorts. These boys wouldn't have been able to see anything incriminating.

Yann studied the scene. The girls were all much older than Zvedan and Lemir. Some of these girls had completely developed. They looked like beautiful young women with every curve on display.

Yann took a step back. "That's all right," he told the boys. "No harm done. I'll leave you alone."

Lemir's head shot up. "You won't tell?"

"Nope." Yann turned back to his wheelbarrow. "You can stay here and enjoy yourselves if you want to."

The boys gaped at him in disbelief. Then they looked at each other with their mouths open.

Yann chuckled to himself and pushed his wheelbarrow back to the stables. He kept grinning to himself. These boys might be magic-users and initiates of a powerful order, but they were still just boys.

From the look of things, they probably didn't get much contact with girls—or any contact with girls.

Those girls must be the Rectors' daughters—which meant their fathers would have been extra protective of keeping them away from the male students.

None of that was Yann's business and these two boys weren't hurting anyone by watching the girls swim and play.

He might have done something if the girls had been changing their clothes, but not this.

He went back to work, and a few minutes later, he spotted Zvedan and Lemir hustling across the courtyard and reentering the monastery as if nothing ever happened.

Yann concentrated on his work. It actually felt pretty good to just focus on this one mundane task.

He didn't have to run and fight and escape collapsing Layers, fight Darklings, and constantly worry about whatever threat was coming after him and his friends next.

He did worry about Eliska, but she wouldn't have to worry about escaping collapsing Layers here, either. She and Yann were safe.

He still hated to let her out of his sight. He would have to bide his time and see if she improved in the monk's care.

He didn't know what he would do if she didn't, but he would have to do something. He wouldn't let anyone harm her or take advantage of her.

Chapter 12

M ilic escorted Eliska up several winding staircases to a huge bedroom with a massive bed in the center. Four carved polished wooden posts held up a canopy with heavy velvet brown curtains draped and tied back on both sides.

A large window looked out over a giant courtyard hundreds of yards across. More windows looked out from rooms all over the walls rising dozens of stories high.

A magnificent terrace covered the bottom floor of the courtyard, but it was like no other terrace Eliska had ever seen. It didn't have any plants or trees, not even growing in pots.

Stone walkways passed between walls, statues, and gazebos. Some of these walkways even created mazes with beautiful sitting areas along the route.

A large pool occupied one side of the courtyard. A high stone wall surrounding the pool to stop anyone from looking in from any direction except from directly above.

A bunch of girls played around in the water, splashed it at each other, and laughed. They sure acted carefree. Eliska never would have been able to do that.

Milic got her attention. "You can make yourself comfortable here for an hour. You have an appointment with Rector Miloji and the other senior Rectors in the Tenth Library after that. They'll assess you and decide on a course of training."

Eliska nodded. "Thank you. You can tell them I'll be there."

He left and she sank onto the bed. This was by far the nicest bedroom she'd ever laid eyes on, but she didn't want to stay here without Yann.

She opened her hand window and located him in the servant's quarters downstairs. He was talking to a stout older woman in a cook's apron while she showed him the dormitory. At least he wasn't too far away.

Eliska had an hour before she needed to be anywhere. She could have gone to see him, but that could wait. She'd only been here for a few minutes.

She used her Coil projection to read the layout of the whole fortress. This place really was massive.

She located the Rectors' families living in the Tenth Wing. Those girls down there belonged to a school class taking a recreational break.

The Rectors kept boys and girls strictly separate with the boys entering the order to receive their education. The Rectors ran a separate school for the girls so they didn't mix with initiates of any age.

Eliska couldn't argue with the order's methods. All those girls were magic-users who got exactly the same training as the boys. They just did it separately.

In fact, the girls didn't socialize with any boys other than their own brothers in the privacy of each family's apartment.

The order took special pains not to let the sexes mix until a person got married and the couple moved into their own apartment.

Eliska didn't let herself think about how the Rectors selected spouses for their young people.

She used her hand window to watch the initiates at their training. They used advanced magical techniques Eliska had never seen anywhere else.

Everyone in the fortress used these magical crystals to channel their power. The size, color, and brilliance of the crystal depended on the person's power and abilities.

She also saw groups of Rectors surrounding individual students in the same circle they used to transport Yann and Eliska through the Layers.

The Rectors were in the process of doing this with a young man of about sixteen. He held his hands out to both sides with greenish-yellow crystals shining above both hands.

The Rectors' magic throbbed with light and the young man's crystals got brighter. They must be enhancing his magic.

Just then, someone knocked on her bedroom door. She shut her hand window in a hurry.

"Yes?" she called out.

Miloji opened the door, stepped inside, smiled at her, and looked around. "It's so good to see you settling in. If you come with me, I'll show you around and we can get acquainted before your first session."

"Milic said I was supposed to meet you in an hour."

"Your session starts in an hour," he corrected. "I thought we could talk and get more familiar with each other before that."

She shrugged. "Why not?"

She followed him outside and they set off down the corridor.

"This is the Seventh Wing," he told her. "This is the residential wing for older initiates—although we don't usually get new students who are as old as you are."

She looked around at older teenagers all wearing floor-length black cassocks. "I can see that."

She could also see that all the initiates in this wing were boys. She was the only girl here.

She assumed that must be because the order didn't take any girls from the outside. The Rectors educated their daughters together, but women didn't enter the order.

Miloji read her mind. "You're special, young one. We always hoped we would find you again, but we didn't find you until we started tracking this Dark force you're carrying."

"I would really appreciate it if you didn't call me that," she blurted out.

He raised his eyebrows. "Call you what?"

"Young one," she repeated. "It's a term of familiarity. We don't share that familiarity—not yet. Just call me Eliska."

"I beg your pardon. We call all our junior initiates that until they become Rectors. It's simply our custom."

"Then make an exception for me. I don't like it."

He shrugged it away and kept walking. "As you wish."

She cringed when he fell silent. She should have treated him more politely considering he was offering to heal her from this Darkness.

He remained silent for so long that she really started to worry that she might have offended him. Maybe he would throw her out.

At least she would be able to continue her travels with Yann after that. She wouldn't have to dread that these people might be doing something to him behind her back.

She checked her hand window and spotted him downstairs in the stable courtyard. He stood under one of the carved stone colonnades watching the monks exercising the horses.

Miloji interrupted her thoughts. "Your friend seems very kind and attentive."

"He's a member of the Black Watch. He's a good man."

Miloji nodded. "I'm glad you found good people to travel with. I hated to think of you out there alone all these years."

She looked away. She had been alone—until recently. A bunch of faces flashed in front of her eyes. Wesh. Yvan. Barsali. Niyazi. Anthane.

Then she remembered Anríq and Marine. Traveling with them had been the greatest privilege of her life.

Now she only had Yann left and he wasn't even here.

She stiffened at the thought. He was right downstairs in the same building, but for some reason she couldn't put her finger on, she felt more alone now than she ever did in all the years she spent growing up in the Coil.

Threat and danger charged this monastery with a sense of danger she couldn't identify. Did she only imagine it?

Miloji turned off into another corridor and showed Eliska into a huge library. It wasn't as big as the library Marine used in the Guardian Temple nor was it as big as the Hall of Magical Learning.

This one was still plenty big enough with twelve landings surrounding a central rectangular chamber. A sweeping staircase rose from each level to the one above it.

Initiates in cassocks worked, read, and studied at desks all over the library. They also used feather pens dipped in ink to write in large books. The Keepers of the Dawn didn't use computers or machines to do anything.

The hum of studious activity filled the library with what should have been a peaceful air. Nothing here gave Eliska any reason to think this place was dangerous.

The dangerous feeling didn't come from the people, the books, the building, or anything else. Maybe it was just the same instability she'd been sensing ever since the Hall of Magical Learning.

That instability permeated everything now—or maybe she only became aware of it since she'd been carrying around this Darkness.

Dark recognized Dark.

"This is the students' library," Miloji told her. "You can come here and do any studying you want to when you aren't in session with the Rectors."

She nodded. She didn't tell him she didn't know how to read. This library would be useless to her.

Miloji wandered through the library looking at everything in a way that told Eliska he expected her to look at everything, too.

He kept stopping at certain desks to see what the students were working on. Eliska did the same thing and copied him like she'd never seen anything so fascinating in her life.

He finally left the library and wandered through a bunch of different other wings and departments of the school.

He showed her the junior wing where the youngest boys did their training, but it was nothing she hadn't already seen in both her projection and in her hand window.

He showed her the sports arena where the older boys used their magic to spar against each other in mock battles to train for the real thing.

"What are you doing with all your power?" she asked once Miloji finally decided it was time to head for the session with the Rectors in the Tenth Library.

He cocked his head to one side. "What do you mean?"

"Why are you training all these powerful magic-users?" she asked. "What's your mission?"

He frowned. "I don't understand."

"You must plan to do something with this power. The Voyant Mendicat is out there collapsing the whole Coil. The Guardian Templars are trying to fight him and stop him. So is the Chivalric Order of Custodians. What are you doing?"

He waved that away. "No one can stop the Voyant. "

"How do you know if you don't try? So....you aren't involved at all—like not at all?"

"Our objective is to train both ourselves and our students in the use of magic. Our task is to perfect our magic as far as possible, to hone our skills, and to attain the highest level of power and proficiency possible."

"That's it?" she asked. "That's your whole objective?"

He frowned at her. "What else is there?"

She shut her mouth and didn't answer. She didn't tell him that he and his order could have been doing so much good in the world with all this magical power they were perfecting, honing, and training.

Chapter 13

Miloji opened the door to another library. This one was much smaller. It bore a striking resemblance to some of the smaller libraries she'd seen in the Templars' cloud tower.

Ten Rectors waited there for Eliska and Miloji to show up. "If you'll just take your place in the center there....." Miloji directed her to the middle of the circle.

"What are you going to do?" she asked. "Are you going to heal me from the Darkness—like right now?"

"We have to assess you first." Miloji stepped into line with the others.

"But I don't use those crystals," she pointed out.

"Raise your staff instead. Channel your magic into that."

She didn't know what to expect, so she raised her staff with both hands.

The Rectors formed a circle, combined their magic through their hands, and created crystals exactly the way she'd seen them doing with the young student.

She sent a flow of magic into her staff and it started to throb, but the magic didn't stay in the staff. It pulsed up her arms and through her. She felt her power building to the breaking point, but it didn't fly out of control nor did it tap the Darkness inside her.

The tension mounted. More and more of the Rectors' magic flooded through her until she couldn't stand it. Her Darkness was already strong enough. She didn't want anything to make it stronger, but once the ritual started, she couldn't break free to stop it.

The torrent flowing into her from all their crystals spiked off the charts. She screamed trying in every way to tear her hands off her staff. She succeeded and the staff fell onto the stone floor with a loud clatter, but the stream of magic didn't stop.

It pulsed into her from all sides, combined with her magic, and threatened to detonate her into a million pieces.

She tossed and thrashed in the middle of the circle. The words, *Make it stop!* kept repeating in her mind, but she couldn't say a word.

The torrent became excruciating. It thrashed her in all directions until she couldn't bear it a second longer.

Without warning, the flood cut off without warning and she collapsed on the ground in a heap. She could barely keep her eyes open.

Every pore and hair sizzled with unimaginable power, but she could already feel that the Rectors didn't give her any power she didn't already have. They just enhanced her own magic to make it stronger—like it needed to be stronger.

Her body twitched and shivered barely containing all that energy. The slightest touch or breath of air would shatter her.

She heard the Rectors talking to her, but she couldn't understand them. Their voices sounded a million miles away.

She jolted when someone picked her up, but she lacked the strength to resist. She went limp when they lifted her off the floor, carried her back to her room, and laid her on the bed.

She felt more people touching her, talking to her, and even sending healing magic into her, but she didn't need that.

She tingled with magic she never imagined existed, much less that she might be able to contain it within herself.

The session didn't touch the Darkness. Whatever the Rectors did, they didn't take the Darkness away.

Whatever they did was no assessment, either. They could call it whatever they wanted. They did it to enhance her magic and make it stronger. Why?

They left her alone and she collapsed into an exhausted coma. She woke up in darkness. Night must have fallen over this Island.

She dragged herself out of bed. She felt wrung out, but at least her strength was starting to come back.

She crossed to the window and looked out at golden light shining from all those windows. It cast a ghostly, almost romantic glow over the courtyard. The other girls weren't around anymore. No one was.

She left the room and wandered the halls planning to go visit Yann.

She stopped when she passed the library.

The Rector's treatment did something to her magic. It increased her own power, but it also increased her intuition about herself and the world around her.

She went in, climbed a few landings, and passed down the stacks.

A dozen older initiates worked around the library even at this late hour. None of them paid any attention to Eliska. They didn't act like a girl staying here bothered them at all.

She didn't plan to do anything in this library, but she stopped at a random shelf and stared at the books on it. These books meant something. She couldn't figure out why, but she couldn't leave until she found out what was in them.

She passed her hand in front of the spines and pulled out a big, thick book bound in brown leather. She couldn't read the writing on the cover.

She took the book to one of the lecterns, flipped it open to a random page, and passed her hand an inch above the text. Her magic radiated to the words and told her what they said even though she couldn't read them.

This book listed all the specific details of Yimichi Ocuron's reign as King in the White Spire. Marine had been right. Historians and accountants followed the King, his Queen, and the whole royal family around day and night recording everything they did every minute of the day.

Anríq had also been right about Yimichi being a Barbarian. So was Noleron Kupuro, the man who would become Yimichi's affiliate after Queen Hubua died.

The records didn't indicate that Noleron even went into the White Spire until after her death. Noleron had been living with the Barbarians in the Sojourner's Sanctum until mere days before she died.

Then he went to the White Spire, took the second Shard of Hotha, and became Yimichi's second affiliate.

Eliska used her magic to scan a few more pages. She froze with her hand above the page when she came to historical accounts about Hubua herself.

Yimichi and Noleron didn't have a drop of royal blood between them, but Hubua did. She was the daughter of one of the Kings in the Hallowed Veils.

That made even less sense than a Barbarian becoming King in the White Spire. Eliska could understand a Barbarian marrying a Barbarian woman and them taking the Shards together. That made more sense than him marrying a princess.

Eliska glanced around the library. She didn't want to disturb the other initiations, but right then, she spotted one of the Rectors.

This was an older man—much older than Miloji. The man let his greying hair grow long and walked with a stoop. He'd been in the session earlier where the Rectors enhanced Eliska's power.

The Rector was talking in low murmurs to one of the initiates and obviously giving the young man some pointers on whatever the guy was writing in his book.

Eliska waited for them to finish before she intercepted the Rector. "Um...excuse me. I wonder if could ask you a few questions."

The Rector turned around, smiled at her, and held out his hand. "Of course, young one. Anything you need, I'm happy to help. My name is Velimir...and you're Eliska, aren't you? Of course we all know all about you."

She tried to brush that off and didn't correct him for calling her 'young one'. For some reason, him calling her that didn't bother her as much as when Miloji did it.

She only said, "Thank you. I was just doing some research on the King in the White Spire and the succession of Voyants. Would you be able to explain something to me?"

His smile slipped only very slightly. "What would you like to know?"

She led him back to the book in question. "This says the last king was Yimichi Ocuron and his wife Hubua was a princess from the Hallowed Vales."

"Yes?" Velimir asked. "What about them?"

"Yimichi Ocuron was a Barbarian—and so was his second affiliate after Hubua's death. How did that happen? How did a Barbarian become King and marry the daughter of one of the Kings in the Hallowed Vales? It doesn't make sense—because we've seen other genealogies where the Kingship is handed down from father to son."

Velimir waved that away and turned to leave. "It makes perfect sense. The previous king must have died without an heir, so they had to find someone else. I must go now, young one. If you have any other questions, don't hesitate to ask."

He walked out of the library and left her standing there with her jaw on the floor. He didn't answer her question at all. What was wrong with him? Did he not understand or was he deliberately trying to mislead her?

The previous King must have died without an heir. Yimichi wouldn't have become King at all if the previous King did have an heir. The Kingship would have gone to the King's son if he had one.

That did nothing to explain why and how some random Barbarian from the Sojourner's Sanctum became king.

If the King in the White Spire died without an heir, the easiest way to replace him would be to take whichever random person happened to be standing around the spire at the time.

Any page boy or maidservant could have taken the Shard of Hotha. It would have saved millions of lives and years of instability and collapse.

So why not do it that way? Why would the Voyant go to so much trouble to find someone no one could find? Why put the whole Coil in danger—unless he really did want to destabilize the Coil for some reason?

It didn't explain how Yimichi came to marry a princess, either, nor did it explain why Yimichi had to go out to the Sojourner's Sanctum to get Noleron to take the second Shard.

Yimichi must have had plenty of advisors standing around when Hubua died. Yimichi could have taken any of them as his affiliate.

This book didn't answer any of Eliska's questions, so she put it back and left the library. She planned to go find Yann and talk to him about it.

Two tall initiates waylaid her on her way out the door. "It's dinner time," they told her. "Come get some food. You must be hungry after your session."

"Um....thank you. I am."

Both initiates smiled at her. One of them had coal-black hair and glittering, narrowed black eyes. He showed all his powerful white teeth when he smiled at her. "I'm Ivico and this is Dusan."

She shook hands with both of them and found herself smiling at them. "Good to meet you. I'm Eliska."

"Let's go," Ivico urged and the three young people left the library. They joined a throng of other initiates all heading in the same direction.

They talked, joked, and bantered back and forth. None of them acted like Eliska being the only girl in the crowd meant anything. Most of the other initiates ignored her. They acted like she'd been here all along.

Chapter 14

Yann tilted his wheelbarrow against the stable wall and propped his shovel next to it. He'd been working for hours and the sun was starting to go down.

The novelty of cleaning these stables was starting to wear off after two days of nonstop work. He worked around the square of stables surrounding the courtyard.

By the time he got back to the starting point, the horses had mucked up their stalls again and he had to start all over.

He didn't see Eliska that first day. He hadn't seen her today, either, and it was almost sunset. Did the monks do something to her?

He went inside the fortress, but he didn't use the servant's entrance the way he usually did. None of the servants were allowed to go up-stairs into the actual monastery unless those servants worked on the housekeeping crew.

Yann went into a side room where the monks kept their water pump. It was an old-fashioned hand pump. The Keepers of the Dawn didn't use any kind of advanced machines or devices to do anything.

He pumped water over his head, stripped off his uniform, and scrubbed down his body to get the feeling of manure off him. He stood there in his underwear and washed his uniform in the water trough.

He could have asked Vesna for another set of clothes and to send his uniform to the monastery laundry, but he didn't want to wear any other clothes while he waited for his uniform to come back.

He was still a member of the Black Watch. If he took off this uniform, he would lose that. He would become nothing but a stable boy. He needed his uniform to remind him that he didn't belong here.

He wrung it out as best he could and put it back on still wet. He really didn't care about how uncomfortable it made him feel.

He wanted everyone who saw him to understand that he wasn't a servant here—not in that way.

He finally went inside and joined the other servants at a big table in Vesna's kitchen while they ate their dinner.

The heat from the fireplace dried out his uniform enough. The water cooled him more than he realized and actually made him more comfortable in the stuffy kitchen.

A few other servants exchanged pleasantries with him, but he avoided conversation whenever possible. He didn't get involved in their discussions unless they asked him a specific question first.

As soon as the dinner broke up, he went to look for Eliska. He actually went back upstairs to the entrance foyer, and from there, he explored the monastery's many levels.

No one stopped him or asked his business or told him to go back downstairs where he belonged. No one even seemed to see him.

He looked in on a bunch of different study halls full of Rectors and a bunch of training halls full of students sparring against each other.

They all used the same colored crystals to shoot their magic at each other. The students used the crystals to manipulate their magic to grab themselves and each other, throw themselves to different places around the training ground, and move and manipulate objects in the course.

Yann watched them for a while, but he lost interest because Eliska wasn't there. Did the monks bring her down here for this kind of training? He would only find out by asking her.

He climbed a few more sets of stairs and looked in on long dining halls full of initiates eating dinner together. They talked and joked and laughed, but Eliska wasn't with them.

He tried not to mind that everyone in the whole monastery was male—apart from the servants. Eliska would have stuck out a mile if she'd been here at all.

The housekeeping crew was made of all men, too. Yann realized in that instant that the only female servants all stayed downstairs in the kitchens, laundry, and other areas. None of them ever went upstairs for any reason.

That realization set off Yann's alarm bells. He started walking faster. He spent less time checking to see what the students, initiates, and Rectors were doing.

He glanced into each room just long enough to satisfy himself that Eliska wasn't there before he moved on. He searched most of the fortress and still didn't find her. Now he was really starting to get worried.

He made it all the way to the top of the fortress and stopped on the roof. A high parapet separated the roof from the vast wasteland stretching away for thousands of miles in every direction.

He thought fast. Eliska wasn't in the fortress. Could she be downstairs in the servants' quarters—or maybe even the stables? They were the only places he hadn't searched.

He hustled downstairs and went through the servants' quarters, the kitchen, the laundry, and the storerooms one after the other. That left the stables.

He'd spent all day out there. He would have seen her if she was there, but he had to check.

He made a complete circuit of the stables and looked into every single stall. The horses gave him strange looks. Eliska wasn't there, either.

He stopped in the courtyard. Where had he not looked? She better still be here. These idiot monks better not have done anything to her.

He was just about to storm back upstairs, track down Miloji, and demand to see Eliska when Yann remembered.

He went out to the manure ramp. It extended from the fortress wall to the canyon floor and looked directly out over the rocky countryside at the bottom of the canyon.

Eliska wasn't on the ramp or anywhere in sight in the surrounding landscape.

The sun had set completely now and cast the sky in darkness. The last trace of light gleamed behind the horizon. The stars covered the rest of the sky and the wind dropped in temperature. He had no choice but to go back inside.

He puffed out his cheeks in a deep, shuddering breath. What would he do if he did lose Eliska?

He would have no way to rejoin the others or even to continue his mission to find the White Spire. He would have to stay here. He would have no other way to get out of this Island.

He was just about to turn away when he spotted a flash of light in the distance. The light came from some caverns in one of the nearby cliffs.

These caverns must have formed naturally. Whoever constructed the monastery didn't carve these caverns. Their jagged walls and low entrances were too uneven.

The ground leading up to the caverns crossed rocky terrain with fissures and boulders blocking the way. No one had made a path up to those caverns, but something was definitely in there.

Yann's curiosity got the better of him. He scrambled over all the obstacles and scaled the cliff to the cavern entrance.

The flash of light got brighter as he drew nearer. Roars, booms, and high-pitched shrieks echoed from inside.

He crept right up to the entrance and his blood ran cold when he peered in. Ten Rectors from the monastery stood in the cave.

He knew they were Rectors because they were all middle-aged men—not boys.

They didn't form a circle the way they did when they transported Yann and Eliska here.

The men stood in a disordered line facing a sea of Dark vapors teeming with Darklings. They poured from a breach in the fabric of reality near the back of the cavern.

The Rectors created their magical crystals on their hands, but they didn't use their power to fight the Darklings.

The Rectors manipulated the Darklings to move in different ways. The Darklings started out by roaring at the Rectors and lunging to attack.

The Rectors poured out Dark vapors from their Crystals to take control of the Darklings and steer them to attack each other instead.

Then Yann's world stopped when one of the older Rectors turned into Dark vapor himself, soared across the cavern, and merged with one of the Darklings.

The vapor shimmered through the Darkling's skin and it stopped roaring and plunging immediately.

It hovered there in midair murmuring and growling to itself. It snarled under its breath, but it didn't attack. It turned one way and then the other like it needed to think about something really hard.

Two more Rectors sent their vapors to that Darkling, surrounded it, and then trails of vapor connected the Darkling with those two Rectors. Their eyes closed and they both slipped into a trance.

Yann gulped hard. These monks were communing with the Dark—and using Dark magic themselves. This was not good at all.

The other Rectors in the cave did the same thing with other Darklings. Then two of the Darklings the Rectors entered turned to face each other, transformed into Dark vapor, and merged with each other.

They formed a giant ball of squirming, interlaced black fibers all twisting, knotting, and tangling with each other. The ball tumbled in midair while all the other Rectors communed with it.

Yann couldn't watch anymore. He backed away, but he made sure to do it quietly.

He planned to sprint back to the monastery, find Eliska, and get her the hell out of here before this whole thing blew up in their faces.

He made it twenty feet before a brutal roar shook the whole mountain. He didn't think he made any missteps or sound to alert those inside that he was here.

Without warning, a massive Darkling charged the cavern entrance, but it was too big to fit through the opening.

It smashed into the cave mouth on both sides and above and below, reared back bellowing its head off, and lunged again and again, but the same thing happened.

Its ferocious charges shook the whole mountain, but it still couldn't smash its way out.

Yann ran for it, but he didn't dare to run back to the monastery. Those Rectors were the ones manipulating that Darkling.

Its tentacles slashed out of the cavern and whipped and cracked in his direction. He stumbled over broken ground to get out of their reach.

He swerved up the canyon floor, bolted a couple hundred yards away from the monastery, and dove into a side fissure between two towering cliffs in another chasm.

This crack was definitely too narrow for a Darkling to get him, but what about the Rectors? They could use their magic to pull him out—or a Darkling could send its tentacle in here to yank him out.

He backed as deep into the crack as he could wedge himself and hunkered down in the cold night to wait. He didn't know what he was waiting for, but he didn't dare to go out there—not now.

He shivered and tugged his jacket around him more tightly. He wouldn't be able to survive in this Island if he went anywhere other than the monastery. He had to go back there at least to find Eliska.

He kept his eyes plastered open for hours, but he didn't hear any sound coming from outside. After a long, tense wait, he finally rested his head on his arms and fell into an exhausted sleep.

Chapter 15

Yann woke up when the sun came up, pried himself out of the crack in the stone fissure, and inched his way back to the monastery.

He didn't dare to go inside where the other servants would see him, so he went straight to the stables and got to work.

He tightened his belt against the hunger pangs in his stomach. He needed to make sure none of the Rectors came after him.

Then he had to find Eliska no matter what. He didn't care if he had to tear this place apart room by room.

He worked for an hour, but it still wasn't past the time when he would usually start work. He started his usual circuit of the stalls and opened his fourth when Eliska barged into the stall behind him.

"Where the hell have you been?!" she demanded. "I've been searching for you everywhere! I was worried! I thought something happened to you."

"Well, I've been searching everywhere for you. You said you would come and see me every day, but you didn't come yesterday."

"Yes, I did!" she countered. "I came right after dinner, but you weren't here. I searched the whole monastery one room at a time. No one knew where you were."

He stared at her as the pieces clicked. She must have come right after he left.

He compressed his lips. He didn't want to talk to her where anyone from the order might hear him.

He took her arm. "Come over here. We need to talk."

"You're damn right we do. I found some information in the library."

He frowned at her "You don't know how to read."

She waved that away. "Just...hey! Where are you taking me?"

He marched her down the ramp, around the corner, and all the way out onto the canyon floor. He didn't stop until he turned into the same crack where he spent the night last night.

She stared at the high walls with huge eyes. "Um. ...what the hell are we doing here?"

"You have to listen to me," he told her. "The Keepers of the Dawn use Dark magic. I saw them last night. That's why I wasn't in the monastery. I was looking for you and I came out to that ramp and I saw light coming from one of the caves nearby. I went over there and saw a bunch of the Rectors communing with the Dark."

She gasped and her mouth fell wide open. "They can't be!"

"Well, they were. I saw it with my own eyes. They were even creating Dark magic with their crystals. We have to get out of here—like right now. Take us to another Layer. We can't stay here. It's too dangerous."

"I....." She opened her mouth and shut it more than once. "I....just...."

He waited for her to say something. "What's wrong? This place is Dark. Don't tell me you haven't seen or felt something already. You must have."

"I did, but....."

"Then what else is there to say?"

"They haven't healed me yet," she blurted out. "They said they would take my Darkness—and now I know why they want it. They might be the only people in the Coil who *can* take it. I.....I can't leave yet."

Yann compressed his lips again. Of course she couldn't leave. "So when are they planning to do it?"

"I don't know." Her voice cracked and her eyes darted around. She looked scared again all of a sudden.

That scared, desperate, pleading look of hers was really starting to infuriate him. How dare these bastards promise to heal her and then leave her to suffer? They should have done that first.

"I had my first session with the Rectors," she stammered. "It was...they said they had to assess my magic, but they......" She broke off.

He saw and heard everything she didn't say. His fury erupted almost to the breaking point. "What did they do, Eliska? Tell me right now what they did."

"They....they enhanced my power."

His jaw hit the ground. "They.....what?"

"I didn't want them to! I didn't know what they were going to do, and once it started, I couldn't stop it. They fed all this power into me and made my magic even stronger."

"What in the name of all that's holy....."

"I don't know when they plan to take my Darkness. I thought they would have done it by now, but the session exhausted me and I passed out for almost the whole day. That's why I didn't come earlier. Then last light was the first time I had a chance to come and look for you and you weren't here."

Her voice cracked and those words stabbed him in the guts. He took a step toward her and put his arms around her. "I'm sorry I wasn't here when you came. The Rectors sent a Darkling after me and I had to hide before I came back to the monastery this morning."

She huddled in his arms. "I don't know what to do. I don't want to be here, but I don't want to pass up the chance for them to heal me. I might not get another chance. "

"Of course you have to stay. It will be all right. The next time you see them, tell them to do it now. Then we can meet up and leave. Okay?"

He stared into her eyes when she nodded. She was still the same person. He knew everything going on inside her head. He hadn't lost her yet.

He really, really didn't want to let her go back in there. He had to fight himself not to tell her to take them out of this Island right now.

He squeezed her shoulders and then hugged her again just because she seemed like she needed it. She hugged him back a lot harder than he hugged her.

He pushed her back and studied her a little closer. She didn't look any worse than when he saw her two days ago. It seemed like twenty years.

"What did you want to tell me?" he asked.

"Nothing as important as that," she replied. "I used the library...."

"How did you do that?"

"The magic the Rectors gave me—I can use it to scan the books without reading them."

His eyes shot open. "You can do that?"

"I couldn't before, but I can now. Anyway, I found out that Hubua Ocuron was a princess from the Hallowed Vales—which makes it even more outlandish that she married a Barbarian and became his Queen in the White Spire."

"How do you explain that?"

"That isn't the weird part. I asked one of the Rectors about it and he gave me the brush-off. He didn't even try to explain it—almost like he wanted to hide something from me."

"Well, that makes sense. Miloji said they wanted to destroy this Darkness and free you. Maybe they want to take your Darkness for themselves or....." He trailed off. He didn't want to say it.

"Or what?" she demanded. "If you know something, you better tell me. I'm the one in there dealing with these people's magic."

"I don't know for sure, but what if they don't want to take your Darkness at all? What if they brought you here to train you on how to use it so they can turn you to their side? Maybe that was their original plan. If they have enough power to take your Darkness, they could have found you in the Coil long before now. They only got interested in you when you took all this Darkness. They say they want to heal you, but we only have their word for that. Maybe they want to leave you with it, make it stronger, and then turn you around so you do things they want you to do."

She shut her mouth and jerked her head away to look somewhere else. "We don't know that."

"You're right. We don't. Just....be careful, okay? Push them to heal you as soon as possible. Then come and find me and we'll beat it out of here. Okay? I don't want you to stay here any longer than you have to."

She nodded fast. "Okay. I will. Thank you." She threw her arms around him.

He hugged her back and kissed the side of her head. "Come see me whenever you can."

"I will. I better go." She hurried back to the monastery. He stayed out in the wilderness watching her go before he worked up the courage to follow her.

Whatever happened between her and the monks, it wouldn't end well. He knew that now. Every minute he and Eliska spent in this place increased the odds that this would all blow up into another disaster—maybe an even bigger disaster than the ones they'd already been dealing with.

Chapter 16

Eliska sprinted up the stairs two at a time, but she slowed when it came time to enter the Tenth Library. She'd had enough sessions in here to know what to expect.

Miloji, Velimir, and the other Rectors stood in their usual circle. Which of them had been in the cavern when Yann saw them communing with the Dark?

Miloji couldn't have been there. Yann would have recognized him.

That didn't mean Miloji wasn't communing with the Dark.

He was the one who spearheaded the mission to bring Eliska in here in the first place. Miloji was the one who wanted to confront this Dark force—either to destroy it or to harness it for himself.

If Yann was right about the Keepers of the Dawn communing with the Dark, then Miloji would be right there in the middle of it. He would be the one coordinating taking control of her Darkness for the order's use.

Yann's warning rang in her ears when she stepped into the room. This moment would make or break her. She wouldn't go through with another session until they healed her. That was all there was to it.

Finding healing from this Darkness was her only reason for coming here. If the monks couldn't heal her, then she had no reason to stay.

Being separated from Yann like this was becoming unbearable even though they were only a few hundred yards apart.

She would almost rather leave this monastery, wander in the Coil alone with him, and carry this Darkness for the rest of her life than live apart from him.

She never had to wonder if he was turning to the Dark. She never had to wonder if he was doing something against her because he never did. He didn't give a rip about any of this if it put her in danger.

He only came here for the chance to heal her. He wouldn't stay if not for that.

Thinking about him cast these Rectors in a whole new light. She knew absolutely nothing about them except what they chose to tell her.

All their promises could have been lies. She had no reason to trust them or believe a word they said.

Miloji and Velimir came toward her smiling and took her hands. "Welcome back, young one," Miloji exclaimed. "You had such a successful session yesterday. Let's see if we can do it again."

She pulled her hands out of his grasp and didn't waste her breath correcting him on calling her, 'young one' again after she asked him not to.

"We won't have another session until you heal me of my Darkness," she blurted out. "I won't go through any more training until we get that out of the way. You promised to heal me if I came here. Now honor your promise. Then we can talk about whether I continue with my training."

Miloji only smiled at her. "Of course, young one. Of course we understand. Step into the circle, but you'll need to lie down on the floor this time. Keep your staff with you."

The Rectors surrounded her the way they did during the first session. In that moment when they surrounded her, she felt a charge of danger running between them.

They could do anything to her. She understood that in a flash of realization. Once they started, she wouldn't be able to stop them until they finished whatever they started.

They could pour an even bigger mountain of Dark into her. She wouldn't know after the process already started.

She considered walking away right then and there, but the temptation of someone finally healing her overrode everything else.

She stretched out on the floor, laid her staff longways next to her, and closed her hand over it from above.

"Excellent," Miloji told her. "Now try to relax....."

She shut her eyes and felt the surge of power coming from all the Rectors. Their magic flooded her and went straight into the Darkness she'd been carrying all this time.

It erupted out of all proportion. Nightmares blasted into her head and she ran through a thousand horrific scenes from the Symphorian church.

She also experienced scenes of torture, sacrifice, and dismemberment from Vidal's memories, the Corsair massacres, and a dozen other sources, some of which she'd never seen before.

She couldn't stop the torrent and she didn't try. The Rectors' magic rushed into all that Darkness and exploded it to life as never before, but they didn't take it.

She convulsed on the floor with another surge of magic tearing her apart—except that it didn't tear her apart. She really wished it would.

The Rectors kept it up for almost fifteen minutes, but the Darkness never ebbed.

In the end, the members withdrew their magic and left her quivering on the floor barely conscious.

She went through the same process of losing awareness of who she was and what anyone was doing.

Someone picked her up and took her back to her room. She passed out for even longer this time, but nightmares kept invading her sleep. She tossed and turned on the verge of waking up. She didn't really get any rest at all.

Whatever the Rectors did, it didn't take the Darkness away. They just woke it up. Now it raged through her being in the worst possible way.

She woke up sometime in daylight. She couldn't be sure how much time had passed. It might have been hours or days. Was Yann out there worrying about her again?

She tried to sit up, but the Darkness drained her. She rolled onto her side fighting down a wave of nausea as the memories overwhelmed her.

She hung her head over the side of the bed, but at least she didn't puke this time. She lay there panting and fighting back tears as all those awful pictures paraded through her mind.

She finally hauled herself back to the bed, slumped onto the pillows, and threw her arm over her face. She couldn't do this. She couldn't live like this.

Just then, the door opened and a completely different Rector came in. She actually thanked the stars that neither Miloji nor Velimir came to see her. She didn't trust them at all.

This man was maybe ten years younger with short brown hair clipped close to his scalp. He looked nothing like the other Rectors. This guy actually looked kind of nice.

He smiled down at her. "How are you feeling? My name is Mirko. The initiates say you didn't come to dinner. Miloji got called away on business, so I came to see if I should bring you something here.'

"I can't eat anything," she croaked. "I'm sick to my stomach. The Dark....."

"Yes, of course." He sat down on the edge of her bed without asking for permission and laid his hand on her forehead.

He sent a pulse of healing magic into her. The nausea eased, but the weakness didn't go away.

"It will pass, young one," he told her. "Then we can try again."

"You said you would heal me and take my Darkness," she choked. "This is just making it worse."

"It's no worse." He opened his hand, created his crystal, and passed it up and down in front of her body. "The Darkness is the same strength it was when you came."

She looked away. "Fine. It's awake now."

"It's awake the same as it was before, too."

"Then why can't you take it?" She heard herself demanding, but she couldn't take it any longer. "You promised."

"We will honor our promise. We tried, but the Dark is too big for us. You've been living wild in the Coil for too long. You need more training to refine your magic before we can rid you of the Dark completely."

She wanted so desperately to believe that. Could she trust this man? This was the first time he'd even spoken to her.

She felt too wretched even to speak, and in another minute, he left the room.

She would have given anything to see Yann right now, but she couldn't even get out of bed.

She felt how hungry she was, but she fell asleep again instead and woke up at dawn. How many days had she already missed?

She sat up feeling fragile, but at least she could move around. She planned to get some breakfast with the other initiates and then go visit Yann.

On her way to the dining room, she happened to pass the library again. It was empty at this time of day. All the initiates were on their way to eat.

She tiptoed inside. Why was she trying to be stealthy when Miloji already gave her permission to use this library?

The Keepers of the Dawn must be trying to keep information from her—either about themselves or about the Shard of Hotha mystery.

Chapter 17

Eliska used her magic to scan the library, but it always led her back to the same bookshelf. She stood there studying the spines extra closely even though she couldn't read them.

She didn't try to use her magic to read the spines. Instead, she dug deep into her innermost being trying to find....something.

She needed something—some clue. She just didn't know what it was.

She shut her eyes and passed her hand in front of the shelf. She stopped when she felt a surge of magic course through her palm.

She pulled out a book without looking at it first. It was the same book she read that first day on the history of the Yimichi Ocuron's reign.

She took the book down to the lectern and opened it. She didn't try to scan it here, either.

She shut her eyes, extended her hand over the open pages, and let her magic turn the pages for her the way Marine turned the pages of that book in the cloud tower.

She didn't open her eyes until the pages stopped ruffling. It opened to the same page as last time.

She focused on using her magic to translate the text. She read farther down to the accounts of Hubua's death.

The account didn't say how she died, but Noleron showed up at the White Spire just two days before her death—just in time for him to take the second Shard and become Yimichi Ocuron's affiliate. How convenient. There had to be a connection.

Eliska stood back, extended her hand over the book a second time, and shut her eyes.

The pages ruffled again, but when they stopped and she opened her eyes, she realized the book had actually turned itself backward—back to accounts from before Yimichi became King.

She ran her hand down the page and information flooded her brain. Yimichi and Noleron weren't just Barbarians. They actually came from the same Tribe—the Sirki Tribe in the Sojourner's Sanctum.

Goosebumps erupted on Eliska's arms when she read the truth. Yimichi Ocuron and Noleron Kupuro had actually been brothers from the same mother.

Yimichi's father died in a battle when he was just a baby. His mother married another Barbarian warlord almost immediately after her first husband's death.

Yimichi and Noleron were less than a year apart in age and grew up together. They spent every day together—until they both fell in love with the same girl.

Her name was Teyama and the feud drove a wedge between the brothers. They fought more than once and nearly killed each other trying to decide which of them would marry her.

In the end, she convinced Yimichi to leave the tribe with her so they could be together somewhere else.

They left Noleron behind. He never found out what happened to them and lived his whole life hating his brother. He swore an oath in public that he would kill his brother if he ever saw him again.

Yimichi traveled to other Layers and lived with other tribes with Teyama as his wife.

She eventually died when another tribe raided their camp and killed half the population.

Yimichi and some of the surviving warriors moved to a different Layer where they hired themselves out as mercenaries just to make money to survive. They wound up fighting with a Corsair army that was marauding the countryside.

The King in the White Spire brought out his forces to subdue the Corsairs and took Yimichi and some of his Barbarians comrades as prisoners. The previous King Henov took an interest in Yimichi and they became friends.

They were on the battlefield together when the previous King Henov suffered a mortal injury. As he lay dying, he convinced Yimichi to take the Shard of Hotha for the good of everyone in the Coil.

He returned to the White Spire where he discovered four kings from the Hallowed Vale visiting on an embassy to King Henov.

Confusion reigned when the other kings realized that a completely different King had risen to the throne. The new King Yimichi's advisors informed him that he had to take an affiliate right away or risk starting another instability cycle.

One of the visiting Kings offered his daughter as a sign of alliance between the Kingship and the Hallowed Vales. Yimichi married Hubua that same day and she took the Second Shard.

The historians seemed to think the two had a happy marriage until the day before her death when Noleron came out of the woodwork. In less than forty-eight hours, she was dead and Noleron became the affiliate.

Did he kill his brother's wife? Noleron said he would kill his brother, but maybe he changed his mind.

Maybe he decided to inflict the punishment on Hubua instead—to pay Yimichi back for stealing the woman Noleron thought was his own.

If that was the case, why did the histories make it out that Yimichi and Noleron ruled together in harmony for the next twenty years until Yimichi's death?

Eliska took her hand down so she wouldn't take in any more information about this. She needed to think—but she also needed to talk to Yann about this.

Did it really make any difference to know that the Voyant Mendicat got into his position of power by killing the King's wife?

The couples holding hands in those pictures sure looked happy together. The histories didn't say anything about any conflict between Yimichi and Noleron after Hubua's death.

Then again, maybe no one found out about Noleron killing Hubua. Maybe Noleron kept the secret to himself. He got his revenge and he also got himself in line to take the Kingship after his brother's death. What better reward could he ask for?

Eliska opened her eyes and stared down at the book. She put it away on its shelf and went back downstairs. She opened her hand window to locate Yann when Mirko entered the library.

He smiled at her just as kindly. "There you are! I'm so glad you're back on your feet. We have a fun session planned for you today. You should enjoy this."

"I don't think I want to do any more sessions," she mumbled.

"This one will be different. It's a training session—an obstacle course of sorts. You must have seen the other students training." He grinned even more broadly. "You'll enjoy it. The other Rectors won't be there—only me."

She hesitated. Should she? The training sessions did look fun. The other Rectors wouldn't be there to send her extra magic or to interfere with her Dark power.

She followed Mirko out of the room. He went with her to the dining hall to get something to eat, but most of the other students were already leaving.

He sat across from her and talked nonstop about the founding days of their order while she ate in silence.

She didn't really care how the Keepers of the Dawn got started, but she didn't interrupt.

She spent the meal evaluating him. A training session might be the best way to test this new power the Rectors had given her. It increased her intuition, but what if she could actually use it to find out if someone was lying?

She might even be able to magick a person to tell her something they wanted to keep a secret from her. She might even be able to influence them to do things they didn't want to do.

She pushed that thought out of her head. Those were Dark powers. She didn't want to tap those, but it sure would be nice to know if these monks were keeping things from her—and what things they were keeping from her.

After she ate, she followed Mirko to one of the training halls. Half the students in there stopped what they were doing when he walked in. The others kept sparring and leaping around with the help of their magic.

He waved all the other students away and led Eliska into a corner by herself. "I'll open the course and you'll go in alone," he told her.

"What does that mean?" She looked around at the other students. "Aren't I going to train here?"

"The course is magical. Once you go inside, you won't come out until you get to the other end—but don't worry. I'll monitor you the whole time. If you get into trouble, I'll pull you out."

She frowned. "I don't understand."

"You'll understand when you get inside. Just remember it's a training session. It isn't real. Just remember to use the new power we've given you. That's what it's there for. You'll need to use all your power to get through the course."

"What *is* the course?"

"It's a series of obstacles—nothing you can't handle."

"Is there an objective?"

"Just to get to the other end. Then you can leave the course and you'll wind up back here. Are you ready?"

"I guess so."

He passed his hand in a big circle in the air in front of her.

It opened a magical pool looking in on a rocky cavern somewhere. She didn't see any sign of an opening to the outside world.

"Step through whenever you're ready to begin," he told her.

She took a deep breath, tightened her grip on her staff, and stepped through the opening. It closed behind her immediately.

She turned around, but nothing remained. She was alone in this cave.

Chapter 18

F or some reason, light illuminated the cavern from somewhere so Eliska could see where she was going and what she was doing.

She didn't know where to go, so she took a few steps forward in no particular direction.

The cavern stretched in front of her. She couldn't tell if she was walking deeper underground or toward the surface. It didn't really matter in the end.

The cavern narrowed to a tunnel with side corridors cutting off it. Roars came from down there and she even heard the hiss and crack of Darkling tentacles. Where were they? How close were they to attacking her?

She jumped at every sound, but no Darklings came out. Was this just to unnerve her and throw her off her guard?

She continued to the end of the tunnel and came to another enormous cavern.

Dark forces filled the place, but none of them were Darklings. Vapors, strange shapes, and a confused soup of flying debris whirled in a tempest of shadow and wild magic.

She wouldn't have gone into that cavern, but the minute she stepped out of the tunnel, she spotted another group of travelers in a different tunnel leading away at the far end.

The travelers consisted of two families—two fathers, two mothers, and a bunch of small children.

The four adults stood in front of their children to protect them from ten massive Darklings trying to slaughter all of them.

The four adults all used magic in one form or another. None of them used the monks' crystals.

One of the fathers and one of the mothers used staffs. The other father fought barehanded. The second mother used some kind of talisman. Eliska couldn't identify it from here. It might have been a broach or maybe a small gemstone.

The four parents formed a semi-circle hiding their children behind them against the wall. The parents flattened the children there to protect them from the Darklings.

The Darklings surrounded the party and returned every shot with magical pulses from their tentacles.

Eliska didn't wait a second longer. She knew what she had to do now. Those people over there being an illusion didn't make an ounce of difference.

The Keepers of the Dawn knew exactly what to show her to give her an objective to accomplish. She had to save those people.

The rest of the course didn't matter. She had to take those people to the end of the course so they all got out.

She plunged into the hurricane and let her new magic rip. She didn't have to use her hand or her staff to create a shield of protection around herself. She did it with a thought and it stayed up no matter what else she did.

She fired her staff from her right hand and unloaded with her left hand in the opposite direction.

The objects, monstrous shapes, and crackling Dark vapors whizzing around the cavern—they all turned on her and attacked the minute she stepped out of the tunnel.

She'd already experienced this in other Layers. Having inanimate objects come alive and attack her didn't bother her.

Now she knew with absolutely no doubt that she could beat them. She could beat them all.

She dove into the mayhem, but the Dark forces in this cavern turned out to be stronger than she realized.

Vapors snaked and sparked across her shield. More of them slapped down on the glistening surface and started to knit their fibers together.

They ate through the field and it started to disintegrate. Pieces of broken furniture and even whole trees pelted out of the confusion and slammed into the field to weaken it even more.

They hammered it again and again from all sides. Eliska couldn't drive so many of them off fast enough to save her shield.

She made it halfway across the cavern before she felt the shield start to crack. If these Dark forces attacked her without the shield, they would bring her down right here.

She reacted without thinking and unleashed a powerful shockwave of magic. She didn't even think to use her staff.

She just ejected a pulse of magic from....from somewhere. Maybe it came from inside her or maybe it came through her skin. She couldn't be sure.

She blasted outward and hurled all that stuff away from her. She might even have destroyed the trees and furniture, but she couldn't destroy the Vapors. They retreated, but they came diving straight back.

She tried one more time to erect a protective field around herself, but they came too fast and plastered to her skin.

They burned into her and started eating away at her flesh. They would devour her down to the bone.

She tried one last time to throw them off, but they stuck fast.

She screamed, dropped her staff, and her hands flew to her face to claw the vapors off. More and more of them hurtled in from all directions. They glued themselves to every inch of skin they could find.

She turned one way and then the other trying to see some way out of this.

At that moment, Mirko's voice called into her ear from somewhere. *Use your Darkness, Eliska! Unleash your Darkness and take the vapors on yourself to defeat them.*

"NO!" she shrieked.

You can do this! You can defeat them, but only by using Dark against Dark. You can throw them off. Trust me!

She didn't want to, but she couldn't defeat these vaporous any other way. She started to let her Dark magic out of its cage.

The vapors sank beneath her skin and merged with her own power swelling outward.

She felt them increasing her Darkness. The sheer power of it scared the crap out of her and she instantly pulled it back.

That fear released another colossal starburst of magic, but she didn't let her Darkness break loose—not again. She couldn't risk it.

She hurled the vapors off, but they only came pelting back for another assault. She couldn't let them touch her.

She seized her staff, swept it in a circle, and cleared a path for herself through the mayhem. She spun her staff around too fast. The debris and vapors didn't have time to get near her.

She fired her shield outward—just long enough to give her some protection. The Dark powers overcame it, but she sent out another one again and again. She could keep doing this as long as it took.

She didn't have to do it for long because she used that time to work her way across the cavern to the other tunnel.

She dove inside and fired another spell across the opening to stop any of the Dark powers from following.

That left her alone with the two families and all their Darklings.

The Darklings didn't notice her. They had captured the father who used the staff. One Darkling yanked him into the air by his ankle and dangled him over the Darkling's wide-open mouth.

The children screamed and all the other adults tried to attack that one Darkling to free their friend, but that left them and the children too exposed to the rest of the Darklings.

Eliska fired her staff down the tunnel and severed the tentacle holding onto the man's leg. He would have fallen straight into the Darkling's mouth, but she caught him with another blast and transported him back into position with the other adults.

That one shot definitely got the Darkling's attention. Three Darklings turned around to face her. The others couldn't get past their big friends to come near her. They blocked the tunnel. That left the remaining seven Darklings to go after the families.

Eliska couldn't wait any longer. She burst into a dead run heading straight for the Darklings.

She'd fought Darklings all her life. She knew exactly what to do, but this time, she had so much more power to use against them.

She could have annihilated all ten of them in seconds if she unleashed her Dark power, but she didn't even have to do that.

Those three lunged for her. Their tentacles sparked with magic and more sheets of wild magic ran down their skins. So much the better. That would only work in her favor.

The first Darkling lunged for her and she launched herself at it at the same time.

She landed on its nose as it opened hists mouth to snatch her up and devour her.

She stabbed her staff down into its head, but she didn't try to inflict any damage on it. She didn't have to.

She released a pulse of magic—not into the Darkling itself but into the magic surrounding it.

Her magic took control of the energy crackling on the Darkling's skin and turned it against the creature.

She charged up to the top of the Darkling's head and vaulted across the tunnel to the next Darkling in line.

The first Darkling roared in fury and then shrieked in mortal agony as all its own magic turned inward to destroy it.

She didn't look back to see the slaughter unfold. She sensed it happening through her magical connection to her own magic. It tore the Darkling apart one bloody clump of flesh at a time.

The second Darkling whipped its tentacle around and slashed it around her waist to grab her, but she was already flying too fast.

She landed next to it just as the creature stomped its enormous foot down on the floor. She landed on top of its foot and stumbled to catch her balance before she pitched off.

She didn't have time to use her staff that time, so she sent the pulse through her own foot.

It stabbed into the Darkling's skin and the cascade spread over the rest of the Darkling's body.

She didn't have time to pull any fancy maneuvers on the second one, so she dove underneath it, fired one burst of magic into its stomach, and scrambled clear as that Darkling exploded in its death throes, too.

She skidded out from under it right in front of the two families. They were too busy defending themselves to realize what she was doing before she got there.

She didn't have time to jump from one Darkling to another seven times. She backed up with the adults and swept her staff sideways across all seven remaining Darklings.

Her magic glanced off each of them, married with the magic on their skin, and set off the same chain reaction in them.

They roared in distress.

"Get out of here!" Eliska bellowed over her shoulder. "Back away and take your children out of here!"

It took too long to get the group moving. Eliska pivoted in front of them and kept her staff aimed at the Darklings, but she didn't have to shoot a second time.

She backed up the tunnel and listened to the families' footsteps getting farther away behind her. Their footsteps vanished into the maze of tunnels.

Eliska stopped at a distance from the Darklings and watched them disintegrate to the ground in puddles of Dark ooze. Their dying groans faded into the sea of noise coming from the far cavern.

She lowered her staff long before the last Darkling dissolved into the floor.

You could have defeated them so much more easily and quickly if you used your Dark power, Mirko murmured in her ear.

She didn't answer. She didn't need to tap her Dark power to defeat those Darklings.

The Keepers of the Dawn would have to come up with something more challenging than this if they wanted to make her fall back on using her Darkness.

There was nothing more to see here, so she turned and walked the rest of the way up the tunnel. She used her Coil projection to find the families.

They waited in a small stone room at the end of one of the tunnels. "Thank you so much!" the father with the staff exclaimed. "We would have been dead for sure without you."

Eliska didn't answer. These people weren't real. They were a construct the Keepers of the Dawn came up with to trick her. They manipulated her emotions to get her to go through the obstacle course.

She passed her hand in front of the two families and used her magic to make them disappear. She didn't want to see them anymore.

She didn't want to deal with people who didn't exist. She had enough real people to worry about already without these monks inventing new ones.

She stared at the empty place where the two families had just been standing. She already carried the memory of too many other families she couldn't save. They gave her a much more compelling reason to do all of this.

She had no idea if she was in the right place for Mirko to get her out of this course. She didn't care anymore.

She circled her hand in the air and opened the pool herself. It showed her the training hall with the initiates going through their sparing routines and acrobatics.

She stepped through and the pool closed behind her. She came through on the opposite side of the room.

Mirko came over to her right away. He had to dodge multiple fights to get near her. "That was excellent! You accomplished that easily."

She only stared at him. He acted so nice. They all did. How could she ever trust him after what just happened?

Maybe he thought he was doing her a favor, but she could only hate him for this. How dare he twist her emotions—and for what? To make her run through a maze like a pet he was training—a pet animal?

She turned on her heel and walked away. She knew now what these monks wanted. They wanted her to use her Dark power. She just didn't know why.

Chapter 19

Y ann finished work and put his shovel and wheelbarrow away. He went through the same routine every day.

He only stayed because he held out the dim hope of seeing Eliska again. He hadn't seen her in a week. He didn't even know if she was still alive in this monastery, but he wouldn't leave until he found out for certain.

He didn't even know how he would leave. He might not be able to leave at all, but he would just have to find a way.

He went to the pump and washed himself off as he always did at sunset after a long day of hot, dirty work.

He didn't think about the work anymore. He mostly just dwelled on Eliska and what might be happening to her upstairs.

He went into the dining room to get something to eat, but he didn't talk to anyone. He only talked to people when he absolutely had to.

His policy of staying silent and keeping to himself had worn off on the other servants. They stopped trying to engage with him until none of them talked to him at all.

He spent every day alone, but he liked it better that way. He didn't want to get close to anyone here.

He might have been able to find out from one of the housekeeping staff if Eliska was still living upstairs, but he just couldn't bring himself to ask. He would find out another way.

He left the monastery and went out to the manure ramp to watch the sun go down. This had become his nightly ritual. He wanted to sit somewhere alone away from everyone.

If Eliska came looking for him, she would be able to use her hand window to find him here.

She might have been able to find him in the crack where they held their secret conversation, but he liked it better here where he could watch the evening colors take over the rocky wilderness.

He sat with his knees pulled up to his chest and thought things over. How should he go about breaking out of this Island when the time came?

The easiest way would probably be to wait until the Rectors communed with their Darklings, antagonize one of them, and get it to shatter the Layer.

Yann really didn't care if he destroyed the monks' Island with every last person in it. He just had to make sure Eliska wasn't in it when he did it.

Then he would have his work cut out for him surviving the fall through the Layers.

He didn't know if he could survive, but he sure as hell wasn't getting any closer to the White Spire here. He would never get there if he stayed here for the rest of his life.

Anríq and Marine wouldn't be able to find him. They said a million times that they couldn't use Eliska's Coil projection to navigate the Layers—so staying here was no longer an option—assuming Eliska really was dead.

She must be. Why didn't she come to find him?

He would have to take the next step and go upstairs to look for her. If worse came to the worst, he would have to confront one of the Rectors about seeing her.

Miloji promised they could see each other every day and they failed in that promise. Yann would be in his rights to demand to see her at least once.

What would he do if she turned against him to join the order? He shuddered and pushed the thought away.

She didn't stay away from him because she didn't want to see him. He already knew that.

Something must be stopping her from coming. She better not be in danger or he might have to hurt someone.

He stood up resolved in his decision. He would go upstairs right now. The students and initiates would all be going to dinner. If she wasn't in the dining room, he would ask one of the Rectors.

He dusted off his pants, turned around, and froze when he saw Andrija, Milic, and a bunch of other young initiates standing behind him—or they might have been junior Rectors. Yann didn't understand the Keepers of the Dawn ranking system and he didn't really care.

A cruel smile spread across Andrija's face. The Rectors blocked Yann from going back into the fortress.

He read their expressions in a split second. He didn't doubt for an instant that they came here to attack him and he didn't wait for them to do it.

He dove sideways off the ramp, somersaulted on the stone, and tumbled down it to the rough ground behind the wall.

The Rectors unleashed a torrent of magical blasts that pounded the ramp and the rocky ground all around Yann as he fell away.

Those shots followed him, but he made his move too fast. He took them by surprise and somersaulted behind a boulder before they could hit him.

They pounded the boulder and a deadly crack forked through it. This rock wouldn't protect him for long.

He dove for another boulder farther away, sprinted from one covered spot to another, put a little more distance between himself and his pursuers, and took off at a dead run up the canyon to get as far away from the monastery as he could.

He didn't even stop at this old familiar hiding place. He kept running until his lungs exploded from the effort.

The Rectors stopped shooting long before he topped. He still didn't take the chance of them catching up with him.

They could have magicked themselves to his location in a split second. They must already know where he was.

He found another crevice where he could spend the night, but he didn't sleep. He couldn't force himself to relax.

Eliska. He had to go back and find Eliska.

The monks must realize that he would always come back to the monastery as long as she was still there.

She would have been able to use her magic to find out if he was still there. If their situations had been reversed, she would be able to tell in a few seconds that he was still inside the walls and in trouble.

He didn't have her power. He just had to use his wits, but he would definitely go back there.

He couldn't know for certain if the senior Rectors put these young men up to kill Yann. He would bet any amount of money that they did. Why else would they try to kill him except to keep him away from her?

They must know by now that he wanted to get her out of here—and that both he and Eliska suspected them of belonging to the Dark.

God only knew what else they were doing in this place. This whole monastery could have been a training ground for Dark wizards.

Yann had already seen the senior Rectors doing it. What would stop them from training their students to do the same thing?

He waited for morning before he ventured out into the open.

The trip back to the monastery took a long time, but he didn't rush it. He would not go back to working in the stables.

He would walk straight back into the building, go upstairs, and he wouldn't leave until he found Eliska and got her the hell out of here. The monks would have to kill him for real to if they wanted to stop him.

Chapter 20

E liska reentered the Tenth Library. She'd gone through two more training courses. The monks tried to make them harder, but she accomplished each objective easily.

She stopped in front of the Rectors and Mirko came forward to smile at her the way he usually did.

She pulled away from him. "I've done everything you asked. I've refined my magic. I can control it perfectly well. You have no reason to hold off on fulfilling your end of the bargain. It's time for you to heal me from my Darkness the way you promised you would."

"Of course, young one," Mirko replied. "That's exactly why we called you here. It's time. You're ready."

She glared at him. This was another trick. No one had to tell her.

He waved her to the center of the circle. "Lie down the way you did before...."

"No, I'll stand," she fired back. "You don't need me to lie down. Just take my Darkness and be done with it. Otherwise, I'll know you're screwing me over."

None of the Rectors acted offended. Their bland acceptance of everything she said rang her alarm bells more than anything. They would have tried to discipline her if they weren't actively trying to manipulate her.

She stepped into the circle, but she kept herself alert and didn't close her eyes. She started to summon her own power. If these men tried to do anything to her, she would unleash her magic on them and retaliate. She didn't trust them an inch.

They placed their hands above and below each other's hands, created their crystals, and the energy started to vibrate. It entered her and the air charged with tension the way it did that very first time.

Eliska let her magic rise at the same time. She wouldn't let the monks get the jump on her this time. She had to be ready to counter-attack if they tried to take her over or went farther than she was ready to let them go.

Their magic flowed into her, surrounded her, and woke up the Darkness in her, but it caused a different reaction this time.

She waited for the monks to draw it out of her and maybe take it into themselves or at least for them to start removing it. They didn't.

They stirred it up, woke it up the way they did last time, and then, with one catastrophic blast, they expanded it exactly the way they expanded her original magic during that very first session.

Her own effort to make it rise so she would be ready to use it—her own effort worked against her in the end—or maybe the monks took advantage of it for their own ends.

An unstoppable rush of Dark magic flooded her—but it did a lot more than flood her. It exploded her into a million pieces as overwhelming Darkness invaded her being.

The Darkness already brewing in her soul detonated to such epic proportions that it shattered what was left of her. All restrain evaporated. Every defense she ever used to contain it disintegrated in a whirlwind of pure Dark power.

It blasted out of her with incredible force. She reared off the ground roaring, but not in pain.

Fury mixed with lunatic madness through burst her skin. She ruptured to many times her normal size and every part of her morphed into a completely different shape.

She couldn't tell from the inside if she was becoming a Darkling. She didn't think she was becoming anything. She didn't stay one thing for more than a second.

Her face, head, and body twisted with bulbous swellings of Darkness erupting from the inside. They burst out, reformed, and sank as other parts of her went through the same process.

Darkness rippled, undulated, and swelled on her skin in disgusting shapes. Every part of her contorted into misshapen horrors beyond her control.

She writhed and thrashed as the Darkness built beyond the breaking point. Every trace of who she really was dissolved and became nothing before this cataclysmic volcano of Darkness coming from deep inside her.

The monks kept pumping more and more Darkness into her. Their crystals turned Dark and Dark vapors streamed from all the crystals into her.

Those Dark powers sifted through her skin and the poison burst to life with every passing minute.

She didn't try to stop it. The part of her that wanted to stop it no longer existed. She was pure Dark now. She wasn't human. No human being could contain all of this.

She lost track of how long the monks kept it up. She lost awareness of where she was and what they were doing.

Her consciousness snapped into the Dark and she floated in the Layers surrounded by memories, Darklings, and gruesome forces bellowing, slashing, fighting, and obeying her.

Her Darkness floated out of her in more vapors that attacked, manipulated, and interacted with all the Dark Layers through which she passed.

She used her Darkness to form Islands and caused populations to grow up and civilizations to develop in those Islands.

Then she made the Layers collapse on each other, wiped out everyone living there, and returned them to chaos.

She did this a dozen times across thousands of years. Time didn't exist here. She sent Darklings to maraud the countryside. She used the Dark to infect people's minds and sent them to attack and ravage each other.

She controlled whole civilizations through millennia of destruction, development, and decay. It was all part of the Dark.

It didn't enter her head that she shouldn't do it this way. It just happened by itself with an outpouring of Dark energy. It centered her from somewhere beyond her awareness and poured out of her in an uncontrolled river of time and history.

Why should she control it? It followed the natural order of things that people should rise, suffer, and die. Her involvement didn't change that. She barely existed at all as anything other than a witness.

The Dark would go on without her either way. It flowed through her. It didn't touch her and nothing it did touched her.

Without warning, she slammed down on a cold stone floor and came back to her senses shivering with brutal cold.

She scrambled to sit up, but she couldn't control her limbs. She tried to pick up her staff, but her hands shook so badly that she couldn't close her fingers on it.

She trembled all over and huddled there with her hair hanging in her eyes. She became aware of the monks still standing in their circle where they'd been during her session. They weren't creating their crystals anymore or pumping her full of Dark magic.

The poison she took from Barsali and from the Symphorian people had grown to something so huge she couldn't even think about it anymore. It overpowered everything she was. She couldn't think clearly—about anything.

Someone came toward her and she jerked away from them. She couldn't focus her eyes well enough to see who it was, but some instinctive part of her sensed that it was the monks who did this to her.

Her instincts told her they did exactly the opposite of what they said they were going to do. They didn't take her poison. They quadrupled it or maybe even more.

She lacked the mental clarity even to act. The session wrecked her mind and left her barely coherent enough to understand where she was. She couldn't stand. She couldn't even look around at the people standing nearest her.

The person tried again to pick her up, but she spasmed away and kicked out to push the person away. She didn't want anyone near her—not them, anyway.

She had to think. She had to decide on something—something important. But her thoughts wouldn't form any coherent order.

She felt someone using their magic on her. She couldn't focus well enough to see who it was except that it was no one near enough for her to do anything. She wouldn't have been able to do anything anyway.

A magical ball of energy surrounded her, lifted her off the floor, carried her to her room, and put her on the bed before the ball evaporated. One of the monks stood her staff against the bed nearby.

She couldn't lie down. She kept jolting from one direction to another, spinning around and trying to see something, and struggling to form some coherent thought. Something was wrong—seriously wrong.

Her Darkness was wrong. It was too big and too powerful now. She tried to fight it under control, but she couldn't even touch it.

It seethed in a pocket of its own. It flowed in her blood. It would burst out any second now and she wouldn't be able to do a thing to stop it.

She sat hunched and tense on top of the bed with her legs drawn up to her chest while she floundered to think—of something, anything.

She jumped when someone came in and placed a plate of food on the bed next to her.

She turned her back on it and the person. She didn't even recognize who it was. It could have been anyone.

The thought of food made her sick. The poison stung her throat. It burned her from the inside.

It destroyed everything about her from within. She couldn't stop it. It invaded her mind with random thoughts and ideas. She wanted to hurt something or maybe herself.

She tried her hardest to push that away, but different thoughts kept intruding on her awareness whether she wanted them to or not.

She saw herself as a Darkling storming across the landscape or swallowing towns. She roared at tiny people scurrying to get out of her way.

The insane feeling flooded her of snatching them and devouring them. Their fear exploded her with strength even more Darkness.

Their memories joined with the river of poison and made it expand beyond measure. It would never stop.

Somewhere in all that confusion, rage, and murderous fury, she happened to pass through the memories of herself, Marine, and Anríq the day Yvan Dilnao died. They all stood back and watched Yann sobbing over his father's grave.

The memory only passed through her mind for a split second before it vanished under a torrential avalanche of other memories coming from thousands of years of human history.

She seized that one instant with all her might. Yann. She had to find Yann. He was the only person who could get her out of this.

She took ages to clear her thoughts enough to decide to leave her room. She kept blurring out into memories and Dark Layers of timeless confusion, jolting back into her room, and jerking sideways trying to see someone coming near her.

Images of people invaded her awareness. People she only met for a few hours decades ago appeared in her room and tried to talk to her. She couldn't remember anything about them, not even their names.

The next instant, all their memories, nightmares, secrets, and horrors blasted into her head out of control.

She might have screamed and grabbed fistfuls of her hair trying to stop the torrent, but nothing could stop it. She didn't even have the defenses to try. The idea of trying didn't exist anymore.

Darkness came to her unbidden. It entered her with no barrier. Dark married with Dark. It existed outside of her. It existed inside of her. There was no separation between the two anymore.

Chapter 21

Y ann inched up the ramp and stopped outside the stable courtyard. The last monks were just putting their horses in their stalls
and going inside the monastery for the night.

He stayed outside the walls until all those men went inside. Silence
fell over the stables.

The stars came out and night blanketed the rocky countryside.
Another day.

Yann had taken another day to walk back to the monastery. He took
his time getting here and he took his time before he worked up the
nerve to go inside.

Someone would almost certainly try to kill him when he did go
inside, but he no longer had a choice about that. Eliska was in there
and she obviously needed him.

He wouldn't leave until he found her. He didn't care if he had to
fight people, Dark wizards, or even if they killed him in the process.
He wouldn't leave her in danger.

He took a deep breath, stepped inside the courtyard walls, and
turned up the colonnade heading for the monastery.

All the servants would be in the kitchen eating dinner right now.
He would make it to the stairs and up to the entrance foyer before any
of the servants saw him.

He picked up his pace.

Some of the horses snorted at him as he passed. Did they wonder where he had been all day and why he didn't come around to clean their stalls?

Never again. He didn't work here anymore.

He made it halfway down the colonnade when he happened to pass an empty stall. It had always been empty since he and Eliska first came to this fortress.

He didn't look into it because he didn't expect to see anything inside it.

A slight hint of movement caught his peripheral vision. He stopped dead in his tracks when he saw Eliska crouching in the far corner. Her hair hung over her face and she sat half-turned sideways so she faced the other wall.

He froze at the sight of her. How many times had he seen Marine sitting like that?

His blood ran cold when she jerked a few times, spasmed out of her skin, and spun her head sideways in a sudden movement to look at something that wasn't there.

He swallowed hard. This couldn't be happening. He never should have waited so long to try to find her, but at least he didn't have to go looking for her.

He took a fraction of a second to decide what to do, stepped into the empty stall, and shut the door behind him. Now no one would see either of them—as if the monks wouldn't be able to find them if they really wanted to.

The monks tracked Eliska through multiple Layers. They followed her Dark power. They would be able to find her here.

He inched across the stall and squatted down at a safe distance from her. "Hey!" he breathed. "It's okay! I'm here! You're with me now. It's going to be okay. I'm here. I'm with you. You found me."

He didn't know what the hell to say to her, but he could see plain as day that it was not okay nor would it be. Jesus, what happened to her? He didn't want to think about it.

Just for a second, he imagined what Anríq would say if he ever saw Eliska again. He would thrash Yann for letting this happen to her.

Yann kicked himself for letting her down so badly. He never should have left her alone with wizards he knew belonged to the Dark. He should have insisted that she stay with him—like he might have been able to stop this.

He scooted just a little bit closer. "Hey!" he murmured. "Can you look at me? Can you talk to me? What's going on? Can you hear me and understand me? Give me some sign. Oh, man, what am I saying? You found me so you know who I am. We have to get out of here. Then we can work on taking care of you. Can you do that? Can you get us out of the monastery?"

She didn't respond. He looked around the stall, but he didn't see her staff.

He cringed when he thought about what it must have cost her to come and find him. What had the monks been doing with her this last week?

He took a chance and slid the rest of the way to the wall she was facing He sat against it in front of her, but she didn't acknowledge him.

She didn't make eye contact. She just kept shuddering, jumping from one direction to another, and gasping for breath every time she did it.

He used one finger to comb her hair out of her face. He didn't see any injuries on her—not physical injuries. She looked unharmed on the outside.

Her features spasmed when he looked at her this closely. Her eyes darted back and forth seeing nothing, but she didn't raise them. She knew he was here. Maybe she felt ashamed of what she was.

He couldn't bear the see her like this, so he leaned back and put his arms around her. He didn't know what else to do. He only knew he couldn't let her out of his sight again.

He had her. He found her—or she found him. They just needed to get the hell out of this Island now, but they couldn't do that until she regained the use of her magic.

He wouldn't be able to take her too far away. He would need to be able to sneak back into the monastery to steal food and any other supplies they needed to survive in this Island until she got ready to leave. How long would that take?

He shut his eyes and prepared himself for the long haul. Exhaustion from last night's attempt on his life caught up with him.

He would have liked to take her out of the monastery right now. He didn't trust her inside the walls nor did he trust the monks not to come after her. She was too valuable to them.

He didn't want to disturb her more than she already was.

She trembled in his arms, but she didn't try to fight him off or push him away. She didn't tear away from him. She knew. She knew where she was and who she was with.

That thought gave him just enough comfort to squeeze her tighter and kissed her hair. "I'm here," he whispered. "I'm here. You're with me now. We're going to take care of you and make it better. I promise."

He must have drifted off because he woke up sitting in the same position with his head tilted back against the wall.

Eliska lay against his chest, but she didn't shiver and jolt anymore. She felt like she must have passed out, too.

He heard activity outside the stall. Some of the monks must be out there exercising the horses. It was daytime again.

Yann glanced around. Should he wait for another night before he moved Eliska?

The minute he woke up, she stirred, groaned, and stretched. She sat up with her hair hanging over her face, but he saw right away that she was much better than yesterday.

"Hey!" he breathed. "How do you feel?"

She refused to look at him, but at least she didn't twitch and jerk and glance around.

She opened her mouth to say something, but no sound came out.

"It's okay!" He raked her hair back and kissed her on the forehead. God, she was a mess! "It's going to be okay. We're going to leave the monastery. Then, when you're feeling better, you can take us to another Layer. Okay? You don't have to do anything right now."

She blinked down at the floor, but he saw that she understood. She wasn't as crazy today as she was yesterday.

"I'm going to go into the monastery, get us some food, and find your staff and my glaive, okay? Then I'll come back and we'll leave. We'll go out into the wilderness and you can recover there until you're ready to do something else. Nod if you understand."

She nodded without looking up. He would have left right then, but at that moment, she lunged for him, threw her arms around him, and crushed him in a brutal hug.

Her head fell on his shoulder and she burst into pathetic sobs.

"Hey!" he murmured in her ear. "Okay! It's okay! It wasn't your fault. Everything's okay. You're the same person you were. We'll deal with this. It will be okay."

He couldn't stand to hear her cry. He kept kissing the side of her head and running his fingers through her hair, but he heard the pain and betrayal in those tears.

These monks really knew how to twist the knife. They promised the one thing she most needed in the world.

Instead, they wrecked her even more than she already was. Could she even use her magic anymore? Did they take it completely?

Maybe that was the problem. Maybe she didn't even have her magic anymore.

He really didn't care. He just had to get her out of here and help her recover from this. Everything would be better as soon as he took her away from the monastery.

He held her for a long time. She cried and cried and cried. Poor thing.

He didn't try to comfort her or make it stop. She might be this messed up for a long time. He didn't know and he didn't care as long as he stayed with her.

She finally unwound her arms from his neck and sat back, but she didn't stop crying.

She sat there sniffing and grimacing in misery. She twisted her hands together and crushed the corner of her cloak in a white-knuckle grip.

The agitation in her tormented him even more. Maybe she wouldn't get better. Maybe whatever the monks did to her would plague her for the rest of her life.

He kissed her on the side of the head one more time. "I'm going to get your staff," he murmured. "Then we can leave. You'll be okay here by yourself for a few minutes, won't you?"

She nodded. "I'm sorry...!" she wailed.

"Don't you be sorry," he whispered. "You have nothing to be sorry for. This isn't your fault. You had every right to want the monks to heal you of your Darkness. You were right to stay. You had no reason to think this would happen."

"I just....." she broke off and cast a desperate glance around at nothing.

"Stop it," he breathed. "There's nothing wrong with you. You're beautiful and perfect and priceless.....and I love you."

He blurted out the words before he even thought to hold them back.

As soon as he said it, he knew it was true. He didn't even try to figure out how he loved Eliska differently from Marine. None of that mattered.

His heart exploded with love for Eliska. Nothing mattered but taking care of her and protecting her from whoever did this to her.

"I'll be right back." He kissed her one last time, got to his feet, and left the stall.

Chapter 22

Y ann made sure to stall shut the door behind him and then set off at a fast walk for the stairs leading into the monastery.

He climbed up to the dormitory, got his glaive out of the servants' quarters, and then went into the pantry.

He took a cloth shoulder bag from a hook behind the door and loaded it with any food he could lay his hands on.

He tried to concentrate on dried meats, cheeses, and hard biscuits—anything that would keep out in the wilderness, but he didn't plan to make the food last very long.

He would just raid the monastery kitchen whenever he needed more—at least until Eliska felt strong enough to take herself and Yann somewhere else.

Finding her staff would be more difficult because he had no earthly idea where she'd been staying all this time.

He decided to skip it and went into the broom closet instead. She'd used a broom handle as a staff before. She could do it again.

He set his glaive against the wall and selected a mop with a thicker handle than any of the brooms. He had to use a pair of scissors from the wall to cut the thick cord holding the mob head onto the shaft.

The process took longer than it should have, but he finally got a passable staff. Eliska wouldn't care as long as she could use something.

He picked up his glaive and walked out of the panty. At least he wouldn't have to go upstairs and deal with the monks again.

He turned to leave the boom closet when Vesna blundered in behind him. They came face to face and her jaw dropped when she saw him.

"What are you doing here?" she demanded.

He froze for a second, but the next instant, he realized he just didn't care anymore. He picked up his glaive, stepped around her, and walked out without a word of explanation.

He headed back to the stairs leading to the courtyard. He had no more reason to stay here.

His heart lifted on the way down the stairs. He couldn't wait to take Eliska and leave this god-forsaken place.

He made it halfway down the stairs before a blast of magic erupted behind him. It hit him in the back and sent him tumbling head over heels down the stairs all to the way to the bottom.

He dropped his glaive and the mop handle and crashed onto the stone floor at the bottom of the stairs.

He didn't have a chance to lie there or even check to see who attacked him. More blasts ricocheted down the stairs and smashed into the floor all around him.

One of the shots hit him, but it hit the bag that happened to fall over his stomach right then.

The shot scorched a hole in the bag and bought him just enough time to somersault out of the way.

He would have somersaulted toward Eliska's stall, but he didn't think of it in time and wound up rolling in the opposite direction.

He scrambled to his feet just in time to see five monks rushing down the stairs to close on him. He took off running down the nearest colonnade.

He remembered to head back toward Eliska's stall this time, but a dozen other monks from the courtyard materialized out of nowhere and cut him off.

Jets of colored magic fired across the courtyard and exploded the columns right next to his head.

He wheeled away and bolted for cover in any direction where the monks weren't shooting at him. He realized a second too late that he was running all the way to the other side of the courtyard—away from Eliska.

He no longer had either his glaive or her staff, but he wouldn't have been able to fight these monks with either weapon anyway.

He ducked under another barrage that imploded the ceiling above his head. Rock and shrapnel peppered his face and hammered into his head.

He veered sideways and almost collided with a horse that happened to be standing there with its saddle on.

Yann dodged, dove behind the creature, and the next shot from one of the monks exploded the animal into a cloud of blood and splintered bone.

Yann never stopped running, but he would never be able to get away from these monks.

They magicked themselves all over the courtyard, appeared in front of him, and whizzed in every direction to cut him off. He barely stayed one step ahead of their constant bombardment.

The moment inevitably came when they cornered him in the very opposite end of the courtyard. He was as far away from Eliska as he could possibly get.

Five monks appeared out of nowhere to block him from running down the other side of the courtyard. More monks advanced on him from behind.

A wall of twenty men blocked the courtyard. He wouldn't be able to go out there without getting his head shot off.

He backed up again and wound up wedging himself into a corner. There was no way out and he was completely unarmed.

One of the horses in a nearby stall went nuts right then. The creature shrieked and squealed.

It kept kicking the wooden stall door trying to get out. Its thumps of hoof strikes set Yann's' nerves on end, but the monks didn't notice.

They closed in. Every one of them created their crystals on their hands getting ready to fire on Yann. They would finish him off. Then Eliska would be totally defenseless.

Yann's mind kicked into overdrive. He took a few deep breaths to charge into the open even though he already knew it was hopeless. He just had to give it one last shot and hope for the best.

He pushed himself off the wall. All those monks advanced on him until they joined in a complete semicircle to surround him.

He measured each one and chose the shortest, youngest, and monk. Yann would just have to rely on speed and sheer lunatic audacity to get through their line before they took him down.

A tall, powerfully built monk with shoulder-length black hair stepped out of line to advance on Yann. The man raised his crystal and it turned from deep lustrous green to black.

It pulsed with Dark power. Yann plunged for the monks' line to break through and all those crystals opened fire at exactly the same instant.

Matching jets of magic blasted from every crystal, but they only made it halfway across the space before they stopped.

They hung suspended in midair between the crystals and Yann's face. He stared at them in disbelief trying to understand what was happening.

At that moment, Eliska blinked into existence behind the monks. Yann never once expected her to get involved in this.

She materialized out of nowhere, shot her arm behind her, and the mop handle zoomed across the courtyard to thump into her hand.

The monks spun around to gape at her—and so did Yann. She stood straight upright with not a trace of insanity in sight. She glared at the monks in outright fury.

Magic crackled from her hair and a hot, foul wind tossed it and her clock away from her body.

That wind surrounded her. It didn't disturb anything or anyone else in the courtyard.

The monks opened fire on her, but their magic didn't touch her. She didn't have to raise her staff or even look at them.

All their magic ejected from their crystals—and then stopped halfway between them and her.

The monks went ballistic when their magic didn't hit her. They doubled down their efforts and shot again and again, but the same thing happened.

She just stood there without moving. She glared at the monks in fuming rage, but she didn't acknowledge them in any other way.

One of them gave up trying to shoot her, rushed out of line, and tried to get near her. He blurted out, "Eliska....."

She reacted with unimaginable fury. An ear-splitting boom of magic blasted out of her. She didn't raise her staff or wave her hand or make any other movement.

That blast caught all the frozen shots the monks fired from their crystals and turned them back on their owners.

Eliska's magic drove the shots back inside the crystals and all those crystals exploded in brilliant shards of flying magic.

The same blast destroyed columns up and down both sides of the courtyard and the wall behind Yann's back burst.

The shockwave hurled him into the horse's stall behind him and he cracked down on the floor at the horse's feet.

He must have passed out because he woke up alone in the stall with no one but the horse for company.

The creature swiveled its head around to study him while Yann lay sprawled on the floor.

The creature blinked at him and flared its nostrils in Yann's direction. He stared at the horse and then groaned when he sat up and ran his fingers through his hair.

Everything sounded quiet out in the courtyard. This horse had been the one kicking at its stall door, but the creature stood quietly now—too quietly.

Yann stood up, brushed the dirt off his hands, and strained his ears to listen, but he didn't hear any sound coming from outside.

The horse got his attention by snorting at him. Yann stroked its muzzle and then its neck. "Where is everyone?" he whispered, but the horse didn't answer.

Yann tiptoed to the stall door, listened again, and then eased the door open.

He stepped through it and stared all around him. He wasn't in the courtyard anymore. In fact, he couldn't even be sure anymore that he was in the same Island.

He stood in a giant underground cavern, but a different kind of stone made up the rock walls. This wasn't the same Island where he'd seen the Keepers of the Dawn communing with Darklings.

He eased out of the stall and looked around everywhere. He was definitely alone. The cavern met up with a series of tunnels leading to more caverns.

He stopped at the entrance to one and stared in at a massive garden growing in the middle of the cave. A high stone ceiling covered everything. He was still underground, but glowing daylight shone into the cavern from somewhere.

Towering lush jungle trees, vines, flowers dripping from the branches, and trees loaded with fruit covered the expansive floor as far as the eye could see.

A small creek meandered across the floor down there. The music of falling water mingled with the sounds of insects and birdcalls.

He didn't want to go out there. Stunned curiosity made him explore the tunnel system a little more. He halted at another cavern with a completely different landscape in it.

This one was a vast city full of astounding machines, flying vehicles, and a bunch of other stuff Yann didn't recognize. He didn't go out there, either.

He followed the tunnel system to five more caverns, each with a different landscape in it. Where the hell was he? Was he lost in the Layers somewhere?

He didn't know where he was—which meant he was lost with no way to get out of here.

Chapter 23

A starburst of magic burst in front of Eliska's eyes and she magicked into one of the larger training halls in the Keepers of the Dawn's monastery.

She tightened her grip on her staff and looked around everywhere for the monks she'd just been fighting down in the courtyard. They weren't here and she wasn't in the courtyard anymore.

She stormed through the room looking everywhere for Yann, but he wasn't here, either.

Her fury started to get the best of her, but she fought it under control and forced herself to think. The monks attacked him in the courtyard downstairs.

She stopped them from killing him, but they must have let off some kind of protective discharge to transport themselves, Yann, and her somewhere else.

None of the students sparred or trained in this hall at the moment. It was deserted which made no sense at this time of day. There should have been a hundred students in here all working on their exercises.

She opened her Coil projection and narrowed it to the monastery itself. She scowled when she didn't see Yann anywhere in the diagram.

He better not be hurt or dead. She would have liked to kill every living soul in this rotten place, but she had to find Yann first.

He would be in danger wherever he was—especially now that the Keepers of the Dawn understood how important he was to her.

She expanded the projection to include all the surrounding Layers, but she didn't see him in any of them, either.

She went through them Layer by Layer. When that didn't work, she traced hers and his movements from every Layer collapse they'd been going through lately.

She traced them all the way back to the mountain cave where the Keepers of the Dawn first attacked the pair.

She followed the lines to the monastery. Neither of the lines left this Island. He had to still be here....somewhere.

Her intuition told her that he wasn't dead. She hadn't yet perfected this new power, but she felt it getting stronger. Yann was alive and he was trapped in this Layer.

He didn't show up inside the fortress or in the surrounding countryside The monks must be concealing him somewhere.

Her temper started to rise against the monks who did this. She would have liked to tear the monastery apart brick by brick, but that might put Yann in danger.

She took the next best option, stalked out of the training hall, and headed for the Tenth Library. These idiot monks had some explaining to do.

They made a big mistake by giving her the power to destroy them all. None of the monks in this monastery could beat her now—not if she really tapped her Darkness.

They wanted her to do it. Now they would pay the price for messing with her and Yann.

She barged out of the room.....and stopped on the threshold. The training hall didn't open onto the landing leading to the Tenth Library.

Instead, she walked out into a long stone tunnel somewhere underground. The tunnel fed into a giant cavern made of a different kind of stone from the rest of the monastery Island. Was she even in the same Layer?

She turned off to one of the caverns and stared at a mountainous landscape with a tiny, crude village clinging to the steep hillside. The people there wore sheepskins tied around their legs and bodies to keep them warm in the freezing climate.

They herded their livestock up and down the hills while the animals grazed. None of those people realized that a tunnel met up with this landscape and led into a completely different mountain.

She explored the rest of the tunnel system and looked into a dozen different landscapes, each one different from the others.

None of them looked magical. Some of them looked so ordinary that she questioned if they belonged to the Coil at all.

She wandered the tunnel system for half an hour looking into one landscape after another. She didn't see Yann anywhere.

She consulted both her hand window and the Coil projection. Her own line disappeared in the monastery the same way Yann's did. Was she in the same labyrinth where the monks concealed him?

She was just starting to wonder how she could find him when she remembered. The monks gave her this power. They were also the ones concealing Yann from her.

She released a torrent of magic into the Coil projection and it expanded beyond anything she'd ever created before. She pulled up the same image of the monastery, but Yann still didn't show up.

Her patience snapped and she unleashed an even bigger rush of magic into the image. To hell with these rotten monks.

She shattered the image and used her magic to break the conceal-ment. She located Yann deeper inside these caverns....and then the concealment lifted off the rest of what was in here.

Dark forces seethed and marauded through the tunnels. They sur-rounded Yann and made him run from one magical cavern to another. The Dark forces pinned him down only for him to split away and run somewhere else.

Eliska's protective fury burst out of control and she magicked her-self into the tunnels right behind him.

The instant she got there, a Dark ball of twisting fibers hurtled out of nowhere and almost collided with her.

She raised her hand to deflect it and knocked it away inches before it surrounded her face. The ball plastered the nearby tunnel wall, the fibers burst apart, and Andrija slammed down hard on the floor.

He bounced up immediately, but Eliska knew now what was going on. The monks must be using their Dark magic to attack Yann and come after Eliska.

She swiveled her staff forward and fired at Andrija before he got off the ground.

The shot only seemed to give him extra strength. He levitated back onto his feet and rocketed at her head way too fast.

He spread his arms, created two white crystals on each of his hands, and blasted his magic back at her. He bombarded her, but he couldn't touch her.

One thought from her blocked his attack. She didn't have to acti-vate her magic to create a field of protection around her.

She fired all his power back at him and surrounded him in a differ-ent ball of squirming fibers—bright white ones. They crackled over his skin, lifted him off the ground, and helped him in place while he thrashed and struggled to get away.

Her magic counteracted whatever Darkness he'd been trying to use against her. He shrieked in pain, but she didn't release him.

"Where's Yann?" she demanded.

He was yelling too loudly to answer, and right then Milic, Ivico, and Dusan came out of one of the side tunnels to attack her.

They all unloaded on her from different colored crystals in their hands, but none of them could overpower her.

She waved her hand over her head and hurled Andrija at them. He smashed into them and all her fibers spread to the rest of them.

She snaked them into their skin and let her tendrils eat away and react with their Darkness exactly she attacked the Darklings in the obstacle course.

All four men convulsed and writhed in their death throes on the floor. Eliska didn't even look at them. She stormed past them to go look for Yann.

She heard Darklings roaring in the distance and also crashes and explosions that sounded like a Layer collapsing. She didn't have time to screw around with this.

She left the four initiates writhing on the floor and put them completely out of her mind, but she only made it ten steps before someone called her name from behind.

She froze when she recognized the voice. It was Miloji—the man who promised to heal her and give her the answers and training she most wanted.

She took a long time before she decided to turn around and face him. When she did, she discovered Velimir and Mirko standing with him at the far end of the passage.

The rest of the monks from the Tenth Library came with them. Were these the Dark wizards Yann saw communing with Darklings and Dark forces?

She really didn't care. She would rather have gone to get Yann, but the architects of this maze would give her the answers sooner.

All her weakness and confusion evaporated as the Dark poison welled up inside her. It took over her being and broke whatever flimsy bonds of control she might have once used to try to control it.

She stalked over to the monks and planted herself in front of them. What fools they were ever to think they could control her.

Miloji actually had the nerve to smile at her. He had no idea he was about to die in the worst possible way.

"We're so proud of your progress so far, young one," he told her. "You're more than we ever thought you could be."

"You just need to learn to control your power, " Mirko told her. "You could become the most powerful wizard in the Coil once you do that."

"Where's Yann?" she snapped, but in the same breath, she realized she already knew.

The flood of memories and pictures that kept drowning her mind—they flashed to a different cavern in this tunnel system.

Dark forces surrounded Yann and one of them knocked him down on the floor. He no longer had his glaive. He had dropped it out in the courtyard when the monks first attacked him.

She saw it all in a sudden flash of insight. These senior Rectors brought Eliska here so she would have no choice but to use her Dark power to save Yann.

Then the Rectors hoped she would go completely over to the Dark so she would join them—or maybe so they could use her for their own aims. They didn't have a clue.

Miloji's smile broadened when he saw the light of understanding spread over her face. "Now do you understand why we had to do it this way? You wouldn't have come if we told you the truth."

Her rage erupted to volcanic proportions. "You lied to me," she snarled. "You promised me healing and you betrayed me."

"We didn't betray you," Velimir countered. "We brought you here to fulfill your highest potential. You can become even greater, but you have to go through your training. You're one of a kind, Eliska. You're like no one else who has ever lived in the Coil before."

She couldn't listen to this. She would have inflicted a slow torturous death on all of them, but the Dark forces about to destroy Yann didn't give her enough time for that.

She magicked herself to him and materialized in front of him to protect him.

She would have unleashed her magic to hurl the Dark forces away. They took the shape of bizarre shapes all tangled up with twisting Dark fibers.

They morphed and reshaped themselves again and again in between sending out tendrils to snatch and spark on anything they touched.

She couldn't take the time to throw these things away, so she unchained her Dark power and blasted it at the shapes in front of her.

Her Darkness sucked all their fibers into herself and the shapes turned back into initiates from the monastery. Some of them were only young boys completely consumed by the Dark.

They collapsed as soon as she took their Darkness away from them. They fell unconscious on the floor, but more older initiates and junior Rectors came out of every tunnel to surround her.

They unloaded on her from all sides, but she only took their Darkness, too. She could take it all, but she couldn't control it.

It expanded beyond anything she ever thought possible. It tore her apart from the inside.

The next instant, all awareness of who and what she was disintegrated in an almighty outward explosion of pure hate and murderous fury.

She enveloped the monastery and even the whole Layer in all the Dark power coursing through her veins. It flowed into her, out of her, above her, and in every direction. Nothing could check it.

She lost track of what Darkness belonged to her and what Darkness just came from the Coil itself. Was there even a difference anymore?

She no longer had any choice about what it did or where it flowed.

One thought haunted her mind.

She had to destroy the Keepers of the Dawn town to the last child. She had to leave nothing alive so they could never rebuild and carry on their corrupt work somewhere else.

The Darkness exploded outward from her with a catastrophic boom and the shockwave ripped her out of the tunnels. She pitched head over heels and slammed down hard on the ground in some wasteland many Layers away.

Chapter 24

Yann hit the ground, roared in pain, and scrambled to turn over to see where he was.

The countryside looked disturbingly similar to the mountain village where all the people kept disappearing.

A different village stood a few hundred yards down the hillside, but he didn't see any people. Maybe they all disappeared, too.

Bitter cold wind howled down the mountains and chilled him through his uniform, but that wasn't the worst part.

He pushed himself up onto his knees and swallowed hard when he saw Eliska huddled nearby. She went through the same process of jerking around, darting her eyes here and there, and staring at the world from under her hair hanging in front of her face.

She went farther this time. She snarled, slashed her teeth at invisible enemies, and even kicked at them before she fell into incoherent muttering.

Yann pulled himself to his feet and heaved a broken sigh when he looked down at her. He got her back. They made it out of the monastery Island, but at what cost? Would she ever come back from this?

She acted as insane as Marine ever did, but something told him this was different. Eliska didn't act like this because she was communing with Darklings—not willingly.

The monks did something to her—something bad. They broke her in every possible way—which was exactly the last thing in the world that she needed.

He didn't know what she did to them or their monastery. He would never ask.

He studied her for a long time before he decided what to do with her. What *could* he do with her?

Now he was really alone—much more alone than he'd ever been with Marine. She at least made eye contact with him and talked to him through her familiars.

Eliska wouldn't be able to do any of that. He didn't understand how he knew this, but he felt it in his bones. She was a complete disaster inside and out.

The wind gusted over the mountaintops just then and made him shiver. He narrowed his eyes at the rugged landscape. He couldn't stay up here, but he would be damned if he left Eliska alone.

She saved him from the monastery. She saved him more than once.

She might even have driven herself insane like this just to save him. He wouldn't have been even marginally surprised if that was what pushed her over the edge.

He walked off and left her there, hiked down the hillside to the village, and searched the place. He didn't find anyone or even any sign that people had lived here in years.

Dust covered every surface and he didn't see any food on a single shelf in any of the houses. He also didn't see any firewood stacked against the walls. The whole place echoed as silent as the grave, but at least no one would bother him and Eliska here.

He went back to get her. She was in the process of kicking at some invisible enemy when he returned.

"Come down to the village there, Eliska," he told her. "We can stay in one of the houses. We can't stay out here on the tops. It's too cold and too exposed."

She didn't respond at all. He tried the old trick of walking away, but she didn't follow him the way Maine would.

He took a few steps toward her to see if she resisted him, but she didn't even see him.

In the end, he wrapped his arms around her and picked her up off the ground. She didn't react at all except to continue her insane jolting and spasming. She muttered and snarled in his ear all the way back to the village.

He put her on the bed in one of the houses, left her there, took an axe, and hiked downhill to a wooded valley where he chopped an armload of firewood.

He went back to the house, built a fire in the fireplace, and left again. Eliska didn't move the whole time except to scoot to different parts of the bed. She faced the wall when he came in the second time.

He went through the whole painstaking process of bringing up water from the nearby spring, hunting a biturong to eat, and loading in as much firewood as he thought he would need to keep the house warm overnight.

It was already getting dark by the time he returned and put the biturong on the spit to cook. Then he spent a few hours cleaning the house, shaking the dust and cobwebs out of some blankets, and getting the bed ready for him and Eliska to spend the night.

He didn't try to talk to her while he worked. He had no idea what to expect from her or if she would stay like this forever.

When he finally finished all his chores, he sat down on the bed next to her and watched her. Her mutterings sounded more coherent now, but he might have just been fooling himself about that.

He didn't fool himself about how bad she looked. He made up his mind right then and there to stay in this Island for as long as it took for her to recover.

If she didn't recover—if she stayed like this forever—then he would just live in this house by himself and take care of her for the rest of his life—or for however long this Island stayed intact before it collapsed, too.

He couldn't do anything else. He didn't have the magic to leave nor did he have the magic to heal her of whatever the hell was wrong with her.

He already knew what was wrong with her. The Dark took her over. The monks used the Dark against her. They unleashed her Darkness beyond what she could tolerate and it made her snap.

He could have killed them all for that, but maybe she already did. He would probably never know.

It didn't matter because he already knew what he had to do. He found a plain clay cup on the shelf, filled it with water, and pulled a wooden chair toward the bed to act as a table.

"Here. Drink this," he told her and put the cup in front of her.

She snatched it and pounded the water in loud greedy mouthfuls.

"Are you hungry? Here. Eat some food."

He sliced the bituroung meat into a bowl and she did the same thing when he put that in front of her.

She scarfed the meat and gulped it down without really swallowing it. He served her three big bowlfuls before she started to slow down.

He sat back and watched her lick the juice off her hands. She did it in a crude animalistic way without looking at him.

He used one finger to comb the hair out of her eyes, but it only fell over her face again.

"Everything is going to be okay," he murmured. "I'm going to take care of you until you start to feel better. We're out of the monastery. Those monks can't hurt you here. You can rest here as long as you need to. There's no hurry. You're alone here with me. You're safe now."

She didn't respond, but he didn't need her to.

He ate some of the food himself, drank some water, and then went through the room cleaning up and putting everything away from the night.

This house actually felt comfortable—a lot more comfortable than the monastery.

Whatever made the people disappear didn't haunt this Island with the same oppressive sense of foreboding the friends had been experiencing lately.

He approached the bed to go to sleep, wrapped a blanket around Eliska's shoulders, and tucked it under her chin.

"Try to get some rest, okay?" he told her. "You're probably exhausted after fighting the monks. Maybe you'll feel better in the morning. I'll be right here with you if you need me. Okay?"

He didn't expect an answer and she didn't give him one. He kicked off his boots, pulled off his jacket and shirt, and climbed onto the bed behind her. She took up half of it by sitting on the edge of the mattress.

He crawled under the blankets. She sat next to him with her back to him.

He started to drift off when she tipped over, curled up on top of the mattress with her back to him, and tightened herself into a fetal ball.

He smiled, rubbed her shoulder once, and kissed her hair from behind. He never loved her more than now. She sacrificed everything for him. He would never forget that and he would never, ever abandon her—not ever.

Chapter 25

Yann woke up the next morning, stripped the rest of the meat off the bituroung carcass, ate some of it, and left the rest for Eliska while he went out hunting.

He had the whole day to accomplish half the work he finished in a few hours yesterday. He spotted some waterbuck tracks near the spring yesterday.

He worked steadily through the morning to do all his chores. Eliska woke up while he was out of the house.

He came in carrying another bucket of water and found her sitting on the edge of the bed, but she didn't jerk and startle the way she did before. She just stared blankly into space.

He put the bucket down in front of her and pulled the chair over to the bed. "You look much better this morning," he told her. "I told you a good night's sleep would make you feel better. Let's get you cleaned up."

He dunked a rag into the bucket, wrung it out, and started wiping down her face, hair, and neck.

She didn't respond at all nor did she make eye contact. He talked to her the whole time about everything he was doing, everything he'd seen out in the mountains, and everything he planned to do to make their lives here more comfortable.

She didn't respond to any of it. She barely shut her eyes when he passed his rag across her eyelids to clean the sleep dust out of her eyes.

He left for a few hours, hunted a waterbuck, and then spent several more hours carrying it back to the village, stringing it up, gutting it, and skinning it.

He returned to find Eliska sitting in exactly the same position. He talked to her while he worked in the house, but she never answered or even blinked to show that she heard him.

He crossed the room, but she didn't follow his movements or even realize what he was doing.

He could live with this small improvement. If she kept improving every day, he wouldn't ask anything else.

He ransacked the rest of the village until he found a large iron cauldron one of the previous housewives must have used for laundry.

He also found one house where the resident must have been an educated person. They left behind a bunch of books on a wide variety of subjections.

He took everything back to the house, heated water, washed his uniform, and dried it by the fire in the main room.

Then he went through the same process of taking off Eliska's clothes, washing them, drying them, and redressing her. She didn't move or react at all through the whole process.

He dumped out the water by the time the sun went down. He went inside, carved a haunch off of the waterbuck, and hung the rest of the carcass up the chimney to smoke overnight.

He cooked dinner for himself and Eliska, fed her, and then settled back in his chair while he decided what to do next.

He went through the stacks of books until he found one he liked. "This one looks interesting," he told her. "It's a field guide to wide edible plants in the area…and it lists the habits of local wildlife, too.

That should come in handy. Let's see what it says. It lists the water-buck, biturong, and a few different gar species. This is interesting. It also lists three different varieties of hog. I haven't seen that. Maybe you should come outside and get some sunshine tomorrow. I don't want you stuck in the house all the time. What do you say?"

She didn't respond, but a second later, she lifted the blanket off the mattress next to her, wrapped it around her own shoulders, and curled up on the bed in exactly the same position where she slept last night.

The sight of her twisted his heart. She was all right. She was coming out of this little by little.

He went over to her, rubbed her arm, stroked her hair, and kissed her on the head. "Good night, young one. Sleep well. I love you. I'll see you in the morning."

He returned to the table where he continued reading, but he kept looking up at her sleeping face every once in a while.

He thought nothing of saying he loved her. He did. He would gladly live here with her for as long as it took even if it took forever.

He woke up first the next morning and slipped out of bed trying to be careful not to wake up Eliska.

He got dressed and went out into the mountains. He didn't go hunting because he already had enough food to last a long time.

He tracked the waterbuck for a while and then used the information from that book to find a family of hogs living in the same forest.

He followed them for a few hours to find out where they went, where they wallowed, and where they rested under the trees. He would need to know all of that if he ever wanted to hunt them in the future.

He also gathered a long, straight stick to make a new staff for Eliska and a bunch of branches the book said made good cordage. The book included pages of useful diagrams on how to process the bark and braid it into rope.

He returned to the house, dumped everything on the ground outside, and went inside to get a knife. He stopped dead in his tracks when he saw Eliska sitting up.

She no longer stared into space. Her eyes darted around the room again. She definitely knew where she was and why.

Her eyes snapped to his face before she immediately looked away. Her features spasmed in an excruciating grimace of terror, confusion, and desperate pleading.

He dropped what he was doing and rushed over to her. "Hey!" he breathed. "You're better! This is great! How are you? I was so worried." He burst out in relieved laughter.

She opened her mouth, but she couldn't speak. She tried more than once, but her confusion and terror got in the way.

"That's okay," he murmured. "Don't worry about it. You're getting better. That's all that matters. We're in a stable Island, so you don't have to worry about anything. We're going to stay here until you're ready to leave. Understand? Don't push yourself harder than you need to. I'm taking care of everything."

She tried again to say something and her cheeks screwed up in misery when she failed.

"Stop," he whispered. "You don't have to try. Just concentrate on getting better. Do you want to come outside for a while? I found some instructions in that book on how to make rope. Why don't you come with me? It will do you good to get out of the house for a while. Come on."

He took her hand. She resisted at first, but she eventually stumbled after him to leave the house.

He couldn't get over the pure relief that she was actually responding. He never thought he would ever get her back as much as this.

He pulled a bench over from the house wall. "Here. Sit here. I'll talk to you while I work and explain everything to you."

She stopped in the middle of the yard while he revolved around her in a whirlwind of activity. He probably shouldn't have made such a big fuss about her coming back to her senses, but he couldn't stop himself.

She didn't sit down. He got a block of wood from one of the other houses to use as a stool and another to use as his work surface.

"The book says you have to peel off the bark, scrape away the tough outer bark, and then weave the inner bark into the braid," he babbled. "We'll see if it works. Maybe I'll figure it out by the time I actually need a rope."

He dove inside, got the knife, and returned to find her still standing there. She looked around at everything, but she didn't sit down.

He considered encouraging her to sit down again, but the look on her face stopped him.

She surveyed the town and then, like something out of his fondest dreams, she threw back her head and shut her eyes into the sunshine. Her hair fell back away from her face.

Yann bent over his work so he wouldn't stare at her. She would get better. He knew that now.

He picked up the first branch, slit his knife down the length of the shaft, and peeled the bark away from the branch the way the book instructed. Then he used his knife to scrape off the outer bark.

When he finished, he wound up with a cut cylinder of tough rubbery white inner bark. It didn't look like anything anyone could use to make rope.

He got the hatchet from the woodpile and used the flat butt to pound the cylinder. It split apart into fibers. He knotted them together at the top and started braiding them.

He made it four inches down the braid before Eliska opened her eyes and sat down on the bench he brought forward for her. He looked up and she made eye contact with him.

He burst into a huge smile, and for the first time, she smiled back.

He didn't want to push this success too far, so he turned back to what he was doing.

"This actually isn't that hard. I thought it would be way more complicated. I guess people had a lot more free time to do stuff like this before they started living in cities and using computers and all that."

Eliska didn't respond. He didn't look up to see what she was doing. He never dreamed she could improve as much as this.

Anything was possible. She might get back to full functioning.... but he knew better than to hope for that.

She would carry this Darkness forever. She was worse now than when Anríq brought her back from the cursed city.

Yann didn't let himself hope that she would ever completely recover, but he could look forward to these small improvements. At least she knew who she was and where and why.

He finished braiding the fibers and started peeling the next branch. The process went faster as he got the hang of it.

He paused after the third branch to get himself a drink of water, but before he could go get it, Eliska stood up and paced a few yards down the street to study the town.

"There are quite a few resources left behind in these houses," Yann called after her. "I've only found some of them. We could make a more careful search for anything we might need to use. Who knows? There might be other villages in the area that aren't deserted like this one. There might be other people living nearby. We might not be alone out here."

She didn't answer. She went over to one of the nearby houses, threw the door open, and went inside.

He got his water and kept working until she came out and paced around for a while. He didn't see her acting any differently from a normal person except that she couldn't talk.

He didn't see her using her magic, either. Maybe she couldn't. Maybe she didn't have magic at all anymore.

He didn't care too much if she had magic as long as her mind came back.

He tried not to pay too much attention to what she was doing. He didn't want her to feel any pressure to straighten herself out before she was ready.

He finished pounding the fibers from the fourth branch and started to weave them into his braid.

Just then, a strong gust of freezing wind blew through the town from the west. That sting of cold bit Yann's cheeks and he looked up.

His heart stopped when he saw the Voyant floating in midair a dozen yards out of town.

Chapter 26

Yann shot to his feet and seized the hatchet at his feet. He didn't have any other weapon.

He barged forward to plant himself in front of Eliska, but he didn't get there fast enough.

An outward breaking wave of upheaval ejected from the Voyant's halo. The instability hit the ground and it heaved out of position.

That wave rolled toward the village and then a bone-crushing smash of chaos blasted out of the Voyant's halo to tear the landscape apart.

The shockwave hit the houses on that end of town, blew them to matchsticks, and the village evaporated in a hurricane of flying debris.

Another blast slammed Eliska backward and she crashed into the house behind her. She didn't get up.

Yann sprang in front of her to face down the Voyant alone. God only knew what Yann would be able to do against a magic-user as powerful as this.

Yann raised his hatchet and stormed up the hill to close with the Voyant. He hovered there with the same scowl on his face. Did he even see Yann?

The Voyant didn't raise his hands or wave the way Yann had seen other wizards use magic.

Then again, Yann had also seen Eliska using magic lately without raising her hands at all. The Voyant must do it that way, too.

Yann tensed all over. Maybe he should rush the Voyant, but everyone else who ever did that wound up burned to death or destroyed in the chaos.

Yann halted at a distance while he decided how to defend Eliska from this monster. Yann finally found a safe Island. He wouldn't let the Voyant ruin it, but Yann lacked the power to stop it.

The instability surrounding the Voyant spread outward, rippled through the ground, and tore the mountains apart. Rock exploded out of the high cliffs in deafening booms.

Deep cracks burst apart the hillsides and a hurricane wind ripped the houses off their foundations. None of them was strong enough to withstand the onslaught.

Yann raised his left hand in front of his face to protect his eyes. Hurricane winds knocked him a few steps back. He sidestepped in front of Eliska and tried to take his eyes off the Voyant long enough to see if she was badly hurt.

The Voyant drifted a little closer. His ferocious expression didn't change....until he opened his mouth to speak.

A brutal concussion shot from his halo as soon as he opened it. It translated through the bedrock underfoot and ruptured the landscape for miles around.

The Island completely dissolved. All the house blasted apart into smithereens and the torrential wind plastered Yann off his feet.

He barely had time to drop his hatchet, dive on top of Eliska, and grab her in his arms before both of them wheeled off into the Layers.

He realized as soon as he touched her that she was out cold. That first blow must have knocked her out. She flopped in his arms and didn't respond—which meant she couldn't use her magic to save herself or Yann.

The village Island vanished in the whirlwind, but the Voyant didn't. He stayed hovering the same distance away even when Yann and Eliska hurtled through catastrophic tempests of flying shards, Dark forces slashing and attacking, and raging Darkling battles.

None of the Darklings came after the pair, not even when the Voyant fell into Darkling Layers.

Yann tucked his head against Eliska's shoulder and concentrated all his effort just on holding onto her. Whatever happened to her better happen to him. He really didn't care what that was as long as nothing separated them from each other.

They smashed down into another grassland landscape, but they were both falling too fast to stop themselves from splattering on the ground.

Yann tensed all over and tightened his grip on her. He yelled, "Hold on Eliska!" even though she couldn't hear him.

He turned his back to the ground in his last desperate bid to protect her. They slammed into the ground full force and broke through into another Layer—a Layer full of water.

They plunged in and Yann immediately started to flounder trying to find the surface so he could breathe. He had to drag Eliska along with him, but gravity kept tugging him down, down, down to the bottom.

They fell and broke through another Layer into a world consumed by fire. It scorched all around them and seared Yann's skin through his uniform. He bellowed in pain, but he didn't dare to let go of Eliska.

He spotted the Voyant's halo following them to this Layer, too, but the Voyant didn't have to attack. The fire would kill both Yann and Eliska any second now.

Dark forces whipped through the flames. Monstrous faces and shadowy tendrils of fire moved with unnatural determination to come after the two travelers.

A brutal slash ripped across Yann's face and left a burned cut running from his forehead down to his jawline. He jerked away, but more of the same deadly threads came out of nowhere to cut, slash, and pummel him everywhere.

He shut his eyes and prepared for the worst, but not quickly enough before a hurtling projectile streaked across his line of sight. He cringed away expecting it to attack him, but instead, a jet of magic fired from somewhere and a ball of light surrounded him and Eliska.

Yann's eyes snapped wide open when he saw what looked like a person somersaulting, cartwheeling, and pitching all over the Layer. He took another eternal second to realize it wasn't just a person. It was a woman.

She somehow landed on the flames and used them as solid springboards to propel herself back and forth across the blistering landscape. She fought the Dark forces with two short sticks in either hand. Neither of them was more than two feet long.

Yann didn't see anything special about them. They were made of smooth wood.

This woman channeled her magic through them, pounded the Dark forces back, and kept jetting streaks of magic at Yann and Eliska to protect them from assault.

Yann blinked hard. He still couldn't believe this person was actually protecting him and Eliska from the Dark forces, but he had bigger problems right now.

Voyant kept hovering there in the distance as the ball plunged through the fire Layer and slammed down.

It hit something solid, but Yann didn't see what it was. Flames surrounded the ball until it broke through into a clear blue sky over a grassy countryside full of plowed fields, neatly paved roads, and a few small villages.

The ball slowed its fall as soon as it entered this Island. It kept falling, but it drifted slowly to the ground. That gave Yann as much time as he needed to see the landscape....and the woman who fell through the Layer along with him.

She plunged through the breach and landed right on top of the ball, but her weight didn't make it fall any faster.

She stabbed both her sticks down into its glistening surface and directed the ball sideways until it landed in an open field.

The ball burst and Yann finally let go of Eliska. He laid her on the ground, but she didn't wake up.

He scrambled to his feet to thank the woman who saved him and Eliska from the Dark.

He froze and the words died on his lips when he saw the person standing in front of him.

Advanced age had turned the front of her hair white. Only the bottom few inches showed that it had once been chocolate brown.

She had braided it into millions of tiny braids that had long ago matted into dreadlocks. They hung almost to her waist with a leather thong tying them together behind her neck.

She wore an ancient brown leather vest with no decorations at all, but she kept it laced up the front instead of wearing it open the way Anríq did.

Tattoos covered the woman's body from her neck all the way down to the exposed midriff of her stomach.

Deep wrinkles scored her face, hands, and neck. She was old—beyond old—but Yann couldn't deny the evidence of his own eyes.

This old woman—the woman who saved Yann and Eliska from the fire Layer—was a Servant.

Chapter 27

E liska jolted awake and actually screamed when she felt hands touching her.

"Easy," Yann murmured next to her. "You're okay. You're all right. We're in another Island. The Voyant isn't here. I'm with you."

He clasped both her hands in his....so he couldn't be the one touching her. She jerked the other way and froze when she saw an ancient woman sitting next to her.

A beautiful smile radiated out of the woman's deeply lined face, but her hands gripped every part of Eliska's body with unnatural strength.

Eliska's awareness widened and she wilted in relief when she saw the woman's dreadlocks, leather vest, and the tattoos vanishing under her clothes. She was a Servant—an extremely old Servant.

The woman smiled so kindly that Eliska couldn't help but smile back. The woman kept flooding Eliska with healing magic.

It cleared some of the confusion and desperate terror that had been haunting Eliska ever since she left the Keepers of the Dawn.

"Do you feel better?" Yann asked.

Eliska dragged her awareness back to him. His eyes brimmed with so much concern.

"I....." Eliska struggled to find the words.

"Don't worry about it," he told her. "You go hit by the Voy-ant—and you weren't in the greatest shape before that. Do you re-member the house where we stayed in the mountains?"

She couldn't find the words, so she just nodded. She remembered everything including using her Dark power to destroy the monastery and everyone inside it.

"Here. Drink some water.'"

He scooped his arm behind her head and helped her sit up so she could drink from a roughly carved wooden bowl.

He put her down and her eyes darted to the Servant sitting nearby.

Hand-carved beads, stones with holes drilled into them, pieces of polished wood, and carved shells hung from parts of her hair, clothes, and the leather gauntlets around her wrists.

Her gauntlets didn't completely conceal the blocks and blocks of parallel lines that indicated this woman's great age.

"This Servant saved us from a fire Layer after the Voyant destroyed the village," Yann went on. "She's been working on you ever since. "

Eliska tried again to thank the woman, but something in Eliska's brain wouldn't connect the words in her head to her mouth.

The woman only smiled, pressed her hands together, shut her eyes, and bowed her head. She didn't speak even to say she would serve.

Eliska waited, but the woman didn't respond in any other way.

Yann read Eliska's mind. "She doesn't talk the way Anríq does," he murmured under his breath. "We've been here for almost two days and she hasn't said a single word."

The old Servant pivoted in her seat, turned aside, and poked some sticks into a fire burning next to her. She adjusted some dead animal roasting on the spit.

Eliska found herself studying the woman. Eliska had never seen a Servant as old as this.

The woman went through all the usual camp activities. Nothing she did appeared out of the ordinary from how Eliska, Yann, Anríq, or anyone else would do anything. Eliska didn't even see this woman using magic to perform her tasks.

Eliska watched the woman in fascination. Her sewn-up vest hid the Servant's mark, but it had to be there under her clothes.

This woman carried all the same hallmark signs of being a Barbarian, but she was as much a Servant as Anríq if not more so.

Anríq had deviated so far from the traditional Servant's rules. He talked all the time now. Did that make him something other than a Servant? Eliska refused to believe that.

Yann got to his feet. "I'm going down to the river to get some more water. I'll be back in a few minutes."

He walked off and left Eliska alone with the woman. Eliska would have liked to ask the old Servant's name, but the woman wouldn't answer. She would probably only smile and bow again.

The woman took a different bowl out of the coals—a metal one this time.

Steam billowed from the top. The woman blew on it, brought it over to Eliska, and the woman went through the same routine of jamming her arm under Eliska's shoulders, lifting her up, and supporting her while she held the bowl to Eliska's mouth.

Eliska took a few deep gulps of scalding hot soup. It tasted salty and incredibly good.

Eliska collapsed back on the ground before she realized she was lying on a bunch of blankets underneath her.

Three more blankets lay over her even though the sun shone out of a clear blue sky.

Warm breezes kept blowing through the long grass nearby. Yann and the old Servant had made camp in the middle of an open field with tall grass surrounding them on all sides. Eliska couldn't see over all the grass to see what kind of Island this really was.

Yann came back, put a wooden bucket on the ground next to the fire, and sat down on Eliska's other side.

"We think this Island is suffering from the same problem with people disappearing," Yann began. "There seems to be a lot of that. The few villages we've seen still have people in them, but not enough. Everyone is giving up and watching their families vanish one person at a time."

Eliska tried to answer, but just then, the old Servant extended her hand and placed it on Eliska's forehead.

Anríq had done that a million times, but this old Servant's touch felt different. Her magic was much stronger even than his.

It blasted into Eliska's brain and a switch flipped in her mind. She could actually think clearly for the first time since she left the monastery.

Her eyes popped wide open and she spun around to stare up at the old Servant. The woman only smiled at her, and this time, the old woman actually laughed with a big, beaming, toothy grin.

"Thank you!' Eliska gasped.

"Are you okay?" Yann asked. "You can talk. That's great."

"Um…I'm all right. I can think. Thank you so much." She sat up out of the blankets and moved over by the fire. "I feel…. kind of normal."

"You still look drawn," Yann remarked. "You aren't completely back."

Eliska experienced a quick flash of all the Dark memories—and even more from the monastery itself.

The monks gave her power a massive boost—and they also added a ton of Dark magic to what she already had.

The old Servant stabilized it so Eliska could tolerate it enough to think clearly, but nothing would ever make that Darkness go away.

Eliska took one glance at the woman and knew. This Servant might mean well, but she didn't have the power to heal Eliska.

That would have been a monumental task when she left Symphorian. I would be even harder now after the monks made her Darkness so much bigger and stronger.

The old Servant didn't even try to touch Eliska's Darkness. The woman must have seen it when she healed Eliska of her injuries, but the woman couldn't heal the Darkness and didn't try.

The woman went through a detailed procedure of taking the animal off the spit and dividing the food between all three of them. She gave equal portions to herself, Yann, and Eliska.

They both thanked her, but she didn't reply even to bow.

"It's so strange," Eliska murmured. "I'm used to Anríq. It's eerie not being able to talk to her—about anything."

"I know what you mean., but she's been nothing but kind to us since she found us." Yann turned to the woman, pressed his hands together, and bowed to her. "Thank you.'

She bowed back.

"Maybe....." Eliska murmured and then she turned to the woman and took a deep breath. "We're trying to defeat the Voyant Mendicat. We're trying to find the Shard of Hotha so we can stabilize the Coil. That's our mission. We've been trying to find our way back to the Layer with the White Spire in it. Maybe you could help us."

The woman pressed her hands together and bowed again.

"Does that mean you'll serve?" Eliska asked.

The woman bowed again.

"Thank you so much!" Eliska exclaimed. "We've tried everything—and a bunch of our friends have already died on this quest. We don't know where to find the Shard or the Sacred Shrine. We were just starting to think we might need to go through some magical process or that the Sacred Shrine might be hidden in the Layers. Would you know anything about that?"

The old Servant only smiled at her. It was one of the kindest smiles Eliska could ever remember, but it didn't tell her and Yann anything they didn't already know.

"The question is how to get there," Yann remarked. "Do you still have your magic?"

Eliska blinked into thin air for a second. She still had her magic. She never thought she didn't. "Yes, I still have it."

He gasped and passed his hand across his forehead. "Phew! I was worried."

"Why?" she asked.

"I thought the monks might have done something to you—and you never used your magic since you left the monastery. I thought ....I don't know what I thought. I was prepared for the worst."

"I'm okay." She broke off. She wasn't okay.

She caught Yann looking at her sideways, so she changed the subject by opening her Coil projection.

She actually had to stop herself from adding too much magic to it. It got too big before she restrained herself to make it smaller.

"The White Spire has moved to another Layer," she announced. "It's in another city, but that city is already falling to instability."

"Maybe we should be trying to find the information about how to access the Sacred Shrine," Yann suggested. "If you're right that it's a magical dimension that can only be accessed by magic, then maybe we don't need to go to the White Spire at all. Maybe we can get there by going through the Layers."

Eliska's head shot up. "You're right! I didn't think of that."

She opened her projection again, and this time, she let all her magic pour into it. It expanded and she zeroed in on individual Layers. She ran through hundreds of them. "I'm not seeing anything here that might be the Sacred Shrine."

"Can you locate the Shard?" he asked.

She did the same thing, but again came up with nothing. "Sorry. It must be hidden."

"Does that mean it could be concealed in the Layers or that it *isn't* in the Layers?"

"Either one. The records were pretty specific that the Sacred Shrine and the Hall of the Light were both located in the White Spire."

"But neither of them was on that diagram we saw. So they must be concealed by magic, too."

Eliska frowned. "There's something here we're missing."

"Yeah—the Shard. If we could just find out where it is, we would be set."

She found herself grinning at him. Not even the bad memories could dampen her relief. She could actually think and function. She didn't know how well she could function, but anything was better than the way she was before.

Their conversation turned to other matters. The old Servant sat in silence through it all, but she cocked her head to one side and listened to every word they said.

Eliska got tired much sooner than the other two. She stretched out in her blankets and Yann tucked her in. He kissed her on the head.

"It's so wonderful to get you back at last," he murmured. "I couldn't lose you."

"Thank you—for everything." She choked on the words.

She would have liked to tell him that she loved him, but she just couldn't cross that line—not yet.

Would she ever be able to? Would she ever be able to tell him how much she really valued him? How would he ever find out if she didn't tell him?

What if something happened to him before she told him—like it happened with Yvan and the other Watchmen?

That would be terrible—as terrible as it was to lose them before she got a chance to tell them all how much they meant to her.

She ached from gratitude just to have Yann in her life. He didn't need magic—not that kind anyway. His own precious heart made him more valuable than pure gold.

He sat next to her talking about things he'd seen in the landscape since they came to this Island. He knew more than she ever wanted to know about the local people, the locations of towns and farms, and where all the local roads led.

She drifted off midsentence, and for the first time, she collapsed into an exhausted sleep without nightmares, thanks to the old Servant's healing.

Chapter 28

Yann woke up, sat up by the dying fire, and stared down at Eliska's sleeping face. God, he loved her so much!

He almost wanted to cry from relief that she was okay—or more okay than she had been.

She could hold a steady conversation and think clearly. She could also use her magic—not that he wouldn't have been glad to get her back without it.

The old Servant woke up next, walked off the river, and came back with her hair wet.

She and Yann went through the morning chores in silence. Eliska slept for a long time. Yann and the old Servant did everything quietly to let Eliska sleep as long as possible.

She finally sighed, rolled over, and sat up before she looked around and scowled at the surroundings. "It's late. Why didn't you wake me up?"

"You needed to sleep," Yann told her. "We'll camp here for as long as it takes until you get your strength back."

"I have it back now. I don't want you to delay because of me."

Yann made a face at her. "You've been a mess lately. Don't rush off to do it all again—please."

She couldn't hold back from smiling at him. "Really. I feel okay. Can't we at least travel across the countryside and see what happens? We can stop if I get tired. I don't want to sit around doing nothing. We've delayed too long already."

Yann glanced at the old Servant. She watched Eliska with a keen eye.

The old woman didn't indicate by any sign that she objected to Eliska getting up and moving around.

Eliska must have understood the woman's silence as that, too. Eliska opened her Coil projection. "The White Spire is back in a different Island. It's in the Far Reaches."

"How do we get there?" Yan asked.

"We can cut through these Layers here. It will be dangerous, but with both of us working together, we should make it all right."

Yann glanced at the old Servant again. She still didn't offer any objection. Would she ever? How would she communicate her objections if she didn't speak up and voice them?

Eliska had been unconscious when the old Servant fought the Dark forces in the Layers. Eliska didn't see just how powerful this woman was. Was she strong enough to get into the White Spire?

Eliska shut her hand and the projection vanished. The old Servant started packing up the camp.

She put the bowls into her shoulder bag and picked up the two sticks she used as weapons.

Eliska blinked at her, "Don't you have any weapons?"

"She fights with these sticks the way you fight with your staff. She doesn't use traditional Barbarian weapons like Anríq does."

"You mean....?" Eliska trailed off.

Yann couldn't explain anything else about the old Servant, so he went back to work.

She waved one of her sticks at the blankets and they vanished the same way they appeared when she first saved Yann and Eliska and brought them to this Island.

Eliska stared at everything the woman did. Yann distracted her by holding out the new staff he'd carved for Eliska. "Take this. I made it for you.'

She beamed him and then rushed him, hugged him, and kissed him on the cheek. "You're the best!"

He blushed and looked away. "Now if I could just get my glaive back, we would be ready to go."

"I have it here."

Eliska stuck her hand into her pocket, pulled out what looked like a pebble, and it expanded into Yann's glaive—the glaive he lost in the monastery courtyard.

He gasped when she held it out to him. "Where did you get this?"

She grimaced. "You don't want to know. I found it. Don't ask me where. I magicked it into my bag so I could give it back to you—but I got a little distracted."

"This is wonderful! Thank you so much!" He rotated the glaive around examining it from all sides. "I love this glaive."

She turned bright red and looked away. "I know. That's why I brought it for you."

The group moved out, headed for the nearest road, and passed through one of the small villages.

No one came out to accost the old Servant and ask for her help. She'd already visited all the nearby towns while Eliska had been recovering.

The three travelers passed through the village and farther down the road before Eliska consulted her projection again. "This should be a good spot. We can break through the Layer here to the Far Reaches."

Yann and the old Servant gathered around her. She stood her staff on the ground and tapped it a few times.

"What are you waiting for?" Yann asked.

Eliska frowned to herself and didn't answer. She looked down at the soil at her feet.

"Eliska?" Yann prompted. "Is something wrong?"

Her head shot up and she narrowed her eyes at the landscape around her. "He's coming!" she hissed.

"Who?"

"The Voyant!" She spun her staff up, gripped it in both hands, and looked everywhere. "He's coming! He'll be here any...."

She broke off when the Voyant's halo burst to life a mile away. He hovered over the hillsides behind where the party had just been camping.

His arrival set off an immediate upheaval in the surrounding countryside. The hillsides undulated out of position. Bizarre shapes traveled up and down the line moving away from the Voyant before coming back.

Jets of magic sprayed from his halo and plastered houses in the village, fences, livestock, and even the surrounding hills. Some of those shots came perilously close to hitting the three travelers.

Yann stiffened, but before either he or Eliska could do anything, the old Servant sprang in front of them.

She whirled her sticks in front of her face and deflected dozens of shots coming from the Voyant's halo.

She sent them zooming back toward him, but his assault only escalated the longer she tried to defend the two young people.

The woman advanced a few paces to put distance between herself and Yann and Eliska.

Eliska moved forward to help the old Servant, but before Eliska could do anything, the old Servant started firing bolts of magic from her sticks.

She didn't point the sticks at the Voyant. She thrust them out long ways and at different angles. The blasts came from the long edge of each stick.

She fired a rapid barrage, but her shorts only vanished inside the halo.

The outward spreading chaos overtook the village. The ground rose and fell in giant mountains falling to deep troughs.

Eliska roared out, "NO!!" and charged forward.

A bone-crushing, earth-shattering blast ejected from her. Yann didn't see her even raise her staff. That concussion caught the forward-breaking edge of the upheaval and forced it back.

The cracks closed up on all the hills and valleys returned to their normal position.

Eliska's magic couldn't repair destroyed houses, fenceposts, and dismembered livestock, but it did push the instability all the way back to the Voyant.

Just as many shots blasted out of his halo, but those shots froze in midair before they hit the travelers.

She halted ten feet in front of the old Servant. A crackling starburst of energy surrounded Eliska. It spouted from her hair and skin. It bombarded the Voyant just as hard—and he vanished.

Silence fell over the landscape and Yann heard Eliska rasping for breath. Sweat drenched her forehead and trickled down her neck. The Voyant was gone.

Yann strode forward to her side. "Are you okay?" he whispered.

She nodded fast, but she wouldn't stop searching the surrounding countryside. "I should have asked him......" she croaked. "I should have asked him...."

"You couldn't ask him while he was attacking you," Yann pointed out. "Maybe next time."

Her eyes snapped to his face, but she immediately looked away. They both turned around to find the old Servant standing behind them.

She pointed to the ground where Eliska had been standing before—the spot where Eliska had been planning to break through to the lower Layers.

Eliska let out a shuddering sigh. "Right. Here we go."

She returned to the spot and tapped her staff against it again.

"Do you want to use a binding spell to hold us together like you did before?" Yann asked.

"I don't need to. I can just take us there."

"You mean...." He trailed off when he realized what she meant. She could magically transport herself through the Layers. She didn't have to fall through them or shatter an Island to leave it.

His eyes met hers when he realized. The monks must have given her incredible magic—even more than she already had. They must have magnified her magic beyond anything he could even imagine.

At that moment, both Eliska and the old Servant spun the other way. They stared across the countryside in a completely different direction.

Yann followed their gaze and his heart stopped when two figures strode over the nearby hills. One figure was a man walking straight upright with a giant battle axe slung across his back.

The other figure crouched in the grass and scampered every few paces to keep up with him.

Yann's throat tightened. He couldn't move, but the old Servant didn't have that problem.

She sprang forward and took off at a fast pace heading straight for Anríq. Both of them burst into huge grins and then laughed when they met. The old Servant jumped up and threw her arms around him.

His face shone with laughter as he hugged her. Marine cowered in the grass nearby glaring at everything from under a mat of filthy hair.

Yann gulped hard. He never let himself believe he would ever see Anríq and Marine again.

Marine looked just as insane as ever, but Yann didn't care about that. She was all right—which meant she could get her sanity back sometime.

Anríq put the old Servant down and they held each other at arm's length still laughing. They beamed at each other grinning and their eyes sparkled.

They clasped each other by the hands before they both came walking back to where Yann and Eliska waited.

Anríq laughed again when he saw Yann and Eliska gaping at him and the old Servant.

"This is my grandmother—the one I told you about," Anríq announced. "Her name is Aja. I haven't seen her since I first left the tribe to follow the Servant's path. I should have known you would meet up with her."

"We were just.....we were just about to go to the Far Reaches to find the White Spire," Eliska stammered. "We lost track of you. We didn't know if you and Marine were even still alive."

He turned to smile at her and his expression chilled when he saw her.

Yann watched the realization sink into Anríq's head. Did he realize how much worse she had gotten in the short time he'd been away from her?

Anríq's eyes darted to Yann. Yann cringed when Anríq's eyebrows came together in the middle, but he shrugged that off, forced himself to smile at Eliska, and then stepped forward to hug her, too.

He kissed her on the cheek. "I missed you. I hoped you would find me."

"I tried," she choked. "I tried a million times."

"Never mind," he murmured. "We're together now." He glanced at his grandmother and burst into another full grin. "So what's the plan? What are we going?"

"We were just on our way to the White Spire, but the Voyant just attacked us," Yann explained. "Maybe he knows when we're planning to try to go there."

"He's attacked us at other times when we *weren't* planning to go there," Eliska pointed out.

Anríq looked back and forth between them and then nodded at Eliska. "Can you use your projection to find out what he's doing?"

"I never tried to use it to track him, but I'll try." She opened the projection and wilted. "The Far Reaches are already collapsing. The spire will only move somewhere else now."

"It's moving around a lot more quickly now," Yann pointed out.

"What do you want to do?" Eliska asked. "There doesn't seem to be much point in going there when it will only wind up in another Layer. It might even move to another Layer before we got there."

"Let's stay put a little longer," Yann replied. "I wasn't completely comfortable with you traveling so soon anyway."

He realized a second too late that he said this in front of Anríq, but one glance at Anríq told Yann all he needed to know.

Anríq would have to be dead not to realize there was something wrong with Eliska—something a lot more wrong than whatever happened to her before.

Aja turned away first and headed back up the road to the same spot where she, Yann, and Eliska had just been camping.

Aja sat down by the remains of the fire, added some twigs to it, and started building it up even though it was still morning.

Anríq squatted down next to her and surveyed the area. "This is one of the most stable Layers I've seen so far. We've been here for a few weeks and I haven't seen any sign of instability."

"Neither have we," Yann replied. "Not just until just now when the Voyant showed up."

"Where have you been?" Anríq asked. "How did you get here?"

Yann glanced at Eliska. Yann didn't want to be the one to explain to Anríq what happened at the monastery—mostly because Yann didn't know what happened at the monastery. He hadn't even dared to ask Eliska himself.

Anríq saw that glance. His expression hardened when he looked at Eliska, too. She cast her eyes down and refused to look at him at all.

Yann braced himself for the moment when Anríq cornered Yann alone somewhere, got in his face, and demanded answers the way Yann demanded them from Anríq. Yann didn't have the foggiest notion what he would say that that happened.

Just then, Marine yowled out in the grass somewhere. She didn't come near the camp.

"Has she been like this the whole time?" Yann asked. "Did she come out of it at all?"

"No, she never came out of it even once," Anríq replied. "She never talked to me through her familiars, either. Do you remember how she used to try to talk to you when she first met up with the Watch? She used to make eye contact sometimes or respond when people tried to talk to her. She doesn't do any of that now—and she never used her magic to help me when we got into trouble. I don't think she was even aware of it. I was the one protecting her when she couldn't protect herself."

"Did something happen to her?" Yann asked. "Did she get hurt or.....?"

He trailed off, and this time, he didn't give himself the option to look at Eliska. No way in hell would Yann tell Anríq about her losing her mind.

"She didn't get hurt," Anríq replied. "I tried healing her, but there's nothing wrong with her. She's as whole now as she was back then. She's just farther out in the Dark. I don't know what will bring her back or if anything will bring her back. I've just gotten used to her being like this. She never changes—not around me."

Yann frowned at the flames. Would he ever get Marine back? He'd known for a long time that he would lose her eventually.

Which would be worse—to see her go completely out of her mind or watch her marry another man?

Chapter 29

Yann came back to awareness and realized Anríq was still staring at him waiting for Yann to explain himself. Anríq's voice crushed Yann under an unbearable weight.

Anríq only said two words. That was all it took. "What happened?"

Yann didn't look up. He couldn't meet Anríq's gaze.

Eliska made a choking noise. Movement caught Yann's peripheral vision when she looked up to face Anríq.

"I...." Her voice broke and all the torment came pouring out. "Me and Yann.....we were traveling....and we got attacked.....We met....some monks.....from the Keepers of the Dawn...."

Anríq furrowed his brow. "I've never heard of them."

"They said they met me when I was little and they tried to teach me some magic, but I disappeared after only a day or two. They said they could heal me and take my Darkness away and leave me whole....and I believed them...." She strangled on the last words and looked away.

Yann would have put his arm around her, but he never got a chance to move before Anríq swiveled over to sit next to her.

He put his arm around her and murmured into her ear from an inch away. "Tell me what happened. Maybe I can help."

She shook her head fast and bowed her head over her clenched hands. "You don't understand. They were Dark—the monks. Yann saw them communing with the Dark. He tried to warn me to leave the Island, but I was desperate for them to heal me, so I stayed. They didn't heal me. They made my power stronger ....and then they fed even more Darkness into me—even more than I took in Symphorian....They said they wanted to make it as big as possible.....and it went out of control—exactly the way I was trying not to let it..... They tried to kill Yann....."

Anríq's head snapped around and his eyes locked on Yann. Yann couldn't look away this time. Now Anríq knew. Eliska got like this by saving Yann.

"They would have killed him.....and I....." She faltered before she blurted out, "I let my Darkness loose....and I destroyed the monastery with everyone inside it.....I went out into the Dark....for about a week, I think. Yann knows—he was there. He took care of me....and then the Voyant attacked us and we wound up here."

"Your grandmother saved us," Yann added. "Eliska got knocked out and we were falling through the Layers when she found us and brought us here."

Anríq's eyes darted around the circle of faces. Yann dreaded Anríq saying anything about this.

When he did, he lowered his voice to a husky murmur right into Eliska's ear. "It's all right," he breathed. 'You did the right thing to destroy them. Of course you wanted them to take your Darkness. You can't blame yourself for that."

"They....they were Dark!" Tears spilled out of her eyes and streaked down their cheeks. "They did things—in the Dark—and now all their memories are in me now. I keep seeing them...."

"It's going to be all right,' he murmured. "You coped with it before and you're coping with it now. You don't have to let it out again—not like that...."

"I did!" she blurted out. "I let it out when the Voyant attacked. He was going to kill your grandmother—and I saw him about to destroy the village. I couldn't stop it....."

"I keep telling you this power could be a good thing," Yann interrupted. "Someone has to have the power to defeat the Voyant. Maybe this is it."

She wouldn't stop shaking her head. "I can't. I could have transported us to the White Spire, but I don't dare to. This Darkness gets stronger every time I use it. What if it gets so strong that I can't control it? What if I go completely over to the Dark?"

"You won't," Anríq told her. "You care too much. The fact that you care about protecting people proves that you aren't Dark."

She bowed her head and barely mumbled, "I did hurt people—a lot of people—and I do want to. I *am* Dark."

"No!" he breathed and kissed the side of her head again. "You aren't. You wouldn't be here with us now if you were."

"You wouldn't have destroyed that monastery if you were Dark," Yann interjected. 'You would have stayed there and joined them. It would have been the perfect opportunity, but you didn't. You came after me and sacrificed yourself for me."

Anríq's eyes stabbed into Yann's being. Was Anríq jealous?

Anríq put his big arms around Eliska and pulled her into a hug. Her head fell on his chest and he cradled her there.

Yann forced himself to look away. He might have done the same thing if Anríq hadn't been here. Yann had done it a million times and thought nothing about it.

Did Eliska think she betrayed Anríq by relying on Yann for comfort?

The party went about their usual routine to make camp. Anríq helped out with all the chores and then went hunting.

He came back near sundown. Then came all the little tasks of getting ready to spend another night here.

Yann refused to look at Anríq and Eliska when he sat down next to her.

Yann pretended not to hear Anríq whispering to her. He kept murmuring encouragement and assurance that she did the right thing and that she was still a Servant precisely because she went through all of this.

Night fell and he eventually made her lie down and go to sleep. He stayed sitting up, ran his fingers through her hair, and rubbed her back until she crashed hard.

He even placed his hand on her forehead, but Yann didn't see Anríq do anything to help Eliska.

In a few minutes, Aja stretched out on the ground and went to sleep, too.

Anríq looked up like he just noticed Yann sitting there. "You should go to sleep, too, Yann. You look tired."

Yann spun around. "What are you doing?" he demanded.

Anríq startled. "Excuse me?"

"What are you doing with Eliska?"

Anríq frowned. "I'm not doing anything with her. I'm trying to help her. "

'No, you're trying to do more than that. You're giving her mixed signals when there's no chance you could ever get together with her."

Anríq made a face and looked away. "Is that what you're worried about—that I'll get together with her? I have never stood between you and Eliska, Yann. I've told her a million times that you would be a much better choice for her. It seems to me you're a lot closer to her than I am."

Yann fought his voice to a strained whisper. "This isn't about me. I would say the same thing about a total stranger. I can't let you get into a position where you might hurt her, even if you hurt her by caring about her. You're making her think she could have something with you."

Anríq turned around extra slowly and his tone dropped a register into his chest. His voice sent a shiver up Yann's scalp. "There is no chance I could ever get together with her, Yann—not now."

"I wouldn't care if you got together with her," Yann snapped. "I care that you're leading her on when we both know you don't intend ever to follow through on it."

"I won't. You have nothing to worry about."

"Then why are you making her think you will?" Yann demanded. "Have you ever done anything to give her the impression that you wanted more than friendship?"

Anríq turned to gaze down at her sleeping face. Anríq's features trembled. "I kissed her—once. She was trapped in a Dark Layer. I kissed her to bring her back and to make her realize that people on the outside still needed her."

"Then you admit that you're giving her mixed signals. If you aren't serious about her, then just leave her alone. She's been through enough and she's already struggling under a heavy enough burden without you making it harder for her."

"I would never hurt Eliska, Yann, or make it harder for her."

"Then you'll do the right thing and make it clear that you aren't interested in more—because from where I stand, it looks an awful lot like you're telling her the opposite."

Anríq shut his eyes and bowed his head. "If that's the way you feel, I won't do it again. I won't do anything with Eliska ever again unless something changes between us and it becomes possible for us to take our relationship further. I don't see how that ever could be possible now."

Yann would have liked to go off on him again, but Yann couldn't think of anything else to say. He'd already said it all.

He honestly didn't care about Anríq and Eliska getting together. Yann couldn't think of any man he would rather see her get together with.

He just couldn't stand to see her get her heart broken.

He couldn't explain to himself how he knew that this relationship was all wrong—if it even was a relationship.

Anríq made it sound like it wasn't, but there was something going on there—something more than just them being close and caring about each other.

Yann's attitude toward Anríq came more from Yann's feelings about her than anything Anríq did or said. Yann just wanted to protect her—from everything.

This would never be about Yann getting together with her in Anríq's place because Yann didn't think of her that way. He loved her, but he couldn't really think of her in the romantic sense.

Whatever they shared while they were alone together—it might have gone there if they'd stayed alone together and never met back up with Anríq.

If Anríq demanded to know if something happened between Yann and Eliska, Yann could honestly say that it didn't.

His relationship with her deepened. It turned to love, but it never went beyond that. He never tried to make it into something more.

For some reason, they'd already seemed to travel beyond all of that.

In a way, Yann had come to the point exactly the same as Anríq articulated just now. Nothing like that could ever happen between Yann and Eliska—not now.

She was too hurt, too damaged, too fragile. His role in her life would always be one of a loving protector and caretaker—unless something changed—which it wouldn't.

He found himself staring down at her sleeping face and feeling something for her that he never felt even for Marine.

He could almost love Eliska more like this—more than if he'd actually married her and committed his whole life to her.

Anríq's voice drifted out of the dark. "She loves you," he murmured. "She always has."

Yann shrugged that away and turned back to the fire. "She loves you, too."

"I know she does,' Anríq replied. "She has a heart as big as this Dark power of hers. She must have if she can contain all that. I could kill the people who did this to her. I'm glad she did it so I don't have to break the Servant's vow by hunting them down and murdering them all."

"She didn't tell me," Yann blurted out. "She didn't tell me what happened …in the monastery. She told you, but she didn't tell me. She saves that for you."

"I wish I could give her what she needs," Anríq husked. "It kills me to know that I can't."

Yann swallowed the lump in his throat. "Me, too."

"You're the best thing for her right now, Yann," Anríq told him. "She needs you."

"We're both the best thing for her right now."

"You care about her," Anríq insisted. "You take care of her. She needs that."

"She needs as many people taking care of her as she can get. Don't stop doing what you do just because I'm doing it, too."

Anríq finally looked up. His eyebrows trembled. "You're right, Yann. She deserves the best from both of us."

Yann looked down into the flames and let the silence grow. He couldn't pinpoint exactly when it happened, but it sure looked like he was taking over as something equivalent to Watch Commander of this group, too.

He didn't really have any reason not to tell Anríq what to do. Yann always considered Anríq the better man, but all of that seemed to pass under the bridge along with everything else.

Yann had been Watch Commander of two different cities now. He took care of Eliska and Marine. Why shouldn't Yann take command of Anríq, too?

"We'll go find the White Spire," Yann decided. "We're in the best position we'll ever be to get inside it, now that we have four magic-users with us instead of three."

Anríq nodded. "That sounds like a good plan."

Yann let himself smile up at his friend. "I'm really glad you're back. It really sucks when you aren't around."

Anríq burst into a huge grin and laughed. "Yeah. It sucks when you and Eliska aren't around, too."

Those words stung. You and Eliska.

Anríq said those words almost as if Yann and Eliska were a couple—almost as if Anríq knew what Yann had been doing with her all this time.

Yann hadn't been doing anything with her—not anything more than just taking care of her and being there for her.

It went beyond that, though.

Yann didn't think of Eliska as his—not in any way that pushed Anríq out.

Anyway, it didn't matter because neither of them could have her—not like that. Yann didn't want her like that. He didn't feel that way about her.

The task of taking care of her looked so insurmountable. Yann was becoming more and more certain every day that none of them would even survive this war.

Then the question would become irrelevant because no one would get together with anyone else.

Chapter 30

Eliska pried her eyelids open and stiffened when she saw Yann and Anríq standing at a distance from the camp.

Aja squatted by the fire doing something with all the knickknacks from her bags.

Yann and Anríq murmured to each other in an undertone. Eliska couldn't hear what they were saying from this distance, but their conversation floated into her mind through the Dark connection between her and everyone else in the world.

They were talking about Marine and everything that happened between her and Anríq while they'd been alone together.

Eliska didn't listen to the conversation. She studied the two boys instead.

She had been thrilled to meet back up with Anríq, but something in the way the two boys talked to each other rang her alarm bells.

Yann had been acting so protective of her while they'd been alone. His behavior was nothing more than the way he had always acted around her.

Why should it bother Eliska or Anríq now?

Her relationship with Yann had definitely developed into more than that. He told her he loved her and she knew it was true.

She loved him, too. She knew that now.

She never said or even thought that about Anríq even though they acted exactly the same way toward each other.

Both boys taking that place in her life should have turned them against each other, but it didn't. She would almost rather it did.

Yann spotted her first, broke off the conversation, and came over to squat down next to her.

"Hey! Good morning!" He rubbed her back. "How are you feeling? You slept well last night."

She nodded. "I'm okay."

"Make sure you eat your breakfast. We'll be traveling this morning and you'll need fuel."

He pulled forward the wooden bowl the three of them had been using since they started camping here. It contained a pile of the meat Anríq hunted for the four travelers last night.

"How do you feel about using your magic to transport us across multiple Layers to the White Spire?" Yann asked. "You've never done that before, have you?"

She shot one glance at Anríq and concentrated on the food in front of her.

He stood off to one side and listened while Yann talk to her. Anríq didn't come near her while Yann was there.

She had heard their conversation last night even though she was asleep. It drifted through her dreams and blended with all the memories of everyone else trapped in her head.

She experienced the conversation through the memories of both boys.

Anríq didn't hold it against Yann that Anríq couldn't progress his relationship with Eliska. He agreed with Yann that she was too far out in the Dark for either of them to do anything with her.

He saw that and understood it even before Yann said so. He only articulated a conclusion Anríq already came to on his own.

He didn't even resent Yann taking care of Eliska in his place. Anríq didn't care who did it as long as someone did.

Anríq considered Yann the better man just as Yann considered Anríq the better man.

Anríq would have been doing and saying exactly the same things. What difference did it make if Anríq did it or Yann did it as long as someone did it to take care of her the way she needed it?

She couldn't decide how to feel about that, but if they didn't mind, why should she?

Neither of them had a clue how bad her Darkness really was. She wouldn't have wanted to get together with either of them—not when she was like this. She wanted to protect them both from it as much as she could.

She mumbled down into the bowl. "I suppose I could."

"Just make sure you don't push yourself too hard, okay?" Yann told her. "Tell us if you start to get too far out of yourself."

She nodded again and both boys got to work breaking camp exactly the way they did yesterday.

The subject dropped and neither of them brought it up again, so it must be officially dead to all three of them.

They returned to the same spot and Eliska, Yann, Anríq, and Aja gathered in a circle.

"The four of you will use your magic to assault the White Spire's defenses as soon as we get to the riverbank," Yann told them. "You'll have to break the barrier so I can swim across the river. Then you'll distract the wolves while I get to the tower. As soon as I start climbing, you'll have to find a way to keep up with me because the defenses will follow me up there."

"What did you do last time?" Eliska asked.

"Marine defended me last time. She followed me all the way up the wall to the top turret."

She frowned to herself. "There has to be a better way."

"Like what?" Yann asked.

"There has to be another way to get inside the spire. Climbing the outside is silly. "

"What do you suggest?" he demanded. "Did you see an exit door in the spire wall when you were there?"

"No, but we saw one on that diagram in the library, didn't we? There were all kinds of entrances all over the place."

"Maybe this is one of the defenses," he suggested. "Either way, I don't have your magic so I have to climb up the outside—unless you can come up with some other way to get me inside."

He waited. When she didn't answer, he turned back to the others. "Are there any questions?"

No one said anything. Anríq shook his head.

Yann glanced down at Marine. She crouched in the grass fifteen feet away growling, biting, and muttering.

"I don't know if she'll come out of the Dark long enough to help you, so you three will just have to make it work without her if she doesn't."

"I'll magic us somewhere far enough away from the spire," Eliska offered. "That way, she won't be in danger if she doesn't get involved,"

"Don't magic us too far away. We need to begin our assault the instant we get there." Yann nodded at her. "We're ready when you are."

She pulled her staff forward even though she didn't really need to use it anymore. Anríq lifted his axe off his back and Aja took out her fighting sticks.

Yann cast one last glance at Marine. If she didn't understand what was happening from listening to the group's conversation, nothing would make her understand.

Eliska met Yann's gaze one more time and he nodded. He sure was taking over this group. Anríq did everything Yann said.

She raised her staff. She didn't know exactly how to transport herself and other people across Layers, but the Keepers of the Dawn did it, so she must be able to do it, too.

She sent her magic flowing into her staff, it sprayed upward from the top end, spread outward, and curved downward to form a net around the party the way she magicked them with binding spells in the past.

She included Marine in the sphere of protection inside it.

Then, without really thinking about it first, she magicked the ball through the grass, through the soil, and through the bedrock to the next Layer below this one.

She didn't have to shatter the Island. The ball's magic melted into the Layer and passed straight through it taking the whole party with it.

The ball entered a chaos Layer, but Eliska's magic protected everyone from harm. None of the wind, debris, or Dark vapors touched the party.

Not a breath of wind ruffled Eliska's clothes or hair.

The ball fell faster and faster. Layers whipped past too fast for her to see what they were. She opened her Coil projection with her other hand, located the White Spire in another Layer, and headed for it.

She could direct the ball through the Layers just by thinking about it. It whizzed through multiple Layers flying faster and faster.

She could have flown it even faster if she really wanted to. She could have magicked the ball there with a single thought if she really wanted to let her Dark poison out of the bottle.

She didn't want to do that—not unless she absolutely had to.

She lowered the ball onto the riverbank opposite the wolves. Nothing else about the place looked any different even though this was a completely different Layer.

The Layer had been an ordinary city scene before the most recent Layer collapse brought the White Sire here. The Voyant sure liked his cities.

Marine's expression cleared as soon as the ball descended through the clouds. She returned to her senses, stood up straight, looked around.

Eliska let the ball disintegrate when it touched the scorched earth on this side of the river. The wolves turned to snarl and raise their hackles at the friends.

Without warning, without any reason Eliska could see, an almighty blast smashed across the landscape. It swatted all five of the friends a hundred yards backward.

Eliska slammed down hard on the ground and blinked the stars out of her eyes trying to figure out what happened.

Aja recovered first and sprang up unbelievably fast considering how old she was. She launched herself off the ground, brought both her fighting sticks forward, and soared toward the river.

Constant streams of magical bursts erupted from her sticks. She aimed for the Wolves, but she wound up hitting the invisible barrier over the river instead.

She hurtled straight for it. Eliska jumped up to help her, but Marine got there first.

She took one step forward then a million projectiles and tiny whizzing creatures pelted out of the trees behind the party.

Eliska didn't see Marine do anything to make those creatures and projectiles attack, but they did. A funnel of fast-moving air ripped them all up into a stream of bombarding missiles.

They shrieked past Aja, smashed into the barrier, and shattered it just as Aja made it to the river's midpoint.

She would have hit it, but Marine took it down and Aja dropped the rest of the way falling straight for the wolves.

They turned on her and bared their teeth to attack. She arced over the river and descended to land right in the middle of the pack.

Eliska couldn't wait a second longer. She couldn't let Aja and Marine face the wolves alone.

Eliska grabbed Yann and Anríq, one in each hand, and magicked them both across the river in a heartbeat.

"Get to the spire, Yann!" Eliska yelled over her shoulder and turned to confront the wolves.

The wolves dove in to pounce on Aja the minute she came within range. They lunged for her roaring snapping her teeth.

She spun from right to left hitting them with a rapid barrage of shots from her sticks. She also struck out with the sticks to land blows on the wolves' faces and bodies.

Those blows let off powerful booms of magic exactly the way Anríq's club and axe did.

He stormed into the group, raised his axe, and started hacking his way through the pack.

Eliska charged forward to join them and Yann took off sprinting between the wolves heading for the Spire.

He scrambled onto the white marble wall, grabbed hold, and started scaling it.

Long, undulating vines of something like scaly reptile tentacles snaked out of the ground and looped around to attack him.

The flying missiles Marine sent to protect him swirled in the air between him and the tendrils as they tried to snatch him off the walls.

Eliska reacted without moving and fired on those tendrils to drive them away from him.

Marine lifted off the ground and floated to stay level with him, but the Voyant's defenses overpowered her magic.

The tendrils turned on Marine. More and more of those undulating vines came out of nowhere and then more of them came out of the tower wall itself.

These didn't look so much like they might belong to some creature anymore. These new tendrils were pure magical power.

They ejected from the walls, grabbed Yann to stop him from climbing, rained body blows all over him, and then burst farther out to go after Marine.

That first yell from Yann triggered Eliska's defensive fury.

She shot off the ground blasting her staff at all those tendrils. She could sever and destroy the scaly ones, but not the magical ones.

As soon as she started shooting them, they came after her, too. They launched themselves at her at blinding speed. Dozens of them stabbed at her face and body from all directions.

She had to twist and turn in every possible way just to keep up with them and hold them off. Their escalating assault drove her to desperation and she panicked.

She let off a deep pulse of magic to drive all those tendrils back inside the tower.

It worked, but as soon as she forced them inside the walls, another bone-crushing explosion of magic pulsed out of the spire, hit all five friends, and plastered them away across the landscape.

Eliska smashed through what felt like a brick wall and slammed down hard on the ground.

A tempest wind of flying chaos slashed her face the minute she landed. She struggled onto her hands and knees and saw all her friends nearby—Aja, Anríq, Yann, and Marine. They were all here.

Marine screeched, whipped around, and slashed her teeth at a Dark vapor hissing toward her from somewhere nearby.

Eliska couldn't see anything else in the landscape besides all these vapors swirling around her. The wind peppered her face with sand and splinters.

She squinted into the distance and staggered over to her friends.

"Stay near me!" she roared. "I'll get us out of here!"

She surrounded them with the same ball and the wind died instantly, but the chaos outside the ball only seemed to build to an explosive pitch.

She opened her Coil projection to find out where the party was now.

"I don't see any sign of the White Spire," she remarked. "The Voyant must have moved it."

"Maybe our attack caused the Layer to collapse, so the spire had to move," Yann suggested.

Eliska opened her mouth to tell him that the group wouldn't be able to go after the spire again. That was the moment she saw something in her projection.

"What is that?" Yann asked.

"It's a town," she husked. "It's surrounded by instability."

She didn't wait or ask if she should or could. She magicked the group to the edge of town, but she still couldn't see anything with all the chaos flying around.

She rotated her staff to the front and the ball of projection around the group vanished in the blink of an eye.

She fired a powerful stream of magic in the direction where she knew the town was. She still couldn't see it, but she let her intuition guide her.

Her magic reacted with the Dark forces whipping back and forth across the Layer in front of her. Dark forces pelted out of the confusion, but she didn't stop until she battled her way to the edge of town.

A brick wall surrounded it. The Watchmen and a few magic-users up there tried to fight off the Dark forces, but those few people couldn't hold the chaos at bay.

Eliska flooded the town with her magic, but the Layers only pulled back a little bit. She couldn't fight the whole Coil.

The collapse escalated to the breaking point. It would overpower her in a second.

A low thump vibrated the earth at her feet. Anríq rushed to her side and smashed his club into the ground. The outward boom translated through the bedrock and into the walls surrounded the town.

The Layer quivered back just a little bit and then Aja launched herself toward the wall.

She soared through the air in another high somersaulting arc, landed on top of the wall, and raced down it fighting Dark forces away from the Watchmen.

Eliska and Anríq followed her, took off running for the town, and jumped up there to drive the Dark forces back.

Anríq vaulted high in the air to land on a different part of the wall, but fighting those Dark forces wouldn't save the town.

Eliska levitated into the air .....and saw the edge of the Layer. The travelers' efforts had pulled it back from the town just enough to leave some of the streets clear.

She didn't even try to go in there. She aimed her staff at the Layer's forward edge and stabbed her magic into it the way she fought the margin away from Tenby.

Her magic erupted off the charts, but she still didn't tap the full depth of her Darkness.

She could have taken that Layer away in a split second just by absorbing it into herself, but she didn't do that. She probably would never have regained her sanity if she did that.

She leaned back and pulled her staff with her. The Layer shuddered and then snapped back with a crack like a gunshot.

It stung her in the face as the Layer whipped across the countryside, left the town lying there untouched, and the impact hurled Eliska down on the ground.

Chapter 31

Yann rushed over to Eliska. "Are you all right?"

She writhed on the ground groaning and baring her teeth, but she rolled up onto her knees in a second. She turned her frenzied eyes toward the town.

Her hair streaked across her face, but he saw right away that she was all right. She searched the town to make sure the Dark layer was gone.

He rested her hand on her back as she got to her feet. "Good job," he told her. "You did it."

She barely heard him. Aja and Anríq stood on the top of the wall still armed and ready to defend the town.

Anríq scowled down at Yann and Eliska, but the Dark no longer assaulted the town.

She opened her projection. "The Layer is holding off, but it isn't gone. It will come back."

Yann faced the town. The Watchmen and magic-users on the wall stuck their heads up, looked around, and started to realize what just happened.

Yann guided Eliska forward. Some of the Watchmen said something to Anríq and he turned away to talk to them.

Yann and Eliska advanced to the gate in the wall. It was a wooden gate constructed of thick timber planks bolted together with iron nails and heavy forged straps. It wouldn't keep out Dark forces as powerful as that.

As soon he got closer, Yann realized that the people he thought were Watchmen were actually just ordinary townsfolk. They wore regular brown and grey work clothes instead of uniforms.

They carried old-fashioned melee weapons, too. They didn't have guns—as if guns would do anything against the Dark.

The townspeople opened the gate from the inside, and for some reason he couldn't figure out, they came right up to him. "Thank you so much!" a man in his forties exclaimed. "You don't know how desperate we've been!"

"I can imagine," Yann replied. "How long have you been under attack?"

The guy scratched his bushy dark beard and frowned. "I'd say about two and a half years now."

"That's how long since the instability started," Yann remarked. "Has it always been as bad as this? Why hasn't the Dark wiped out your town completely by now?"

"It's never been as bad as this. It got worse just...oh, I'd say in the last week."

"I'm glad we could help."

Yann looked up at the wall to see Aja and Anríq talking to the town defenders—or rather Anríq was talking to them while Aja listened.

Yann was just making up his mind to ask them and Eliska if the party should stay in this town.

"Your friends are Servants," the man remarked. "We have a bunch of wounded. We would be eternally grateful if you would heal them."

Yann nodded. "It looks like they already are. Come on, Eliska. This could take a while."

The man lunged for Yann a second time and pumped his arm off his shoulder. "Thank you so much! I'm Nello Dumont. Welcome to Laval."

"Are you the mayor of this town or something?" Yann asked.

Nello burst out laughing. "The mayor?! I'm just a carpenter, but so many people have died that none of us can get any work done. We have to man the walls every waking minute."

"I'm sorry to hear that. Maybe we can change that, now that we're here."

The man brightened up, but his expression slipped when he looked at Eliska.

Yann saw the wheels turning in Nello's head and steered the conversation somewhere else. "I'm Yann Dilnao and this is Eliska. She's the one who saved your town just now. I didn't have anything to do with it."

"Oh." Nello frowned. "I didn't realize."

"I'm an imp like you," Yan went on. "I don't have any magic—certainly not any magic strong enough to pull back that Layer. Eliska says the Layer is holding off for now, but it hasn't gone away. We'll stick around for a while if it's all the same to you. We can help defend you if and when it does come back."

Nello seized Yann's hand in another crushing grip. "Oh, thank you! You don't know what this means! We've been so desperate....."

Yann pushed forward and Nello took the hint. He babbled on the way inside. "This is Malo Naquin. We've been doing what little we can to organize the defense, but these attacks have been going on for so long and we've lost so many people. The Barbarians don't ever let up."

Yann stopped in his tracks and spun around fast. "The Barbarians?"

Nello nodded. "They've been attacking us for years. It almost seems like they wait until the Dark forces weaken us. Then Barbarians come in and it takes all we have just to stay alive."

Yann stopped himself from passing his hand across his eyes This was so much worse than he thought.

"So what defenses are you using ?"

"The magic-users would be able to tell you that. We would have been dead long ago if not for them—but the Barbarians usually bring magic-users, too. "

Yann nodded again. "I figured that."

"It usually winds up with the magic-users on both sides fighting each other. That leaves us against the Barbarians—which doesn't go so well if you know what I mean. We have more people lying dead in the graveyard than are left alive to defend this town."

"Don't worry. We're going to help you." Yann put out his arm to steer Eliska inside the gates.

They stood open to a normal little country town. It brought back fond memories of Middleborough with its quaint, cramped houses and dusty streets.

The town showed plenty of signs of recent attack—both magical and conventional. Multiple walls had fallen down and no one had taken the time to repair them.

Yann also saw blood stains on a few walls and the shattered remains of a wagon lying across the street. No one cleaned up any of that. These people really must be hanging by a thread.

He took a few steps forward when Anríq strode out of town from the inside. He wore his axe hanging across his back now. He wasn't coming to fight.

He made eye contact with Yann for a split second. The surrounding townspeople parted to let him through.

Yann pushed Eliska forward to meet up with Anríq, but just then, a screech distracted Yann into turning around the other way.

Marine crouched at the base of a small hill twenty feet away. She kept her back to the group and didn't engage in the conversation.

"I'll just get my other friend," Yann told Nello.....

Nello's eyes popped. "That?! You can't bring *that* inside the walls! It's a Darkling!"

"She isn't a Darkling," Yann snapped. "She's a member of the Guardian Templars and she's our friend. She's coming inside or all five of us will leave you to fend for yourselves. She's one of the kindest people I know. She can help us."

Anríq caught up with them just then. He pulled to a stop next to Eliska and heard the end of the conversation.

Nello waved his hands and started to back away. "No, no, no. We can't let a Darkling inside the walls. We have to protect ourselves."

"I'm telling you she isn't a Darkling," Yann countered. "If you take these Servants, you have to take her."

Yann didn't wait to listen to anything else. He headed over to Marine and bent down to take her arm. "Come on, Marine. We're going inside."

He spun around and froze when all the townspeople rushed forward raising their weapons. They formed a blockade to stop Yann from bringing Marine any closer.

Anríq and Eliska reacted just as fast and sprang between the townspeople on one side and Yann and Marine on the other.

Anríq raised his club and Eliska brought her staff forward. "Lay a finger on them and I'll flatten your town myself," Eliska snarled. "I took that Layer away. It will come back the minute I leave."

"Keep that Darkling away from our town!" Nello fired back. "We have enough problems without taking them inside the walls to stab us in the back while we sleep."

"You bastard!" Eliska roared, but right then, Marine screeched again.

She reared away from Yann, slashed her teeth at him, and at the same time, she let off a powerful burst of magic.

It blasted out of her mouth the same way she hit Yvan in the mountain cave.

She hurled Yann away from her and he crashed into a nearby tree. He staggered to catch his balance, and before he could move, Marine scuttled off into the undergrowth.

Eliska crossed the area and helped him stand up. "I guess she's gone."

The townspeople lowered their weapons, but they didn't stop scowling in Marine's direction. "We'll kill her if she comes back," Nello growled.

"You'll have to get near her first—which you won't," Eliska snapped. "I'll make sure of it."

Yann held up both hands. "Okay. Marine isn't here and she obviously doesn't want to go inside the walls anyway. If you want us to help you, we will. Otherwise, we'll go somewhere else."

Nello studied each person one after the other. He softened when he faced Anríq. "We need you too badly. Come inside. We need all the help we can get."

Chapter 32

Nello led the way back to the gate. Yann hesitated on the threshold before he let himself cross it.

He already knew how this would go, but at least he, Eliska, and Anríq were together this time. He wouldn't have to spend his time in this town wondering and worrying if they were okay.

Anríq led them back to where Aja was already starting to heal the sick and injured townspeople.

Most of them lay in their beds in their houses. Half of them suffered from wounds sustained during armed battles against the Barbarians.

Others lay under Dark curses, either from continuous attacks by Dark forces or inflicted by the Barbarian magic-users.

The party found Aja in a hotel where the townspeople had assembled the largest group of patients. She went from room to room on the second floor healing people packed in ten to a room.

"Why are the Barbarians attacking you?" Yann asked Nello.

The man only shrugged. "They don't need a reason. They'll attack anything that moves."

"That makes no sense," Eliska interrupted. "The Barbarians are looters. They only care about stealing goods to enrich themselves. They don't go around inflicting random violence for its own sake. If you're already under siege, then you wouldn't have anything of value for them to take."

"They're Barbarians," Nello sneered. "All they care about is killing."

Yann glanced over at Anríq. He didn't add anything to contradict. Aja pretended not to hear and went right on healing everyone.

When no one argued, Anríq turned into the same room and went over to one of the patients' beds.

"You're a magic-user," Nello told Eliska. "Aren't you going to do anything?"

"Everyone in this room is cursed," she told him. "Show me where I can find some people with normal injuries and I'll heal them."

Nello walked off to a different part of the hotel. Yann hung back and watched her while she started healing people, but he eventually turned away.

He found Malo by his side. "Take me out to the wall and let me see your defenses," Yann told him.

The two men walked off together. Malo jerked his thumb over his shoulder toward the hotel as they left the building. "Your friends must be pretty useful to have around."

"Useful isn't the word I would use for it." They stopped in the middle of the street and Yann surveyed the wall. It showed as much damage on the inside as it did on the outside. "So the Barbarians have gotten inside, have they?"

"They can get in whenever they want," Malo replied. "We can't stop them."

Yann frowned again. "Something about this doesn't make sense. Are you telling me they wait until after the Dark forces finish attacking the town? The Barbarians don't attack at the same time?"

"Why would they?" Malo asked. "The Barbarians don't want to get caught in the same upheaval."

Yann pinched his lips shut to stop himself from answering. He was starting to see Eliska's point of view on this. Why would the Barbarians attack a town that didn't offer any spoils?

It also made no sense that they would attack more than once. If they really wanted to inflict pointless destruction on the town, why not attack, raze it to the ground, kill everyone, and leave the place scorched and dead for nothing to ever rise again?

Why leave the town intact at all? It couldn't be so the Barbarians could attack again and again and again. What was the point of that?

Yann also didn't believe that the Barbarians were mindless animals who did things for no reason. They must have a reason to attack this town—a reason other than simple lust for violence.

He made up his mind to ask Anríq about it later. Even Eliska knew more about the Barbarians than Yann did.

She also knew more about the Barbarians than these townspeople did. They never even stopped to ask themselves why the Barbarians were attacking.

Maybe the townspeople didn't think of it—what with the Dark Layers taking over the town every other day.

He stepped forward to go back to the wall when Eliska came hustling out of the hotel behind him. She cast a sidelong glance at Malo and pulled Yann aside.

"What's up?" He studied her extra closely. "I don't want you healing anyone who's under a curse. Understand? You can heal people from conventional injuries. Stay away from the Dark. That's an order."

She burst into a rare grin and blushed. "I won't. I promise. That isn't what I wanted to talk to you about."

"What is it?"

She drew him farther away from Malo and lowered her voice. "We're...we're in the Sojourner's Sanctum. We thought it got destroyed, but we must have been wrong."

"Who's we?" he asked.

"Me and Anríq. We were in the Sojourner's Sanctum when we were alone together and instability hit the Island. We thought it got destroyed, but it didn't—not in that way. It must still be suffering from instability because....this is it."

She waved her hands around her on all sides.

"So....what are you telling me?" he asked. "Does the Layer we're in make that much of a difference?"

"Listen to me," she whispered. "Yimichi Ocuron and Noleron Kupuro originally came from the Sojourner's Sanctum."

He frowned. "I'm still not seeing how that's relevant."

"I checked a book in the library at the monastery. Yimichi and Noleron were actually brothers—and they fell in love with the same woman. They fought over her and then she ran off with Yimichi. Noleron swore revenge—and then he showed up at the White Spire less than two days before Hubua Ocuron's death. She dropped dead almost the minute he walked in the door and he took her place as his brother's affiliate."

Yann's eyes fell out of their sockets. "Are you telling me Noleron killed his own brother's wife—out of revenge or something?"

"That was my first thought, too. It looks awfully suspicious if you ask me."

"Why didn't you tell me this before?" he asked. "Why did you keep it to yourself?"

She opened her mouth and her features spasmed. Her eyes darted around the town, but she couldn't make a sound.

He saw it all in a split second. She'd been so busy fighting the monks and then dealing with this overwhelming Darkness. She'd been unconscious most of that time and barely sane enough to think straight the rest of it.

"It's all right," he murmured and put his arms around her. "I understand why you didn't tell me—and it doesn't really matter anyway. I know now. That's what matters."

She squirmed out of his arms. "The Barbarians who are attacking this town—they might be from the same tribe—the Voyant's home tribe. He may have sent us here for some reason—to find out something about how Yimichi became King. You're in a position where you can ask these people about it."

"These people don't know anything about the Barbarians," Yann pointed out. "You saw that yourself."

"Just try, okay, Yann? Just keep your eyes and ears open for anything that might shed some light on this. Yimichi stole his brother's sweetheart and then she died within days of Noleron showing up at the White Spire. The Barbarians might know something."

"All right. I'll try, but I can't promise anything."

She forced herself to smile again. "Thanks. This could be the breakthrough we're searching for."

He watched her walk back to the hotel, but her remarks didn't put him at ease. He didn't think this could be the breakthrough the friends were searching for.

Yann didn't see how getting information on how Yimichi Ocuron became King could help anything. It certainly wouldn't weaken the Voyant or make him easier to defeat. It might even make him worse to remind him of the woman he lost to his brother.

Malo took Yan out to the wall, but Yann saw right away that the town really didn't have any defense at all.

The wall was just a regular brick wall less than ten inches thick. The townspeople of Laval had set up ordinary wooden benches behind the wall for the defenders to stand on. They didn't have to stand any higher than that to see over the top.

Apart from that, the town was utterly defenseless except for four inexperienced magic-users.

Malo introduced Yann to the four of them.

The first was a bullish man of twenty-five. His heavy eyebrows, thick beard, and powerful shoulders would have intimidated anyone.

His name was Huges and he worked as a blacksmith when he wasn't using his magic to help someone.

Cuts and bruises covered his face and arms. Blood soaked different parts of his shirt and he carried his left arm in a sling, but he didn't go to the hotel or even mention his injuries.

"You should go get your injuries taken care of," Yann told him.

Huges shrugged that away. "I'll sleep when I'm dead. I've been standing the wall for four weeks straight. I don't have time to sit still long enough for anyone to heal me."

The second magic user was a thirteen-year-old boy with tousled dirty-blonde curls. His name was Perrick kept shivering, grimacing, and quaking in terror every time anyone looked at him sideways.

The other two magic-users were women named Helien and Natach.

Helien was an early-twenties blonde wispy-frail slip of a girl who laughed away too easily considering the circumstances.

She would have reminded Yann of Marine except that Helien didn't seem to have a serious bone in her body—not even when a dangerous situation like this called for her to have one.

Natach was a sturdy, dark-haired woman of twenty-seven. She scowled at everything like she'd seen it all.

She also sported several poorly healed injuries on different parts of her body.

Her homemade dress had ripped in places, but she didn't seem to notice. She had a powerful, muscular, get-out-of-my-way kind of air about her that instantly made Yann like her the most of the whole group.

"As soon as my friends finish healing everybody, I'll send one of them out here to help you erect a magical barrier around the town," he told the four of them.

"That won't hold off the Layer," Natach pointed out.

"No, nothing can do that, but it might stop the vapors from getting inside—and it will help defend the town against the Barbarians."

"We'll need more than that," Huges rumbled.

"Do you have any spare weapons?" Yan asked.

"We barely have enough to go around," Malo replied. "We're lucky we're even still on our feet."

Yann nodded. "Huges, you and Natach go into the hotel and get Eliska to heal your injuries. Don't come out until you finish."

Huges glared at him. "Don't tell me you plan to defend the wall by yourself."

Yann only smiled at him. "I don't have to because Malo will still be here and you'll be back in a few minutes."

Huges snorted. "No healer is that good."

He and Natach stormed off together. Malo wrung his hands watching them go. "What are we gonna do?! This is bad."

"It isn't as bad as it seems. Eliska will take care of them and then we'll think about defending this town. "

"What do you want to do about....?"

A powerful wind blasted into town and silenced him.

Before anyone could move, the curtain of magic and flying shrapnel pelted out of the countryside. It came from the same direction where Eliska pulled the Layer back just a few minutes ago.

Yann turned to the wall. He didn't have time to go over there to see how bad the situation was before he spotted the Voyant's characteristic golden halo caught in the mayhem out there.

Chapter 33

The Voyant didn't come near Laval. Yann couldn't figure out why.

The Voyant stayed out there in the confusion at least five miles away from the town. He didn't come any closer.

Yann rushed the wall. "Get into position! Get that barrier up, Helien!"

She sprang up on one of the benches next to him, but before she could do anything, another Dark shadow dropped down from directly above the town.

It spun and twisted between a bunch of different buildings, exploded windows out of their panes, and sent debris flying.

The same Dark force caught the bench, pitched it over, and toppled the defenders into the dirt.

Yann slammed down on the ground, and at that instant, the gate flew open. It swayed on its hinges, slammed back against the walls on both sides, and left the gate standing wide open to the outside world.

Hurricane winds screamed into town tearing the whole place apart. Yann dragged himself up and saw shapes forming in the Darkness outside.

The shapes became more distinct. Were Darklings about to ravage this town?

At that moment, an explosion went off behind him and a jet of white lightning blasted into the sky.

Yann spun around ready to defend his life—and froze when he saw Eliska standing on the hotel roof. How the hell did she get up there?

She planted her feet on either side of the gable, thrust her staff into the air, and dumped massive bursts of magic into the sky.

They fountained from the end of her staff, detonated when they collided with Dark forces pounding down from above, and then the lightning burst apart into a million sparkling raindrops.

They floated down in a curtain around Laval, surrounded the town, and the wind died down.

The Dark forces went insane the way they usually did when anyone put up any kind of defense. The Dark attacked in fury and the hammering explosions on that field built to a deafening pitch.

The field shuddered, but Eliska didn't budge. The wind ripped her hair and clothes nearly off her body, but she didn't even blink.

She stood there staring up at the end of her staff as a steady geyser of magical power emptied into the atmosphere.

Yann couldn't tell from here if she even realized the Voyant was out there, but she didn't try to attack him. She didn't try to attack any Dark force.

She surrounded the town with her curtain. The eerie light shone almost as bright as day with shadow and Dark energy whirling around the perimeter. It couldn't get inside.

Yann glanced toward the gate. The Voyant still hovered off at the same distance. He didn't come after the town. Did he even want to? Maybe he was busy doing something else and just happened to come too close.

Yann pulled himself to his feet. Eliska's curtain stayed where it was. Did she plan to hold it there forever? The mayhem and instability outside didn't slacken at all.

He inched over to the gate. Nothing penetrated her field.

He shut the gate and Perrick rushed over to help Yann barricade it from the inside. Yann lost sight of the Voyant, but the noise didn't subside.

Yann helped Helien stand up, propped the bench next to the wall, and looked over the top. A solid sheet of chaos, debris, and Dark forces blocked him from seeing anything outside the walls.

At that moment, another crackle went off from the hotel roof. Eliska cut the flow of magic coming from her staff, but the veil of sparks didn't die away. It stayed there with the Dark vapors snapping, whipping, and exploding all over it.

She lowered her staff, stared at the curtain of light for another minute, and then looked down to see Yann standing there.

She blinked at him. She didn't seem any the worse for using this power.

Just then, Huges and Natach came rushing out of the hotel. "What the....?" Huges looked up at Eliska standing on the roof.

He and Natach gaped at her with their jaws on the ground, but she didn't react at all.

She shook her hair out of her eyes, took a few steps to the edge of the roof, and jumped down.

She dropped thirty feet and landed next to Yann. "Thank you," he exclaimed. "I guess you guys don't have to set up a barrier around the town after all."

"Did you see the Voyant out there?" Eliska asked. "He didn't come after us this time. He was way over there."

"I saw. I guess he's too busy causing chaos everywhere else. Maybe he doesn't have time for us."

She frowned and cocked her head, but she didn't say anything.

"What?" he asked. "Did you see something up there?"

"No, nothing you didn't see."

"If you can do all that, you probably don't need us," Huges suggested.

"You could go into the hotel and help Aja and Anríq heal the rest of the patients," she replied. "I can cover the defenses from here."

The four magic-users stared at her with their mouths open for a minute before they all went into the hotel.

Huges no longer had his arm in a sling, but he didn't look much better than he did before.

Yann chuckled to himself. "You're gonna put them out of business if you aren't careful."

She didn't hear him. She narrowed her eyes at the gate and then up at the sky. "I've been thinking....about the Voyant...."

"What about him?"

"I don't know what to think anymore.....ever since you suggested...." She gulped and didn't say it.

"You mean about him maybe being connected to you somehow?"

"Maybe I'm just letting the idea get inside my head. I know he's our enemy and everything, but ......"

"But what?" he prompted. "What's on your mind? No one will hold it against you if you are related to him. I mean, Jesus, everyone thinks *I'm* related to him somehow, too."

She didn't take the joke. Everything he said went straight over her head.

"I've been thinking....if losing the second Shard—or whatever you want to call it....if the instability cycle starts when the second Shard holder dies—maybe he doesn't have a choice about causing instability in one place or another. Maybe it just happens."

Yann frowned at her. "Do you think so?"

"I don't know what to think, but what if he isn't trying to hurt anyone? What if he's only looking for us because he wants to find us—and the instability happens out of his control?"

Yann shook that off. "That still doesn't change anything for us, does it? The fact remains that he *is* putting all these people in danger. The only way to stop that is by stopping him—taking both Shards away from him and putting someone else in his place."

"Or one single person could just take the second Shard," she pointed out. "Maybe this doesn't have anything to do with killing him or even defeating him."

"I see what you mean and I also understand why you would see it that way—especially if there's a connection between you—but think about it. It really doesn't change anything. We still have to find the Shard and one of us has to take it—or find the person who will take it. We still don't even know if one of us *can* take it. I don't see why he would be looking for one specific person unless that is the only person who can take the Shard. If you're right about him not doing this maliciously, then that would indicate that I'm right. Whoever this person is that he's looking for must be the only person who can take the Shard."

She tried to shrug that off, but she wound up squirming instead.

Just then, Huges and Natach came back. "Your friend says all the cursed people are taken care of. Now it's just the injured. He's asking you to come inside and help him."

Eliska gave Yann one more pointed look and followed Natach and Huges into the hotel. That left Yann with plenty on his mind.

Chapter 34

Eliska sat on the floor in what she hoped would be an out-of-the-way corner of the hotel. The five travelers had started using this hotel as their headquarters for some reason.

The sick people started here, but almost all of them had already gone home after Aja and Anríq healed them.

It took Eliska only a few minutes to heal the injured. She didn't dare to go near any of the cursed people.

Anríq wouldn't let her near them even if she wanted to. The thought of even touching Dark magic again made her sick to her stomach.

She tilted her head back, rested it against the wall, and shut her eyes. Images of Laval kept flashing through her mind along with all the memories and nightmares that had been plaguing her these last few days.

The memories didn't go away— not ever. Now she saw other things—landscapes and Layers of the Coil.

Her projection seemed to have gone inward. She no longer needed to project it into her hand to see what was going on out there.

She tried again and again to stop herself from seeing, but it happened automatically now.

She became conscious of everything happening in almost every Layer of the Coil. She didn't even have to open her eyes.

She saw the streets of Laval outside and her field holding off the Dark forces. She didn't have to go outside or do anything to keep that field in place. She could do everything with her mind.

The Dark forces slackened when the Voyant disappeared and went somewhere else.

She was really starting to dread ever running into him again in any kind of battle situation.

What if Yann was right and she really was related to him somehow? Why did that bother her so much?

She didn't even know if it was true, but just thinking it might be changed everything. She couldn't think of him as her enemy.

She really needed to stop sympathizing with him. She had no idea why he did anything.

He could be as malicious and destructive as the friends originally thought. He could be out there destroying, murdering, and slaughtering just for the fun of it. She had absolutely no reason to think otherwise.

This idea would not leave her alone. She couldn't get rid of it once it took root in her mind.

She just wanted him to be one of the good guys. If he was related to her, she wouldn't be able to stand it if he did all this to hurt people—especially people she cared about.

She tried more than once to put the thought out of her head.

She had to fight him. He was her enemy whether he meant to be or not. He was the one causing the instability. She would have to use her magic to defeat him.

That was the part that scared her the most. What if the Keepers of the Dawn gave her the power to defeat the Voyant?

She would have to tap her Dark poison to do that. She shivered at the thought.

She didn't trust herself to use her Dark poison for anything—not even to transport her friends from one Layer to another.

Forget about summoning all that power to defeat the Voyant. She just couldn't go there. Just thinking about it terrified the ever-loving crap out of her.

Right then, Helien came breezing around the corner and saw Eliska sitting on the floor by herself.

"Hi!" Helien chirped.

Eliska barely looked up. "Hi."

"Don't you need to defend the wall?"

"I am defending the wall," Eliska mumbled. "I can do that from here."

Helien blinked at her. "You can? How?"

"Never mind." Eliska looked away. She really didn't want to talk to anyone right now, especially not someone as cheerful as Helien. "Besides, it's peaceful out there, so we don't need to defend the walls right now anyway."

Helien frowned, but that expression still came across as comical. "It is?'

Eliska waved to a window at the end of the hall. "Take a look."

Helien walked down the hall and bent over to peer out the window. Eliska didn't have to get up or even glance in that direction to know what Helien was seeing. Eliska could see it all in her visions.

The instability faded and left the landscape quiet outside the walls. The upheaval ruptured hillsides, carved deep fissures in the surrounding fields, and left a bunch of dead livestock in its wake.

At least the wind no longer tore the place apart. No Dark vapors drifted down from the clouds.

Helien craned her neck to squint up at the sky. "Where did those shadows come from?"

"The Dark Layer is still hovering at a distance from here," Eliska told her. "It will come back eventually."

Helien jolted. "It will? Should we do anything about that before it comes?"

"Like what?" Eliska asked. She already knew the answer.

"I don't know," Helien asked. "You're so much more powerful a magic-user than I am."

Eliska changed the subject by getting to her feet, but fortunately, Natach showed up and saved the day just then.

"Huges wants you downstairs, Helien," Natach ordered. "It's your turn to monitor the Barbarians and make sure they aren't trying to approach Laval again."

"They aren't," Eliska interrupted. "But they are planning to make another campaign in the next couple of days."

Both women spun around to stare at her. Eliska realized a second too late that she probably shouldn't have said that.

She was used to spending time with Yann, Anríq, and Marine. They didn't question her using this new power in new and frightening ways. Eliska wasn't used to spending this much time around people who didn't know her.

Helien blinked a few more times before she recovered her usually good humor. She burst into a big grin that somehow didn't look right under the circumstances. "Okay! See you around, Eliska!"

Helien sailed off up the hall and vanished down the stairs leading to the ground floor.

Eliska really didn't like Helien's cheery attitude at all. Marine balanced her sense of humor with seriousness.

She knew exactly how serious any situation was and she handled it with the same gravity. She never joked unless the situation called for it.

Eliska cast one last parting glance in Helien's direction....and froze when she saw Natach studying her with a very different expression on her face.

Eliska marveled that two women could be so radically different from each other. Natach's dark eyes drilled Eliska to the core.

Eliska didn't have to wonder if Natach realized the depth of Eliska's Darkness.

Natach didn't have the magic for that, but she probably had enough life experience to see the signs.

Eliska looked away first and headed off down the hall so she wouldn't have to stand here with Natach staring at her.

"Where are the others?" Eliska asked over her shoulder.

"Your Servant friend is down in the kitchens repairing some damage to the furnace. His grandmother is going from house to house healing the last of the patients. The Watch Commander is gathering up any available weapons to use against the Barbarians and organizing the patients who are strong enough now to help us fight."

Eliska froze when Natach called Yann the Watch Commander. The townspeople did that in Tenby, but it still sounded strange.

Eliska nodded and entered the stairwell, now that Helien wasn't there anymore.

Natach followed Eliska every step of the way. "Where are you going?" Natach asked.

"I guess I'll go outside and get to work repairing the damage to the buildings. I should have thought of that before."

"Shouldn't you be defending the wall?" Natach asked.

Eliska heaved an almighty sigh. "I am defending the wall."

"How can you be when you're sitting up here by yourself?"

Eliska lost her grip on herself for a minute and spun around to confront this woman. "Do you want something from me?"

Natach skewered Eliska with another penetrating stare. "You have powerful magic."

Eliska turned away in the other direction. "I know that."

"How did you get it?"

"Does it matter how I got it?" Eliska barked over her shoulder.

"I wish I had magic like that," Natach remarked. "I could do so much good with it."

"You don't want magic like this," Eliska muttered. "Trust me."

"You could have cured all the cursed people in a few minutes," Natach pointed out. "You probably could have healed the whole hotel without ever setting foot across the threshold."

"You're right. I could have."

"Why didn't you, then? You wouldn't even go in the same room with the patients."

Eliska whirled around again. She couldn't understand herself. She really should not be talking to this woman at all.

"Where did you get *your* magic?" Eliska snapped. "Huh?"

Natach frowned. "I was born with it. I didn't get it anywhere."

"There you go. I was born with it, too." Eliska walked away, but Natach only followed her.

"Could you teach me how to use it?" Natach asked. "Could you teach me how to use my magic the way you do?"

Eliska stopped, turned around much more slowly, and leveled the woman with a direct stare. Should she?

Something in the woman's constant questions struck a chord with Eliska. Natach didn't come across as nearly so airheaded as Helien.

Natach didn't come across as airheaded at all. Eliska would have sent Helien packing if she asked Eliska to teach her how to use magic.

Natach didn't have anything particularly spectacular when it came to magical powers, but she meant well. Eliska sensed that right away.

Natach wanted to learn magic so she could help her town. That much was obvious.

Eliska opened her hand and created a pool of magic. "Can you do this?"

Natach glanced down and her jaw dropped. "The Barbarians! They're arming!

Eliska looked into the pool at a view of the Barbarians camp on the other side of the surrounding hills.

The Barbarian warriors all stood up, gathered their weapons, and got ready to leave their camp to trek across the countryside to assault Laval, but the Barbarians didn't leave right away.

She saw at one glance that they weren't in any big hurry to leave. Maybe they were worried about getting caught in another instability wave.

They milled around their camp, talked a lot, made a big show of adjusting and checking their weapons, and had to go back into their tents more than once to organize their supplies.

They also took way too long to say goodbye to their families considering the men were only crossing a few hills and a dozen miles at the most.

"We have to do something to stop them! We have to prepare." Natach's eyes shot up to Eliska's face. "You have to help us! You have to help us defeat them. You don't know what it's been like living under their constant attacks."

"So....they've never told you why they're attacking?" Eliska asked.

Natach frowned. "How could they tell us? We've never spoken to them. They come, they kill a bunch of people, and they leave."

Eliska kept walking down the stairs. "We'll see about that."

"What do *you* know about them?" Natacha asked over Eliska's shoulder. "Do you know why they're attacking?"

"I don't know why, but I bet you anything there's a reason. You and your people and Nello and whoever has been in charge around here should have at least taken the time to negotiate with them. You could have avoided dozens of attacks if you only asked."

"What could they possibly want? We don't have anything but the clothes on our backs—and the Barbarians never take food or supplies."

"That proves it." Eliska made it to the bottom of the stairs just then—just in time to meet up with Anríq coming up from the kitchens.

"The Barbarians are just leaving their camp," she told him. "Come out to the wall when they get here. Let them see you and maybe negotiate with you."

He nodded. "I was planning to."

Eliska looked around. "Where's your grandmother?"

"I'm not sure. She's in one of the houses, I think."

Natach followed the friends out of the hotel just as Yann approached them from a side street. He carried an armload of weapons and deposited everything on the hotel porch.

"The Barbarians are just leaving their camp now," she told him. "They won't be here until tomorrow at the earliest."

"I've been asking around," he replied. "No one knows anything."

Her shoulders slumped. "That's a shame."

He squinted up at her and then glanced at Anríq. "Maybe Aja and Anríq can find out for us."

"Find out what?" Anríq asked.

"We're in the Sojourner's Sanctum," Eliska explained. "I don't know how, but we are—and before you ask, yes, I already checked and your family isn't here. None of the Dinu Tribe is here."

He clenched his jaw and looked away. She would have squeezed his arm, but she didn't do it in front of Yann and Natach.

"I asked Yann to ask around to see if anyone around here knows about Yimichi Ocuron, but it seems like no one in Laval ever talks to the Barbarians. That's why I was hoping you could do it—to find out about Yimichi and also to find out why the Barbarians keep attacking."

"That's basically what I found out, too," Yann added. "No one in town ever thought to ask the Barbarians what they want—and no one knows anything about Yimichi or his family. The townspeople don't interact with the Barbarians."

"Are you serious?!" Natach interrupted. "You actually think.... like.....the Barbarians.....*want* something from us—something other than to loot our supplies?"

"You're the one who just said they don't take your supplies," Eliska pointed out.

"Then they just want to kill us," Natach pointed out.

"Then why haven't they? They could have. They could have burned this place to the ground with everyone trapped inside the wall. They want something else."

"I'd like you two to spend the rest of the time going through town and helping Aja get as many able-bodied people back on their feet as possible." Yann gave Eliska a pointed look. "Just do it safely."

"I will," she told him.

"What do you want *us* to do?" Natach glanced at Eliska. "There isn't much we *can* do with *her* around."

Yann laughed at her. "I'm sure there's plenty you can do. Round up everyone who is strong enough to fight and make sure they're armed. If they don't know how to handle their weapons, you can get Eliska to show them."

"Show them how?" Natach asked. "We don't have time to train everyone."

"She doesn't need to train them. She can transmit the knowledge to them magically."

Natach's mouth fell open in another gasp. "You can do that?!"

Yann waved her away. "You better go do it. We have a lot of work to do before the Barbarians get here."

The party split up. Anríq and Eliska didn't take long to find Aja. Newly healed patients bustled around almost every house.

Half the town was still in bed as she worked her way from one house to the next.

Anríq and Eliska separated to cover more ground, but she didn't even approach some of the houses. She sensed the level of Darkness radiating through the walls. She left those patients for Aja and Anríq to heal.

Eliska concentrated on the injured and she didn't find any shortage of those. By late evening, she worked her way all the way back to the hotel and met up with Aja, Anríq, and the town defenders.

Eliska looked around. "Where's Yann?"

"I haven't seen him," Anríq replied. "I've been indoors almost all day."

"He left," Natach interrupted.

Eliska whipped around. "He....what?"

"He went outside the walls. He said he would be back in a little while."

"What is he doing out there?"

"I don't know. He didn't say and I didn't ask. He just said to lock the gate behind him and not to open it until he came back."

Eliska gulped. "At least tell me he took his glaive with him."

"Yes, he did."

Eliska glanced over her shoulder toward the gate. The heavy beam lay across it to barricade the townspeople in and all the dangers out there.

Yann was out here.

She shut her eyes tight—and saw where he was. She immediately turned away and steered Anríq back toward the hotel. "I'm hungry. Let's go get something to eat."

Chapter 35

Yann looked over his shoulder at the town of Laval in the distance. It didn't look like anything special.

No upheaval or instability disturbed the place now. The town looked peaceful from this distance.

He stepped into the trees and kept walking until he couldn't see the town anymore. He probably shouldn't have left when so many dangers threatened to attack.

He wouldn't have been able to defend the town from inside the walls anyway—not from the deadliest assault.

Anríq, Aja, and Eliska would defend Laval against whatever came. This was more important right now.

He hunted through the trees for a while until he heard a scuffling noise nearby. He followed the sound and located Marine huddled next to a giant rock outcropping in the middle of the woods.

Thorns and undergrowth had ripped her dress to shreds. Leaves and twigs stuck in her matted hair.

She sat in a pile of dry leaves and occasionally shuffled her feet on the ground underneath her.

That rustling sound gave the only indication that she was even still conscious. She didn't respond at all when he sat down next to her.

He had to get control of himself before he dared to try to talk to her. He swallowed down the lump in his throat.

He took one look at her filthy face, her tangled hair hanging over her eyes, and the black dirt under her fingernails. He looked away with a pained grimace. "I don't know if you can hear me....." he croaked.

Nothing.

He clamped his eyes shut, gulped again, and forced himself to turn around and face her.

"If you can hear me....if you're even in there anymore at all....just give me one sign....Give me anything. Just tell me you're still there.....I need you....I need to know you're still there....I love you, Marine....."

He broke off and squeezed his eyes shut tight to hold back the sting of tears. He couldn't lose his composure now—not with the fate of another town resting on his shoulders.

He had to go back to Laval and face....everybody,

She didn't reply. She didn't respond at all, not even by moving. She didn't look up at him or snarl or bite at him.

A thousand words came rushing into his head. He would have liked to pour out how much he missed her—how much he needed her support and company right now.

He would have liked to tell her how he needed her so much more than he needed Anríq and Eliska. He couldn't even explain why because he loved them both with all his heart.

He stared down at Marine with a heavy weight sinking into the pit of his stomach. She wasn't there. He sensed that.

Whatever they had in Savaré was long gone. It would never come back.

He always knew this day would come. He just never thought it would hurt this much.

He would almost rather have taken her back to her father's kingdom and stood in the crowd to watch her marry another man. Anything would be better than this.

He summoned every ounce of resolve he had left, but he still didn't manage to keep his voice steady.

"If you don't look at me or talk to me or give me some sign right now, I'll assume you can't. I don't believe you would leave me sitting here like this without giving me something. If you don't, I'll assume you're gone and I'll go back to the wall...."

He broke off. He couldn't go on anymore.

She didn't look at him or say anything or give anything sign. She sat there glaring at the rock surface and shuffled her feet exactly the same way.

He waved his hand in front of her eyes. She didn't even blink. He snapped his fingers right next to her ear. She didn't hear.

He stared down at her for longer than he needed to. He didn't even recognize this creature.

This wasn't Marine. This wasn't the beautiful, vivacious girl he started to care about so much in Savaré.

She was gone. He would never get her back.

He would spend the rest of his life dreaming about her.

He really had no reason anymore not to take his oath to the Black Watch. He would never find another woman like her.

He could care about Eliska. He could even love her, but she would never take Marine's place in his heart. He didn't want Eliska to and he sure as hell didn't want to find someone else.

He would rather live alone and dedicate himself to helping people. It sure looked like his life was going in that direction anyway.

He turned away from her—this mud creature without a brain. This wasn't a person anymore. It was a block of wood or maybe some kind of animal. It definitely wasn't Marine.

Even after he turned his head and stopped looking at her, he still couldn't bring himself to leave. He sat there next to her and thought about her—the real her—the Marine he used to sleep next to in Savaré.

He would just spend these last few minutes remembering how fantastic it felt to fall asleep at night with his arms around her—and to wake up in the morning with her lying in the same position.

He remembered her deep kisses, her arms around his neck, her body trembling against his. Those were the days.

He would have liked to describe them for her, but she wouldn't hear.

Whatever part of her remembered was somewhere else. Talking about it would only make it harder.

He would stand up and leave in a few minutes. He wouldn't come back out here.

He just had to satisfy himself that his worst fears really had come true. She was gone exactly the way he always knew she would be.

He didn't want to hurry the moment of departure. He just wanted to sit here and swim in a sea of memory—memories of her.

Maybe she wouldn't come back when the war ended. Maybe she had gone completely over to the Dark. It might have wiped out any trace of who she really was. She might not come back at all.

He cursed Brother Matherus for ever recruiting her to commune with the Dark to fight the Voyant.

Brother Matherus couldn't have known then how much it would cost her. Brother Matherus cared about Marine too much to do that—or maybe Brother Matherus did know.

Maybe Brother Matherus thought Marine's sanity was a small price to pay for a chance to defeat the Voyant.

The thought propelled Yann to his feet. He couldn't sit here a second longer. He strode back across the woods without looking back. Marine was gone for good. Now he just had to live with it.

The Laval defenders saw him coming a long way off. They unbolted the gate to let him in and Perrick barricaded it behind him.

"Where were you?" Nello demanded. "We were worried something might have happened to you."

"Nothing happened to me. Where are Anríq and Eliska?'

"They're at the hotel eating dinner. Eliska said to tell you to come there when you got back. I wasn't sure you would...."

Yann walked away without explaining himself. He didn't want to talk to anyone about where he went and why.

He found Anríq, Aja, and Eliska eating together in the hotel kitchen. They sat at a small round table in the corner by themselves.

"Pull up a chair," Eliska told him. "Everyone in town is in a tizzy because you went outside the walls."

"Please tell me *you* aren't in a tizzy about it," Yann countered more harshly than he should have.

"I wasn't," she told him. "I don't think Anríq is capable of tizzies .....are you?"

She glanced at him and he burst out laughing. "Define 'tizzy'."

All three of them laughed....and then Yann caught Eliska scrutinizing him.

She didn't say why she hadn't been worried about him.

That one moment of eye contact answered his question for hm.

She must have been watching him either through her hand window or her Coil Projection. She was the only person in town who knew where he went and why he went there.

He saw in her eyes in that moment that she knew. She already knew she couldn't hold a candle to Marine. Eliska didn't want to hold a candle to Marine. Eliska never once considered taking Marine's place in Yann's life.

Eliska's expression betrayed nothing. She wouldn't do that in front of the other two—as if Anríq could possibly not know.

Yann bent over his food and tried to avoid looking at anyone for the rest of the meal.

He couldn't regret them knowing. At least someone did.

He didn't have to pretend it was all okay with him when it was as far from being okay as it could possibly get.

He caught Aja glancing at him a few times, too. That would be just stellar—if she knew, too.

Chapter 36

Eliska jumped and used her magic to lift herself onto the hotel roof. She could see the whole countryside for miles around from up here.

She didn't have to open her hand window or use any magical sight to spot the Barbarians approaching Laval.

They came in force, but she saw right away that these Barbarians didn't belong to the Dinu Tribe.

She already knew that. She'd already searched every square inch of the Sojourner's Sanctum—and the rest of the Coil into the bargain. She never found any trace of Anríq's tribe or any of their relatives.

She couldn't explain how this section of the Sojourner's Sanctum survived the upheaval that separated her and Anríq from the tribe.

She couldn't even be sure that the Voyant's tribe survived it, but she and the rest of Laval were about to find out.

She and the rest of Laval were about to get all the answers they ever wanted about what the Barbarians really attacked this town.

She stayed standing on the roof as they emerged from the distant trees. They came in all their finery. Their studded clothes, beads, and weapons glittered in the sun.

The Barbarians went all out to make their hair spikes and scalp horns as big and intimidating as possible.

It worked. Their arrival sent a tremor through the townspeople behind the wall.

Yann, Anríq, Aja, and the principal defenders stood on a scaffold behind the wall. Yann had gotten a bunch of the newly able-bodied former patients to construct it so everyone could see over the top and so the Barbarians could see them.

The other townspeople hid behind the wall and only showed their eyes and the tops of their foreheads.

Yann and the two Servants stood right up there where the entire Barbarians horde could see exactly who they were dealing with.

The Barbarians lined up just outside the trees. The Barbarians stopped there to make sure they cast the right impression on their would-be victims.

Yann waited for a minute and then waved up at Eliska. The friends had already discussed this confrontation at length. Eliska knew how Yann wanted to carry it out.

She jumped down from the roof and joined him, Aja, and Anríq at the gate. The townspeople scrambled to lift off the big beam to unlock it.

Nello rushed after them talking a mile a minute. "You don't have to do this. At least take some of our men with you."

"I need you behind the wall in case they get hostile," Yann replied over his shoulder. "We're going out there to talk to them. The more people we take, the more threatening we'll look."

"But.....are you sure?" Nello stammered. "There are only four of you."

"I'm aware of that. Thank you," Yann returned. "Go back to your post and be ready to defend the town if you need to."

Yann walked away and didn't look back. Eliska followed him on one side. Aja and Anríq took their positions on Yann's other side.

The four friends strode out of town through the gate and the defenders slammed it shut behind them.

The Barbarians didn't move until the gate closed.

The Barbarians started forward in a long thin line stretching the width of the field.

They could easily have flanked the four friends and rushed the walls. Eliska and her party wouldn't have been able to stop this many Barbarians.

The friends advanced and the Barbarians came forward to meet them, but the Barbarians didn't charge.

Eliska kept a sharp eye on them, but they didn't even raise their weapons.

Good. Yann's plan was working. The Barbarians couldn't possibly see these four people as a threat.

The two groups closed with each other, but when they were still a hundred yards away from each other, an explosion went off in the trees to one side. The Barbarians on that end of the line spun around and then they really did raise their weapons to defend themselves.

A loud boom went off in the trees and a giant trunk split. The tree toppled over with a deafening crash and Eliska spotted a flash of white in the undergrowth.

She caught one glimpse of Marine scooting from one bush to another. She barely got there before another burst of magic erupted in the foliage.

Eliska tried for one split second to check to see what Marine was doing in there. Marine never used her magic like this while she was communing with the Dark—at least she didn't do it before.

Marine had never gone this far out into the Dark before. Eliska couldn't even tell if Marine had control of her magic anymore—especially not after the way she completely ignored Yann. That wasn't like Marine at all.

She charged through the undergrowth, and this time, she swerved and veered toward some of the Barbarians at that end of the line.

Two Barbarians magic-users rushed out of line, darted back to the woods, and boxed her in on both sides.

She didn't see them until she got too close to one of them. She would have run straight past him, but he panicked when he saw how dirty and crazy she looked.

He raised his hands and bombarded her with a burst of his own magic. It hit her, but it didn't harm her. She never even stumbled in her headlong charge to get away from these two men.

She bolted straight for the magic-user who shot at her, roared in his face, and unloaded a torrent of Dark power that flattened him instantly.

She kept running and even stepped on him in her haste to get away.

The other Barbarians saw their friends under attack and rushed into the trees to help.

She spun around, bellowed to shake the earth, and laid thirty Barbarians on the ground with a torrential jet of magic spilling from her mouth.

Then she whirled the other way and vanished into the trees.

Eliska saw the Barbarians about to go after her. Eliska couldn't let that happen. Marine was already in enough trouble without a bunch of murderous Barbarians hunting her down.

Eliska magicked herself in front of the Barbarians and held up her hand to stop them. She chose the Barbarians with the biggest hair spikes and materialized right in front of him.

"She's crazy!" Eliska blurted out. "She's out of her mind. She doesn't know what she's doing. Leave her alone. She isn't part of this.

You don't want to go to war against one girl. Come on. Let her go. She won't bother you if you don't bother her."

The Barbarian chieftain glared at Eliska and then glared into the undergrowth, but he didn't go after Marine.

He eventually came back to scowling at Eliska. "Who the hell are you?"

"I'm nobody. I'm just a traveler passing through." She waved behind him. "My friend here is Commander of the Black Watch in Laval. He wants to negotiate with you."

"We don't negotiate with anyone!" the chieftain snarled. "Especially not anyone from *that* hellhole!"

"We aren't from Laval. Like I said, we're only passing through. Just hear what he has to say. You have nothing to lose. If you don't like what he says, you can assault the town anyway, right? No one can stop you—certainly not us."

He kept glaring at her as she backed away. She didn't magick herself back to her friends. She walked there so all the Barbarians could see her carrying nothing but her staff.

"What's going on?" Yann murmured when she got there.

"Marine popped off at them, but she's gone now. The Barbarians are on edge and the chieftain doesn't want to listen, but at least he knows now that we aren't connected to this town. If he doesn't listen to you, he won't listen to anyone."

Yann narrowed his eyes at the Barbarians. They came out of the woods and lined up in the same place where they'd been standing just a few minutes ago. Marine was nowhere in sight.

Eliska pivoted back into position standing next to him. The friends waited until all the Barbarians lined up. They didn't lower their weapons this time. Marine couldn't have made her appearance at a worse time, but the friends would just have to make the best of it.

Yann stepped forward and the Barbarians advanced to match him. They met in the center of the field.

Whatever the Barbarians chieftain had been planning to do or say, it all went out the window when he saw Aja and Anríq.

"You're Servants!" he exclaimed.

"We all are," Yann replied. "My name is Yann Dilnao and I'm a member of the Black Watch. I'm here to help these people defend their town, but I'm not one of the residents. My friends and I were just passing through when these people asked us for help."

"Then you're our enemies!" the chieftain spat and rounded on the two Servants. "I call on you to hear our grievance against this town. We've tried for generations to negotiate and compromise with them. If you truly serve humanity, you'll hear our side and defend our claim as much as theirs."

"That's what we're here for," Yann replied. "I understand from speaking to the townsfolk that none of them has even asked what your grievance is. They don't understand why you're attacking their town. They never thought you had a reason at all." He waved at Eliska and then at the two Servants. "That's why we're here. We want to talk to you and find out what it is you want from this town."

"This *town* as you call it...." The chieftain curled his lip at the wall. "This land is ours! It belonged to our tribe for a thousand years before these people invaded and built their town in our territory. My father and grandfather before him both sent embassies to the town to try to reason with them, but the townspeople attacked our embassies outright and slaughtered our parties."

"So the townspeople never even let your father and grandfather explain what the problem was?" Yann asked. "That's terrible."

"These people will all die under our blades!" the chieftain fired back. "We'll level this town and then the land will be ours again."

"If you wanted to level the town and kill everyone, you would have done that long ago. Your father and grandfather would have done it before you. That's the Barbarian way, but none of you has done that. I believe you actually want peace with these people. I can get it for you—and I can get your land back, too, if you at least let me try."

"You're a liar and a fool!" the Chieftain wrinkled his nose at Yann. "You're just a boy."

"I'm a boy who has taken over the defense of that town. I'm Commander of the Watch now, so if you go against that town, you'll be going against me."

"So you're a coward," the chieftain snapped. "You want to avoid fighting because you know you can't win."

Yann had to bite his lip to stop himself from laughing. "Our magic-users could have wiped all of you out the minute you showed your faces here. If you attack that town, you won't get anywhere near the walls. I'm offering because I believe we can come to some solution that works for both you and the town."

"The only solution is for all of them to pack up and leave this Island," the Chieftain fired back. "When they're gone and their buildings and wall destroyed, then we'll be satisfied to let the matter rest. That is the only solution we'll accept."

"If you attack the town, more of your men will die," Eliska pointed out. "You'll weaken your tribe and expose yourself to attack from neighboring tribes. Maybe that's the reason you haven't attacked this town with enough force to destroy it. If you attack now, you'll lose even more men. If you compromise and come to a peaceful solution that satisfies everyone, you can walk away without any further bloodshed."

"I don't care about bloodshed," the Chieftain barked.

Yann didn't say again that he didn't believe that. He already said it once and now everyone knew it. The chieftain didn't want another battle any more than the townspeople did.

"I'll go back to the Laval and tell the townspeople about your claim to the land," Yann went on. "I'll find out what they say and we'll discuss how we can accommodate your demands. Does that satisfy you? You can stay out here and lay siege to the wall until we come up with an answer. Just promise me you won't attack until I have a chance to negotiate on your behalf. Can you do that?"

The Chieftain narrowed his eyes and scowled even more ferociously. "Who the hell are you, boy?"

"I already told you. My name is Yann Dilnao and I'm a member of the Black Watch—but I notice you didn't tell me your name. That makes it harder to consider you a friend and an ally."

"We aren't friends or allies," the chieftain snapped.

Yann shrugged. "Then maybe the best we can do is to avoid being enemies. I'll go see what the townspeople say and we'll take this discussion to the next level. Thank you for meeting us."

He turned around and started walking back toward the town. Eliska didn't want to turn her back on the Barbarians, but she didn't come out here to threaten them—not unless they needed someone to threaten them.

She hesitated before she turned away to follow Yann. Aja and Anríq both lingered for a second before they turned away, too.

"Hey!" the chieftain yelled after them. "Watch Commander!"

Yann turned around extra slowly. "I already told you. My name is Yann. You don't have to call me anything else.'

The chieftain furrowed his eyebrows in concentration and then growled, "My name is Morix."

Yann burst into a grin. "It's very nice to meet you. Maybe we can be on a first-name basis from now on." He waved at the surroundings. "Feel free to camp here if you want to. Make yourselves at home."

Yann walked away. Eliska didn't have to turn around to keep an eye on the Barbarians. She would have found it virtually impossible to turn her back on them if she hadn't been able to see them in her mind's eye.

Morix scowled at the back of Yann's head as the party walked away.

The townspeople scrambled to unlock the gate. Yann didn't mention it when a bunch of armed men stormed out and pointed their weapons at the Barbarians while Yann and the others passed through the gate.

The defenders backed away with their weapons raised until Perrick and the others shut the gate and barricaded it behind them.

Nello actually trembled in front of Yann when it was all over. "Well....what did he say?"

"He says that your ancestors trespassed on Barbarian land and built their town here without even checking to find out if the land belonged to someone else. He says his father and grandfather both sent embassies to Laval to negotiate with your ancestors, but your ancestors attacked first and slaughtered the diplomatic parties without even waiting to hear their grievance. They want you to evacuate the area and give the land back."

"We can't do that!" Malo exclaimed. "We've lived here all our lives!"

"You know, you could have spared yourselves untold loss of life if you just talked to the Barbarians before now. They've gone out of their way to avoid wiping you all out—which is what they should have done in the first place. That's the Barbarian way. They've been far more accommodating than they need to be—and they're sitting out there right now—not attacking—so I could come in here and tell you what it is that's bothering them. You might have the decency to at least consider their side of the story."

No one said anything for a minute.

"How can we come to any compromise?" Huges asked. "Why should they get what they want and not us? How can we pack up and just leave? Everything we have is here. If someone did them wrong, those people are long dead. It isn't our fault."

"I'm not saying one party has to win and the other has to lose," Yann replied. "I'm saying we could come to a solution that satisfies both of you."

"What solution is that?" Nello countered. "You explaining their grievance only makes it seem more impossible."

"It makes it *seem* more impossible, but it isn't," Yann replied. "There's always a solution."

"Then what is it?" Malo asked.

"Would you be willing to compromise if I came up with one?" Yann turned in all directions and eyed everyone near enough to listen to the conversation. "Would you be interested in ending this conflict if I find a way that works for both sides?"

The townspeople exclaimed glances. "You mean....compromise with....with Barbarians?" Malo made a face.

"Would you rather pass down this war to your children and grand-children? You would be sentencing them to death, dismemberment, and a lifetime of conflict—for nothing. End it now by growing up and coming to the table in good faith." Yann swiped his finger at everyone. "Get back on watch and keep an eye on them. Raise the alarm if they do anything."

He headed back to the hotel. The two Servants went off in different directions.

Eliska stayed where she was until the townspeople dispersed.

She didn't have to get up on the wall to see what the Barbarians were doing. They went back into the trees and eventually wandered back to their camp at a distance from Laval.

They only murmured to each other along the way. They weren't expecting to meet someone like Yann.

She found herself marveling at the way he handled himself—in everything. He'd become something beyond anything she ever could have imagined.

Chapter 37

Eliska passed down one of the corridors in the hotel's upper floors. She looked in on cursed people—the last ones left that Anríq and Aja hadn't cured yet.

She barely had to glance into the rooms to know more than anyone could possibly know about these sick people. They were all too Dark to survive.

A bunch of their family members stood out in the hall watching and waiting for Aja and Anríq to come back and heal the sick people.

Eliska only had to glance at the relatives to know everything about them, too. Their memories poured into her, joined the overflowing cascade already storming inside her, and they all blurred together in a sea of humanity.

In a way, all these memories fighting for her attention made it easier for her to cope with it all.

She didn't have to focus on any one memory for very long—or to put it another way, it made it easier for her to ignore them or for any random thing to come along and distract her from thinking about them.

It did make it nearly impossible for her to interact with anyone. She found herself getting lost in the person's memories instead of paying attention to the person in front of her.

She couldn't ignore these people, though. They all turned around when she got to the landing. They must have been waiting a long time because they rushed her and surrounded her.

"When will the Servants come back?" one man blurted out. "My father has been getting worse every day. I'm really worried. Perrick said the Servants would come to our house to heal him, but they never came. Then Helien and Huges came to move my father here."

"The same thing happened to my cousin," a woman chimed in. "She was too sick to move, but they brought her here anyway so the Servants could heal her—but the Servants don't come."

Eliska took a deep breath. "I'm very sorry to tell you this, but all these people are here because they're too cursed to heal. The Servants can't help them. It's too late. I'm sorry. No one can heal your loved ones."

"Why did Helien and Huges say that the Servants would heal them here, then?" The first man narrowed his eyes at Eliska. "Could *you* heal them?"

She didn't squirm under his gaze. "I could, but I won't be able to. I would have to take the curse on myself. I would kill myself by trying and I might not even be able to save them at all. In fact, I'm certain I couldn't because your relatives are too far gone. I'm sorry, but we just didn't get here in time to save everyone. If I was in your place, I would use the time you have left telling your loved ones how much they mean to you, saying goodbye....... and maybe you could tell them you're sorry for things you did wrong or give them the chance to say they're sorry for things they did wrong. I wish I could help you and them, but maybe that's the best anyone can hope for now."

She blurted it all out in a rush and panted to a stop so she wouldn't say anything else.

She probably shouldn't have said that, but it was the only comfort she could give these people.

She must have gotten through to some of them. They turned away, peered through the bedroom doors, and then drifted inside. Each able-bodied relative separated and sat down next to one of the sick people.

She watched them from the hall. She didn't have to go anywhere near those people to hear every word they said to each other.

This Darkness—it didn't change the fact that people were going to die. The power the Keepers of the Dawn gave her—it could do a lot, but it couldn't stop death.

She turned away toward the last room in line. It was one of the rooms the people of Laval gave the four travelers to stay in.

She went inside and sat down on the bed, but she kept seeing and hearing everything going on in the adjacent rooms.

The man sat down next to his father, but his father was too out of it to see his son sitting right next to him.

A river of memories washed over the son when he looked down at his father's haggard face.

The father worked all his life as a butcher. He woke up in the early hours of the morning, worked hard all day, and came home late just to snatch a few hours of rest before he did it all over again.

The son grew up watching his father slave every day to provide for his family. The son got to spend an hour with his father every day at the absolute most, but the son cherished those moments as the most precious minutes of his day.

The father went out of his way to play with his son, talk to him about all his cares and concerns, and even went without food to make sure his son got enough.

The son started out by holding his father's hand in both of his, pressing it, and then the son broke down in tears when he kissed his father's knuckles.

The son couldn't speak to express his love and gratitude, now that his father lay on his death bed too insensible even to look at his son.

All those memories bled Eliska's heart. Tears sprang to her eyes when she felt the overpowering love pouring out of the son through his tears.

Eliska clung to those memories. She never wanted to remember the other things. She wanted to dwell in that love forever and never think or see or feel anything else ever again.

Even losing the father felt like the greatest blessing imaginable. The son guarded the memories of his father's life in the most protected corners of his heart. The son cherished those memories above everything else in his life.

Now the father would die and leave behind a legacy of love, care, and admiration. Nothing would ever tarnish that image the son carried of his father. The father would live forever in the halls of glory.

She heard other family members moving around out in the corridor and some people crying, but she focused all her attention on that one man and the outpouring of love he felt for his father. She used it to block out everything else.....including footsteps coming closer.

She didn't hear anything or notice anything until Anríq stepped into the room and saw her sitting on the edge of the bed with tears in her eyes.

He took one look at her and his weight compressed the mattress when he sat down next to her.

"Did you tell them?" he murmured in an undertone.

She nodded down the floor. Helien, Huges, Perrick, and Natach should have been the ones to break the bad news to their own neighbors. These people shouldn't have had to hear it from a stranger, but Eliska didn't say that.

Even this somehow felt like a blessing—being the person to finally tell these people the truth about their loved ones' chances. At least she gave them a few more minutes to say goodbye.

Anríq broke in on her thoughts again. "Aja and I want to go through the town and find the source of this curse. We'd like you to help us if you can find a way to do it without hurting yourself."

"You don't have to," she mumbled. "The curse is nothing more than instability coming from the Island itself. It's nothing you can break."

He looked up at the side of her head. She didn't raise her eyes to meet his gaze. "So will it keep coming back?" he asked. "Will more people keep getting sick?"

She shrugged at nothing. The memory of his conversation with Yann about not giving Eliska any ideas burned a hole in Anríq's mind every time he looked at her. He couldn't stop thinking about it. It nagged him until it drove him insane.

The agitation radiating off him right now blasted straight into her brain. He fought himself every minute to stop himself from putting his arms around her and kissing her the way he did in Symphorian.

Yann's warning stopped Anríq from doing anything.

Her power showed her everything he saw when he looked at her. She was too messed up for him to touch her even to give her the smallest comfort. He didn't want to cross the line.

He didn't think he went too far in Symphorian, but things changed when she came back from the monastery. She was a lot worse now—even worse than he realized.

Neither of the boys would go near her—not until something changed.

She also felt the unbearable love both of them felt when they looked at her. They wanted nothing but the best for her, but they held themselves back.

They didn't even hold themselves back from each one. Anríq didn't keep to himself because Yann warned him away. Neither of the boys did.

The boys loved and admired each other too much to care about that.

This was all about her. She was too fragile to go there even though she loved both of them more than she could stand.

She clamped her eyes shut and buried herself in the excruciating love Anríq felt for her.

He sat over there looking at her and barely holding himself together from the agony of not being able to do anything to help her—and from the agony of not being able to be near her.

An impassable barrier separated them from each other even when they sat right next to each other on this bed.

He would never be able to touch her like that again—not in any way that really communicated how he felt.

He would always keep it platonic from now on—probably forever. They would never go back to the way they were before.

Without warning, he raked his fingers through her hair to pull it back from her face, ran his hand down her back, and rubbed.

It was such a comforting gesture. It flooded her with warmth and relaxation—if anything could relax her.

He did it so lovingly, but it was also the most brotherly move he could possibly make. It was exactly the same platonic, caring, brotherly touch he'd been using on her since the beginning.

He even kissed the side of her head—exactly the way Yann always did. Neither of them ever took it any further. They wouldn't.

The resolution settled into both of them with the granite certainty of the ages. Both of them locked themselves into this decision and dug in for the long haul. Neither of them would change anything—not until something changed in her.

Anríq practically read her mind, but he couldn't read her mind—not the way she could read his. He knew just enough to ask the right questions.

"How are you feeling? You seem better these last couple of days."

She didn't give herself the option to look up or make eye contact with him.

"It's getting stronger," she croaked. "I use the Darkness and it gets stronger. Then there's more of it to use and it keeps getting stronger. I don't see how it can ever go away."

"Is that a bad thing?" he murmured. "I don't see you losing control of it and I don't see you turning the power against anyone else. You've used it for nothing but good as far as I've seen."

She twisted her shoulders inside her clothes She didn't want to talk about it, but she had to talk to him. She would always have to talk to him. She could never keep anything from him.

"That's the thing," she husked. "I don't have a problem controlling it."

"That's good," he exclaimed. "Then you don't have to worry about using it for the wrong reasons."

"Is there a right reason?"

"Of course. Helping people is always the right reason. I haven't seen you using it for anything else."

She found herself turning her head away. "Maybe I should do more."

"Like what—like healing those people? We both know that isn't possible."

She shrugged again. She didn't seem to be able to sit still.

"You have your hands full just trying to live with this power. I don't think you should be trying to do more than that." He cocked his head to one side to study the side of her face. She still found it impossible to look at him. Just sitting next to him cost her everything she had. "You seem to be living with it better. Maybe things will improve when you get used to it."

She couldn't answer. She wasn't sure if she was living with it better or not.

"I'm glad you had Yann with you at the monastery....and I'm glad he had you there to get him out of it. I wouldn't trust either of you with anyone else....."

He broke off when they heard more footsteps coming down the landing outside. These definitely didn't belong to the loved ones out there.

Anríq took his arm down immediately and sat straight on the bed so he left a few inches of space between him and Eliska.

The footsteps beat a steady rhythm coming straight down the hall heading to this room. They didn't stop.

Eliska stiffened for just a second when Yann walked in. He froze on the threshold and his eyes darted back and forth when he saw Anríq and Eliska sitting next to each other.

His eyes registered in a split second that Anríq wasn't touching her.

The slightest hint of bite crept into Yann's tone. "Did you find out about the curse?"

"There is no curse," Eliska told him. "The instability is allowing the Dark to creep into this Layer. That's all."

"So will these people keep getting sick?" Yann asked.

"That's what I was just asking," Anríq added.

"Nothing can stop the Dark as long as the Coil keeps destabilizing," she replied. "Stabilizing the Coil is the only long-term solution. Things like this will just keep happening until someone stabilizes it."

Yann barely acknowledged her at all. He turned to Anríq. "I need you to take over supervising the defenses for a while. I can't be sure, but I think Huges and Helien might be talking about us behind our backs and convincing the townspeople not to listen to us. I need you to keep an eye on them...."

"They aren't," Eliska interrupted.

His eyes swiveled over to lock on her. "Are you sure?"

"Huges and Helien are talking to the townspeople about us behind our backs, but not about that. They're trying to find a way to convince us to stay so we don't leave when this is all over. They think we can save this town from what's happening."

"But....you just said nothing can stop it—not until someone stabilizes the Coil."

She nodded. "That's right.

He shrugged that off. "Well, I still need you to take over the defenses—both of you."

"Are you going somewhere, Yann?" Anríq asked.

"I need to take care of something. I need you to...."

"Don't worry," Eliska cut in. "The Barbarians aren't going to attack and I'll do what I can to hold off the Dark if we suffer another incursion. You don't have to worry about Laval or us."

Anríq turned around to frown at the side of her head. She didn't acknowledge him.

She looked up at Yann and saw exactly what he planned to do. She didn't say anything to stop him.

He just said, "Thanks," and left the room.

Chapter 38

Y ann pretended to search Laval for any sign of weakness in the defenses. Eliska's comments about the town slowly falling to the ongoing instability didn't paint a very hopeful picture—for anyone.

He circled the town inspecting the wall at close range. It really was the flimsiest defense he had ever seen. It might as well not be there at all.

He took way too long studying the wall and all its bricks and the mortar in between them. Nello, Malo, and the four magic-users finally left him alone to go do their own thing.

He made it back to the gate, climbed up on the scaffold, and hopped over the side.

He landed in the fields outside Laval and set off walking fast toward the trees in the distance. That wasn't the direction he wanted to go, but he wanted to get out of sight quicky before anyone from Laval saw him.

He was beginning to get the impression that Eliska already knew what he planned to do, but she didn't stop him. She must approve of this plan.

He struck off north and cut through the woods until he found open countryside. He didn't have any trouble following the highway of tracks all the way back to the Barbarian camp.

He paused at a distance from their camp and looked down on a bunch of tents constructed of sewn-together animal skins tied to wooden frames. Men, women, and children went about their business down there.

They looked so peaceful from up here. He could ignore their hair spikes, tattoos, leather studded harnesses, and all their giant weapons.

They acted like any normal people when they interacted with their families, sat around, talked, ate, and lounged in the sunshine. They didn't look dangerous at all.

He found it difficult to imagine Anríq ever living like this. Maybe that was the point.

He never really fit in with these people. They counteracted each other and drove each other apart.

Yann took a deep breath and started climbing down the last hill—right where the Barbarians could see him.

His arrival electrified the warriors. They all stopped what they were doing, jumped up, grabbed their weapons, and formed up in ranks to confront him.

They could all see that he came alone. He brought his glaive, but not even that posed any threat to them.

They treated him as the non-threat that he was. None of the Barbarians raised their weapons. They just squared their shoulders and threw back their heads to watch him come.

Someone must have run off to tell Morix that Yann was coming. Morix ducked under the flap of his tent and narrowed his eyes up the hill at Yann coming closer.

A surge of confidence and certainty settled over Yann on his way down that hill. This was his now. He was the man in charge—of everything. He wound up taking charge of everything no matter where he went.

It started when he chose to become a Servant and fight Simion Mihaili. Then he took command of the Watch in Tenby. Then he took responsibility for Eliska and Marine.

He just couldn't stop himself from taking over everything. It happened whether he wanted it to or not, but he did want it to. He was the best man for the job. He couldn't explain why, but he knew that now.

Morix kept his giant battle axe with him when he advanced to join ranks with his men, but he didn't raise it, either.

Yann got to the bottom of the hill and had to pass through another clump of trees to get to the camp.

The Barbarians pivoted sideways to block the way. He had to stop there facing down all those men, but the sight of them only made him happy. Even their hostility gave him a surge of hope.

Morix broke the uncomfortable silence. "What are you doing her e.....Yann?"

Yann couldn't help but grin at him. "I was hoping I could talk to you—without any of the townspeople from Laval around."

Morix pretended to look around him. "You didn't bring your friends—your Servant friends and....that other girl."

"No, I thought we could just talk—just you and me." Yann made an executive decision not to look at all the other Barbarians.

"Did you get the townspeople to agree to leave the area and give us our land back?"

"That's what I wanted to talk to you about."

"Then the answer is no," Morix countered. "What more is there to say?"

"Actually they didn't give me an answer because none of them knows what to do—but I think I know a solution that will satisfy all of you."

"There is no solution that will satisfy all of us," Morix returned. "We've already discussed this enough. We don't need to talk about it again. If the townspeople aren't willing to abandon this town, then we have nothing more to talk about."

"You don't want to go to war against Laval—not any more than you already have. You've already lost too many people. Another battle will only get a lot of your people killed. My friend and the two Servants will have no choice but to defend the town with their magic. You already know this. I shouldn't have to explain it to you. It isn't like we can just walk away and leave the town unprotected."

Morix frowned at him. A bunch of the other Barbarians shifted their weight and exchanged glances.

Of course none of them wanted to confront a bunch of magic-users. Fighting townspeople was one thing. None of these Barbarians stood a chance against Eliska by herself.

Aja and Anríq would flatten the Barbarians, too.

"If you continue to wage war against Laval, there's a good chance you'll never get the land back at all," Yann went on. "You'll just hand down this war from father to son exactly the way your father and grandfather handed it down to you. It won't accomplish anything, but coming to a compromise will."

"What compromise is that?" Morix demanded. "What compromise could possibly make up for them stealing our land right out from under us?"

"No one alive in Laval stole anything from any of you. If someone stole something, it happened decades ago. Everyone who did the stealing and everyone who had something stolen from them are all long dead. The only question is what we're all going to do about it now—but I can promise you one thing. You stand to profit a lot more by establishing a trade relationship with Laval than by fighting a battle you can't win."

"Trade relationship!" One of the other big Barbarians snorted. "That is never going to happen."

"It will never happen if you tell yourselves it will never happen. You have resources the townspeople want and they have resources you want."

"They have nothing we want," Morix snarled.

"They have the ability to trade with you. You could profit from this—a lot more than you would profit from the land itself. The land is poor at best—especially compared to your territory. I've seen the land, believe me. It's rocky, dry, and barely sustains any kind of animal life. That land would be worthless to you, but as long as the town is there, you could profit from the townspeople's efforts and vice versa."

No one moved for a second. Morix kept scowling at Yann, but the same simmering level of tension didn't run through the Barbarians.

"How do you plan to pull off this trade relationship?" Morix finally demanded. "They would think we were weak if we dropped the challenge now."

"I'll negotiate with them on your behalf....and then you would have to come into town and meet them. You would all have to get to know each other....."

"That's ridiculous!" a different Barbarian snapped. "We are NOT getting to know a bunch of spineless worms."

"It will be difficult at first. I'll grant you that," Yann went on. "I don't think you need to worry about them thinking you're weak because you aren't doing this to stop them from defeating you. In a way, you could see it as them capitulating to you. Think of them as your clients....or tenants on the land. They're over there making a living on your land. Trading with you will be a way for them to repay what they owe you in rent."

Morix snorted. "That's the stupidest thing I've ever heard."

Yann shrugged. "You're the ones who are so insistent that the land is still yours. It can still be yours by right. It can still be part of your territory. You can just make up your minds that you're going to let them use it in exchange for the profit you would gain by trading with them."

"How could we profit if we're trading with them?"

"You have to buy and sell from someone, don't you? Laval is right there on the other side of those hills. Who do you trade with now? How far away do you have to go to get there? These people are so much closer."

Another silence answered him. Morix kept glaring at Yann and furrowing his brow in thought.

Then some of the surrounding warriors glanced over at Morix to see how he would take it.

Morix finally shrugged and looked away. "I guess it's worth thinking about."

"That's all I ask," Yann replied. "It's a simple enough matter for you to get to know the townspeople and for them to get to know you. You can discuss what you might trade and how to go about it. I would bet that relations between both sides will vastly improve as soon as the townspeople realize that you don't want to attack them anymore."

"That town has nothing worth trading for anyway," one of the other Barbarians interrupted.

Morix pretended not to hear and waved behind him. "Come to my tent and share a meal with me. You've come all this way. We can talk about something else while I think it over."

Yann hesitated. He had to stop himself from looking behind him. Should he get out of here as quickly as possible?

He didn't understand the Barbarians' hospitality rules, but he didn't want to antagonize Morix by refusing.

Chapter 39

The Barbarians parted to let Yann through so he could follow Morix back to his tent. Yann didn't know what to expect.

The Barbarian warriors followed Yann into a large tent full of tables standing in rows two feet off the ground. Cushions lined both sides of each table.

Yann didn't see any beds or any other furniture to indicate that anyone lived here—not in any normal way. This was more of a formal ceremonial hall.

Morix sat down in the center of a table on the far side of the one big room. He sat with his back to the wall so he could face out and see everyone else.

He waved to the cushion next to him. "Sit here."

Yann lowered himself onto the cushion, and at that signal, all the other Barbarians sat down, too.

Yann kept a close watch on everyone around him, but he couldn't keep a very close eye on Morix when the man sat right next to him.

Once they got into that position, Yann realized almost for the first time how much bigger Morix was.

Morix dwarfed him by a mile. Yann felt like a young child sitting next to a fully grown man.

Yann didn't get a chance to think too much about it before a bunch of other Barbarians came in carrying countless trays loaded with all kinds of food. Yann didn't recognize most of it.

The servers piled the tables with more food than these people or even the whole tribe could eat in their one sitting.

Morix helped himself and started stuffing his face.

"I'm surprised a man of the Black Watch would negotiate with Barbarians," he mumbled out the side of his mouth. "Most men of the Watch won't come near us. They stand the wall and attack us whenever we come near their towns."

"You can't exactly blame them, can you?" Yann pointed out.

Morix chuckled and wound up coughing on the food in his mouth. "I guess I can't, but it still raises the question. You might be the only man of the Watch in existence who would consider negotiating and compromising with Barbarians." Morix cocked his head to study Yann more closely. "Where you do you come from?"

"I came from a town called Middleborough a long way from here. We got attacked by Darklings and the town got lost in the Coil—and I suppose you could say *we* go to lost in the Coil, too."

"Who's we?"

"My father the Watch Commander, six Watchmen, and me—and Eliska—the girl you met earlier. She was with us. We've been wandering in the Coil ever since." Yann helped himself to one of the pastries in front of him, but he had to study it before he figured out how to eat it. "I suppose I never would have considered negotiating with Barbarians before, either. A lot has changed since then."

"You aren't with the Watch now." Morix raised one eyebrow at Yann's uniform. "Where are your father and Watchmen now?"

"They're all dead. I'm the last one."

"You could find another station and stand the watch there. You don't have to keep wandering around the Coil by yourself."

"I'm not wandering by myself. I guess that's the point. I'm standing the watch with these people instead."

Morix frowned again. "I don't understand."

"I guess I don't understand it, either, except that I'm committed to these people and they're committed to me. We're on a different mission. If my path takes me back to the Watch, so be it, but this is more important right now."

"So what's the mission?" Morix asked.

Now it was Yann's turn to cock his head and look up at the much bigger man. "Do you know a man named Yimichi Ocuron?"

Morix nodded. "Sure. I know him very well."

Yann's eyes fell out of their sockets. "You do? What do you know about him?"

"He grew up in this tribe. We grew up together as boys."

Yann's jaw dropped. "Seriously? You mean....?" His eyes traced the tent and outside to the rest of the camp.

He found it nearly impossible to believe that one of these Barbarians actually rose to become King in the White Spire. Actually two of them did.

"So....do you know his brother, Noleron Kupuro?"

Morix nodded again. "Of course. We all grew up together."

Yann shut his mouth with difficulty. This was the absolute last thing he expected.

"They were good men," Morix went on and frowned again. "What do you want to know that for?"

"Did you know Yimichi became King in the White Spire?

Now it was Morix's eyes that fell out of their sockets. "You're joking!" Then he burst out laughing. "Stop it. That isn't funny."

"It's true. Noleron became his secondary. Yimichi died and now Noleron is Ruler of the Coil in his brother's place."

Morix made a face. "I don't believe you. That's impossible.'

"That's what we thought. That's one of the reasons I wanted to come and talk to you. My friend found records indicating they both loved the same woman—a girl from their home tribe. They fought over her, and when she left the tribe to marry Yimichi, it caused a rift between the brothers. "

Morix turned back to his food. "I wouldn't know anything about that."

"So you never heard about any hostility between the two of them? Did you ever find out why Yimichi left the tribe?"

"I never heard anything about it—and I don't think anyone else heard anything about it. He just left one day."

"Did any girl from the Tribe leave around the same time?"

Morix only shrugged. "I can't remember anything, but I suppose it's possible. I didn't really keep track of what everyone else was doing. I had my own business to attend to. What do you want to know all that for?"

"That's the mission my friends and I are on. We're trying to find information about the last King—and his secondary—who turned out to be the King's brother. They both loved the same woman and she wound up with Yimichi. We think the younger brother took revenge on his brother by doing something to cause his wife's death."

"Then how could the Noleron become the King's secondary if they hated each other so much?"

"That's what doesn't make sense. That's why I wanted to ask—to see if you or anyone here could shed any light on it."

"Sorry," Morix replied. "I can't help you. Does that mean your mission is dead in the water?"

Yann fiddled with his food. "I guess not. I should probably get back. Come to Laval tomorrow and we'll move on to the next stage of our negotiation. If this works, none of us has to fight each other anymore and you can deploy your resources somewhere else. Thank you for your hospitality."

Yann started to stand up. Morix scrambled to get to his feet at the same time and all the warriors copied him.

The crowd parted to let Yann out of the tent. Morix stopped him in the outside and held out his hand. "It's a pleasure doing business with you."

Yann shook it. "Thank you. Likewise. If this works, it could be the best thing for all of us. I'll see you tomorrow. Thank you again."

Yann walked off and started climbing the last hill. He didn't worry too much about what happened when Morix and all his spiky Barbarians showed up at the wall of Laval tomorrow.

Yann dwelled on the Yimichi Ocuron mystery all the way back to town. Yann didn't know what to think of Eliska's theory that Noleron killed his brother's wife and took her place as Yimichi's affiliate.

The Barbarians turned out to be no help at all. They didn't even know that Yimichi became King or that he and his brother had any conflict over a girl.

It didn't really make any difference, though, did it? Yann came to that conclusion by the time he returned to the wall.

How Yimichi became King, how Noleron became the Voyant Mendicat, and how Hubua Ocuron died didn't really matter in the end.

When all was said and done, it didn't even really matter if the Voyant was doing all of this for the sake of inflicting rampant carnage on the people of the Coil or if he was another innocent victim in all of this.

The friends still had to find the Shard of Hotha.

Finding and meeting up with Yimichi's home tribe and even finding people who grew up with him and Noleron—none of that got the friends any closer to locating the Shard or the Sacred Shrine.

The townsfolk rushed to the wall and pointed their weapons at Yann long before he got near Laval. Then Nello had another nervous breakdown when he saw Yann returning.

"We thought you were dead for sure that time!" Nello quavered.

"Why would I be dead?" Yann asked. "I went to see the Barbarians."

Nello, the surrounding defenders, and the local magic-users froze with their mouths hanging open. "You did what?" Huges growled.

"They're coming back tomorrow to negotiate with you. You're going to seal a trade relationship that will benefit both of your peoples."

"Like hell we will," Malo snapped. "We won't have anything to do with them! They're murderous fiends."

"Then you can all go home, say goodbye to your wives, and kiss your children because you'll all be dead the next time the Barbarians raid this town." Yann turned away. "I'll go tell my friends that you don't need us anymore."

"Hey!" Nello shrieked. 'You can't just leave us like this! What kind of Watchman are you?!"

"I'm the kind that risked my neck to save all your worthless lives. None of you had the balls even to talk to the Barbarians to find out why they were attacking you. This trade agreement stands to benefit both sides instead of getting a whole lot more people killed. If you don't want to get on board with that, then you don't need us. We didn't come here to save a bunch of people who are in a hurry to rush off to fight a battle they can't win and get themselves killed for no good reason."

He turned away a second time. He really had better things to do than mollycoddle these idiots.

Nello and Malo hurried after him talking fast. "How can we negotiate with people who have been at war against us for generations?"

"You'll negotiate with them the same way they'll negotiate with people who have been at war against them for generations," Yann replied over his shoulder. He didn't stop walking. "They didn't start this. Your ancestors did. They want to stop it as much as you do. This is the solution you've all been looking for. It's the best way to end the attacks and get you all living in the same territory—which I would remind you is their territory. They're doing you a favor by letting you negotiate at all—so I expect all of you to be gracious and polite tomorrow. Anyone who isn't could be putting the whole town in danger."

Chapter 40

Eliska stood on the hotel porch, leaned on her staff, and watched Yann at the city gates. They stood open to the outside world.

He had disarmed all the men who usually guarded the wall. They gathered around, but they couldn't defend the city unless they absolutely had to.

Yann's glaive rested against the wall next to Eliska. She could magick it to him in a blink if this whole scene went down the pipe in a big fat hurry.

A hundred massive Barbarians stood across the field at a distance from Laval. The Barbarians definitely came armed. They seemed to have gone out of their way to make themselves look as scary as possible just for the occasion.

The townspeople couldn't fail to understand the obvious threat. They trembled in their shoes and kept looking around like they wanted to locate something each person could use as a weapon if he needed it.

Yann didn't look around. He walked through the gate alone and stopped on the open ground beyond the threshold. He never looked at anything other than the Barbarians.

He stood there waiting for a few minutes. Dead silence hung over Laval. Even the birds out in the field fell silent. Tension quivered in the air.

Aja and Anríq stood off to one side, but they came fully armed, too. They didn't take their weapons out, but both Servants could grab them whenever the need arose.

The Barbarians started forward to cross the field. They swept over the rises in a long, shoulder-to-shoulder line like they usually did when they attacked.

A shiver went through the assembled townsfolk. The Barbarians approached the wall with the gate standing wide open. Nothing stopped the Barbarians from entering.

Yann advanced a few paces and stopped again to wait for the Barbarians to meet up with him.

He stayed where he was until the big chieftain halted right in front of Yann. All the warriors stared through the gate at the townspeople cowering behind Yann's back.

All at once, Morix and Yann both burst into matching grins. Morix laughed and the two men hugged in front of everyone.

No one but Eliska could hear the two men from here. "I can't believe you actually convinced me to come here," Morix growled low.

Yann crushed his shoulder. "I'm glad you did. Come inside and let's see what happens."

Morix glanced past Yann's shoulder and made a face. "They're worms."

"Then you won't have any trouble taking charge of the place."

Yann took Morix's arm. All the Barbarians followed the two men inside.

They halted just inside the gate and, fortunately for everyone's sanity, no one closed it with the Barbarians inside.

"Which one of you is in charge here?" Morix demanded.

"They don't have anyone like that," Yann explained. "Everyone who was in charge has died. They've been suffering from Dark forces assaulting—as I'm sure the rest of this Island has been, too. This is Nello Dumont. He's the closest person these people have to anyone who can negotiate with you."

Morix strode over to Nello. Morix towered over the poor man.

Morix stuck out his hand. "I hope we can come to an agreement that benefits both our peoples."

Nello had to think really hard before he decided to shake Morix's hand. "Um...I hope so, too."

Morix cast another flinty glance around. "So.....what would you like to trade?"

Nello exchanged glances with those nearest him. "We don't have anything."

Yann interjected. "What would you like to trade, Morix?"

Morix waved to the warriors behind him. Three men came forward carrying large, rolled bundles wrapped in blankets and tied with lengths of rope twisted out of dried grass.

The three warriors laid their bundles right in the middle of the street, untied them, and unrolled them to reveal a bunch of other much smaller packages wrapped in leather pouches.

The Barbarians got to work unwrapping everything and dumped piles of hand-carved gemstone beads, gold trinkets, and a few luxury items of housewares and clothing accessories.

None of these expensive items could have come from the Barbarians. They must have stolen them from travelers or sacked towns.

Helien broke out of line first, squatted down in front of the gemstone beads, and picked up a blue one.

She held it up to the sunshine and gasped when a shaft of brilliant color radiated through it. "It's so beautiful! I love this red one, too. Oh, look! You're wearing one in your hair, aren't you? Did you make these yourself?"

She actually put out her hand to the man displaying the beads. She fingered a string of similar beads hanging tied into his dark brown hair.

A few other local women came forward to examine the gold jewelry. That set off everyone else.

People gathered from all over town, crowded around the Barbarians' goods, and everyone started talking and haggling in a seamless river of voices.

A few people rushed off to their houses and came back with items of their own. One man raced to the kitchen door behind his house, vanished inside, and came back with a wooden crate full of flecked stone arrowheads.

Another man brought out a box full of wooden children's toys with the marks of a pocketknife still on them.

Three warriors pounced on the box and actually started arguing amongst themselves over which of them would get to trade for which toys.

The noise built to a steady throb as more townsfolk rummaged in their houses, brought out things they wanted to trade for the Barbarian's goods, and other people stepped in either to offer higher prices or different items in exchange.

The crush of bodies around the Barbarians got so thick that Yann backed out of the crowd. He hesitated there and then headed for Eliska's porch.

"That was absolutely incredible," she told him when he got there. "You really missed your calling."

He laughed. "Greed wins again. I knew they would come around once they started talking to each other."

She smiled up at him. "Now you can run for mayor of this town.'

"Naw." He nodded down at her hands. "Did you do what I asked?"

She nodded back at him. "Are you sure you want to do this?"

"I'm sure." He waved at Anríq across the street and Anríq nodded. He and Aja broke off from watching the Barbarians and came over to the porch to join Yann and Eliska.

"Let's get out of here, " Yann told them. "We don't need to stay here anymore."

Eliska didn't raise her staff nor did she cast any binding spell around the party. She wanted to keep the group's departure understated.

Yann had asked her last night to find an Island for the friends to travel to when they left Laval. He didn't want to say goodbye. He just wanted to disappear once the townsfolk and the Barbarians started cooperating with each other.

She magicked the four friends down through the porch and into a Dark Layer shifting with shadows and powerful forces.

She cast an invisible ring of protection around the four of them. Nothing could penetrate that field. Her magic had grown too powerful for that.

She concentrated on the Layer where she'd located the White Spire. It started as a beautiful, thriving landscape full of flowering trees and singing rivers rushing through majestic valleys.

It became a charred, lifeless hellscape as soon as the White Sire appeared there.

She braced herself to fight whatever magical defenses the Voyant set up to defend the spire this time.

The ball of protection broke through three different Layers. It came to a chaos Layer full of rampaging Darklings. Only one Layer remained before the four friends made it back to the White Spire.

At that moment, a powerful hand clamped on Eliska's arm and a torrent of unbelievable magic rushed into her before she even realized enough to protect herself from it.

The fingers crushing her arm felt too bony to belong to either Yann or Anríq. Aja's hand left a skeletal imprint of every bone in her powerful fingers.

Eliska shuddered at the sensation of those bones pushing into Eliska's arm through parchment-paper skin.

The charge of magic coming from the old woman reacted instantly with Eliska's magic and yanked the ball in a completely different direction.

The ball hurtled across the chaos Layer, dodged multiple Darklings, and crashed through a dense wall of Dark power.

Eliska barely had time to see where Aja was sending the party before the ball broke the surface and plummeted out of the sky in a completely different Island.

Eliska didn't have to check her Coil projection. The White Spire definitely wasn't here.

Chapter 41

Eliska's protective ball floated down through the clouds and landed right on the outskirts of a microscopic town.

No more than twenty houses lined a single street that met up with a road twisting and curling into empty countryside from miles in any direction.

"Um....where the hell are we?" Yann demanded.

"I'm not sure." Eliska opened her projection just in case.

She located the Layer Aja had brought the group to, but Eliska didn't see anything about it that would make the old woman bring the friends here.

"Why are we here?" Yann asked. "You said you would take us to the White Spire."

"I tried to, but...." Eliska opened her mouth to explain.

She stopped when Aja burst into a big smile, pressed her hands together, and bowed to all of them.

"She brought us here," Eliska husked. "She used her magic to change our direction through the Layers. She transported us here instead of to the White Spire."

"Why?" Yann turned to Aja. "Why did you bring us here?"

Anríq looked at Aja, too, but the old woman didn't say anything. She just smiled, bowed, and started walking toward the town.

It was really hardly even a hamlet. It wasn't even a village.

Country people in old-fashioned clothes worked in their yards. A man used a stick to herd a bunch of milk cows down the one street and out into the fields.

Eliska didn't see a single fence anywhere. The cows just milled around grazing where they wanted. The man collapsed on the ground nearby and lounged in the sunshine while the animals grazed.

Housewives did their laundry outside. When the three travelers looked in that direction, a different woman opened the window of her house and tossed a pan of dirty water onto the grass.

"It looks like a nice enough Island," Yann remarked. "I wonder why she brought us here."

"It looks like we're about to find out. Look," Eliska pointed out. "She's going into one of the houses."

Aja approached one of the houses. Eliska didn't see anything exceptional or different about it, but every house in the place looked occupied.

"Maybe she knows people here." Yann turned to Anríq. "Do you know this Island? Does your grandmother know people here?"

"I've never been here before," Anríq replied. "She's been a Servant for so long that I wouldn't know where she's been or who she knows. I can't imagine why she would bring us here when she knows we're trying to find the Shard."

"We better go see what she's up to," Eliska suggested. "She must have brought us here for a reason."

She and the boys stared forward. The country people who lived here all nodded and smiled at the three young travelers. Everyone here seemed really nice and friendly—unlike just about every other place the friends had visited.

Eliska picked up their memories. None of these people was haunted by the Dark They had the usual combination of memories, fears, and worries, but nothing close to what she'd seen elsewhere.

The three young people stopped at the door where Aja stood waiting for them. She didn't knock.

She pushed the door open and let it swing inward. Then she stood back and cast the most beaming smile imaginable on all of them.

"What are we doing here?" Yann asked. "Why did you bring us here?"

Aja shut her eyes, pressed her hands together, bowed, and turned and walked away. She headed up the road heading east.

Eliska, Yann, and Anríq all turned to look inside the house. It was uninhabited, but it wasn't empty.

A crushing grip of something like fear or maybe sinking inevitability took hold of Eliska's heart when she looked into that house. Whatever was in here must be really big—even bigger than the Dark power at the Keepers of the Dawn's monastery.

Some mysterious force pulled her across the threshold. She felt her legs taking steps to enter the room and then her body turning to look around.

A collection of quaint, tidy, comfortable furniture filled the front room. It looked similar to the cottage where the friends spent the night in the Island of the lost.

This house was bigger with a rocking chair by the fire and more space between the big table, hewn wooden benches, and large, glass windows letting sunshine stream in from outside.

The house didn't have a bed in the main room. Three good-sized bedrooms split off from the main room.

The house even had a small library attached to the living room. A big wooden desk and a bunch of books on bookshelves gave the library a cozy, warm, inviting feel.

The sunshine twinkled on rows of colorfully painted plates standing on the kitchen dresser. A white porcelain sink sat embedded in a polished wooden counter on one side of the living room.

A single wooden door separated the kitchen from a small pantry on the back of the house. It connected to a broom closet and the back door leading outside into the fields.

A man's coat hung from a hook on the back of the front door. A woman's apron lay folded on the kitchen counter right next to the sink along with a hand towel.

A knitted woolen blanket draped over the rocking chair. A tiny wooden cradle sat next to the rocking chair with a child's wooden stool there, too.

A hand-stitched rag doll lay in the cradle under a patchwork quilt. The doll smiled up at the world with big, embroidered yarn eyes and a sewn-on mouth.

A wooden rocking horse occupied a place near the fire. Someone had pushed the horse against the wall to make more space in the living room.

Not a speck of dust covered any surface in the whole house. Every inch of it shone with freshness. All the beds had been made perfectly and the kitchen counter and table scrubbed to a high shine.

Eliska, Yann, and Anríq spread out through the house. Eliska didn't see anything out of place—not at first.

This agonizing sinking feeling in the middle of her chest—it only got stronger as she passed from one item to the next. She looked into each of the bedrooms......and stopped in front of the fireplace.

The bottom dropped out of her world when she saw a bunch of pictures on the mantel shelf.

They showed a family of four—a mother, father, a little boy, and a baby girl barely old enough to walk.

The first picture showed the mother sitting outside in the sunshine with the little girl on her lap. The boy leaned against his mother's side with his arms wrapped tightly around her arm.

The father stood behind them with one hand resting on his wife's shoulder and the other on his son's shoulder.

Eliska's heart stopped at the sight of the man. She would have recognized him anywhere. It was Yvan Dilnao, but he looked twenty years younger than she remembered him.

He wasn't wearing a uniform from the Black Watch. He couldn't have. He wouldn't have a wife and children if he'd been a member of the Watch.

The picture changed before her eyes. Someone had put a spell on the picture to make it change.

It morphed and the people in it changed their appearance. The two parents started to age—and so did the children. They got bigger. The girl grew too big to sit on her mother's lap.

The picture changed so it showed the woman standing up with the two children standing in front of her.

Her husband laid his arm over her shoulder and put his other hand in front of his son's chest to hold him in position.

The children kept growing. The parents' faces became lined and weathered. Grey hair appeared at the corners of Yvan's forehead. The pouches under his eyes drooped as he aged.

The children grew taller. The boy grew taller than his father. The boy's shoulders widened and his features became more chiseled and distinct. His hair grew and formed a cap of brown curls on top of his head.

The girl got taller, too—taller than her mother, but not as tall as her father or her brother. Her hair got darker.....and longer......

The boy started out wearing regular country clothes like everyone else in this town, but after a while his clothes changed—and so did his father's. The picture showed them both wearing uniforms of the Black Watch. Yvan wore a gold oak leaf on his collar.

Eliska swallowed hard, but she couldn't move in any other way. Her awareness zeroed in on the picture of the girl.

She developed a haunted look around her eyes and mouth. Her jawline became hardened with intensity and guarded determination.

Her clothes changed to a patched collection of ragged castoffs. She wore a black cloak around her shoulders and she carried a long wooden staff that she rested on the ground at her feet.

She leaned on it in the picture and started out at the of the picture with a challenging, resentful expression.

Eliska was staring at a picture of herself.

Chapter 42

Yann covered his face with his hand and rubbed his eyes. He still struggled to accept what he'd seen in that house. He and Eliska were brother and sister.

Yann forced himself to look up and open his eyes. He surveyed the countryside surrounding the little hamlet.

It looked so serene and untouched—like nothing bad could ever happen here. Something bad did happen here. It must have.

He spotted one speck of greyish-white in the landscape at a distance. Something sat against a hillside far away. He couldn't exactly see what it was from here. He didn't have to see. Marine must have followed the travelers here. Of course she did.

He had to summon every ounce of his willpower not to go out there and talk to her.

He already knew what he would find if he did. He didn't hate himself enough to put himself through that kind of torture.

He rubbed his eyes again. He really didn't want to be conscious right now. He couldn't cope with everything going on in his head right now.

Just when he thought his ordeal couldn't get any worse, Anríq walked up to him and stopped at Yann's side.

"Where's your grandmother?" Yann asked over his shoulder.

"She's gone. I've searched the whole town. She must have traveled to another Layer. She isn't here anymore."

"So she brought us here...so we could find out about this?" Yann snorted. "Great."

"I assume she brought us here to heal Eliska."

"Heal Eliska!" Yann heard his voice rising. "How is *this* supposed to heal Eliska? It didn't take her Darkness away, did it?"

"No, not that. I meant the other thing."

Yann spun around to glare at his friend. "What are you talking about?"

"She needed healing—before—before I ever met her. I assume it was there before *you* ever met her. It had nothing to do with her taking Barsali's Darkness or anything like that. It was something else—something she's been carrying around for a long time. I couldn't heal her of it. I don't know if this will do it, but she needed something—something none of us can give her."

Yann whirled the other way. He couldn't stand to look at Anríq. He knew too much—about all of them. He knew the worst and yet he just kept sticking around.

He kept witnessing every terrible thing that happened to both Yann and Eliska. Anríq was the one person who stayed with them through it all.

His heavy hand fell on Yann's shoulder. "Maybe you needed healing, too. Maybe you needed to see this. In fact, I know you did. You didn't know where you stood with Eliska and now you do. That must be why Aja brought you both here."

Yann couldn't think. He stared out at the countryside and did his best not to see Marine out there.

"So much of this makes sense, you know?" he husked. "It all makes sense somehow—all except the part about my father not telling me the truth. I mean, obviously he couldn't tell me the truth because he didn't know who she was. She went into the Coil alone when she was just little and I remember him in Middleborough when I was little. He couldn't have known who she was."

"Of course not," Anríq replied.

"Do you want to know the weirdest part?"

"What is that?" Anríq asked.

"He was like a father to her. She didn't like him at first, but after a while, he became the father she never had. It was eerie to see them together. I thought at the time...." Yann trailed off.

"Did you think there was anything wrong about it?" Anríq asked.

"No, nothing like that. I thought it would be good for her to have someone like him. She needed that.....but it was just strange. It was.....it was almost like it was meant to be.....and then he died...."

Yann choked and turned all the way away to hide his anguish from Anríq.

Yann tried to block out his father's dying words, but they came back anyway. They would haunt Yann for the rest of his life. *I'm sorry.....I should have told you......*

What should Yvan have told Yann before he died—that he had a sister somewhere? Or a mother?

Yann clamped his eyes shut against a tide of pain. His father was dead. Now Yann would never be able to ask all the questions crowding his mind.

Who was Yann and Eliska's mother? Where was she? How did Yvan get separated from her and Eliska? Did Yvan and his wife have other family somewhere else?

Anríq took a deep breath like he had to build up his courage to speak again. "I need you to come back to the house with me."

"What for?"

"I need you to help me help Eliska. She's in trouble."

Yann whipped around fast. "How is she in trouble?'

"This truth—it's bringing up her Darkness. She's trapped in it and she can't get out."

"I don't understand."

"Come with me and I'll show you."

Yann turned away with a heavy sigh. He would have to live with this information for the rest of his life—and with all the information this discovery didn't bring him.

None of that would get resolved.

They would have to leave this Island soon. He would take all this information with him.

He would probably never get the answers he wanted because his father wouldn't be around to give them.

The two boys headed back into town. Yann dreaded seeing Eliska again. He didn't know how to deal with her.

Their relationship had been borderline romantic before she took on all this Darkness. He had been able to see himself getting together with her so many times.

Even his brief romance with Marine didn't really change his impression that he would probably wind up with Eliska.

He never once entertained the possibility that he and Marine might wind up together. That was never going to happen—and now she was completely out of her mind.

Now he lost Eliska, too—but also gained her in ways he never had her before.

He'd been an only child all his life. In a way, he'd been the only child to all the other Watchmen, too. Each of those men treated Yann like his own son.

Yann always wished he had a sibling—at least one. Should he be happy about this or not?

He really didn't want to find out what was wrong with Eliska. Anríq made it sound like she wasn't taking this very well—and who could blame her? Yann wasn't taking it very well, either.

He really hoped this didn't tear them apart. He hoped their feelings for each other didn't change because of this—and yet they already had changed.

He and Eliska couldn't possibly stay the same, now that they knew the truth about themselves and each other.

The same collection of country people smiled, nodded, and greeted the boys on their way back to the house—the house Yvan shared with his wife.

Yann didn't even know her name. He didn't know his own mother's name. Who was she? How did they meet?

No way in hell could Yann asked Eliska to use her Coil projection to find out. If she didn't look on her own, he couldn't ask.

At least this settled the question of the Voyant being her father. Yann almost wished he was.

The two boys passed down the street. Just before they turned into the garden path leading to the front door, a different older woman approached them from the other end of the village.

She burst into a big grin when she saw Yann. "It's so wonderful that someone is taking an interest in this house. It's been standing empty for so long—and the people who lived there were so nice.'

"Did you know them?" Yann asked.

"Of course!" the old woman exclaimed. "I helped them move in! They were such a nice young couple then."

"Soo....." Yann's heart started racing. "Was that before they had children?"

"Oh yes!" The woman beamed. "They were just young lovers—and so in love! They couldn't take their eyes off each other."

"Do you remember the woman's name?" Yann asked.

The old woman frowned. "Hmm.... Let me see.....The boy's name was......

"Yvan," Yann interrupted.

She exploded in a huge smile "Of course. I remember now. Yvan and Alexiane. Alexiane LaFauve. She was beautiful—and he wasn't too bad to look at, either." She blushed and burst out laughing.

Yann found himself smiling at her. "Do you remember what happened to them? How long did they live here before they left?"

"Oh, I'd say it must have been about five years. They had the little boy first and then the little girl."

"So what happened? Why did they leave?"

The old woman's features darkened, "I couldn't tell you exactly, but we started to have a few spates of instability—nothing serious, you know—just enough to throw the countryside into chaos. Then it all settled down. It was during one of those when the father and the boy disappeared."

Yann's heart sank. "And the little girl?"

"I don't know what happened to her or the mother. They both vanished without a trace. We just woke up one morning and they were both gone. That was about a year after the man and the boy disappeared. We figured the mother took the little girl back to her own people. She was heartbroken when her husband didn't come back. She waited, but you could see it wearing on her more and more every day to carry on alone. Everyone around here tried to help her, but eventually we all just told her to take her daughter and go back to her family. It was for the best."

Yann glanced toward the house. "Something must have happened. They must have gotten caught in another upheaval."

The woman frowned. "What makes you say that?"

"Never mind. I'm just thinking out loud."

She brightened up immediately. "Do you boys plan to stay in the country? This old house needs people to look after it."

"I don't know what our plans are. Thank you for telling us about the people who lived here. I really appreciate it."

She squeezed his arm. "Anything I can do to help. I live right over there. Let me know if you need anything."

She bustled off down the street heading somewhere else. Yann stayed where he was starting at the house—the house where he'd been born.

So he and his father got separated from the other two during an instability cycle. Yvan must have taken Yann to another Layer and gotten stuck there. He didn't have the magic to find his way back to his wife and daughter.

Eliska must have gotten separated from her mother in another upheaval. Yann couldn't think of any other logical explanation for why their mother would abandon a little girl in the Coil.

Eliska said she searched for her family for years and never even found the Island they came from. She said the Layer collapsed long ago.

The Layer might have gone through waves of instability that concealed it or at least stopped her from finding it.

She couldn't use her gold and silver lines back then. She would have no way of knowing which Layer was the right one.

The Island could have traveled anywhere in the Coil. It must have traveled somewhere she couldn't find it.

Yann's heart twisted at the thought of her wandering alone all those years. She must have been desperate and so lonely.

Yann wanted to cry when he thought about her as a little girl with no one. He would have given anything to find her and take her home to the Black Watch's house in Middleborough.

Yvan must have been suffering the same torment—except that he didn't know his daughter was alone. He never found out what happened to his wife and daughter.

He would have given anything to help her, too, if he only knew. He would have raised Yann and Eliska together. They would have grown up together. She would have learned to fight on the wall with the Watchmen.

She wouldn't have grown up thinking she would become one of them, though.

Yann couldn't imagine what she would have become if she'd had a father, a brother, and a bunch of Watchmen looking after her.

She wouldn't have become this grim, hardened Coil rat. She might have been as fun-loving and lighthearted as Marine if things had only played out differently for all of them.

Chapter 43

Eliska sat in her mother's rocking chair, cradled the doll in her arms, and rocked in front of the fire. She stroked her finger down the doll's cheeks and let the memories wash over her.

Alexiane LaFauve sat in this chair and rocked baby Eliska in her arms just like this. Alexiane stroked baby Eliska's hair just like this and sang to her.

Alexiane held Eliska against her body while the mother put little Yann to bed.

She kissed him, petted his face and hair, rubbed his arms and back, and murmured to him how much she loved him before she blew out the candle to darken the room.

Eliska swayed in the halo of all those memories. She experienced the rush of love when Yvan came back to the house at the end of his day's work.

She suffered soul-crushing happiness when she laid her baby daughter in her cradle and rocked the little girl to sleep.

That magical, blissful curtain of love surrounded Eliska and blocked out everything else.

Her own Dark power didn't let her remember anything else from anyone else. None of the other memories intruded on this beautiful world overflowing with love. She never wanted to leave and now she never had to.

She didn't let herself find out where Yvan and Alexiane came from.

She didn't let herself find out how they met or if they had any other family or even what happened to them afterward that separated them from each other.

Eliska didn't want to know any of that and she never had to.

She shut herself off from everything outside this one room. She could preserve baby Eliska and little Yann in this bubble of love and happiness. She poured out all the mother's love on both children.

Eliska didn't have to feel the aching terror, rage, and longing of living without her family all those years. She wasn't Eliska. She was Alexiane preserved in this memory forever.

She also didn't have to feel the desperation and hopeless resignation when Yvan realized he could never get back to his wife and daughter.

She didn't allow herself even to look at the memories of how much he struggled against despair when he had to raise Yann alone with only the other Watchmen for help.

None of that existed in this room. Eliska occasionally slipped into her own infant memories of gazing up at her mother's face.

Awe and angelic worship overpowered her senses. She loved her mother beyond comprehension, but Eliska's mind hadn't been able to understand anything else.

She'd barely registered that she had a father and it took her a long time even to understand what that meant. She didn't understand at all that she had a brother.

All the other memories in this room came from Alexiane. She showered both children with constant care and affection. She attended to every discomfort and distress. She soothed all their fears and surrounded them in an endless bath of blissful love.

Eliska felt all of that when she gazed down at the doll, but she didn't see a doll. She saw an immaculate baby girl with bottomless brown eyes and a fuzz of brown hair on her velvet-soft head.

The baby's tiny fingers and ears enchanted her beyond anything she'd ever experienced in her life.

She thanked Heaven every day for her children. She could sit and gaze at them for hours.

Then came the memories of Yvan coming home from work. Then all four of them basked in the angelic clouds of love radiating between all of them.

Both parents overflowed with love for both children and for each other.

The children only enhanced the bond between Yvan and Alexiane. They adored each other and clung to every day, every hour they got to spend together.

They loved each other desperately, graspingly—almost as if they both knew it couldn't last.....

But Eliska didn't let herself think that.

She rocked the chair and hugged the baby close while she sang songs. She picked them up from different memories of all the people she'd absorbed in the last few days.

Her magic blocked every detail of those people's memories except the songs and how to sing them. She poured all her emotion into the songs.

Her voice resounded through the house and Yann stirred in the bed nearby, but he didn't wake up. He just settled down and sank deeper into a peaceful sleep.

Any minute now, that door would open and Yvan would come home from work. He would bend over her chair, kiss her, and then kiss the baby.

The love between them would pass between his eyes and hers. They would share all the knowing and heartfelt connection of two souls bound together for all eternity. Nothing could ever change the way they felt about each other.

The door opened. She looked up and burst into a huge smile when she saw him. He looked so handsome and strong.

His brown eyes found hers, but he didn't smile. He stepped into the room.

Just for a second, the sunshine streaming through the door from outside thinned the veil between reality and illusion. It wasn't night-time. He should have been at work.

He advanced halfway into the room, but he didn't smile or kiss her or even look at the baby.

Actually he did look at the baby. He glanced down at the bundle in her arms and his features spasmed in a disgusted grimace.

A pang of doubt stabbed her in the heart and then the worst thing of all happened when a tall, broad-shouldered Barbarian walked into the house.

He wore his hair long with beads, shells, and colored stones tied into his dreadlocks. His leather vest hung open to reveal the Servant's mark tattooed across his chiseled body.

He narrowed his eyes at her, too. "You have to leave here, Eliska," the Servant told her.

"What?! No!" She tried to sit a little deeper in her chair. "You can't make me leave my family!" She spun around and yelled up at her husband. "Tell him, Yvan! Tell him we can't leave! We have to stay here and take care of the children! You promised we would."

Yvan's face spasmed in misery. "This isn't you, Eliska," he husked. "I'm not Yvan. I'm Yann. I'm all grown up and you're Eliska. You aren't Alexiane. Alexiane and Yvan are gone and..." He choked on the words. "Yvan is dead."

"NO!!" she bellowed. "He can't be!"

He and the Servant advanced toward her chair. They were going to do something terrible—like take her baby away. She saw it all in the hardened cruelty of their expressions.

"You haven't lived in this house since you were a baby," Yvan went on. "You got separated from your mother—and Father and I got separated to Middleborough. He never found out what happened to you. That's how you wound up alone in the Coil. It was an accident."

His voice broke and tears sprang to his eyes at those words, but that only made her panic even more. She shot out of her chair clutching her daughter tighter.

"You stay away from me! Don't you dare come near my children!" She backed up closer to Yann's bed. He still didn't wake up even though she bellowed at these strangers at full volume.

Yvan and the Servant flanked her on both sides. She cast a desperate glance from left to right trying to find something to fight them with, but she couldn't do that holding the baby in her arms.

She couldn't keep track of both Yvan and the Servant at the same time. They widened their positions so she had to face one or the other. She couldn't confront them both.

She jerked right and left trying to keep them both in sight.

The instant she faced Yvan, the Servant did something. She didn't see what it was. A shimmering pulse of magic covered her for a split second—just long enough to immobilize her.

He charged her from the side, collided with her, and seized her just as the spell evaporated.

She screamed and then roared at him struggling with all her might to break free, but he overpowered her easily.

She kicked out and he lifted her feet off the ground. She thrashed in all directions trying to wrench herself out of his arms, but he only tightened them to crush her against his enormous, rock-sold frame.

Yvan charged her from the other side. The instant the Servant grabbed her, Yvan tore the baby out of her arms, took one last disgusted look at it, and tossed it on the bed.

It landed face down and bounced. In that awful moment, she saw for one instant that little Yann wasn't there. He wasn't lying asleep where she left him.

The baby girl turned into a ragdoll and fell on its side with its arms and legs tangled up with each other. Its yarn mouth kept smiling at nothing.

The next instant, the illusion flared to life as strong as ever and wiped out what she'd just seen. These fiends were trying to take her children away from her.

Yvan couldn't be dead. No way. She loved him too much. She needed to spend the rest of her life with him. He had to come back.

The Servant backed across the living room. She went ballistic when she saw him trying to get her toward the door to take her outside.

She shrieked and thrashed and roared and kicked. Yvan moved the furniture out of the way to make room for them.

She couldn't overcome the Servant's strength. He held her in front of him so her feet could only kick in one direction—away from him.

He angled through the door and hauled her outside into the light of day where all the neighbors could see and hear exactly what was going on.

Chapter 44

Yann went through the little house, tucked the doll back into its cradle, and positioned the tiny patchwork quilt over the doll's chest.

He put it back into the position it had been lying when he and Eliska first entered this room.

He found himself lingering over the doll and letting his fingers trail through its hair and down its cheeks.

He didn't have to think too hard about what Eliska saw in her hallucinations or how she got trapped in memories of the past. She must have been so precious as a baby.

The look of pure love and happiness on her face when she looked down at the doll in her arms—Alexiane must have loved Yann and Eliska beyond anything.

Who wouldn't want to stay in that memory forever? Yann really wished he could.

He hated to take Eliska out of it, but Aja didn't bring Eliska here so she could disappear into the past. Aja didn't bring either Yann or Eliska here for that.

He went through the whole house, straightened all the beds, and wiped any dust off the table, the kitchen counter, and all the bookshelves.

He stopped in front of the mantelshelf and looked at the pictures for the last time.

They kept changing as Yann and Eliska grew up and Yvan and Alexiane aged.

They didn't grow up and grow old as a loving family the way they appeared in the picture. They couldn't because they were never together as adults.

Who magicked this picture to show them all as they would appear now? Did Alexiane do it? Was she a magic user? How else would Eliska become one?

Alexiane might have magicked the picture so she could see Yann and Yvan after they got separated from her. Maybe Alexiane thought they would never come back and she wanted to watch Yann grow up even if they weren't here.

Now Yann and Eliska had to face the future no matter what it brought.

Yann had become something more than her brother these last few weeks. He'd taken charge of this group—for whatever that was worth.

Anríq and Eliska both needed Yann to step up and be the man his father raised him to be. Yann had become that man ever since he left Middleborough.

He couldn't let his father down now—or any of the other Watchmen down.

Eliska needed Yann more than ever now. She needed a brother who would take care of her exactly the way Yann had been taking care of her all this time.

He watched the picture come to the point where Yann and Eliska were both fully grown. Yann stood three inches taller than his father. They both wore uniforms from the Black Watch.

Eliska leaned on her staff and glared out at the viewer with that same expression of hostile contempt he recognized from her very first night in Middleborough.

Then the picture changed back to Alexiane sitting down with baby Eliska on her lap and little Yann leaning against her side while Yvan stood behind them.

The cycle started all over again with the picture changing to each stage of the family's growth and ageing process.

Yann watched it for a long time. He didn't want to leave, either. He wanted to stay here forever, but his parents' absence ruined the illusion.

Their family didn't live here. They might have lived here for a few years before they got separated. They had never really been a family here—not in any way that meant anything.

He really just wanted his father back. Staying here hurt far worse than losing Yvan in the first place. Staying here slapped Yann with the unavoidable fact that he would never see his father again.

Yann would never again feel how much his father loved him. Yann would never again get that feeling that his father was proud of him. Yann would rather go out into the Coil alone than face the nightmare of staying in this house another second.

He returned to the front door and cast one last long look around the room. He and Eliska could have had such a beautiful childhood if the Coil hadn't shifted and separated them from each other.

He took a step back and closed the door on those memories. They would stay here entombed in the past, never to rise again.

No one could give Eliska back the childhood she should have had. No one could give Yann his mother back or tear down the wall Eliska built around herself to protect her from all the dangers she must have faced.

Now Yann was all she had left. He couldn't take himself away from her—not ever again.

He headed out of town on the eastbound road—in the opposite direction the friends had entered this town.

He didn't give himself the option to talk to or even make eye contact with any of the neighbors. They were all part of his past.

Eliska was his future. She was his only future.

He followed the road over a hill and spotted Anríq standing under a tree to the left. Anríq leaned his beefy shoulder against the trunk and stared off into the countryside.

Yann stopped at his side. Anríq didn't move. He kept his narrowed eyes locked on a tiny figure in the distance.

She sat on a fallen log a few hundred yards from the road. She kept her back to the world and her shoulders hunched.

She looked so lonely out there all by herself.

"Have you tried to talk to her?" Yann asked.

Anríq didn't turn around. He kept looking at her and her alone. "You better do it. She needs you right now, not me."

Yann didn't want to face her, but he couldn't leave her out there alone.

She needed him, but as soon as Anríq said those words, Yann realized the terrible truth. He needed her just as much if not more.

She was the only family he had left. She was the last thing in the world he could truly call his own. He'd already lost everyone and everything else that ever meant anything to him.

Irresistible magnetic gravity pulled him toward her.

She was his sister.

Those words burned a hole in his mind all the way across the fields to where she sat. His sister.

The words did something to him—something that could never happen from him putting his arms around her or kissing her hair or falling asleep with her on the boat.

She didn't react at all when he sat down on the log next to her. She kept staring across the countryside with tears streaming down her cheeks.

Overpowering love tore him in half at the sight of her. This precious child had been all alone.

She had been all alone even when her father and brother had been standing right in front of her. That's when she was the most alone.

He didn't hesitate to put his arm around her. He hugged her tight against him and kissed the side of her head. The feeling pouring out of him when he did it—he could barely survive it. He loved her beyond words.

"I'm glad I know now," he murmured in her ear. "I'm glad I know and I'm glad we're together. It explains why I love you the way I do.....and now I can love you as much as I want to. I'm glad I have you. I never want to lose you—not ever again. I want to give you everything.....and be everything to you that you need me to be. What happened before—whatever happened with our parents—it didn't have anything to do with us—but we can be like that again. We can be like that now. We can be the way we were back then—because I love you."

She didn't make a sound. She didn't acknowledge even by a sound that she heard what he said.

She kept her eyes locked on the distant hills while tears streaked down her cheeks one after the other. She didn't try to wipe them away.

He already knew what she saw out there. He even knew what she felt about it and he didn't try to stop those tears.

These tears of hers were a drop in the ocean compared to what she must be thinking and feeling right now.

He squeezed her tighter one last time and kissed her again. He didn't ask her to stand up and move on. He just sat there with her in the silence of all those memories.

They had both been loved beyond words. Yvan loved Eliska as much as if she was his own daughter. Yann knew that even while Yvan had been alive. Yvan would have sacrificed his own life to give her back just a little of what she lost.

Yann settled in to wait as long as it took for her to be ready to go.

He stared off into the distance and let a thousand memories wash over him.

He remembered every detail of his childhood in Middleborough. He remembered every word, every look, every command, and every embrace his father ever gave him.

Yann grew up worshiping his father and wanting nothing but to be exactly like him.

Yann even remembered things he couldn't possibly know—like memories of Yvan's marriage to Alexiane when Yann and Eliska were small.

Memories from the Watchmen got all mixed up in those memories—and memories of the party's journey through the Coil—memories of the Watchmen's interactions with Eliska—and all the times she helped them and they helped her.

They had become a family—as much a family as Yann could ever want. Those memories gave him as much peace as he could ever ask for from the pain of losing all of them. He still had them with him.

Without warning, Eliska leaned over and rested her head on his shoulder. She let her weight fall against him and she softened in his arm and sniffed.

That feeling of her finally releasing herself in him—he couldn't stand it. He kissed her hair again and let his mouth linger on her scalp.

He shut his eyes and let all that emotion flood him. He had her. She was his last, most precious treasure and now he had her.

Chapter 45

Yann pulled Eliska's cloak a little tighter around her shoulders and pushed against her shoulder even though she was already lying down on the ground. She curled up on her side next to the campfire. The flames glowed on her cheeks.

He let his hand run down her hair, rubbed her back once, and sat down next to her. He left his hand resting on her shoulder.

"Go to sleep," he told her. "We'll have plenty of miles to cover tomorrow before we leave this Island."

She shut her eyes immediately. She'd been walking around in a numb trance all day while she and the two boys trekked across the countryside.

Anríq could have taken the three friends out of this Island to another Layer.

He and Yann probably could have brought Eliska out of her stupor enough to locate the White Spire in whichever Layer it happened to be now.

Neither of the boys mentioned it. Neither of them even suggested leaving this Island.

They just got Eliska as far away from her hometown as possible so she wouldn't slip back into the illusion that tapped her there.

Yann waited until he felt her melt into sleep. Her breathing length-ened before he took his hand off her shoulder. He turned back to the fire and stared down into the flames.

Anríq sat across from him and worked on his axe in his lap. He unwound the leather strap from the handle, tightened it, and used the thumb of his other hand to hold it in place while he rewrapped it.

Yann watched him for a while until Yann decided how to break the silence. "I'm sorry," he blurted out.

Anríq's head shot up. "What for? You have nothing to be sorry about."

"I'm sorry....for what I said about you and Eliska....about you lead-ing her on. That was wrong of me."

"Not at all," Anríq insisted. "You were right. Nothing can happen between us now. She couldn't tolerate it."

"You should," Yann insisted. "I think you should."

Anríq gaped at him across the fire. "You can't be serious—not when she's like this."

"She needs you. She needs you more than she needs me. I'm sorry I came between you two before. I knew something was developing between you and I felt threatened by that."

"No, you didn't," Anríq countered. "You said it because you were concerned that our relationship would hurt her—and you were right."

"No." Yann shook his head. "It won't hurt her. It might be the only thing that can heal her. Did you ever think of that?"

Anríq bent over his axe, started rewinding the strap again, and compressed his lips. "I can't heal her, Yann. I wish I could. You don't understand...."

"I understand." Yann heard the ice in his voice. "I understand a lot better than you think—and I know she needs you. She needs all of you.

She needs to know that you feel the same way about her that she feels about you."

Yann shook his head fast. He had to say this, so he poured it all out in a rush.

"Listen to me. We both thought she was too hurt to do any-thing—and that was a mistake. Don't you get it? She needs to know you love her as much as you do. I know you do. She needs to see that she isn't so messed up that you won't go as far as she needs you to go—because she isn't too messed up. She's been through a lot, but she's stronger than any of us realizes. If she can survive all those years alone in the Coil, she can damn sure handle getting together with you. No way can you convince me otherwise. Getting together with you could be the best thing that ever happened to her. How can you hold that back from her? How can you hold anything back from her when it might be healing for her? What else could possibly heal her besides you loving her?"

Anríq scowled down at his hands. He didn't stop working.

Yann waited for him to say something. Anríq didn't break the silence.

Yann might have crossed a line here. In fact, he knew he did. He crossed a line that could never be uncrossed, but he had to do it for both of them.

"I can't think of any man I would rather see her get together with," Yann finally finished. "She deserves you and you deserve her. You were made for each other."

"You're a much better man than I am, Yann," Anríq muttered.

"Well, I can't get together with her. I'm her brother, so it's up to me to make sure the man who does get together with her is the best that she deserves. Who else would that be besides you? Who else in the world loves her as much as you do? Who else could possibly love her the way you do?"

"I have nothing..." Anríq broke off with a choking sound.

"You have you. She doesn't want anything else. You know she doesn't. You're already everything she wants and needs. You know everything there is to know about her. I wouldn't trust her with anyone else."

Anríq fell into a long silence. He finished tucking in the strap on his axe handle, checked it a few dozen times, clenched his fist around it, and eventually he laid the weapon aside.

He didn't speak. He stared into the flames with his brow furrowed in thought.

Yann watched him for a while and then turned to look down at Eliska. Just looking at her face confirmed more than anything that he was right. She didn't need Anríq holding himself at a distance to protect her.

She needed him. She needed to know she was good enough for him. She needed to know that he would go to any lengths for her—because he would.

Just looking at her sealed something that Yann hadn't been sure of before. Now he was sure. She and Anríq belonged together.

Them getting together repaired something that had been broken before. It was still broken because they weren't together yet.

It would be repaired as soon as they got together. Yann wanted that more than anything. He wanted it for both of them.

They would only become healed and whole once they both gave themselves to each other with nothing holding them back. It was the only healing left for either of them.

Anríq snapped Yann out of his thoughts. "I'm sorry, too, Yann......I'm sorry about Marine."

Yann clamped his eyes shut against an unbearable tide of anguish and loss. This was so much worse than anything he experienced when he found out about his parents.

Marine had been that for him. She had been the missing piece—and now she was gone. He didn't even know where she was.

Wherever she was, she was gone. The beautiful princess he loved so much—she got lost under all that insanity. She wouldn't come back—not the way she had been before.

Whatever healing he got from talking about his doubts with Anríq—that was nothing compared to this.

No one would ever be able to heal Yann from this because the cure was gone.

Anríq's voice floated out of the darkness. Yann couldn't even look at his friend—the one person who understood.

"I think we should take Marine to the nearest order of the Guardian Templars," Anríq murmured. "I don't think we should let her travel with us anymore. The Templars will be able to look after her. It's too dangerous for her to go back to the White Spire with us. Eliska's magic will be strong enough for us to confront the Voyant if anyone's magic is strong enough for that. We won't be doing Marine any favors by letting her stay out here."

Yann gulped down a lump in his throat and his vision blurred. He couldn't see Eliska anymore, so he turned back to the fire. Another cascade of memories from his time with Marine in Savaré overwhelmed him.

He knew then that his time with her was limited. He'd been a condemned mean even then, but at least he got to enjoy her while it lasted.

Anríq got to his feet, took a few steps around the fire, and crushed Yann's shoulder in a death grip.

That sensation shot a lightning bolt through Yann's being. Despair dragged him to the ground. The next minute, Anríq walked off into the dark and left Yann sitting there alone with all those memories.

No one would ever admire or appreciate Marine ever again. She would never marry a prince or have a bunch of little princes and princesses or wear all her finery to church the way she should have.

Yann would have paid any price to see her like that on the arm of another man just to know she was happy instead of some raving lunatic lost in the Coil.

Where was she now? Was she floating in some Dark Layer? Was she sleeping on the ground out in the cold dark night right now?

He buried his face in his hands and shuddered at the thought. What he wouldn't give for just one more hour with her—just one more look into her eyes gazing back at him with that mischievous twinkle he knew so well.

Chapter 46

Eliska opened her Coil projection and pointed to one of the silver lines. "There she is. Marine's right there. She's only half a mile away from us. She's following us the way she did before."

Anríq pointed to a blur of instability right next to a burst of magic erupting out of the Coil at the end of Marine's line. "What is that?"

"It's her magic. She must be shooting off at someone or something—or maybe no one. I'm not picking up anyone or anything near her."

Yann winced. "Just find the nearest Temple we could take her back to. She said the Temples block Dark magic. She should recover once she gets back inside.?

"Then what's to stop the Templars from sending her back out?" Eliska asked.

"We'll just have to explain the situation to them. We'll have to explain that she went too far out into the Dark and she needs to stay in the Temple for the duration of the war."

"She won't like that," Eliska remarked.

Yann fought his voice under control. "I really don't care if she likes it or not."

She rested her hand on his arm. "Okay," she murmured. "We'll take her to safety. It's the best thing for her."

Yann pinched his lips to stop himself from losing his composure completely. "Just find the Temple. Please."

She turned back to the projection. Something had happened to Yann—something more than just finding out that Eliska was his sister and Yvan Dilnao had been their father.

Yann had become increasingly touchy on the subject of Marine. His conversation with Anríq last night had pushed him over the edge.

She didn't look at him again. She concentrated on finding the closest Guardian Temple, but she felt his agitation building to the breaking point.

He needed to take Marine to safety for his own sanity. He couldn't stand to see her lurking in the Coil and gnashing her teeth at Dark forces.

She pointed at a different Layer. "The Layer is unstable, but it isn't collapsing completely. The Temple is under assault from Dark forces."

"It looks like the Temple itself is holding steady," Anríq pointed out.

Eliska revolved the projection somewhere else. "I don't see any other intact Temples—none that are in as stable an Island as that one. That one looks like our best bet."

"So we'll have to fight our way inside," Yann remarked.

"I'm afraid so. The Temple's defenses will block me from magicking us straight inside the walls, so I'll have to transport us somewhere in the instability. Then we'll have to get past the instability and breach the defenses and any other Dark forces hanging around before we get in."

Yann puffed out his cheeks. "Maye this isn't such a great idea."

"I think we should do it. We would want her and anyone else to do the same thing for us if we were in her position. She's gotten us this far. She needs to get somewhere safe before she gets hurt or before she can't come back from the Dark at all."

Yann nodded down at the projection. "Just do it. Do whatever you have to do."

She closed the projection. "I'll magick us to her location, use a binding spell to grab her, and then magick all of us to the Layer where the temple is. Then it will all be on while we fight our way through the defenses."

Anríq took down his axe. "Do it."

She raised her staff. Transporting the four friends to the Guardian Temple would be easy. She could transport them across the Layers to the Temple with just a thought.

She couldn't imagine what would happen when she transported them all into the instability, but the three friends committed themselves to this path.

So did Marine. She was the one who encouraged all of them to follow this path so at least one of them could take the Shard of Hotha at the end of it.

Marine probably never imagined she would be the first to fall. Now it was happening. Eliska didn't want to face that moment when she left Marine behind and set off alone with just the two boys.

The four of them had been a unit for so long. Eliska didn't want that to end, but it was too late to back out now.

She took a deep breath and blinked all three of the friends to Marine's location.

She was in the middle of a thicket somewhere between two larger towns. She crouched in the bushes snarling and hissing at her Dark forces while workmen plowed a field just a few dozen yards away from her.

She kept blasting off random magical charges that disturbed the undergrowth. The workmen saw the commotion and it bothered them, but they didn't realize what caused it.

They kept shooting sidelong frowns toward the woods before they plowed away to the other side of the field.

Eliska magicked herself, Anríq, and Yann into the thicket right next to Marine. The three travelers crashed down in the dry shrubs and practically landed right on top of her.

The three friends broke branches and startled Marine out of her wits. She shrieked and spun around.

Her magic must have flown totally out of control. Anríq dove in to grab her and she plastered him in the face with a fountain of wild magic shooting from her mouth.

Her hair spun around her head when she whipped right and left trying to attack all three friends at once.

She flattened Anríq in a split second and Yann rushed her from behind in an exact reverse move of the one the boys pulled on Eliska in her mother's cottage.

Marine turned her eruption on Eliska next. Yann got his arms around Marine, but she ejected another concussion out of her back and sent him flying.

Eliska ducked to avoid Marine's torrent. Marine whirled the other way trying to target all three friends at once and also shoot at invisible enemies who weren't there at all.

Eliska flung both arms out to her sides, magnetized both boys inward with a powerful binding spell, and squashed all four friends into a tight cluster before she magicked all of them away.

She did it so fast that Marine didn't have time to defend herself. Neither Yann nor Anríq had time even to get to their feet before they crashed inward and all four friends slammed into each other full force.

Both boys roared in pain and so did Marine. Another geyser of magic blasted from her mouth when she yelled out. She would have destroyed all three of her friends.

She thrashed and jerked back and forth in the cluster. Eliska saw Marine about to annihilate the two boys. Eliska could have defended herself, but she had to stop this.

She dove for Marine, plastered her hand across Marine's face, and forced all that magic back down inside Marine's body.

She exploded in a catastrophic convulsion of insane struggling, jerking, and trying to tear herself out of the binding spell.

Eliska was really starting to worry about Marine hurting herself, but at that instant, the party materialized in the instability a mile from the Guardian Temple.

Eliska had been planning to get the group closer than this, but the instability shifted too fast. It moved the Temple around inside the Layer.

The structure of the Layer distorted to make locations closer and farther away from each other at the same time.

The friends crashed down in a chaos whirlwind slashing and pummeling the travelers in from all sides.

Eliska released the binding spell immediately—mainly to get herself and the boys far enough away from Marine to stop her from killing all three of them and maybe even herself.

"Come on!" she roared over the noise. "We have to move out. Follow me."

Chapter 47

Yann ran over to Eliska, but Anríq turned sideways to swing his axe at a Dark vapor hurtling out of the mayhem.

It headed straight for him, morphed into multiple different shapes, and would have collided with him.

He hacked his axe at it and a boom of magic sent the vapor twisting and whipping away into the swirling clouds.

More dark Forces came out of nowhere. The chaos in this Layer exploded off the charts when the four friends showed up here.

The Layer had been churning in a jumbled soup of forces, creatures, rapidly transforming objects, debris, and even sections of landscapes, trees, buildings, and hunks of machinery caught in the confusion.

Eliska held out her staff on her left side and raised her arm on her right side.

She tried to erect a ball of protection around all of her friends. She got it up, but a split second later, Marine wheeled around and vomited another outpouring of magic from her mouth.

The noise coming from her mouth drowned out all the din of thousands of shrieking, roaring, screaming, thunderous voices pounding in Eliska's ears.

Marine hit Eliska from behind and knocked her off balance. Her protection dropped and all the Dark forces hurtled in to attack the party.

Those forces attacked Marine, too. She was too out of her mind to realize that Eliska was trying to protect her.

Yann grabbed Eliska to steady her and she put her protection up again, but Anríq stood too far away. He couldn't stop striking Dark forces with his axe to drive them away from the others.

He hacked a giant house that widened its door to gobble him. A wall of rock twisted and morphed out of the vapors, changed shape into a giant monster, and would have flattened the party.

At that moment, another black curtain of Dark magic sizzled across the Layer from somewhere behind the cliff face.

The curtain overtook the cliff, dissolved it into a million grains of sand, and the whole thing smashed into the four friends with the force of a hurricane.

Eliska crouched under the onslaught, squinted trying to see where she was, and stumbled closer to Anríq to envelop him with her protection.

That inevitably made her and Yann move too far away from Marine, but Eliska couldn't think about that right now.

Marine kept spouting off random bursts of magic. They exploded from every part of her body.

Those bursts hammered Eliska's protective field with just as much force as the Dark entities flying around in this Layer.

Eliska had to protect herself and the boys as much from Marine as from the Dark itself.

Eliska couldn't worry about Marine—not as much as the boys. Yann stayed right by Eliska's side. He even grabbed her cloak and shirt in his fist to hold onto her so he wouldn't get separated from her.

That feeling of having to pull him along actually made her feel better. He was the only person she didn't have to worry about.

She charged over to Anríq and her ball surrounded him. All three of them dropped back inside and Anríq's shoulders chest and heaved from the effort of trying to catch his breath.

Marine fell behind.

"Come on!" Eliska bellowed again. "We have to move toward the Temple. Let's go!"

She set off across the landscape—what little of it she could actually see. Only a few features remained after the instability tore apart whatever had been here before.

Her magical awareness told her where the Temple was, but she couldn't see much around it because there wasn't much around it.

Vast reaches of this chaos Layer surrounded the Temple, but its magic stabilized the building and the surrounding mountains into an isolated Island in a landscape of pure chaos.

Dark forces pounded the fortress, the mountains, and everything else. They all dwarfed Eliska's tiny ball of protection.

She fired a thread of magic behind her. She didn't have to raise her hand or her staff.

She wrapped the thread around Marine to pull her along behind the party, but Eliska didn't make the mistake a second time of trying to bring Marine inside the ball. She was too dangerous—to everyone.

She didn't seem to have any problem fighting the Dark forces out there. They bombarded her just as fast as they bombarded Eliska's ball.

A Dark vapor whip-cracked out of the mayhem, turned into some monstrous shape, and then transformed back into a vapor. It widened, its outer shadowy edge became rough, spiky, and those spikes sprouted grasping fingers.

Marine no longer seemed aware of what she was doing or what she was shooting at—or maybe she understood the Dark too well.

She unloaded in every possible direction. She wound up hitting Dark forces before they got near her. In some cases, she destroyed them before they even fully formed enough to attack her.

A wall of those grasping fingers raced through the vapors to grab her, but she bellowed a deafening hurricane of magic from her mouth and scoured all of them backward away from her.

Her magic fragmented the fingers into millions of Dark wisps.

They scattered in the wind, but more Dark forces always came out of the Layer to form, disintegrate, reform, and come back at her again and again.

They did the same thing to Yann, Eliska, and Anríq. The three travelers would have been dead a million times over without Eliska's protection blocking all that crap from getting near them.

Eliska couldn't wait any longer. She took off running, but she had to grab Anríq and pull him along the same way she pulled Yann.

Anríq kept turning back to belt his axe at some Dark force that got too close. He could hit them through the ball, sent them flying, and cleared the way to stop them from clustering too thickly on that side.

Eliska unloaded from her right hand on the right side, but the sheer murderous fury of the storm only escalated to match their efforts.

"We can't do this!" she hollered over the noise. "We're too far away from the Temple!"

Yann bent close to his ear closer to her mouth. "WHAT?"

She couldn't take the time to explain. She seized all four of her friends in another binding spell. She didn't have time to protect them as well as she needed to, but she had to do this now.

She magicked all of them right to the base of the Temple steps, but she couldn't go anywhere. "We can't go any further! We have to break the defenses! Come on, Anríq! Yann—get Marine!"

Eliska didn't take the time to make sure the boys obeyed her. She charged up the steps, brought her staff forward, and fired a bone-crushing blast into an invisible field across the entrance.

Anríq rushed to her side and nailed his axe into the same field a few feet away.

A watery sheen of magic rippled over the field. It trembled and reestablished itself.

"Together!" she roared.

"Now!" he yelled back.

They both struck at once, and this time, Eliska tapped a little more of her Darkness to get the job done.

The field exploded in her face, hurled her and Anríq all the way back down the steps, and they crashed at Yann's feet.

He took advantage of Marine constantly twisting and turning in circles. He grabbed her from behind and ducked his head behind her neck so she wouldn't hit him with all that magic pouring out of her mouth.

Yann ducked under the shockwave, but he and Marine had been far enough away from the blast. It didn't hit them the way it hit Anríq and Eliska.

Anríq sprang to his feet and grabbed Eliska. "The field is down!" he yelled. "Come on! We have to get inside now!"

He and Eliska rushed back to the steps only for more Dark vapors to come out of nowhere.

Anríq spun left to belt them away with his axe. Eliska turned to the right. Yann wrestled Marine to the steps.

She went the whole way bellowing, kicking, and shrieking, and unloading her magic on everything, anything, and nothing.

Yann fought her every step of the way all the way up each and every stair to the Temple entrance.

Anríq and Eliska flanked him on both sides. They had to fight their hardest to hold the chaos at bay.

Eliska didn't dare to put a ball of protection around them in case Marine hit one of the friends inside it.

Yann made it to the top of the steps. Eliska sprang over to them, pumped a wicked burst of magic into the doors, and one of them flew inward with an echoing crash.

She shoved Yann and Marine across the threshold. She and Anríq backed in just as another brutal impact smashed the doors, hurled everyone inside, and the doors slammed shut behind them.

Chapter 48

Yann buckled onto a stone floor and collapsed trembling in exhaustion. He couldn't hold onto Marine any longer.

She sprawled on the cold granite flagstones next to him and immediately scrambled into her usual crouch. She screeched, hissed, and bared her teeth at him and everyone else.

A bunch of Templars stood around gaping at the friends in abject shock, but at least Marine didn't shoot all that magic from her mouth—or from any other part of her body.

Anríq lay across the floor, too. Yann didn't see what was wrong with him, but Anríq didn't get up.

Eliska dove over to him, passed her hands up and down his body frantically searching him for injuries, and finally came to rest on the back of his neck and spine.

"It's all right," she panted. "I got you. Just lie still."

He groaned under his breath and then wilted when she started to straighten him out.

She pressed one hand into the back of his neck and the other into the base of his spine where it met up with his hips.

She pushed her hands outward and he screamed once before he collapsed whimpering on the floor.

Yann couldn't get up to go over there to make sure Anríq was all right. Yann couldn't take his eyes off Marine.

Coming to this Temple seemed to have made her worse if that was even possible—or maybe Yann just saw her that way because of how the Templars were looking at her.

Eliska finally took her hands off Anríq, patted him a few times, kissed him on the side of the head, and got to her feet.

She left him lying there and took a few steps toward Marine.

Eliska halted ten feet away and stared at Marine. She crouched on the ground yowling at everyone who looked at her.

Eliska's eyes darted to Yann once before she slumped. "It didn't work," she croaked. The Temple's magic doesn't protect her anymore."

"Um......excuse me." One of the Templars advanced out of the crowd, cleared his throat, and looked back and forth between the four travelers. "Excuse me, but what is the meaning of this intrusion? Who are you and how do you come to invade our Temple with this.....this Darkling?"

He curled his lip at Marine. She screeched and slashed her teeth at him, but she was sat too far away to threaten him.

"She isn't a Darkling," Eliska explained. "She's an initiate of the Guardian Templars. Her order trained her to commune with the Dark and that's exactly what she's doing. She's been trying to fight the Voyant Mendicat, but as you can see, she's gone a little too far out into the Dark. Now she can't come back."

The man gasped and stared at Marine in horror. "My God! It can't be!"

"We brought her here for her own safety—and so she can regain her sanity," Eliska explained. "She's been traveling with us and helping us for weeks, but it's too dangerous now, I'm sorry we had to break in like this, but this is the only Temple we could find that isn't being taken by the instability."

The man made a face. "This Temple *is* being taken by the instability. I don't know how long we'll be able to hold out."

"Just do what you can for her. Please." Eliska hesitated and then held out her hand. "I'm Eliska. This is Yann Dilnao of the Black Watch and that's Anríq. He's a Servant."

The man blinked at her hand and then down at Yann and over at Anríq. "I can see that."

Eliska stood there with her hand out and waited, but it took the guy a long time to come to his senses enough to remember to shake it.

"I'm Master Levil," he finally stammered. "I....I don't know if we'll be able to help her.....She's so Dark."

"I know. Just...please try. That's all we ask.....and keep her here. Don't let her go back out into the Dark to wander the Coil."

Eliska crossed the floor and helped Yann stand up. "Is Anríq all right?" he asked.

"He isn't now, but he will be. He needs to recover for a little while."

Yann turned his attention to Marine, but he found it hard even to look at her. "Is it really so hopeless?"

"We don't know that," Eliska replied. "There's always the chance she could come out of it."

Yann winced when he heard her say exactly the same thing about Marine that Anríq said about Eliska.

Master Levil was still standing there blinking in disbelief and staring at everyone when two other elderly masters came hustling out of somewhere.

The first man was considerably shorter than the other with close-cropped grey hair.

He seized Yann's hand and pumped it hard. "Welcome, welcome! Any man of the Black Watch is welcome here! I'm Master Phiric and this is Master Zitro. We're in charge of hospitality to strangers in this Temple. We're so pleased you made it! We weren't expecting anyone to get through the instability."

Yann waved at his friends. "Eliska and Anríq did it. I just came along for the ride."

Master Phiric's smile slipped when he glanced first at Eliska and then at the other two. "Yes...well....." he stammered. "We better get you inside and take care of your friend's injuries. A Servant is more valuable in this day than they've ever been before. We can't let anything happen to him."

"He doesn't need healing," Eliska interrupted. "I already did that. He just needs a bed to rest in for a few hours."

Master Phiric squirmed just from looking at her. Then he forced a smile. "Right. We can give him that. Follow me and we'll take him somewhere he can rest."

The two Masters went over to Anríq, but Eliska got there first. She crossed the floor, put her hand on his back, and bent over to talk to him in front of his face.

"The Masters are going to take you to a room where you can sleep. Don't move. I'll transport you there so you don't hurt yourself."

She rubbed his back a few times before she stood back, aimed her staff at him, surrounded him with her magic, and lifted him off the floor.

She held his body perfectly immobilized and he floated upward to hang in mid-air. "Where would you like me to take him?" she asked.

The two newly arrived Masters went into a flurry of activity. They had to push their way through a mob of pupils, initiates, and older Brothers to lead the way.

Eliska followed them with Anríq floating along behind her. She created an even bigger halo of magic around him so none of the surrounding onlookers would bump him accidentally.

Yann stayed behind. The crowd murmured and exclaimed over Eliska's magic and how long it had been since any of them had seen a real Servant and how they couldn't let anything happen to him.

Yann waited until they left and the crowd started to disperse. Then he went over to Master Levil. He still stood there staring down at Marine.

Levil didn't seem to have heard anything the other two Masters said to Eliska about taking Anríq away. Levil didn't seem to be aware of much at all apart from how awful Marine looked.

"Can you do anything for her?" Yann asked. "Can you help her at all?"

Levil cleared his throat, glanced at Yann once, and went back to staring at Marine. "I'm not sure if we can do anything for her. She's gone so far out into the Dark. We can try, but I can't promise anything."

"Just try," Yann repeated. "And keep her here. None of us wants to see her in danger out there anymore."

"Of course not," Levil murmured. "I can't believe actual Templar Masters would send an initiate out into the Dark to do this."

Yann flinched again. "It seems her order did a lot of things the other orders don't agree with."

Levil finally came out of his trance enough to look up. He studied Yann a little too closely. "You should get some rest, too, young man. You look dead on your feet."

Yan looked away. He'd gotten plenty of rest lately.

No amount of rest took away the constant tension and stress of going through all of this.

He would never be able to truly rest until this was all over—whenever the hell that turned out to be. He was really starting to think it never would be.

He would have to keep wandering in the unstable Coil for the rest of his life—which might not last as long as all that considering the way things had been going lately.

Eliska came back just then and stopped next to Yann. She looked up and studied him extra closely, too. Then she placed her hand on his shoulder and squeezed.

She didn't say anything about how bad things were with Marine, but she must have known. He saw that in her eyes. She knew so much more than she ever said in words.

Her Darkness made her fragile, but it also made her infinitely more understanding about everything wrong with everybody.

Her intuition told her more than Yann could possibly imagine about everything going on with everybody.

She left her hand there and turned to Levil. "Do you have somewhere I can take Marine—somewhere private where everyone won't stand around staring at her?"

Levil nodded, but he found it difficult to make eye contact with Eliska. How much could Levil tell about her condition?

He mumbled, "Follow me," and turned away.

Chapter 49

Eliska magicked the same binding spell around Marine. Marine burst into another fit of shrieking and thrashing to get out of it, but Eliska ignored her and carried her a few feet off the ground to follow Levil out of the entrance foyer.

Levil led the way through the crowd of onlookers. It was already starting to thin and these people didn't follow Levil, Eliska, Yann, and Marine.

They passed down a bunch of lofty colonnades and hallways identical to the other Temples Yann had seen in the past in the cloud tower and in Savaré.

Levil walked a long way through the Temple, down a bunch of stairs, and eventually turned off into a long, low, narrow hallway lined on both sides with small bare rooms.

He entered a close little room at the far end of the hall away from everyone else.

"You can put her in here," he told Eliska.

"What is this place?" Yann asked. "Don't tell me you plan to keep her locked up in here."

Levil opened his mouth to say something, but Eliska answered for him. "They aren't locking her up—not in that way. This is one of the Brothers' quarters. It's the same accommodation all the Brothers and

Masters of the order get. Marine will be used to something like this."
She turned to Levil. "Thank you, Master. This will be perfect."

Eliska lowered Marine onto the floor and released the spell. Marine yowled again and scampered into the corner where she huddled, glared, and bared her teeth at the three people looking at her.

"We will need to keep her locked in," Levil explained. "We can't have her wandering the hallways and interfering with the pupils and initiates. It's for her own safety and everyone else's. She's too unpredictable to leave her at large."

Eliska smiled at him. "We understand. Do what you can to help her."

Levil gave her a strange look and studied Marine for a minute. "We would have to combine our magic to drive out a Dark force as strong as this. I'm not sure how well it will work....." He trailed off and turned away to leave the room. "Step outside and I'll lock the door from the outside."

Yann grabbed the guy as he walked past. "Wait a minute. We need you to help Eliska, too. You could combine your magic to take her Darkness. She needs your help as much as Marine does."

Levil grimaced and his eyes darted in Eliska's direction before he looked away. "No. I'm sorry, but we would definitely not be able to do anything about *that.*"

Levil shook off Yann's hand and marched out of the room much more determinedly than he entered it.

He left Yann standing there with those fateful words hanging in the air.

Eliska only shook her hair out of her eyes and crossed the rest of the way to stand in front of Yann. "Don't worry about it," she murmured. "Thank you for asking, but these men don't have the magic to heal me."

"That's ridiculous," he countered. "There must be a hundred Masters in this place. They could combine their magic and....."

He broke off when she looked away. "I don't think so. Anyway, just leave it alone. I'll be all right." She looked up and frowned at him. "Are *you* going to be okay....with *this?*"

She inclined her head ever so slightly in Marine's direction.

Yann couldn't look at Marine or Eliska. "I guess I'll be as okay with this as you are with your Darkness. No one can fix it, so I just have to be okay with it."

"Come on. Let's get out of here. The Templars might be able to bring her back."

"And then the three of us will have to leave her here." Yann gulped hard and turned his back on Marine. "I always knew this would happen."

He didn't give himself a chance to finish. He couldn't keep standing here dwelling on Marine.

He walked out of the room. Master Levil was nowhere in sight.

Eliska followed Yann and she led the way upstairs.

The initiates, students, and other Templars who had gathered in the foyer all returned to their own business. No one stopped to remark on Yann and Eliska passing through the Temple.

She returned to the foyer, followed another corridor, climbed a bunch of different staircases, and passed a bunch of landings before she came to another section of the Temple.

She stopped at one of the bedrooms. It was much bigger and nicer than the Brothers' rooms downstairs.

Five Templars stood around the bed where Anríq lay flat on his face. He didn't move or open his eyes while they worked on him with their magic.

"Are you sure he'll be okay?" Yann asked.

"I'm sure," Eliska replied. "I healed his injuries downstairs. He just needs to rest now. He'll be all right as soon as he gets his strength back. Come on. I'm more worried about you right now."

She led him farther down the hall and entered the room next door to Anríq's.

It wasn't quite as nice as the one in Costico's palace. It might have looked more like Yann's apartment in Savaré, but the Temple used an older style of décor.

Eliska slipped her hand into his and pulled him down to sit next to her on the bed.

She didn't let go of his hand, and in that moment, he really felt the crushing weight of what was happening to him.

He stared at the floor in front of him.....and the world shrank to a pinprick.

The sensation of her holding his hand did something none of the rest of this could do. It brought home the undeniable reality at last.

Marine would stay here. He and Eliska and Anríq would leave. Marine really would pass out of Yann's life forever. Could he really do that?

Eliska's hand made it all too real. He was just as incurably damaged as she was and she couldn't heal what was wrong with him. No one could.

She didn't say anything. She didn't have to. She just sat there holding his hand. Her presence hurt worse than any pain he'd ever felt....because she knew.

She could be there for him in ways no one else could—because he had no one else.

He lost track of how long they sat there together. She didn't try to get up and leave or tell him to go to sleep or anything like that. She might sit here forever.

He really hoped she would. As soon as she stood up from this bed, that would mean the three friends really had to leave this Temple. They had to leave without Marine.

A few hours might have passed before Master Phiric bustled in. "Your friend is sleeping comfortably next door."

Eliska smiled at him. "Thank you. We're grateful for all your hospitality."

"You have a room next door, young lady, if you want to go get some rest yourself."

"I know. Thank you. I'll go in a little while."

Phiric's eyes darted to Yann and back again. "The senior Masters are planning to work on your friend downstairs tomorrow morning. We'll come and get you before then." He cocked his head and frowned at the two of them. "You two should come downstairs for dinner. We'll be eating soon. You don't want to miss that."

"Thank you." Eliska stood up. Yann didn't.

He didn't want to let go of her hand.

She turned around and murmured down at him in that undertone people use when they're talking to someone in emotional distress. "Come downstairs and get something to eat. Don't stay up here alone."

She tugged his hand. His body went through the automatic motions of standing up and following her out of the room.

He couldn't exactly say that moving around made him feel better because it didn't. He just got moving again. He didn't seem to be able to do anything else.

She stopped off at Anríq's room. None of the Masters were in there anymore. She bent over his bed, put her arms around him, and kissed him on the back of the neck.

He didn't respond at all. He must have been really out of it.

She returned with a much lighter spring in her step, now that she knew he was okay—or that he was going to be.

Yann should have gone in there to make sure Anríq was okay, too, but Yann wouldn't have been able to tell what was wrong with Anríq or do anything about it if he did.

Anríq was in the best possible hands. If Eliska said he was all right, Yann trusted that.

Yann followed her and Phiric downstairs. They joined the whole bustling population of students and Templars at the long dining tables while they ate.

Yann and Eliska got lost in the crowd. Everyone was too busy eating and talking about their own business to notice the two gests.

Yann and Eliska sat down next to each other. They stayed sitting next to each other in silence through the meal.

Eliska listened to the conversations flying back and forth across the table and laughter breaking out a few seats down.

Yann stared into his plate. He forced himself to eat even though he didn't feel like it.

Afterward, he followed her back upstairs where she led him to the same room next door to Anríq.

Just before she left Yann there, she put her arms around him and crushed him in a deep hug. He was too numb even to return it.

He just stood there in silence and felt the cruel irony. After everything that happened, she was the one trying to comfort him instead of the other way around.

How did this happen? How did the loss of a girl become the worst disaster of his life?

Yann never even had Marine—not really. He never held out any hope of getting together with her. She started to slip through his fingers before he ever met her. This was all just part of the inevitable cycle he saw coming long ago.

Eliska told him she would be in the room next to his on the other side, slipped away, and left him there.

He sank onto the bed, kicked off his shoes, and stretched out to stare at the ceiling. He let himself get lost in the memories of the time when he and Marine lived together in their apartment in Savaré.

He could trick himself into thinking she was still here lying on the bed next to him.

He shut his eyes and imagined her arms around him and her hair brushing his face when she bent over to kiss him.

That was all just a fantasy, though. She wasn't here and she would never be here again.

Chapter 50

Yann and Eliska followed Master Phiric and Master Levil downstairs. They returned to the long corridor where the Brothers stayed.

They found a mob of older Templar Masters crowding around the door to the room where the friends left Marine yesterday. Her shrieks echoed through the heavy wooden door.

No one said a word when Master Levil passed his hand in front of the doorknob to unlock it. He pushed it back, swung the door inward, and the Masters started to file into the room.

Yann glanced down at Eliska. Her eyebrows came together in the center and she shot him a desperate, pleading look.

"Don't go in there," he murmured. "You should go back upstairs."

She nodded fast. Her lips quivered all over the place. Her features spasmed so badly that she couldn't speak.

He pushed her way. "Go," he whispered. "Go now before they start."

She spun away and charged back up the corridor. None of the Masters noticed.

A wave of relief washed some of Yann's cares away when she vanished up the stairs. She never should have come down here.

Yann didn't want her anywhere near Marine or the Masters when they tried to heal her from her Darkness.

He didn't know what to expect, but he wouldn't let Eliska participate in this. That would be the worst idea in the history of bad ideas.

The Masters crowded into Marine's room. Her screeches escalated when she saw them gathering around her.

Yann could barely fit inside the room. He had to stand on the threshold. Even then, he couldn't see much of what the Templars did.

They all went dangerously still for a minute and then they all shut their eyes and started to sway. They made a humming noise in their throats.

The sound drove Marine out of her mind. She screeched to wake the dead and threw herself violently against the walls trying to get away from the sound.

For some reason, she didn't hurl herself at the Templars. She would have had to break through them all to get to the door.

Yann planted himself there and braced himself to tackle her if he absolutely had to. He even prepared himself to fight her when she bombarded him with her magic.

He would do whatever it took to keep her in this room so the Templars could at least try to heal her of this Darkness.

He didn't want to use force, but he would if it came to that.

She didn't break away for the door. Maybe she couldn't.

She backed away, but she only wound up plastering herself even more tightly against the walls.

She spun left and right trying to keep all the Templars in sight at the same time. None of them opened their eyes as her hysterical howls escalated.

Her voice made the hair stand up on the back of Yann's neck. Something massive was about to happen. Would these men be able to restore Marine's sanity?

He really didn't think he could walk away from her if they did. What would it be like to see her like that just one more time—to see her smiling at him and her eyes glowing with all the approval and emotion he knew so well?

How would he be able to leave that to go back into the Coil without her?

The Templars might send her home to the Hallowed Vales. Then Yann would have no choice but to leave without her.

He didn't want to think about that, but right then, the Templars opened their eyes and moved in on her.

Fifty men crammed into this one tiny room. They had to stand body to body against each other. Now they packed in even more tightly to blockade the corner where Marine crouched.

She exploded into a full-scale meltdown when she saw them crowding in.

The Templars in the back placed their hands on the shoulders of the men in front of them.

Master Levil, Master Phiric, Master Zitro, and two other Masters surrounded Marine at the very front. A continuous connection of hands interlaced all the Templars to each other.

They walled her off from the others and all five of those in the front grabbed her at the same time.

They planted their hands on different parts of her body—the only parts they could access considering her behavior.

Master Levil put his hand on her head. Master Phiric put his hands on her shoulders. Master Zitro grabbed one of her arms.

The other two touched her chest and her ribs.

She cringed, screamed out loud, and tried to shrink from their touch, but they bent over to follow her down to the ground. They never lost contact with her.

They stopped humming and a charge of tension went through the room. Every man furrowed his brow in concentration.

Yann didn't see what was happening, but the minute they all got into that position, some reaction translated through the group. It started with Marine and raced backward to the Templars in the very back.

One of the men pitched out of position, roared in pain, and then started screaming. He toppled over backward onto the floor and convulsed there screeching his head off.

Blood trickled from his nose and it didn't stop. Then another Master jolted away from the group, tore his hands away from the man in front of him, and threw himself backward against the wall. He almost slammed into Yann.

The Templar flattened himself there, spread his arms, and plastered his hands to the wall.

His eyes darted back and forth not seeing anything. He panted, grimaced, and whimpered in terror at something no one else could see.

Three other Masters broke the chain to deal with the situation—and as soon as they broke contact, two other Masters succumbed to the Dark, too.

One of them tore his hands away, bellowed in desperate agony, grabbed his head in both hands, and charged out of the room in a frenzy.

The fourth man buckled on the spot, passed out on the floor, and blood poured from his nose and ears.

The other Templars broke apart instantly, now that their cohort had weakened by the loss of seven of their members.

The five Templars at the front took their hands off Marine and backed away. The remaining Templars filed out of the room while one group scrambled to deal with their injured comrades.

Yann backed out into the corridor to wait.

The Templars burst into a flurry of activity taking the injured men upstairs. They hurried away somewhere else. None of them looked at or spoke to Yann or each other.

The noise and commotion died down. No one but the three Masters remained inside the room. Yann tiptoed back to the entrance.

Master Levil, Master Phiric, and Master Zitro stood near Marine. She crouched in the corner muttering to herself exactly the way she did before. She acted the same way Yann remembered her acting all along.

He knew the truth even before Master Levil said it. "We can't help her. She's too far gone. Our people got hurt trying to bring her back. We can't risk trying again—not for one person. I'm sorry."

The three Masters walked out of the room and left the door standing open. Yann didn't check to see if any of them stayed behind to lock the door after he left.

Their footsteps faded on the stairs down the corridor. They left him alone with Marine—probably for the last time.

He stared at her for a while, but he couldn't feel anything about her anymore.

He would drive himself insane if he tapped the depth of emotion he actually felt for her. He had to shut it off so he could keep functioning.

He didn't even understand why he felt this way about her when they spent so little time together.

He kept coming back to the words he said to Anríq last night. Was it really only last night? It seemed like a million years ago.

She was the only person who could heal whatever was wrong with him. He didn't even know what that was.

He just needed her. He only found out how much he needed her after he lost her.

He went upstairs. He planned to go to his room, sit on the bed, and stare at nothing for as long as it took to wrap his head around everything that happened to him recently. His brain still hadn't caught up with the rest of him.

He paused when he passed Anríq's room. Anríq sat up in bed propped against an enormous pile of pillows. He had his shirt off with the sheet across his stomach.

He didn't sit up when Yann walked in. "Hey!' Yann murmured. "You're back."

"Hardly," Anríq croaked. "I'm a mess."

"What happened?" Yann asked. "Eliska did something to your spine when she healed you."

Anríq's eyes flew open. "She did? I thought the Templars did it."

"No, she said you were already done by the time they got to you. She healed you the minute we got thrown inside the Temple."

Anríq looked away toward the window. "Where is she? I need to thank her."

"I was just about to go find her. She...." Yann trailed off.

Anríq's eyes snapped to his face with brutal intensity. "Where is she?"

"She's fine...at least I think she is. The Templars....they just tried to heal Marine. I sent Eliska back upstairs to keep her away while they were doing it...."

"What do you mean—they *tried* to heal Marine?"

Yann broke eye contact first. "It didn't work."

"I'm so sorry, Yann," Anríq breathed. "Is there anything we can do?'

"There's nothing anyone can do. I......" Yann broke off again. He didn't want to say it, but who else would he say it to besides Anríq? "I don't dare to ask Eliska to help her."

"Maybe you should," Anríq suggested. "Maybe..."

"No," Yann snapped. "Eliska might relapse. We can't risk that—not after everything that's happened lately. She might go out into the Dark and not come back. Then we would sacrifice Eliska to get Marine back. I couldn't do that."

"All right," Anríq murmured. "If that's the way you feel....."

"Marine did this on her own. She's out there because she went there willingly. Eliska.....She's already Dark enough. I don't want to make it worse."

"Okay," Anríq breathed. "I understand."

Yann forced himself to look up. "How long do you have to stay in here? How long do the Templars think it will take you to recover?"

"I should be strong enough to travel tomorrow morning. I just need to rest tonight before we go back out."

Yann nodded. "I better go check on Eliska."

Anríq called after him. "Yann!"

Yann turned around. "Yeah?"

"Could I....could I see her....after you talk to her?"

Yann found himself smiling at his friend. "Sure. I'll tell her you want to see her. Take it easy. I'll come check on you later."

Yann left the room and found Eliska sitting on her bed in her room. She sat with her knees drawn up to her chest while she gazed out the window. It looked out into the swirling chaos vapors.

She didn't turn away from the window when Yann sat down next to her. "You okay?" he asked.

She looked down at her hands then. "I'm fine. I can protect myself from it. I just....if I see her, the temptation to heal her will be too strong."

"I don't want you anywhere near her—and I don't want you to try to heal her any other way. Just leave it alone."

She finally turned around and locked her dark eyes on him. "I'm so sorry....I wish I could do something...."

He turned aside so he wouldn't see the way she was looking at him. "It doesn't matter."

She didn't correct him by saying that it did matter because it did.

She let the silence linger. He couldn't stand it any longer.

He got to his feet and headed for the door. "Anríq is awake. He's asking to see you when you feel ready to."

Yann walked out, went to his own room, and shut the door with himself inside it. He didn't want to talk to anyone right now—about anything, especially not about Marine.

He might have felt the temptation to completely fall apart right then and there if he did talk to anyone about her.

He sat down on the edge of the bed, but he didn't fall apart. He felt.....nothing. He didn't feel anything because she was already gone. She was as good as dead to him.

That thing downstairs wasn't Marine. That thing downstairs hadn't been Marine for a long time. She died to him a long, long time ago.

He could walk away now. He could leave that dead thing behind in the care of the Templars who made her like this. They could deal with the fallout.

She wasn't Yann's problem anymore. He had big enough problems of his own without dealing with that on top of everything else.

Chapter 51

E liska took a long time to work up the courage to go down the hall to Anríq's room where he lay awake on his pile of pillows.

She had been monitoring his progress. She already knew he was awake before Yann told her.

She paused in the doorway when he turned around to look at her. His eyes caught her in a vortex of a million confused memories and emotions.

She already knew the way he felt about her even before she started reading everyone's memories, thoughts, and feelings.

She inched toward the bed and sat down next to him.

"Hi," she croaked.

"Hi," he replied.

She slipped her hand into his and squeezed. He felt as big and strong and safe and protective as ever even when he was hurt.

His hand radiated warmth into her.

She laid her other hand on his chest to check his injuries even though she already knew he was healed and whole again.

"Thank you," he breathed. "Thank you for saving my life."

"Of course," she replied. "What else would I do?'

"How's Yann?" he asked.

"Not very good. We need to leave here as soon as you're ready. Staying here isn't good for him."

Anríq nodded. "That's what I thought."

"Do you think....?" she blurted out. "Do you think I should heal Marine....for him?"

"I suggested that, but he said no. He doesn't want you to. He thinks you might go out into the Dark in her place....."

"I wouldn't," she told him. "I could do it "

"No," Anríq replied "I understand why you want to and I would probably want to do the same thing if I was in your place, but don't do it. Yann has already made up his mind and I agree with him. Marine is on a different road now. She went there on her own and that's where she'll stay."

Eliska squirmed in her seat. "I don't like leaving her."

"None of us do, but if Yann thinks this is the right way, then I'm with him."

She looked down at her fingers tracing back and forth across his knuckles. "I guess so."

He didn't break the silence for a minute before he said, "I'm glad you have him.....and I'm sorry we had to take you out of your mother's house the way we did. I'm sorry if what I did hurt you."

She couldn't look up. "It didn't. Everything else did, but not you."

"Then.....you agree with what Yann said....about us?"

She nodded down at her fingers on his skin. She couldn't form the words to tell him what she really thought.

"I don't want to hurt you," he murmured.

"You won't," she croaked. "Nothing can hurt me. That's the problem."

He raised his other hand without letting go of hers, slipped the fingers into her hair, and pulled her head down on his chest.

She collapsed there in the safety of his arms and shut her eyes in the darkness of his smell. She hadn't fully released herself in this since they left Symphorian.

She didn't know or think about how things would unfold between them, but Yann was right. She needed Anríq. She needed him in ways Yann couldn't give her.

Finding out that Yann was her brother and Yvan Dilnao had been her real father—those two facts healed something in her—something that had been broken for decades.

Yann could go through all the same actions of putting his arms around her, kissing her hair, and pulling her against him in bed.

Those affections would never mean the same thing as when Anríq did them. They meant something different with him. They meant everything.

Chapter 52

Eliska and Anríq came downstairs to find Yann already there. Yann rested the end of his glaive shaft on the floor. Anríq wore all his bags and weapons. He was ready to leave.

"You don't have to do this," Master Levil insisted. "You should stay here. We can protect you."

"You can't even protect yourselves," Yann told him. "This Temple will collapse eventually. We would leave even if it didn't. We have things to do."

"No one can defeat the Voyant Mendicat," Master Phiric added. "He's too powerful in the ways of Dark magic."

"I've heard that before," Yann replied. "Defeating him or at least taking the Shard away from him is the only way to save the Coil. You should know this. You should be out there doing the same thing instead of hiding in here behind these walls."

His comments made the Templars squirm.

"I'm grateful for all your help—and I'm grateful that you're taking care of Marine. We'll come back for her when this is over if we get that far."

"Are you sure you aren't doing this for another reason?" Master Zitro interrupted. "The Voyant killed your father—and now you've lost Marine, too. Is that why you want to risk your life to go out there and defeat him?"

"Think whatever you want about me. I chose this path and I'll keep following it to the end. You won't do it, so someone else has to. I can't turn back now—not without costing millions of lives." He turned to Anríq and Eliska. "Are you both ready?'

Anríq nodded. "I'm ready."

Eliska didn't even have to make eye contact with Yann to know what he was thinking and feeling.

He wanted to get out of here. He wanted to get as far away from Marine as possible. Staying in this Temple only made the pain of losing her worse.

The three friends approached the Temple's big front doors. Eliska took a deep breath. Anríq unhooked his club and Yann raised his glaive.

Anríq pulled the doors open and the three friends charged out into the hurricane of Dark forces.

The friends all plunged in to attack the minute they got outside. Eliska fired a ball of protection around all three of them and defended Anríq while he pulled the doors closed behind them.

She waited just long enough for the lock to click shut. Then she magicked the three of them away, but not before a giant black shape lunged down on top of them.

It started as a wisp of black vapor before it exploded to an enormous size, opened a hideous mouth, and dove down on top of the ball.

She magicked the three friends deeper into the chaos only for her ball to get battered from all sides by more Dark forces.

She didn't wait long enough even to see what they were much less fight them. To hell with this.

Anríq raised his club to defend the party, but she magicked them away too fast.

The ball plunged through multiple Layers. She'd checked her Coil projection before leaving the Temple, but the Layers shifted too fast.

The ball dropped into a Layer full of other magic-users all fighting each other. Eliska didn't see any Dark forces around—or maybe these people were the Dark forces.

They fired magical bursts at each other, deflected them, and a million whizzing missiles punctured Eliska's field.

She returned fire, but she couldn't even see if there were any different sides in this battle or why anyone was fighting anyone else.

Anríq raised his club, but he couldn't decide what to hit or how to defend the group with so many strikes coming from every side.

Some of those shots penetrated Eliska's ball. Others didn't. If she and Anríq tried to confront an attack coming from one direction, they inevitably got hit from another direction.

A spike of what looked like stone punched through the ball and stabbed her in the upper arm.

She roared in pain and whirled around to face whoever shot at her, but she only got hit by another projectile coming from her left.

It embedded itself in her thigh and her knee buckled. "Eliska!" Anríq yelled.

"I'm going to shatter the ball!" she bellowed. "Get ready!"

He raised his club again. She dropped the ball and he swung his club at a cloud of more spikes hurtling at the three friends.

He hit dozens of them out of the air, blasted off a deafening thump of magic, and cleared the air in that direction just enough to protect the friends.

Eliska let off a matching explosion of magic in the other direction at exactly the same instant, bought the friends an instant's reprieve, and magicked them out of the Layer in the blink of an eye.

The ball plummeted downward through a solid sheet of bedrock. She immediately reestablished her ball of protection when the three friends plunged into a chaos Layer full of hideous Darklings all in full-scale battle against each other.

Their tentacles whipped back and forth at each other, pounded the ball, and the Darklings' magic swatted the ball hard enough to hurl the friends against its magical sides.

The ball slammed into one Darkling after another. Yann and Anríq fell on top of each other and then the next strike hurled both boys down on top of Eliska.

Their weight drove both spikes deeper into her muscles. She screamed in pain. They didn't have a chance to get off her before another brutal swat from a different Darkling threw both boys away.

She saw the situation disintegrating before her eyes and magicked the party to a completely different Layer. She had no idea where she was going. She might be sending herself and the boys into another collapse.

She just had to keep moving until they found somewhere stable—wherever that turned out to be.

The ball tumbled through so many different layers that Eliska couldn't keep track of them all. She didn't try.

She concentrated everything on strengthening the sphere around herself and the boys. She couldn't fight the forces tearing the Coil apart.

The ball fell down through another shattering surface of what felt like solid granite and smashed on a steep mountainside.

The ball tumbled for miles down, down, down steep ridges, ravines, fell over waterfalls, and smashed onto rocks before it finally rolled to a stop on a rough, barren, desert expanse.

Eliska let the ball dissolve and she sprawled on the ground panting hard.

Yann and Anríq both fell on either side of her, but Anríq jumped up immediately and rushed her. "Don't move!' he ordered. "Let me take them out......

She shot her arm too fast—faster than she meant to. She wound up knocking his hand away before he touched the spike sticking out of her thigh.

"I'm sorry...." she choked. "I....just....."

Pain obliterated her mind. Blood saturated her pants and shirt. She struggled to think straight.

These spikes were Dark. They set her whole system on edge. She floundered to hold her magic back from merging with them, but she found it impossible not to tap the same Dark power to heal herself.

She grabbed the spike and crumbled in screaming sobs when she pulled it out of her thigh. Her magic surrounded the wound and closed it. The same thing happened when she pulled out the spike in her arm.

She buckled there and lost the fight to sit up straight. Anríq moved in and placed his hands on her arm and her leg, but her own magic already healed her better than he could.

She didn't fight him when he sent his magic into her. He didn't heal the wounds, but he did calm her down and helped clear her thoughts.

She fought to breathe while the three friends looked around. A road crossed the desert heading for what looked like an oasis in the distance.

Monstrous, predatory animals roamed the landscape and snarled at the three friends, but the creatures didn't come any closer.

A few nomad groups passed down the road dozens of miles away. Their shaggy pack animals lumbered along with the groups. None of those nomads came in this direction.

Eliska snapped alert when she saw a curtain of instability crossing the countryside a hundred miles away. It consumed mountains and planes far at the limit of sight.

Anríq grabbed her hand and pulled her to her feet. Yann stood up and all three friends stared at the instability. Eliska's intuition showed her the landscape collapsing out there.

"Is it coming this way?" Yann asked.

"No, it's staying the same distance away, but it could sweep back in this direction anytime. There's no way to predict it."

"What about the surrounding Layers?" Anríq asked. "Are any other more stable Islands nearby?"

She opened her Coil projection just to check. "There are a few, but they're all becoming increasingly unstable. I say we stay in this Island—at least until we make a plan on where to go and how to get there."

Yann nodded and turned toward the road. "Let's get out of here. We need to put as much distance between ourselves and that wave as possible."

Anríq turned away to follow him. Eliska hesitated only a split second before she joined them.

That instant of hesitation gave her the one moment she needed to see a tiny speck of white floating in the chaos over there.

She gasped and seized Yann's arm. "Wait! Look!"

Dark shadows kept surrounding the spot, concealing it, and drifting aside to reveal it again.

"It's Marine!" she husked. "She must have followed us after all."

"The monks should have confined her in the Temple," Anríq pointed out.

"She must have escaped." Eliska sprang forward. "We have to help her. We have to get her out of there."

Now Yann was the one who grabbed her arm. "Stop! Don't go out there!"

"She could die out there!" Eliska fired back. "We can't just leave her!"

He turned very slowly and stared across the countryside. "She didn't follow us—not like that. She doesn't even know we're here."

He fell dangerously silent and squinted at the spot in the distance. Then he clamped his mouth shut and turned his back on the instability. "Leave her. We can't help her. We have our own mission now. Let's go."

He walked off toward the road and didn't look back. He didn't wait for Anríq and Eliska to go with him.

They both stood there looking for what felt like a long time. Anríq left first and hustled to catch up with Yann.

Eliska lingered. She cringed when she sensed the turmoil raging in Yann's middle. He wanted to go after Marine even more than Eliska did, but he didn't go after her.

He turned his back on Marine and walked away. He left her in life-threatening danger......and now Eliska had to do the same thing.

She couldn't help Marine. No one knew better than Eliska did just how out of her mind Marine had become. She really was gone.

Eliska wasn't even sure anymore if taking Marine's Darkness would bring Marine back from whatever Dark wilderness she'd gotten herself lost in.

Eliska couldn't risk that—and Yann knew better than to try. He knew better than to think about a girl who wasn't even there anymore.

Eliska stayed there way too long. She shouldn't have let the temptation creep in, but it reared its ugly head anyway.

She stayed even after she discarded that temptation. She wouldn't go back for Marine. Eliska couldn't go back for Marine. Marine wasn't even there to go back for.

Eliska just watched. She watched in silent witness to the friend who no longer existed—Eliska's one and only friend—the only friend she'd ever had in her entire life—gone—lost in the Coil forever.

The boys brought her back. They still needed her.

They got farther and farther away. Yann never turned around even to make sure Eliska went with them. He already knew she would.

She finally turned her back on Marine, too. Eliska walked away, left Marine in mortal danger, and did her best to put Marine as far out of her mind as possible.

Whatever happened now, Marine wasn't on this journey anymore. She'd fallen along with the others.

The road ahead led Eliska, Yann, and Anríq on an inevitable trajectory to the Sacred Shrine.

Eliska couldn't be sure anymore which of them would survive long enough to take the Shard of Hotha, but one of them would do it.

They had to. They no longer had any other choice. None of them would go through all of this and let Marine's sacrifice go to waste.

End of Book 4.

Keep Reading

Corrupted Coil Series: Book 5: The White Spire

With the Coil collapsing around their ears, Yann, Eliska, and Anríq must follow the last hopeless clues in a deadly race against time to find the Shards of Hotha before the Voyant Mendicat destroys the Coil and kills everyone in it.

The Coil is already dangerous enough, but the worst lies ahead as the three friends' journey takes them into uncharted territories of nightmares, tempting fantasies designed to make them forget their quest, and ultimately, just might turn them into the very evil forces they've been working so hard to defeat.

When the war ends in one final epic battle, none of the friends may have the will or the power to save the Coil at all. They might just be the ones who cause its destruction along with everything they hold dear.

You can find it at your favorite book retailer.

Sign Up Once--Get all Theo Mann's free books including brand new releases

S ign Up Once--Get all Theo Mann's free books including brand new releases

With the Corrupted Coil becoming increasingly unstable and the human world torn apart by war, the Barbarians expects their Chieftain's sons to become his greatest warriors and take over his power after him.

When twelve-year-old Anríq's dormant magic comes to the surface, it will destroy everything he knows about his life, his family, and his future.

When those he most cares about turn against him, he'll have to find a new source of strength within himself and the allies to help him do what must be done before it's too late.

Sign up at www.theomann.com to read it for free

About Theo Mann

I write 70 books per year—and yes, before you ask, all these books are my original creative work. Nothing written under my name is AI-generated or ghostwritten because I write better than AI and any ghostwriter out there.

People don't read fiction for entertainment or to escape from reality. People read fiction to see their humanity reflected in another person's character and story.

This is my promise to you. When you read my books, you'll see your own humanity reflected in the characters and stories. I take this commitment to my readers very seriously. My books are an intimate form of communication between us. I would never disrespect my readers by turning that over to a machine or another writer. This is my bond between me and you as my reader.

I write 20,000 words per day as my daily work output. If anyone with a public platform would like to challenge me to prove this in a controlled environment, feel free to contact me on this website's contact page.

I worked as a professional ghostwriter for fifteen years. Now I'm on a mission to set a Guinness World Record by writing 700 books over the next ten years and 1400 books over the next twenty years, all originally written by me. See my website for the full book list.

I'm also the author of *Proof for the Existence of God* and the *Crimes Against Fiction* blog. You can find all my nonfiction work at www.crimes-against-fiction.com.

If you have a story idea, or if you would like me to explore a series in more depth, or if you'd like me to explore a character by writing a spinoff series about that character or world, leave me a message on my website's contact page. I answer all reader emails, so ask me anything, tell me what you liked and didn't like, and let me know where you'd like your favorite series to go. I would love to hear your ideas and find out what you'd like to read next.

Find out more at www.theomann.com.